From Savannah to the Hollows, from the Big Easy
to Sin City, something wicked has come

UNBOUND!

A pixy and a gargoyle must band together to rescue
the endangered innocent from a psychotic nymph
with delusions of goddesshood,
in **KIM HARRISON's**
Ley Line Drifter

In New Orleans, a pair of undead serial killers is
about to turn Mardi Gras into a horror show—unless
the immortal hitman Bones can hunt them down,
in **JEANIENE FROST's**
Reckoning

Following the slaughter of his parents, J.J. became
an agent of the Light—but now his love for the
beautiful killer who spared his life transforms the
fierce defender into the most perfect predator of all,
in **VICKI PETTERSSON's**
Dark Matters

A nightwalker is slain, and suspicion falls on
Mira—Fire Starter—the last hope of her
immortal race, in **JOCELYNN DRAKE's**
The Dead, the Damned, and the Forgotten

Nice girls don't hunt is Eavan's credo—until a
local drug dealer begins mixing Haitian zombie
powder and selling enslaved women,
in **MELISSA MARR's**
Two Lines

Also by

Kim Harrison
WHITE WITCH, BLACK CURSE,
THE OUTLAW DEMON WAILS, FOR A FEW DEMONS MORE,
A FISTFUL OF CHARMS, EVERY WHICH WAY BUT DEAD,
THE GOOD, THE BAD, AND THE UNDEAD,
DEAD WITCH WALKING

Jeaniene Frost
AN EARLY GRAVE, AT GRAVE'S END,
ONE FOOT IN THE GRAVE, HALFWAY TO THE GRAVE

Vicki Pettersson
CITY OF SOULS, TOUCH OF TWILIGHT,
TASTE OF NIGHT, SCENT OF SHADOWS

Jocelynn Drake
DAWNBREAKER, DAYHUNTER, NIGHTWALKER

Melissa Marr
FRAGILE ETERNITY, INK EXCHANGE, WICKED LOVELY

UNBOUND

KIM
HARRISON

MELISSA
MARR

JEANIENE
FROST

VICKI
PETTERSSON

JOCELYNN
DRAKE

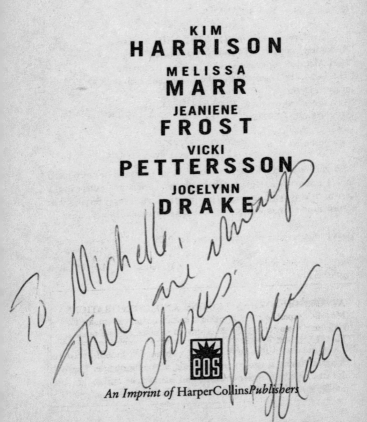

To Michelle, These are always Chorus.

Melissa Marr

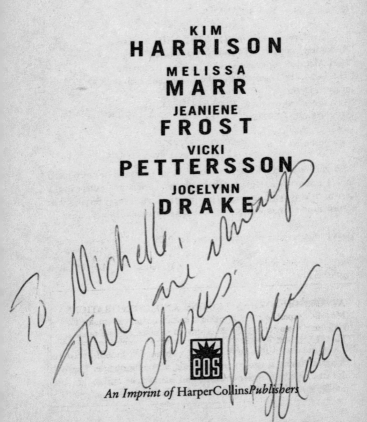
eos

An Imprint of HarperCollinsPublishers

This is a work of fiction. Names, characters, places, and incidents are products of the authors' imaginations or are used fictitiously and are not to be construed as real. Any resemblance to actual events, locales, organizations, or persons, living or dead, is entirely coincidental.

EOS
An Imprint of HarperCollins*Publishers*
10 East 53rd Street
New York, New York 10022-5299

"Ley Line Drifter" copyright © 2009 by Kim Harrison
"Reckoning" copyright © 2009 by Jeaniene Frost
"Dark Matters" copyright © 2009 by Vicki Pettersson
"The Dead, the Damned, and the Forgotten" copyright © 2009 by Jocelynn Drake
"Two Lines" copyright © 2009 by Melissa Marr
ISBN 978-0-06-169993-1
Cover art by Victor Gadino
www.eosbooks.com

First Eos paperback printing: September 2009

HarperCollins® and Eos® are registered trademarks of HarperCollins Publishers.

Printed in the U.S.A.

10 9 8 7 6 5 4 3 2 1

Contents

UNBOUND

LEY LINE DRIFTER

KIM HARRISON

I

The dim gloom was heavy in the lower level of Jenks's stump, only the high ceiling of the cavernous great room still holding the fading haze of the setting sun. Working by the glow of his dragonflylike wings, Jenks hovered in the wide archway leading to the storerooms, feet dangling and shoulders aching as he smoothed a nick from the lintel. The smell of last year's garden drifted up past him: musty dandelion fluff, dried jasmine blossoms, and the last of the sweet clover used for their beds. Matalina was a traditionalist and didn't like the foam he'd cut from a sofa he'd found at the curb last fall.

The rasping of his lathe against the living oak only accentuated the absence of his kids; the quiet was both odd and comforting after a winter spent in his human-size partner's church. Shifting his lower wings to push the glowing, silver pixy dust upward to light his work, Jenks ran a hand across the wood to gauge the new, decorative curve. A slow smile spread across his face.

"Tink's panties, she'll never know," he whispered, pleased. The gouge his daughter had made while chasing her brother was now rubbed out. All that was needed was to smooth it, and his beautiful and oh-so-clever wife would never know. Or at least she'd never say anything.

Satisfied, Jenks tilted his wings and darted to his tools. He would've asked his daughter to fix the archway, but it took cold metal, and at five Jolivia didn't yet have the finesse to handle toxic metal. Spilling more dust to light his well-used tools, he chose an emery board, swiped from Rachel's bathroom.

Late March, he thought as he returned to his work, the sparse sawdust mixing with his own pixy dust as he worked in the silence and chill. Late March, and they still hadn't moved back into the garden from Rachel's desk, on loan for the winter. The days were warm enough, and the nights would be fine with the main hearth lit. Cincinnati's pixies were long out of hibernation, and if they didn't move into the garden soon, someone might try to claim it. Just yesterday his kids had chased off three fairy scouts lurking about the far graveyard wall.

Breath held against the oak dust, Jenks wondered how many children he would lose this fall to romance and how it would affect the garden's security. Not much now, with only eight children nearing the age of leaving. Next year, though, eleven more would join them, with no newlings to replace them.

A burst of anxious motion from his wings lit a larger circle to show the winter-abandoned cushions about the main central hearth, but it wasn't until a sudden commotion at the ground-floor tunnel entrance that he spilled enough dust to light the edges to show the shelves, cupboards, and hooks built right into the living walls of the stump. "If there's no snapped wings or bones sticking out, I don't want to hear about it!" he shouted, his mood brightening as he recognized his children's voices.

"Papa. Papa!" Jerrimatt, one of his youngest sons, shouted in excitement as he darted in, trailing silver dust. "We caught an intruder at the street wall! He wouldn't leave, even when we scared him! He said he wanted to talk to you. He's a poacher, I bet, and I saw him first!"

Jenks rose, alarmed. "You didn't kill him, did you?"

"Naww," the suddenly dejected boy said as he tossed his

blond hair in a credible mimicry of his dad. "I know the rules. He had red on."

Exhaling, Jenks let his feet touch the ground as, in a noisy mob, Jack, Jhem, Jumoke, and Jixy pushed a fifth pixy wing-stumbling into the room.

"He was on the fence," Jixy said, roughly shoving the stranger again to make his wings hum, and she touched her wooden sword, ready to smack him if he made to fly. She was the eldest in the group, and she took her seniority seriously.

"He was looking at our flower beds," Jumoke added. The dark-haired pixy's scowl made him look fiercer than usual, adding to his unusual dark coloring.

"And he was lurking!" Jack exclaimed. If there was trouble, Jack would be in it.

The five were on sentry detail this evening, and Jenks set the emery board aside, eyeing his own sword of pixy steel nearby. He would rather have it on his hip, but this was his home, damn it. He shouldn't need to wear it inside. Yet here he was with a strange pixy in his main room.

Jerrimatt, all of three years old, was flitting like a fire-fly on Brimstone. Reaching up, Jenks caught his foot and dragged him down. "He is wearing red," Jenks reminded him, glad they hadn't drawn blood from the hapless pixy, wide-eyed and scared. "He gets passage."

"He doesn't want passage," Jerrimatt protested, and Jixy nodded. "He was just sitting there! He says he wants to talk to you."

"Plotting," Jixy added suspiciously. "Hiding behind a color of truce. He's pixy trash." She threatened to smack him, stopping only when Jenks sent his wings clattering in disapproval.

The intruder stood with his feet meekly on the floor, his wings closed against his back, and glancing uneasily at Jumoke. His red hat of truce was in his hands, fingers going around and around the brim. "I wasn't plotting," he said indignantly. "I have my own garden." Again, his gaze landed on Jumoke in question, and Jenks felt a prick of anger.

"Then why are you looking at ours?" Jhem demanded, oblivious to the intruder's prejudice against Jumoke's dark hair and eyes. But when Jhem went to push him, Jenks buzzed a warning again. Eyes down, Jhem dropped back. His children were wonderful, but it was hard to teach restraint when quick sword-point justice was the only reason they survived.

At a loss, Jenks extended a hand to the ruffled pixy as his children watched sullenly. The pixy buck before him looked about twelve or thirteen, old enough to be on his own and trying to start a family, married by the clean and repaired state of his clothes. He was healthy and well-winged, though they were now blue with the lack of circulation and pressed against his back in submission. The unfamiliar sword in Jumoke's grip led Jenks to believe the intruder's claim to having a garden was likely not an exaggeration, even if it was fairy steel, not pixy. The young buck wasn't poaching. So what did he want?

Jenks's own suspicions rose. "Why are you here?" he asked, his focus sliding again to his own sword, set carelessly next to his tools. "And what's your name?"

"Vincet," the pixy said immediately, his eyes roving over the sunset gray ceiling. "You live in a castle!" he breathed as his wings rose slightly. "Where is everyone?"

Vincet, Jenks thought, wary even as he straightened with pride at Vincet's words concerning his home. A six-letter name, and out on his own with cold steel. Pixies born early into a family had short names, those born later, the longest. Vincet was the fifth brood of newlings in his family to survive to naming. That he had a blade and a long name to his credit meant that his birth clan was strong. It was the children born late in a pixy's life that suffered the most when their parents died and the clan fell apart. Most children with names longer than eight letters never made it. Jerrimatt, though . . . Jenks's smile grew fond as he looked at the blond youngster scowling fiercely at Vincet. Jerrimatt, his birth brother, and both his birth sisters would survive. Matalina was stronger now that she wasn't having children anymore. One or two more seasons, and all her children would survive her. It was what she prayed for.

Not knowing why he trusted Vincet, Jenks gestured for his children to relax, and they began shoving one another. The earth's chill soaked into Jenks now that he wasn't moving, and he wished he'd started a fire.

"I heard you investigate things," Vincet blurted, his wings lifting slightly as the kids ringing him drifted a few paces back. "I'm not poaching! I need your help."

"You want Rachel or Ivy." Jenks rose up to show him the way into the church. "Rachel is out," he said, glad now he hadn't accompanied her on her shopping trip as she searched for some obscure text her demonic teacher wanted. She'd be in the ever-after tomorrow for her weekly teaching stint with the demon, and of course she'd waited until the last moment to find the book. "But Ivy is here."

"No!" Vincet exclaimed, his wings blurring but his feet solidly on the poker-chip floor, rightfully worried about Jenks's kids. "I want *your* help, not some lunker's. I don't have anything they'd want, and I pay my debts. They'll tell me to move. And I can't. I want you."

His kids stopped their incessant shoving, and Jenks's feet touched the cold floor. *A job?* he thought, excitement zinging through him. *For me? Alone?*

"Will you help me?" Vincet asked, the dust from him turning a clear silver as he regained his courage and his wings shivered to try and warm himself. "My newlings are in danger. My wife. My three children. I don't dare move now. It's too late. We'll lose the newlings. Maybe the children, too. There's nowhere to go!"

Newlings, Jenks thought, his focus blurring. A newborn pixy's life was so chancy that they weren't given names or considered children until they proved able to survive. To bury a newling wasn't considered as bad as burying a child. Though that was a lie. He and Matalina had lost their entire birthing the year they moved into the church, and Matalina hadn't had any more since, thanks to his wish for sterility. It had probably extended Mattie's life, but he missed the soft sounds newlings made and the pleasure he took in thinking up names as they grasped his finger and demanded another day of life. Newlings, hell. They were children, every one precious.

Jenks's gaze landed squarely on Vincet, assessing him. Thirteen, with a lifetime of responsibility on him already. Jenks's own short span had never bothered him—a fast childhood giving way to grief and heartache—until he'd seen the other side, the long adolescence and even longer life of the lunkers around them. It was so unfair. He'd listen.

And if he was listening, then he should probably make Vincet feel at home. As Rachel did when people knocked on her door, afraid and helpless.

A flush of uncertainty made his wings hum. "We're entertaining," he told his kids with a firmness he'd dredged up from somewhere, and they looked at one another, wings drooping and at a loss. Pixies didn't tolerate another on their land unless marriage was being discussed, much less invite him into their diggings.

Smiling, Jenks gestured for Vincet to sit on the winter-musty cushions, trying to remember what he'd seen Rachel do when interviewing clients. "Um, give me his sword, and get me a pot of honey," he said, and Jerrimatt gasped.

"H-honey . . ." the youngster stammered, and Jenks took the wooden-handled blade from Jhan. The fairy steel was evidence of a past battle won, probably before Vincet had left home.

"Tink's burned her cookies, go!" Jenks exclaimed,

waving at them. "Vincet wants my help. I don't think he's going to run me through. Give your dad an ounce of credit, will you?"

His cursing was familiar, and knowing everything was okay, they dove for the main tunnel, chattering like mad.

"I brought you all up," he shouted after them, conscious of Vincet watching him. "You don't think I know a guest from a thief?" he added, but they were gone, the sound of their wings and fast speech fading as they vanished up the tunnel. It grew darker as their dust settled and went out. Chilled, Jenks vibrated his wings for both warmth and light.

Making a huff, Jenks handed the pixy his sword, thinking he'd never done anything like *that* before. Vincet took it, seeming as unsure as Jenks was. Asking for help was in neither of their traditions. Change came hard to pixies when adherence to rigid customs was what kept them alive. But for Jenks, change had always been the curse that kept him going.

Jenks darted to a second, smaller hearth at the outskirts of the room for the box that held kindling. Insurance wouldn't allow a fire inside the church, and the kit had never made it inside. *And if I'm interviewing a client*, he thought, worried he might not make a good impression, *it should be by more than the glow of my dust*. The interview should be given the honor of the main hearth in the center of the room.

Vincet slid his sword away, his wings shivering for warmth as he looked at the ceilings.

"Um, you want to sit down?" Jenks said again as he returned with the kindling, and Vincet gingerly lowered himself to the edge of the cushion beside the dark fire pit. Though never starting outright war, poaching was a plague upon pixy society. Even being used to bending the rules, Jenks felt a territorial surge when Vincet's eyes scanned the dim room.

"I heard you lived in a castle of oak," Vincet said, clearly in awe. "Where is everyone?"

Watching him, Jenks struck the rocks together, whispering the words to honor the pixies who first stole a live flame and to ask for a prosperous season. Matalina should be at his side as he started the season's first flame, and he felt a pang of worry, wondering if it was wrong to do this without her.

"Right now we're living in the church," he said as an ember caught the charred linen, glowing as he added bits of fluff. "We're going to move out this week." *I hope.*

Vincet's wings stilled. "You live inside. With . . . lunkers?"

Smiling, Jenks began placing small sticks. With an instinctive shift of the muscles at the base of his wings, he modified the dust he was laying down to make it more flammable. It caught immediately, and stray bits floated up like motes of stars. "For the winter so we don't have to hibernate. I've seen snow," he said proudly. "It burns, almost, and turns your fingers blue."

Perhaps I could turn one of the storage rooms into an office? he thought as he set the first of the larger sticks on the flames and rose from his knees. But the thought of Matalina's eyes, pained as strangers violated their home repeatedly, made him wince. She was a grand woman, saying nothing when his fairy-dusted schemes burned in his brain. Better to ask Rachel to bury a flowerpot upside down in the garden beside the gate at the edge of the property. Hang a sign out or something. If he was going to help Cincinnati's pixies, he should be prepared.

"I need your help," Vincet said again, and Jenks's dust rivaled the firelight.

"We don't hire ourselves out for territory disputes," Jenks said, not knowing what else the pixy buck could want.

"I'd not ask," Vincet said, clearly affronted as his wings slipped a yellow dust. "If I can't hold a piece of ground, I don't deserve to garden it. My claim is strong. My wife and I have land, three terrified children from last year, and six newlings. I had seven yesterday."

Though the young pixy's voice was even, his smooth, childlike face clenched in heartache. Seeing his pain, Jenks settled back, impressed that this was his second season as a father, and he had managed to raise three children already. It had taken him and Matalina two seasons to get their first newlings past the winter, and no newlings at all had survived that third winter. "I'm sorry," he said. "Food is hard at this time of year."

Vincet had his head bowed, mourning. "It's not the food. We have enough, and both Noel and I would gladly go hungry to feed our children. It's the statue." His head came up, and Jenks felt a stab of concern at Vincet's haunted expression. "You've got to help me—you work with a witch. It's magic. It's driving my daughter mad in her sleep, and last night, when I kept her awake, it killed one of my newlings."

Jenks's wings angled to catch the heat from the fire, and a sudden surge of warmth drove out the chill that had taken him. *A statue?* Leaning forward, Jenks wished he had a clipboard or a pencil like Ivy always had when she interviewed clients. He didn't know what to say, but a pen always made Ivy look like she knew what she was doing. "A statue?" he prompted, and Vincet bobbed his head, his blond hair going everywhere.

"That's how we got the garden," he said, his words faster now that Jenks was listening. "It's in a park. The flower beds abandoned. No sign of pixy or fairy. We didn't know why. Last year, we held a spot of ground in the hills, but lunkers cut it down, built a house, and didn't put in any flowers or trees to replace what they destroyed. I barely got my family out alive when the dozers came. Noel—that's my wife—was near her time. She couldn't fly much. The park was empty. We didn't know the ground was cursed. I thought it was goddess-sent, and now my children . . . The newlings . . . They're dying in their sleep, burning up!"

Jenks crossed his knees, trying to look unaffected by Vincet's outburst, but in reality, he was worried. Rachel always got as much information as she could before saying yes or no. He didn't know what difference it made, but he asked, "What park are you in?"

Vincet licked his lips. "I don't know. I've not heard anyone say the name of the place yet. I'll take you there. It's by a long set of steps in the middle of a grassy place. It was perfect. We took the flower beds, dug out a small room under the roots of a dogwood. Noel brought to life seven newlings. We were even thinking of naming them. Then Vi, my daughter, began sleepflying."

Frowning, Jenks shivered his wings for some light as he sat across the fire from him. "Sleepflying? She'll outgrow it. One of my sons spent a summer waking up in the garden more than his bed." Jenks smiled. There was always some question if Jumoke had been sleepflying, or simply looking for solitude. His middle-brood son endured a lot of good-natured ribbing from his elder siblings due to his brown hair and hazel eyes, rare to the point of shame among pixies.

Vincet made a rude huff, the dust from his wings turning black. "Did your son scream in pain as his wings smoldered while he beat at a statue? Did his aura become sickly, and pale? My daughter isn't sleepflying, she's being attacked. I can't wake her up until the moon passes its zenith. Even if I bend her wing backward. It's been happening every night now that the moon is nearly full."

Vincet's face went riven with grief, and his head dropped. "Last night I kept her awake, and the statue attacked a newling. Noel held him as he died, unable to breathe, he was screaming so. It was . . ." The young pixy's wings drooped, and he wiped his eyes, black dust slipping from his fingers when the tear dried. "I couldn't wake him. We tried and tried, but he just kept screaming as his wings turned to powder and his dust burned inside him."

Horrified, Jenks shifted on his cushion, not knowing what to say. Vincet's child had burned alive?

Vincet met his eyes, begging without saying a word.

"Noel is afraid to let the newlings sleep," he whispered, his hands wringing and his wings still as he sat on Jenks's winter-musty cushion. "My children are terrified of the dark. A pixy shouldn't be afraid of the dark. It's where we belong, under the sun and moon."

Jenks's paternal instincts tugged on him. Vincet wasn't much older than Jax—his eldest now on his own. If he hadn't seen Vincet's fear, he would have said the pixy buck was dust-struck. Taking a stick as thick as his arm, Jenks knelt to put it on the fire, dusting it heavily to help it catch. "I don't see how a statue can cause children to go wandering," he said hesitantly, "much less set their dust on fire. Are you sure that's the cause? Maybe it's a mold or a fungus."

Vincet's dust turned a muddy shade of red as it pooled about his boots. "It's not a mold or fungus!" he exclaimed, and Jenks eyed his sword. "It's the statue! Nothing grows on it. It's cursed! And why would her aura shift like that? Something is in her!"

Jenks's wings hummed as he drew back from the hearth. Making a statue come to life to torment pixies didn't sound like witch magic, but there were other things that hadn't come out of the closet when the pixies, vampires, and witches had—things that would cause humans to raze the forests and plow the abandoned smaller towns into dust if they knew. But a statue? And why would a statue want to destroy itself? Unless . . . something *was* trapped in it?

"Have you felt anything?" he asked, and Vincet glanced at the dark tunnel behind him.

"No." He shifted uncomfortably, looking at his sword. "Neither has Noel. I've nothing to give you but my sword, but I'd gladly hand it over to you if you'll help us. I'm lost. I can defend my land from fairies, hummers, crows, and rats, but I can't see what is killing my children. Please, Jenks. I've come such a long way. Will you help me?"

Embarrassed, Jenks looked at the young man's sword as

Vincet held it out to him, his face riven with helplessness. "I won't take another man's steel," Jenks said gruffly, and the young pixy went terrified.

"I have nothing else . . ." he said, the tip of the sword falling to rest on his knees.

"Now, I wouldn't say that," Jenks said, and Vincet's wings filled the room with the sound of a thousand bees and the glow of the sun. "You have two hands. Can you make a dragonfly hut out of a flowerpot?"

Vincet's hope turned to disgust. "I'll not take charity," he said, standing up with his sword in a tight grip. "And I'm not stupid. You have a castle and a large family. You can make a dragonfly hut yourself."

"No!" Jenks said, standing up after him. "I want an office on the edge of the property, on the street side of the wall that divides the garden from the road. Can you build me that? Under the lilac? And paint me a sign if I give you the letters for it? It's not garden work, and I can't ask my children to make me an office. My wife would pluck my wings!"

Vincet hesitated. His eyes shut in a slow blink, and when they opened, hope shone again. "I can do that."

Smiling, Jenks wondered if Jax had made half as honorable a man. The dust-caked idiot had run off, poorly trained, with a thief. Jenks's last words to him had been harsh, and it bothered him, for once a child left the garden, he was gone forever. Usually. But Jenks's kids were changing that tradition, too. "I'll take a look," Jenks said. "Me and my partner, Bis," he added in a sudden thought. Rachel never went on a run without backup. He should take someone, too. "If I can help you, then you'll build me an office out of a flowerpot."

Looking up at him, Vincet nodded, relief a golden dust slipping from him. "Thank you," he said, sliding his sword away with a firm intent. "Can you come now?"

Jenks looked askance at the ceiling to estimate the light. The sun was down by the looks of it, and Bis would be awake.

"Absolutely. But, ah, I have to let my wife know where I'm going."

Vincet sighed knowingly, and together they flew up the short passage to the sun, leaving the fire to go out by itself.

PIXY SITUATIONS, INQUIRE HERE, Jenks thought as he guided Vincet to the garden wall to sit with Jumoke while he talked with Matalina. What harm could ever come of that?

2

Hands on his hips to maintain his balance, Jenks shifted his wing angle to keep his position as the night wind gusted against him. Before him, the distant evening traffic was a background hum to the loud TVs, radios, and phone conversations beating on his ears in the dark, coming from the brightly lit townhouses across the street. Behind him were the soft sounds of a wooded park. The noise from the nearby city was almost intolerable, but the small garden space with its two statues and profusion of flowers in the middle of the city was worth the noise pollution. The barrage was likely reduced to low thumps and rumbles underground where Vincet had begun to make a home for his young family.

His middle was empty, and as he waited for Vincet to return from telling Noel they were back, Jenks fumbled in a waist pack for a sticky wad of nectar, honey, and peanut butter. His human partners were clueless, but if he didn't eat every few hours, he'd suffer. What Rachel and Ivy didn't know wouldn't hurt them.

"That's the statue, eh?" he said when Vincet rejoined him and they both came to rest on the back of a nearby bench. It was across the sidewalk from Vincet's flower beds, and staying off the greenery made both of them happier—even if he had been invited and was wearing his red bandanna like a belt. He hesitated, and then thinking it might be required as part of his new "helping" role, he offered Vincet a sweetball. He'd never given food to anyone outside his family before. It felt odd, and Vincet blinked at him, clearly shocked at the offer.

"No, thank you," he said, looking confused. "Um. Yes, that's the statue." Vincet pointed at the closest statue, and Jenks slipped the second sweetball away. "It won't attack until the moon is higher," Vincet added, more at ease now that the food was put away. Wings shivering, he glanced up at the moon, a day shy of full. "It attacks at midnight, not the lunkers' clocked midnight, but the real midmoon when it's at its zenith."

Jenks's attention dropped to the twin statues spaced about ten feet apart, surrounded by new annuals and low shrubs. Both had a Greek look about them, with a classic beauty of smooth lines and draping robes. The older statue was black in places from pollution, making it almost more beautiful. Carved ringlets of hair pulled back and braided framed a young-looking face, almost innocent in her expression. Her stone robes did little to hide her admittedly shapely legs from her thighs down. There was a flaccid water sack on her belt, and her fingers were wrapped about the butt of a sword, pushing into the pedestal at her toe.

The second statue was of a young man with smooth, almost feminine features. An empty ankle sheath was on one bare leg not covered by his stone robe. He was lithe, thin, with a hint of wild threat in his chiseled expression. The sign between them, framed by newly planted, honey-smelling alyssum, said that both statues had been donated by the Kalamack Foundation to commemorate Cincinnati gaining city status in 1819, but only the statue of the woman looked old. The other was a pearly white as if brand-new. Or freshly scrubbed, maybe.

A distant argument over burned rice became audible from over the grass between the garden and the nearby townhouses. Tink's tampons, humans were noisy. It was as

if they didn't have a place in the natural order anymore, so
they made as much noise as they could to prove they were
alive. His garden and graveyard stretching an entire block
within the suburbs, now made his by human law and a deed,
was a blessing he'd come to take for granted. Rachel and
Ivy never seemed to make much noise. 'Course, they slept a
lot, and Ivy was a vampire, if living. She never made much
noise to begin with.

"Did you clean it?" he asked Vincet, and the young pixy
shook his head, looking scared.

"No. It was like that when we got here. Vi wakes as
if in a trance, mindless as she hits the base of the statue
until the burning brings her down. Then she screams until
the moon shifts from the top of the sky and the statue lets
her go."

Jenks scratched the base of his wings, puzzled. Though
he didn't move from the back of the bench, his wings
sent a glitter of dust over them. Holy crap, he had to pee
again.

Vincet pulled his frightened gaze from the white stone
glinting in the light of a nearby streetlamp. "I'd fight if I
could. I'd die defending my children if I could see it. Is it
a ghost?"

"Maybe." Pulling his hands from his hips, Jenks crossed
his arms. It was a bad habit he'd gotten from Rachel, and
he immediately put his fists back on his hips where they
belonged.

A sudden noise in the trees above them caught them
unawares, and while Jenks remained standing on the
back of the bench, Vincet darted away, clearly surprised.
It was Bis, returning from his circuit of the park under
Jenks's direction. Jenks was used to giving orders, but
not while on a run, and he nervously hoped he was doing
this right.

With a soft hush of sliding leather and the scent of iron,
the cat-size gargoyle landed on the back of the bench, his
long claws scrabbling for purchase. Bis could cling to a ver-

tical slab of stone with no problem, slip through a crack a bat would balk at, but trying to balance on the thin back of the slatted bench was more than he could manage. With an ungraceful hop, he landed on the concrete sidewalk between the bench and the statues.

"Nothing larger than an opossum near here," the gray, smooth-skinned kid said, his ears pricked to make the white fur lining them stick out. He had another tuft on the tip of his lionlike tail, but apart from that, his pebbly patterned skin was smooth, able to change color to match what was around him and creep Jenks out. He had a serious face that looked something like a pug's, shoved in and ugly, but Jenks's kids loved him. And his cat, Rex, was enamored of the church's newest renter. Jenks sighed. Once the feline found out Bis could kick out the BTUs when he wanted to, adoration was a foregone conclusion.

Bis was too young to be on his own, and after having been kicked off the basilica for spitting on people, he'd found his way to the church, slipping Jenks's sentry lines like a ghost. Bis slept all day like a proverbial stone, and he paid his rent by watching the grounds during the four hours around midnight when Jenks preferred to sleep. He ate pigeons. Feathers and all. Jenks was working on changing that. At least the feathers part. He was working on getting Bis to wear some clothes, too. Not that anything showed, but if Bis was wearing something, Jenks might catch him sneaking around on the ceiling. As it was, all he ever saw was claw marks.

"Thanks, Bis," Jenks said, standing straighter and trying to look like he was in charge. "You grew up around stone. What's your take on the statue? Is it haunted?"

It might have been a jest if anyone else had said it, but both of them knew there were such things as ghosts. Rachel's latest catastrophe, Pierce, was proof of that, but he had been completely unnoticed when bound to his tombstone. Only when it had cracked had Pierce escaped to harass them. Get a body. Become demon-snagged. Confuse

Rachel into a love/hate relationship. Something was wrong with the girl. But now that he thought about it, maybe that's why Vincet's daughter was trying to break the statue. *Tink's a Disney whore,* not *another ghost.*

The gargoyle flicked his whiplike tail in a shrug. His powerful haunches bunched, and Vincet darted back with a flash of pixy dust when Bis landed atop the statue in question, his skin lightening to match the marble perfectly. Looking like part of the statue itself, he scraped a claw down a fold of chiseled hair. Bis brought it to his nose, sniffing, then tasting. "High-quality granite," he said, his voice both high and rumbling. "From Argentina. It was first worked hundreds of years ago, but it's only been here for a hundred and twenty."

Impressed, Jenks raised his eyebrows. "You got all that from tasting it?"

Smirking to show his black teeth, the kid pointed a claw to a second sign. "Just the high-quality part. There's a plaque."

Vincet sighed, and Jenks's wings went red.

Wheezing his version of laugher, the gargoyle hopped to the spot of light on the sidewalk. "Seriously, something is wrong. Both statues are on the ley line running through the park. No one puts two statues on a ley lines. It pins it down and weird stuff happens."

"There's a line?" Jenks asked, seeing Vincet looking understandably lost. "Where?"

Bis pointed at nothing Jenks could see, cocking his ugly, bald head first one way, then the other as he focused on the flower beds. "Lines don't move, but they shift like the tide under the moon—unless they're pinned down. Something is absorbing energy from the line—right between the statues where it's not moving."

"It's the statue," Vincet said, glancing at the shadowed hole beside the dogwood tree where his family lived. "It comes alive when the moon is high and the pull is the strongest. It's possessing my daughter!"

"I don't think it's the statue," Jenks murmured, hands on his hips again. "I think it's something trapped in it." Puzzled, he stared at nothing. His partner Rachel was a witch. She could see ley lines, pull energy off them, and use it to do magic. Bis could see ley lines, too, which made Jenks doubly glad he'd brought Bis with him. "You can see it, huh?" Jenks asked.

"It's more like hear it," Bis said, his big red eyes blinking apologetically.

"It's almost time," Vincet said, clearly scared as he glanced up at the nearly full moon with his fingers on the hilt of his sword. "See? As soon as the moon hits that branch, it will attack Vi. Jenks, I can't move my family. We'll lose the newlings. It will break Noel's heart."

"That's why we're here," he said, putting a hand on Vincet's shoulder, thinking it felt odd to give comfort to a pixy not of his kin. The pixy buck looked too young for this much grief, his smooth features creased in a pain that most lunkers didn't feel until they were thirty or forty, but pixies lived only twenty years if they were lucky. "I won't let any of your children die tonight," he added.

Bis cleared his throat as he scraped his claws the side-walk, silently pointing out the danger in making promises that he couldn't guarantee. Vincet's wings drooped, and Jenks took his hand from his shoulder. "Maybe I should go to sleep," Jenks said softly. "If you kept all your children awake, it would have no choice but to attack me."

"Too late." Bis made a shuffling hop to land on the bench's seat, wings spread slightly to look ominous. "The resonance of the line just shifted."

"Sweet mother of Tink," Vincet whispered, wings flashing red as he looked at his front door. "It's coming. I have to wake them!"

"Wait!" Jenks flew after him and caught his arm. Their wings almost tangled, and Vincet yanked out of his grip.

"They'll die!" he said angrily.

"Wake the newlings." Jenks's hand dropped to the butt of his sword. "Let the children sleep. I'm sorry, but they'll survive. I'll protect Vi as if she was my own."

Vincet looked torn, not wanting to trust another man with his children's lives. Panicked, he turned to a secluded knoll and the freshly turned earth of his newling's grave, still glowing faintly from the dust of tears. "I can't . . ."

"Vincet, I have fifty-four kids," Jenks coaxed. "I can keep your child alive. You asked me to help. I have to talk to whatever is trapped in that statue. Please. Bring her to me."

Hesitating, Vincet's wings hummed like a thousand bees in the dark.

"I promise," Jenks said, only now understanding why Rachel made stupid vows she knew she might not be able to keep. "*Let me help you.*"

Vincet's wings turned a sickly blue. "I have no choice," he said, and trailing a gray sparkle of dust to light the dew-wet plants, he flew to his home and disappeared under the earth.

Watching him, Jenks started to swear with one-word sentences. What if he couldn't do this? He was a stupid-ass to have promised that. He was as bad as Rachel. Angry, he fingered the butt of his sword and glared at the statue. Bis edged closer, his eyes never leaving the cold stone glinting in the moon and lamplight. "What if I'm making a mistake?" Jenks asked.

"You aren't," the gargoyle said, then stiffened, his glowing eyes widening as he pointed a knobby finger at the statue. "Look at that!"

"Holy crap, what is it doing?" Jenks exclaimed, the heartache of a child's death gone as the moonlight seeping through the branches brushed the statue, seeming to make it glow. *No*, he thought as a gust of wind pushed him back. The stone really *was* glowing, like it had a second skin. It wasn't the moonlight!

"Are you seeing what I'm seeing?" Jenks said, dropping to land beside Bis on the bench.

"Yeah." The kid sounded scared. "Something's trapped in that stone, and it's still alive. Jenks, that's not a ghost. This isn't right. Look, I've got goose bumps!"

Not looking at Bis's gray, proffered arm, Jenks muttered, "Yeah, me too."

Across the street, three TVs exploded into the same laugh track. The glow about the statue deepened, becoming darker, less like a moonbeam and more like a shadow. It stretched, pulling away to maintain the same shape as the statue, looking like a soul trying to slip free.

"Fewmets!" Bis barked, and with a ping of energy Jenks felt press against his wings, the shadow separated from the statue and vanished. "Did you see that? Did you freaking see that!" Bis yelled, wingtips shaking.

"It's gone!" Jenks said, unable to stop a shudder.

The bench shook as Bis hopped to the sidewalk and tucked under the slatted wood. "Not gone, loose," he said from underneath, worrying Jenks even more. "Hell's bells, I can hear it. It sounds like bird feathers sliding against each other, or scales. No, tree branches and bones."

Uneasy, Jenks slipped through the slats of the bench to alight beside Bis on the sidewalk where the heat of the day still lingered, watching the same empty air that the gargoyle was staring at. A thin lament rose from the small hummock of Vincet's home. The sound hit Jenks and twisted, and he wasn't surprised when the glow about the door brightened, and in a glittering yellow pixy dust, Vincet emerged with a small child in his arms.

She was in a white nightgown, her fair hair down and tousled. Two wide-eyed children clung to the door, a matronly silhouette beside them, crying and unable to leave the newlings.

The memory of the past night's torment was on Vincet when he joined them under the bench. "It's Vi," he said, grief-stricken. "Please, you said you'd help."

Jenks awkwardly took another man's child, feeling how light she was, stifling a shudder when the girl's unnatural, silver-tinted aura hit him. A piercing wail came from her throat, too anguished to be uttered by someone so young. Bis's ears pinned to his skull, and Jenks shifted his grip, binding her swinging arms and tightening his hold on her.

"Please make it stop," Vincet said, touching his daughter's face to wipe her dusty tears.

Though it went against his instincts, Jenks brought the girl to his shoulder. Like a switch, the child's wailing shifted to an eerie silence. Bis hissed and backed up, the scent of iron sifting over them as his claws scraped the sidewalk until he found the earth.

Jenks shivered. Not knowing what he'd find, he pulled the child from his shoulder and held her at arm's length.

At the shift of her weight, the child opened her eyes. They were black, with silvery pupils—like the sky and the moon—and her weird-ass aura.

"Trees," whispered Vi, clearly not Vi at all. Her voice was wispy, like wind in branches. "This cold stone is killing me."

Bis hissed as he clung to a tree like a misshapen squirrel, black teeth bared and tail switching. Vincet stood helpless, wings drooped and silent tears falling from him to dry into a black, glittery dust. He reached out, and Vi screamed wildly, "I have to get out!"

Jenks held her with her bare feet dangling. It wasn't Vincet's daughter speaking. Under the hatred streaming from Vi's eyes was a pinched brow and a fevered panting. Whatever gripped Vi was drawing the ley line through her. That's why she burned.

"Something is wrong with it," Bis hissed, half hidden by the tree. "The statue is sucking up the line like it's feeding off it, and I can hear it going right into her."

"Who are you?" Jenks whispered.

The young girl's eyes rolled to the moon. "Free me, Rhenoranian!" she begged it. "I beg you! Have I not suffered enough!"

Rhenoranian? Jenks's wings blurred into motion. It sounded like a demon's name. His hands holding Vi were warm from her heat, and he gently set her down, catching her shoulders as she swayed, oblivious to him. "What are you?" he asked, changing his demand as he knelt before her. "You're hurting the girl. Maybe I can help, but you're hurting Vi."

Vi's eyes tore from the moon as if seeing him for the first time. "You can hear me?" she whispered as her wings smoldered, limp against her back. Eyes focusing on Jenks, Vincet, and Bis, Vi seemed to shake herself. "Gracious Rhenoranian! You are wise and forgiving!"

Jenks rocked backward when Vi flung herself at him, her little arms encircling his knees. Bis hissed at the sudden movement, and even Vincet dropped back.

"Please, help me," she babbled, her long hair tangled as she gazed up at Jenks. "I'll do anything you ask. I'm trapped in that statue—a moon-touched nymph put me there, jealous of my attentions to her sisters. Rhenoranian sent you. I know he did. I've waited so long. Break the statue. Quick, before she comes back! She's going to come back! Please!" Vi begged.

Vincet watched wide-eyed as Jenks disentangled himself, pushing her off him and making her stand up. His hands warmed where they touched her shoulders, and he jerked away. "You're burning the child," he said. "Stop, and maybe I can help."

Anger flashed in the girl's face, then vanished. "There's no time. Break the statue!"

"You are *killing* my daughter!" Vincet shouted. "You already killed my son!"

Vi's eyes went wide. Taking a deep breath, she glanced at the second statue of the woman. His jailer, probably, and likely dead and gone. Nymphs had vanished during the Industrial Revolution, long before the Turn, brought down by pollution. "I'm sorry," she panted, but the edges of Vi's wings were starting to smolder. "I didn't know I was hurting anyone. I . . . I can't help it. It's Rhenoranian's blood. It keeps me alive, but it burns. I've been burning forever."

Rhenoranian's blood? Did he mean the ley line?

Behind them, Bis hissed. "Jenks?" he questioned. "I don't like this. It's eating the line. That's wrong like three different ways."

"Of course it's wrong! That's why it burns!" Vi shouted, then went silent, frustrated. "Break the statue and let me out, and I'll never bother the child again."

Eyes narrowing in suspicion, Jenks clattered his wings in acknowledgment to Bis. It sounded almost like a threat. Let it out or else. But the line energy running through Vi was making her tremble, and the higher the moon got, the worse it became. Soon, she would be screaming in pain, if Vincet was right, and his chance to talk to it would be gone.

"Tell me what you are," he said, grasping her wrist and bring her attention to him, but when Vi looked at him, Jenks let go, not liking what lay in the depths of her eyes.

"I'm Sylvan, a dryad," Vi said. "The nymph imprisoned me unfairly. Punishing me for my attentions to her sisters. She believes she's a goddess. Completely touched, but the demons didn't stop her. Why do you hesitate? Break my statue. Let me out!"

Jenks blinked, surprised. A dryad? In a city? Between him and the statue, Bis dropped to the grass, clearly amazed as well. "You're supposed to live in trees," Jenks said. "What are you doing in a statue?"

Twitching in pain, the child looked at Bis then back to Jenks, assessing almost. "I told you, the nymph put me there. She's touched in the head. But I survived. I learned to live on the energy right from a ley line instead of that filtered from a living tree. Though every moment I exist as if burning in Hell itself, I can survive in dead stone. I beg you, break my statue. Free me!" Vi's eyes went to her father with no recognition. "I promise I'll leave you pixies in peace. Forgive me for the agony upon the child. I cannot help it."

Still, Jenks hesitated as he looked at Vi, the hope in her flushed face too deep for her years. Something wasn't right.

Jenks pinned his wings when the wind gusted. He looked up, the scent of honey and gold tickling a memory he'd never had. Vi's eyes widened. "Too late!" she shrieked. Darting to Vincet, she kicked his shin. The pixy yelped, dropping his sword to grasp his leg. Even as Jenks flung himself into the air, Vi snatched the sword up, running, not flying, to the statue. Her nightclothes furled behind her like a ghost, and, screaming, she swung the blade at the stone. With a ping, the fairy steel broke. Using the broken hilt like a dagger, she beat at it, trying to chip the stone away.

"Jenks!" Bis shouted, and Jenks turned, bewildered but not alarmed. Until he saw what the gargoyle was pointing at.

A robed, barefoot woman stood in the middle of the sidewalk, heart-shaped face aghast as she stared at the hush of cars at the edge of the park. Lungs heaving as if in pain, she put a hand to her chest and looked at the distant buildings, their lights twinkling brighter than the stars. A sword was in her grip, and she appeared exactly like the second statue, even down to the braid her black ringlets were arranged in, shining in the light as if oiled. And her aura was *shiny*?

"It's her!" Bis shouted, bringing the woman's gaze to them.

"Who dares defile my sacred grove to free Sylvan?" she intoned, robe furling as she gestured to Bis. "Is it you?" Her arm dropped, and she peered at him in the dark. "What are you?" she asked. "A new demon dog? Come into the light."

"Let me go!" shrieked Vi, struggling now in Vincet's arms. "Let me *go*!"

Jenks darted to help Vincet, and still she fought them, her skin red and hot to the touch. At his nod, Bis awkwardly went to stand in the middle of the sidewalk between them.

"I'm a gargoyle, not a dog," he said, fidgeting like the teenager he was. "Who are you?"

The woman spun a slow circle, dismissing him. "Someone tried to free Sylvan, woke me from my rest. Did you see who it was, honorable . . . ah . . . gargoyle?"

"It was me," Jenks said, grunting when Vi's foot escaped his grip and kicked him. "What's it to you?" Turning to Vincet, he screwed his face up. "I gotta go talk to her. Can you hold her alone?"

Vincet nodded, and together they got the girl facedown on the manicured grass as she howled. Looking miserable, the young father sat on her, wincing as her screams grew violent.

Satisfied, Jenks rose up into the air to the woman's level, frowning when he saw her amusement in her steely eyes. They were silver, like the moon, and just as warm. "A pixy?" she said, laughing. "Leave my sacred grove, little sprite. Return to it, and you will die. Your children will die. I will hunt you down and destroy the very earth you ever walked upon. Go."

Fists on his hips, Jenks sifted a red dust that made it all the way to the sidewalk. "Sprite? Did you just call me a sprite, Little Miss Shiny Aura? What did you do? Eat a roll of tinfoil?"

Claws scraping, Bis edged closer, his white-tufted ears pinned to his head in submission. "Jenks," he hissed, not taking his eyes off the woman. "We should go. She's doing something weird with the line."

But Jenks flitted almost to her nose. She smelled like violet sunshine, and the gold pin holding her robe shut sparkled. "Did you just threaten me, little prissy pants?" he shot out.

Her nostrils flared, and her hand gripped her sword tighter. "You mock me? I am Daryl, and you are warned!"

Jenks snickered, his own hand on the butt of his sword. "I think if you think I'm going to fly away and let you keep some helpless dryad forever imprisoned, burning in a ley line, you got your toga too tight, babe."

Mouth open, she put a hand to her chest. "You . . . you defy me?" she said, wheezing slightly, clearly not doing well. "Do you know who I am!"

Glancing at Bis, who was silently looking up at him, pleading with him to be nice, he said, "You look asthmatic, is what you look like. Forget your inhaler at the temple?"

"I am Daryl!" she stated, then coughed. "Goddess of the woods. I've learned of steel and leather to defend my sisters, and you are . . . warned!" Turning away, she struggled to breathe.

"See, she's touched!" Vi yelled from under Vincet. Struggling, the little girl got an arm free. "Go crying to your demon, Daryl! You're a concubine! A minor nymph with delusions of goddesshood!"

Jenks's eyes widened as the woman's coughing suddenly ceased. Head turning to the base of Sylvan's statue, she straightened. A murderous look was on her, and Jenks felt a moment of panic. "Get out of that pixy, Sylvan," she intoned. "Now!"

Straining, the little girl gestured rudely. *"Ay gamisou!"* she yelled defiantly.

Jenks had no idea what she had said, but he filed it away for future use when the woman staggered back, clearly appalled.

"Jenks!" Bis whispered from under him. "Let's go!"

"I promised to help!" Jenks said, fascinated at the color the woman was turning in her outrage. "And I'm not going to leave Sylvan stuck in a statue by some nymph!"

Daryl's attention flicked to Jenks and Bis, then back to Vi. "I will not allow you to hurt another, Sylvan!" she said loudly, gesturing.

Bis reached up, wings spread as he half jumped to snag Jenks from the air and pull him down. Bis's warmth hit him as Jenks cowered in his hand while a wave of nothing he could see passed over them, pressing against his wings and driving the blood out. His wings collapsed for an instant, then rebounded on his next heartbeat.

Vi screamed, the sound reaching deep into Jenks and driving him to wiggle from Bis's fingers. His head poked free, and he saw Vincet spring into the air with his daughter. Her dust had taken on a deathly shade of black, bursting into a white-hot glow as it fell from her. Again Vi's scream tore the silence of the night as Daryl clenched her fist, her face savage with bloodlust.

"She's killing her!" Vincet shouted, terrified. "Jenks, she's killing my daughter!"

"Get her away from the line!" the gargoyle cried out as he stood his ground. "I can see the energy flowing into her. You have to get Vi out of the line!"

Jenks's lips parted. Cursing himself as a fool, he darted to Vincet, snatching the pain-racked child to him and throwing himself straight up. The line. The entire garden was in the line between the statues! Get her far enough away, and the connection would break!

Vi fought him as his ears popped painfully, thumping her fists into his chest and squirming until she suddenly went terrifyingly limp. "Vi!" Jenks shouted, scrambling to catch her as she threatened to slip from him, a good forty feet up. Her skin was hot, and her face was pale in the glow of his own dust. But a profound peace was on her face, and as he held her far above the dark city, fear struck him deep. The silver tint to her aura was gone.

"Vi," he whispered, jiggling her as the night cocooned them. "Vi, wake up. It's over." Oh God. Had he failed her? Was she dying? Killed by his own shortsightedness? Another man's child dead in his arms because of his failing?

Vi's lips parted, sucking in air like it was water. Her eyes flashed open, green and full of terror in the light of the moon.

"Tink save you, you're okay," he whispered, his eyes filling with tears. She was herself. Sylvan was no longer in her thoughts. That terror of a woman no longer burned her.

With a frightened whimper, Vi threw herself at him, her thin arms cold as they wrapped around his neck. "Don't let him hurt me," she begged as she cried, her little body shaking. "Please, don't let the statue hurt me anymore!"

A clear, healthy glow enveloped them as Jenks held her close, his hand against the back of her head as he whispered it was over, that she was okay, and he was taking her to her papa. He promised her that the statue wouldn't hurt her again and that Uncle Jenks would take care of everything. Foolish promises, but he couldn't stop himself.

Uncle Jenks, he thought, wondering why the term had fallen into his mind but feeling it was right. But below them, Daryl waited on the dark sidewalk. And Jenks—was pissed.

Jaw clenching, he descended more slowly than he wanted in order to give her younger ears a chance to adjust. Vincet met them halfway down, his wings clattering and dusting in fear until he saw Vi's tears. With a cry of joy, the grateful man took his daughter. Vi's sobs only strengthened his resolve.

"Get your family to ground and stay there," Jenks said grimly.

"I can help," Vincet said, even as Vi clung desperately to him.

"I know you can. I'll take the field, you take the hearth," he said, falling back on the battle practices of driving off invading fairies. One always stayed in earth to defend the hearth—to the end if it came to that.

Vincet looked as if he was going to protest, then probably remembering his sword was broken at the base of the statue, he nodded, darting away with Vi to vanish beneath the dogwood.

Free, and anger burning in his wings, Jenks drew his sword and dropped to where Bis was clinging to Sylvan's statue, hissing at Daryl as she stood in a spot of light with a satisfied smile.

"What the hell is wrong with you!" Jenks shouted, darting to a stop inches from the woman to make her jerk back. "You could have killed her! She's only a year old!"

Daryl's thin eyebrows rose. "A pixy?" she said haughtily, then stifled a cough. "Take your complaint to what demon will listen to you. Sylvan is in that statue, and there he will stay!"

"I'll take my complaint to you!" Jenks shouted, poking his sword at her nose.

The woman shrieked, robes furling as she swung her fist to miss him completely. "You cut me! You filthy little mouse!"

Jenks darted back, only to dive in again to slice another cut under her eye. "I'm letting Sylvan go if only to piss you off! You look like a sorority sister in hell week with that discount sheet around you! What is that, a one-fifty thread count? My three-year-old can weave better than that."

Clasping a hand over her eye, the woman shrieked, her voice echoing in the darkness. "I'll destroy you for that!" she cried, spinning to keep Jenks in front of her.

"Jenks?" Bis said loudly, half hiding behind Sylvan's statue. "Maybe we should leave the goddess alone."

"Goddess!" Jenks pulled up a safe eight feet into the air. His sword glinted red in the lamplight, and his wings hummed. Cocky, he dropped back down. "She's no goddess. She's a whiny. Little. Girl."

Angry at the woman's lack of respect, Jenks slashed at her robes with each word.

"Uh, Jenks?" Bis warbled his creased face bunched in worry as she screeched.

"Get out of here!" Jenks yelled at her like she was a stray dog. "Go find a museum or something. That's where you belong! Tell them Jenks sent you."

Panting, the woman came to a halt, staring up at him. Her face was red, and determination was equally mixed with anger. A car door slammed in the distance. Someone had heard her and was coming across the wide expanse of lawn. Oblivious, the woman jumped straight up at him with a fierce yell.

"Holy crap!" Jenks exclaimed, darting up. But the woman had sprung to her statue, scattering Bis and using it to make another leap for him. "Whoa! Lady. Chill out!" Jenks shouted as he darted to the nearby tree. Immediately he realized his mistake when Daryl leapt into the branches, following him.

"I am a *goddess*!" she screamed, her sword thunking into the branches as he dodged her. "You will die, pixy! Your name will be forgotten. Anyone who aligns themselves with Sylvan is a shade still walking!"

Maybe he went too far, Jenks wondered as her blade got closer with each swing, but before he could retreat, his wings unexpectedly froze. He had a glimpse of Daryl blowing at him with her lips pursed, and then he plummeted, falling through the leaves to the cement below.

"No!" Jenks exclaimed as the smacking of leaves against his back ceased and he dropped into free fall. A yelp escaped him when long, thin, gray fingers caught him, pulling him closer to the ashy scent of iron and dry stone. Above, Daryl scrambled to reach the ground.

"Bis!" Jenks said, dazed as he looked up to the gargoyle's red eyes. "Good God. We have to get out of here!"

"Yeah, that's what I've been telling you," Bis said dryly.

In the distance, the sound of car doors slamming and the revving of an engine told him whoever it was, was now leaving. Bis landed again on Sylvan's statue, shaking in fear. Carefully testing his wings, Jenks took to the air. Daryl was again on the sidewalk, her steely eyes watching them both in evaluation.

"You okay?" Bis said as his claws scratched the statue's forehead.

"Yeah," he said, stretching his shoulders and wondering if there was a remaining stiffness. "We have to get this bitch away from the garden before she hurts someone."

"How?"

Bis was trembling, his eyes wide and whirling. Grinning, Jenks rose farther up into the air. "I'll get her to follow me," he said to the gargoyle, then turned to the woman. "Hey, bright eyes! What's your problem with Sylvan? Did the dude bump uglies with one of your girlfriends?"

Jenks shifted his hips back and forth to make sure she knew what he was talking about, and Daryl's eyes narrowed. With no warning, she came at him silently, her robes furling in the wind from her passage.

Adrenaline pushing him, Jenks darted into the green field, leading her away. The city was nearby. He'd get her among the buildings, then ditch her. The cops would pick her up for disturbing the peace. Inderland Security would love bringing in a thought-to-be-extinct species of Inderlander with a goddess complex, but that was their job.

Laughing, Jenks sped across the grass, dark and black with the night. A ripple of wind shifted under his wings, and he looked down. An eerie keening dove down upon him, and in a surge of panic, he found himself tossed in a sudden whirlwind.

His sense of direction vanished. Tumbling, the wind beat at him, almost a living force bending his wings and tearing his breath from his lungs. Starved for air and out of control, he fell out of the sky and slammed into the ground. The wind collapsed on him, bringing him to his knees. Eyes shut, he held his wings to his back, one hand gripping his sword, the other clenched upon the grass to keep him from spinning away.

Just as suddenly as it came upon him, the wind broke into a thousand pieces of shrill voice and vanished. Dazed, he looked up, still kneeling.

Daryl was standing over him, her silver eyes gleaming like a cat's in the dark. Wheezing from the pollution, she raised her foot. "You are rude, and you will die."

"Oh, shit . . ." Jenks whispered.

A dark gray streak slammed into her chest, and, stumbling, Daryl fell back.

"Bis!" Jenks exclaimed as the gargoyle swung back around, plucking him from the ground and holding him close. "Tink loves a duck, you're a great backup!"

"You can't fly," Bis said breathlessly. "You're too light. Let's get out of here!"

"'Kay," Jenks said, grateful but feeling somewhat sheepish. This was the kind of spot he was always getting Rachel out of. He didn't like being carried, but if the woman could whistle up the wind, then he'd be better off with Bis. The moon had shifted, and Vincet and his family would be okay for another day. If the garden was sacred, Daryl wouldn't be likely to tear it apart.

Behind them came an infuriated shriek, and Jenks cringed when the roar of the wind came again. Wiggling, he inched himself up to look over Bis's shoulder, not liking the dips and swerves Bis was putting into his flight. Squinting, he looked behind him expecting to see a frustrated women standing alone, but the grass was empty. Satisfaction filled him. Until he saw the black, boiling cloud bearing down on them, rolling over the grass to leave it untouched.

"Holy shit!" he exclaimed, seeing a tiny white figure at the center. "Bis, she's flying! The freaky bitch is flying!"

Bis's smooth wing beats faltered. Glancing back, he gulped. "She's riding a ley line. Jenks, I don't know how she's doing it or what she is!"

Pointing at them with her sword, the woman clenched her teeth and grinned, clearly eager for battle. Her oiled ringlets lay flat, and her robe plastered to her like a second skin. The chugging of heavy air reverberated off the nearby buildings, but the trees were utterly still.

"Go!" shrilled Jenks, smacking Bis's shoulder. "Go to ground!"

The heat off the street was a wave as they left the park. Town homes gave way to buildings, flashing past and reduced to blurs. Cars were moments of light and noise, and still she came on, leaving the sound of horns and folding metal in her wake. Glass shattered, and Jenks hunched into Bis's protection, a new terror filling him as he realized that to take to the air now would be his death. Bis's flight grew sickeningly erratic among the buildings, and Jenks looked behind him.

They weren't going to make it.

"Down!" he screamed, voice lost in the shrieking wind. "Go to ground, Bis!"

Twisting wildly, Bis brought his wings in close, diving for a gutter drain.

"Oh-h-h-h-h no-o-o-o!" Jenks exclaimed, ducking his head.

Wings back, winging furiously in the sudden dark, Bis hit the wall with a grunt, sliding down to land in a sludge of water and goo. Putrid muck splashed up, coating Jenks in cold. Shaking his head, he lay on Bis and tried to figure out what happened.

I'm in a hole, he realized, his pulse hammering hard enough to shake him. *I'm alive.*

Above him, the wind shrieked, sounding like a woman screaming in battle. Bis shifted underneath him, and Jenks put a finger to his own lips when the gargoyle's eyes opened. Together they listened to the destruction as glass shattered and heavy things hit the earth. Slowly the roaring wind faded to leave the frightened calls of people and the growing sounds of sirens.

Shaking, Bis began to wheeze in laugher. "Holy pigeon poop. That was close," he said, sitting up slowly until Jenks took to the air.

Jenks's flash of anger at Bis's mirth dissolved as he realized they were okay and they would both live to see the sun rise. "Watch this! I'll get her to follow me, Bis!" he said, shaking his wings until a sludgy dust spilled from him to light the hole.

Bis stood shin-deep in the muck, his skin shifting toward pink as he upped his body temp. Appreciating the warmth, Jenks moved to his shoulder and tried to wipe the muck off his clothes. Matalina wouldn't be happy, and he enviously watched the mud dry and flake off Bis.

"Think she's gone?" Bis asked as he gazed up to the rectangle of brighter dark.

Jenks darted to the opening and the fresher air to hover with his head in the opening. Hands on his hips, he whistled long and low. "She tore up the street," he said loudly, looking up at the broken streetlights. "Power's out. Cops are coming. Let's get out of here."

The scrabbling of claws made him shiver, and he made the quick flight to the sidewalk when Bis slid out like an octopus. Bis shook his wings and sniffed at his armpits, then turned black to remain unnoticed. The sirens were coming closer, seeming to pull the distraught people together.

Frowning, Bis somberly clicked his nails in a rhythm that Jenks recognized as Mozart as he took in the tossed cars and broken windows. Fingers shaking, Jenks wedged a sweetball out of his belt pack and sucked on it, replenishing his sugar level before he started to burn muscle.

"Do you think all nymphs were like that?" Jenks asked, glad the muck hadn't gotten to his snack.

"Beats me."

With a push of his wings, Bis was airborne. Jenks joined him, shifting to fly above him where they could still talk. The night air felt heavy and warm, unusually muggy as they flew straight down the street and to the park. Only a small section of the city was without power, and it looked like the park was untouched.

"Maybe we should check on Vincet," Jenks said, and the gargoyle sighed, turning back to the cooler grass to check, but Jenks was already thinking about tomorrow. He had promised to help Vincet, and he would—even if it was a dryad trapped in a statue by a warrior nymph.

He had to help these people, and he had to do so before midnight tomorrow.

3

Even from inside the desk, Jenks could hear Cincinnati waking up across the river. Under the faint radio playing three houses down, the deep thumps of distant industry were like a heartbeat only pixies and fairies could hear. The hum of a thousand cars reminded him of the beehive he'd tormented when he was a child and living in the wild stretches between the surviving cities. It wasn't a bad life, living in the city—if you could find food.

Worried, he sat in his favorite chair, thinking as his family lived life around him. The doll furniture he reclined in had been purchased last year at a yard sale for a nickel, but after stripping it down, reupholstering it with spider silk, and stuffing it with down from the cottonwood at the corner, he thought it was nicer than anything he'd seen in any store Rachel had taken him in. Nicer than Trent Kalamack's furniture, even. Distant, he rubbed his thumb over the ivy pattern that Matalina had woven into the fabric. She was a master at her craft, especially now.

A faint sifting of dust slipped from him to puddle under the chair, but his glow was almost lost in the shaft of light slipping in through the crack of the rolltop desk. The massive oak desk with its nooks and crannies had been their home for the winter, but after Matalina had perched herself on the steeple last night to wait for his return, she'd breathed

in the season and decided it was time to move. So move
they did.

The voices of his daughters raised in chatter were hardly
noticed, as was the bawdy poem four of his elder sons were
shouting as they cheerfully grabbed the corners of the long
table made of Popsicle sticks and headed for the too-narrow
crack.

Matalina's voice rose in direction, and the rolltop rose
just enough. It wasn't until Matalina sent the rest of them
out to scout for a nest of wasps to steal sentries from that
it grew quiet. All his children had lived through the winter.
It was a day of celebration, but the weight of responsibility
was on him.

Responsibility wasn't new to him, but he was surprised
to feel it—seeing as it was coming from an unexpected
source. He'd always felt bad for pixies not as well off as
he, but that was as far as it had ever gone. A part of him
wanted to tell Vincet that he chose badly and he'd have
to move, newlings or not. But Vi clinging helplessly to
him had gone through Jenks like fire, and the smell of
the newlings on Vincet kept him sitting where he was,
thinking.

Jax had been his first newling he'd managed to keep alive
through the winter. Jih, his eldest daughter, had survived
in Matalina's arms that same season. Scarcely nine years
old, Jih had moved across the street alone to start a garden,
and Jax left to follow in his father's footsteps by partnering
with a thief instead of devoting himself to a family and the
earth.

Jenks had never wanted more than to tend a spot of
ground, but four years ago, forced by a late spring and suf-
fering newlings, he'd shamefully taken a part-time job as
backup for Inderland Security, finding that he not only enjoyed it, but was good at it. Working for the man had eventually evolved into a partnership with Rachel and Ivy, and
now he was on the streets more than in the garden. Turning
his back on his first independent job wasn't going to happen.

Blowing up the statue wouldn't be the hard part—it would be getting around Daryl to do it.

A nymph and a dryad, he thought sourly as he sucked on a sweetball in the quiet. Why couldn't it be something he knew something about? Nymphs had vanished during the Industrial Revolution, and the dryads had been decimated by deforestation shortly after that. There was even a conspiracy theory that the dryads had been responsible for the plague that had wiped out a big chunk of humanity forty years ago. If so, it had sort of worked. The forests were returning, and eighty-year-old trees were again becoming common. Nymphs, though, were still missing. Sleeping, maybe?

And what about Daryl, anyway? A deluded nymph, Sylvan had said. A goddess, Daryl claimed. There were no gods or goddesses. Never had been, but there were documented histories of Inderlanders taking advantage of humans, posing as deities. He frowned. Her eyes were downright creepy, and he hadn't liked demons being mentioned, either.

Jenks started, jerking when his chair moved. The breeze of four pairs of dragonfly wings blew the red dust of surprise from him, and he looked up to find four of his boys trying to move his chair with him in it. They were all grinning at him, looking alike despite Jumoke's dark hair and eyes, in matching pants and tunics that Matalina had stitched.

"Enough!" Matalina called out in a mock anger, her feet in a shaft of light, a dusting rag in her hands, and a flush to her cheeks. "Leave your papa alone. There's the girls' things to be moved if you need something to do."

"Sorry, Papa!" Jack said cheerfully, dropping his corner to make the chair thump. Jenks's feet flew up, and his wing bent back under him. "Didn't see you there."

"Dust a little," Jaul said, tangling his wings with Jack's, and Jack dusted heavily, shifting as he pushed him away. "The fairies will think you're dead," he finished, sneezing.

"Come and carry you away," Jumoke added, his wings

lower in pitch than everyone else's. It made him different, along with his dusky coloring, and Jenks worried, not
liking how Vincet had looked at him as if he were ill or
deformed.

Jake just grinned, his wings glittering as he hovered in
the background. Apart from Jumoke, they were the eldest in
the garden now, as fresh-faced and innocent as they should
be, strong and able to use a sword to kill an intruder twice
their size. He loved them, but it was likely this would be
the last spring they'd help the family move. Jack, especially,
would probably find wanderlust on him this fall and leave.

"Go do what your mother said," he grumped, grabbing
four sweetballs from the bowl beside him and throwing
them to each boy in turn. "And keep your sugar level up!
You're no good to me laid flat out in a field."

"Thanks, Papa!" they chorused, cheeks bulging. It kept
them quiet, too.

Matalina came closer, smiling fondly as she shooed them
out. "Go on. After the girls' room, find the big pots and fill
them. Check for cracks. I'm soaking spider sacks tomorrow
for the silk. They've been in the cool room all winter. If
we're not careful, we're going to have a hatching. I'm not
going to make your clothes out of moonbeams, you know."

"Naked in the garden is okay with me," Jumoke mumbled, and Matalina swatted him.

"Out!"

"Remember what happened the last year?" Jaul said,
his words muffled from the sweetball as they headed for
opening.

"Webs everywhere!" Jack said, laughing.

"Yeah, well you're the one that moved the sacks into the
sun," Jumoke said, and they were gone, the dust from them
settling in a glowing puddle to slowly fade.

"How else was I going to win the bet as to when they
were going to hatch?" came faintly from outside the desk,
and Jenks chuckled. It had been an unholy mess.

Slowly their voices vanished, and Jenks watched

Matalina's expression, gauging her mood as she smiled. Wings stilling, she walked across the varnished oak wood to settle next to him, their wings tangling as she snuggled in against him. Slowly their mingling dust shifted to the same contented gold.

"I can't wait to get back into the garden," she said, gazing at the pile of laundry across the room. "I'll admit I don't like moving day, but I'll not set myself to sleep like that again with the fear of guessing who might not wake up with me in the spring." Reaching to the bowl, she deftly twisted a sweetball into two parts and handed him half. "You're quiet. What's got your updraft cold this morning?"

"Nothing." Setting his half of the sweet back in the bowl, he draped his arm over her shoulder, moving his thumb gently against her arm. Remembering the smell of the newlings, he dropped his gaze to her flat belly, not swelling with life for more than a year now. His wish for sterility might have extended her life—but had it also made her last years empty?

Setting her sweetball aside as well, Matalina shifted from him, pulling out of his reach to sit facing him. "Is it the pixy that you and Bis went into Cincinnati to help? I'm proud of you for that. The children enjoy watching the garden when you're gone. They feel important, and they'll be all the more prepared when they've a garden of their own."

A garden of their own, he thought. His children were leaving. Vincet's children were so young. His entire adult life was before him. "Mattie, do you ever wish for newlings?" he asked.

Her eyes fell from his, and her breath seemed to catch as she stared at the piles of clothes.

Fear struck Jenks at her silence, and he sat up to take her hands in his. "Tink's tears. I'm sorry," he blurted. "I thought you didn't want any more. You said . . . We talked about it . . ."

Smiling to look even more beautiful, Matalina placed a fingertip to his lips. "Hush," she breathed, leaning her head forward to touch his as her finger dropped away. "Jenks, love, of course I miss newlings. Every time Jrixibell or any of the last children do something for the first time, I think that I'll never see the joy of that discovery on another child's face, but I don't want any more children who won't survive a day after me."

Worried, he shifted closer, his hands tightening on hers. "Mattie, about that," he started, but she shook her head, and the dust falling from her took on a red tinge.

"No," she said firmly. "We've been over this. I won't take that curse so I can have another twenty years of life. I'm going to step from the wheel happy when I reach the end, knowing all my children will survive my passing. No other pixy woman can say that. It's a gift, Jenks, and I thank you for it."

Beautiful and smiling, she leaned forward to kiss him, but he would have none of it. Anger joining his frustration, he pulled away. *Why won't she even listen?* Ever since he'd taken that curse to get lunker-size for a week, his flagging endurance had returned full force. It had fixed his mangled foot and erased the fairy steel scar that had pained him during thunderstorms. It was as if he was brand-new. And Mattie wasn't.

"Mattie, please," he began, but as every other time, she smiled and shook her head.

"I love my life. I love you. And if you keep buzzing me about it, I'm going to put fairy scales in your nectar. Now tell me how you're going to help the Vincet family."

He took a breath, and she raised her eyebrows, daring him.

Jenks's shoulders slumped and his wings stilled to lie submissively against his back. Later. He'd convince her later. Pixies died only in the fall or winter. He had all summer.

"I need to destroy a statue," he said, seeing the clean wood around him and imagining the dirt walls Vincet was living between, then remembering the flower boxes he and

Mattie had raised most of their children among. He was lucky, but the harder he worked, the luckier he got.

"Oh, good," she said distantly. "I know how you like to blow things up."

His mood eased, and he shifted her closer to feel her warmth. Pixies had known how to make explosives long before anyone else. All it took was a little time in the kitchen. *And a hell of a lot of nitrogen*, he thought. "By tonight," he added, bringing himself back to the present, "to help free a dryad."

"Really?" Eyeing him suspiciously, Matalina popped her half of the sweetball into her mouth. "I 'ought 'ay were cut 'own in the great deforestation of the eighteen hundreds. 'Ave they emigrated in from Europe?"

"I don't know," he admitted. "But this one is trapped in a statue, existing on energy right off a ley line instead of sipping it filtered from a tree. He's been slipping into Vincet's children's minds when they sleep, trying to get them to break his statue." He wasn't going to tell her the dryad had accidentally killed one. It was too awful to think about.

Matalina stood, rising on a burst of energy to dust the ceiling. "A city-living dryad?" she murmured, cleaning wood that would lay unseen for months if Rachel continued her pattern and avoided her desk even after they vacated it. "Tink loves a duck, what will they think of next?"

Jenks reclined to see if he could see up her dress. "Blowing it up isn't the problem. See, there's this nymph," he said, smiling when he caught a glimpse of a slim thigh.

She looked down at him, her disbelief clear. Seeing where his eyes were, she twitched her skirt and shifted, eyes scrunched in delight even as she huffed in annoyance. "A nymph? I thought they were extinct."

"Maybe they're just hiding," he said. "This one said something about waking up. She was having a hard time breathing through the pollution." *Until she came after us.*

Flitting to the opening in the desk, Matalina shook her rag with a crack. "Hmmm."

"She's got this goddess . . . warrior vibe," he said when Matalina returned to the ceiling. "Mattie, the woman is scary. I think if I get the dryad free, the nymph will follow him and leave Vincet in peace."

Again Matalina made that same doubt-filled sound, not looking at him as she dusted.

"Freeing the dryad is the only way I can help Vincet," Jenks said, not knowing if Matalina was unsure about Sylvan or the nymph. "He's only been on his own for a year, and he has three children and passel of newlings. He's done so well."

Matalina turned at the almost jealous tone in his words, the pride and love in her expression obvious. "You were nine, love, when you found me," she said as she dropped to him, her wings a clear silver as they hummed. "Coming from the country with burrs in your hair and not even a scrap of red to call your own. Don't compare yourself to Vincet."

He smiled, but still . . . "It took me two years to be able to provide enough for Jax and Jih to survive," he said, reaching up to take her hand and draw her to him.

His wife sat beside him, perched on the very edge of the couch with her hands holding his. "Times were harder. I'm proud of you, Jenks. None has done better. None."

Jenks scanned the nearly empty desk, the sounds of his children playing filtering in over the radio talking about the freak tornado that had hit the outskirts of Cincinnati last night. Not wanting to accept her words, he pulled her to sit on his lap, tugging her close and resting his chin on her shoulder and breathing in the clean smell of her hair. He could have done better. He could have given up the garden and gone to work for the I.S. years sooner. But he hadn't known.

"You need to help this family," she said, interrupting his thoughts. "I don't understand why you do some of the things you do, but this . . . This I understand."

"I can't do it alone," he said, grimacing as he remembered Daryl controlling the wind, taking the very element he lived in and turning it against him.

"Wasn't Bis a help?" she asked, sounding bewildered.

Jenks started, not realizing what his words had sounded like. "He was the perfect backup," he said, his words slow as he remembered almost being squished, and then Bis's frantic flight in the streets. "He's no fighter, but he yanked my butt out of the fire twice." Smiling, Jenks thought he couldn't count how many times he'd done the same for Rachel. "I'd ask Rachel to help," he said, "but she won't be home until tomorrow."

Still on his lap, Matalina reached for Jenks's half of sweetball and put it in his mouth. "Then ask Ivy," she said as he shifted it around. "She'll help you."

"Ivy?" he said, his voice muffled. "It's my job, not hers."

Collapsing against him in irritation, Matalina huffed. "The vampire is always asking *you* to help *her*," she said severely. "I don't begrudge it. It's your job! But don't be so slow-winged that you won't ask for help in return. It would be more stupid than a fairy's third birthday party for Vincet to lose a newling because you were too proud to ask Ivy to be a distraction."

Jenks thought about that, lifting Matalina to a more comfortable position on his lap. "You think I should ask her?" he asked.

Matalina shifted to give him a moot look.

"I'll ask her," he said, feeling the beginnings of excitement. "And maybe have Jumoke come out with me, too. The boy needs something other than his good looks."

Matalina made a small sound of agreement, knowing as much as he did that his dark hair and eyes would make finding a wife almost impossible.

Grinning, Jenks pushed them both into the air. She squealed as their wings clattered together, and a real smile, carefree and delighted, was on her as he spun her to him, hanging midair in the closed rolltop desk. "I'll teach Jumoke a trade so he has something to bring to the marriage pot beside cold pixy steel and a smart mind," he said, delighting in her smile. "I can teach him everything I know. It won't be like Jax. I'll make sure he knows why he's doing it, not just how. And with Ivy distracting the nymph, I'll blow up the dryad's statue. I already know how to make the explosive. I just need a whopping big amount of it."

Matalina pulled from him, holding his hands for a moment as she looked at him in pride. "Go save them, Jenks. I'll be in the garden when you get back. Bring me a good story."

Jenks drew her close, their dust and wings mingling as he kissed her soundly. "Thank you, love," he said. "You always make things seem so simple. I don't know what I'd do without you."

"You'll get along just fine," she whispered, but he was gone, already having zipped through the crack in the rolltop desk. Smile fading, Matalina looked over the empty desk. Picking up the discarded fabric, she followed him out.

4

The shouts of his kids came loud through the church's kitchen window, their high-pitched voices clear in the moisture-heavy air as they played hide-and-seek in the early dark. The boys, especially, had been glad to get out of the desk and into their admittedly more-cramped-than-a-troll's-armpit quarters in the oak stump. More cramped, but vastly more suited to a winged person smaller than a Barbie doll.

A parental smile threatened Jenks's attempt at a business-like attitude as he stood on the spigot before the window and cleared his throat. Jumoke's apprenticeship had begun, and Jenks was trying to impress on him the sensitivity needed in mixing up some pixy pow. It wouldn't be napalm, which pixies had first used to get rid of weeds—then fairies when it was discovered to their delight that it would go boom under the right conditions. And it wouldn't be C4, C3, or any other human explosive. It would be something completely different, thanks to the dual properties of stability and ignition that pixy dust contained.

"That's it, Papa?" Jumoke said doubtfully as he penciled in the last of the ingredients on one of Ivy's sticky notes. Unlike most of Cincinnati's pixies, Jenks's family could read. It was a skill Jenks taught himself shortly after reaching the city, then used it to claim a section of worthless land before the proposed flower boxes existing on a set of blueprints went in.

"That's it," he said, gazing at his son's hair. It looked especially dark in the fluorescent light. For the first time, he saw it as perhaps an asset. It wouldn't catch the sun as his own hair did, a decided advantage in sneaking around. Perhaps Jumoke was the reigning hide-and-seek champion for a reason.

Bis, newly awake and doing his sullen gargoyle thing atop the fridge, rustled his wings in disbelief. "There is no way that soap, fertilizer, lighter fluid, and pixy dust is going to blow that statue up. It's solid rock!"

"Wanna bet a week's worth of sentry duty?" Jenks asked. "I use it all the time. A pixy handful will blow surveillance lines and fry motherboards, QED. We're just going to need a lot more." Rising up, he eyed the rack of spelling equipment hanging over the center island counter. "Can you get that pot down for me?"

Jumoke made a small noise, and Bis's pebbly gray skin went black. "Rachel's spell pot?" the gargoyle squeaked in apparent fear.

Hands on his hips, Jenks hummed his wings faster. "The little one, yes. Jumoke, go see if you can find Ivy's lighter fluid out by the grill. We need more propellant than we have dust."

The young pixy darted out into the hallway, and Jenks frowned at the worried tint to his son's aura now. Tink's titties, he could use Rachel's spelling equipment. The woman wouldn't mind. Hell, she'd never even know.

Ears pinned to his ugly skull, Bis hopped the short distance from the fridge to the center island counter, jumping up with his wings spread to pluck the small copper pot. It would hold about a cup of liquid and was Rachel's favorite-size spell pot. She had two of them.

"Can I have the other one, too, please?" Jenks said dryly, and the kid's tail wrapped around his feet, his ears going flatter. "I can't touch anything but copper," he complained. "And if I use the plastic ones, they'll smell funny. Will you grow a pair and get the bowl?" he said, darting upward and smacking it to make it ping.

"Don't blame me if Rachel yells at you for using her spell pots," Bis muttered as he plucked it from the overhead rack and set it rocking next to the first. The draft from his wings blew Jenks back when Bis hopped to Ivy's chair at the big farmhouse kitchen table, pulling first the phone book, then *Vixen's Guide to Gathering Guys and Gals* down and onto the seat. The guide was the larger of the two.

"Don't blame me if Ivy de-wings you for using her computer," Jenks shot back as Bis settled onto the stack of books and shook the mouse to wake the computer up. One day he was going to get caught, and then there'd be Tink to pay. Tugging a bowl to the middle of the counter, Jenks felt a moment of guilt. "Rachel will never know. What's the problem here?"

Bis looked up from the keyboard. His thin fingers were curved so his nails touched the keys, and he snapped off Ivy's password without looking. "You didn't ask her."

"Yeah, like you said pretty-please for Ivy's password," he said, and Bis flushed dark black. Smug, Jenks pulled the recipe closer and wondered how he was going to size up the amounts. "I'll polish the stinkin' bowls when I'm done," he muttered, and Bis smirked. "I'm not afraid of Rachel!" he said, hands on his hips.

"And I'm not afraid of Ivy."

They both jumped at the hum of dragonfly wings, but it was Jumoke. "It's metal," he said, his expression going confused when he saw the panicked look on their faces. "What did I do?"

"I thought you were your mother," Jenks said, and Jumoke's wings turned a bright red as he drifted backward, giggling. It didn't seem right to be teaching a six-year-old how to make explosives. The giggling didn't help. But now was the time to start teaching him, not two weeks before he left the garden like he had Jax. There was a moral philosophy that went along with the power a pixy could wield, and he wouldn't make the same mistake with Jumoke as he had with Jax.

Bis stood, stretching his wings until the tips touched over his head. "I'll help," he said, and the two flew out into the hall and then the back living room. The cat door squeaked, and Jenks sighed, glancing at the clock. He'd already called Ivy, but she wouldn't be home for a couple more hours. The three of them would have to make a whopping amount of explosive before she got home; he didn't want Ivy to know he could make this stuff. Word would get out, and then Inderland Security would start drafting them into service. Pixies liked where they were, on the fringes and ignored . . . mostly.

Jenks drifted down until his feet hit the polished stainless steel, harmless through his boots. The squeak of the cat door brought him back to reality, and he pretended to be estimating the depth of the bowl when Bis and Jumoke flew in with the reek of petroleum.

"Because their horns don't work," Bis said. "Get it? Because their horns don't work?"

The thunk of the tin can hitting the counter was loud, and Jenks's hair shifted in the gust from Bis's wings. "Jumoke, what do you think. A cup?" Jenks asked, measuring the bowl off at his shoulder and pacing around the perimeter.

"I don't get it," Jumoke said, and after landing inside one of the bowls, he added, "A cup and a third to the brim?"

"You know, their horns?" The gargoyle reached up and touched the tiny nubs where his would be when he grew up.

"Bis, I don't get it!" Jumoke said, clearly embarrassed. "Dad, what's next?"

Jenks smiled, pleased. A cup and a third. Jumoke had it right. Jenks looked up to find Bis and Jumoke watching him eagerly. Teaching an adolescent pixy and teenage gargoyle how to make explosives might not be such a good idea. But hell, he'd learned when he was five.

"Mmmm, Ivory soap," he said. "Ivy has a stash of it—"

"In Rachel's bathroom under the sink," Jumoke finished, already in the air. "Got it."

Bis was a moment behind, his wind-noisy takeoff making the bowls rock.

"Just one bottle ought to do it!" Jenks shouted after them. "We're blowing up a statue, not a bridge." The Turn take it, they were *far* too eager to learn this.

When the sound of their rummaging became muffled, he braced himself against the copper bowl and pushed it to the can of lighter fluid. Taking to the air, he tapped the can with his sword point, moving down until he heard a sound he liked. Marking the spot with his eyes, he darted back, aimed his sword, and flew at it.

With a stifled yell for strength, he jammed his sword into the canister. The hard pixy steel went right through. His elder children had fairy steel, taken from invaders testing their strength. Jenks's blade was stronger, and the thin sheet of metal was nothing. Grinning as he imagined it was an invading fairy he had just pierced, Jenks put his foot on can for support and pulled the sword out, darting back to avoid the sudden stream flowing out and arching into the bowl . . . just as he had planned.

Wiping his sword on the rag over the sink, Jenks listened to the changing sound to estimate how full the bowl was getting. Little splashes spotted the counter, and he dropped to the floor, slipping into the cupboards by way of the open space at the footboard.

It was a weird world of wooden supports and domestic-ity behind the cupboards, and using his arms as much as his wings, he maneuvered himself to the kitchen's catch-all drawer. Vaulting into the shallow space, Jenks hunched over, vibrating his wings to create some light as he moved to the front, dodging dead batteries and mangled twist ties until he found the spool of plumber's putty. The trip out was faster, and eyeing Bis and Jumoke standing on the counter and panicking about the rising level of lighter fluid, he ex-pertly plugged the hole.

"More than one way to empty a can," he said, vertigo taking him when the flow stopped and the fumes hit him hard. "Don't get too close, Jumoke. I swear, this is the worst part."

"It stinks like a fairy's funeral pyre," the boy said, plugging his nose and backing up.

Standing on the counter beside his son, Bis looked huge. There was a bottle of soap in his grip, and the gargoyle easily wedged the top open. Jenks could have done it, but it would have been a lot harder. "How much?" Bis asked, poised to squirt it out.

Still reeling, Jenks covered his eyes, now streaming a silver dust as his tears hit the air and tuned dry. "Put it in the empty bowl. I'll say when."

"Rachel's spell bowl?" Bis said, hesitating.

"It's soap!" Jenks barked, rubbing his eyes and staggering until Jumoke grabbed his shoulder. Holy crap, it was nasty stuff until it all got mixed together.

The squirt bottle made a rude sound as it emptied, and feeling better, Jenks peeked over the edge to see how much they had. "That's good," he said, and Bis capped the bottle by smacking the tip on the counter. "Jumoke, see the proportion to the lighter fluid? Now all we need is the nitrogen and the pixy dust. Lots of nitrogen to make the boom intense."

"Fertilizer," Jumoke said. "In the shed?" he asked, and when Jenks nodded, Jumoke rose up. "I'll check."

In an instant, he was gone. Glancing out the night-darkened window, Jenks watched Jumoke's arrow-straight path, the sifting dust falling to make a gold shadow of where he'd been. His siblings called out for him to join them, but Jumoke never even looked.

Pleased, Jenks turned to find Bis trying to get the fridge open by wedging a long claw between the seals. It felt good to be teaching someone his skills. Tink knew that Jax had been a disappointment, but Jumoke was genuinely interested. He already knew how to read.

Leaning against the bowl of soap, Jenks scratched the base of his wings, watching Bis hang from a fridge shelf with one hand and pull out a tinfoil-covered leftover with the other. His claws scrabbled on the linoleum when he dropped, and Jenks wasn't surprised when Bis shook the leftover lasagna into the trash under the sink and ate the tinfoil instead.

The rasping sound of teeth on metal made him shudder. Black dust sifted from him, and seeing it, Bis shrugged, crawling back up onto his elevated seat before Ivy's computer. "A gargoyle doesn't live on pigeon alone," he said, and Jenks winced.

Pushing off into the air, Jenks rose into the hanging utensils for his own snack. There was a pouch of sweets for the kids in the smallest ladle. Rachel never used it. Opening it, he popped one of the nectar and pollen balls into his mouth, then grabbed another for Jumoke. The kid had a lot to learn about maintaining his sugar level. Unless he was snacking in the garden. How long did it take to look through the shed, anyway?

Angling his wings, Jenks dropped to the dark windowsill and pocketed the second sweet. Hands on his hips, he stared out into the dark garden and watched the bands of colored light sift from the oak tree. Jumoke wasn't among them. The individual trails of dust slipping down were as pixy-specific as voices, and he knew them all. There'd been no new patterns to learn in years.

No more newlings, he thought, more melancholy than he thought he'd be. He'd done it to save Mattie's life, and it had seemed to have worked. A healthy pixy woman gave birth to more sons than daughters by almost two to one. The size of the brood, too, was telling, which was why only two children were born that first season, none the next, then eight, eleven, ten, twelve . . . then seven—four of them girls. That was the year he panicked, going to work for Inderland Security. Matalina had borne only three children the year he'd met Rachel, two of them girls. None had survived to naming. His wish for sterility had saved her life. Another birth of newlings might have killed her.

What he hadn't anticipated was with the absence of newlings, both he and Matalina had time to spare on other things. He'd gone from side jobs to a full-time career outside the garden, gaining enough money to buy the church and the security that went with it. Matalina had been able to help their eldest daughter take land before taking a spouse, something that only pixy bucks traditionally managed. Not to mention Matalina pursuing her desire to learn how to read, and then teaching the rest of the children—all impossible if caring for a set of newlings. Children were precious, each one a hope for the future. How could they be detrimental?

Frowning, Jenks tried to figure it out, failing. Perhaps he wasn't old enough yet, because it didn't make sense to him. Maybe Mattie could help him. She was the smart one. As soon he got her to take the Tink-damned curse, he'd rest easier. They'd live in the garden for another twenty years, then, watching their children grow, take their places . . .

The sharp taps of Bis on the keyboard stopped, and the gargoyle ruffled his wings. "Listen to this," he said, his high, gravelly voice pulling Jenks's attention from the window. "'Dryads declined with the deforestation, and many ghosts have been blamed on them as they learned to live in statues placed on ley lines.'"

Jenks flitted close, thinking he looked nothing like Ivy. "Kind of like pixies adapting to city gardens. Humans. Learn to live with them, or die trying."

Bis blinked his red eyes at him. "We've always lived with humans. I can't imagine living in the woods. What would I eat? Iron ore and sparrows?"

Ignoring his sarcasm, Jenks moved closer to the screen. Now that he thought about it, gargoyles were dependent on people. The picture of the dryad on the monitor was his size, and he tapped it. "Look at that. It looks like the statues in the park, doesn't it?" He turned, starting when he found

Bis unexpectedly inches from him. *Holy crap, didn't the kid breathe?*

"Yeah . . ." Bis said softly, not noticing he had jumped.

Trying to cover his surprise, Jenks walked across the keyboard to the "down" arrow, scrolling for the rest of the article. " 'Because they declined before the Turn,' " he read aloud, proud that he could, " 'little is written about them without the trappings of fairy tale, but it's commonly accepted that they live as long as the tree they frequent does, perhaps even hundreds of years. Though generally thought of as meek and gentle, Grimm has placed them several times in the position of wildly savage.' "

Chuckling, Jenks put his hands on his hips. "Yeah," he said as Jumoke flew in trailing a disappointed green dust. "And the freak had kids shoving witches into ovens, too." Scraping his wings for his son's attention, he tossed Jumoke the pollen ball.

Catching it, his son tucked it away, saying, "It's not there. I think Rachel used it."

"Crap on toast," Jenks swore, using one of Rachel's favorites, but pleased that Jumoke had indeed been tapping off his sugar level. The kid had a head on his shoulders. "She did. I remember now. She put it around the azaleas this spring." Frustrated, he rose up as his wing speed increased. "I hate it when people use stuff and don't replace it. How am I supposed to make a bomb without nitrogen?"

Bis brought up a serious-looking black screen and started deleting evidence of Web sites and searches. "How about mothballs?" he asked, and Jenks laughed.

"You've been watching TV again. No, mothballs and pixy dust don't mix. Besides, that would make something more like napalm, and we want inward destruction, not outward devastation. Vincet wouldn't thank me for destroying his garden." Jenks frowned. Ammonia, maybe, but Ivy didn't keep that on hand like she did the soap and lighter fluid. "We want a nice simple pop, and for that, we want fertilizer."

"How much?"

Jenks looked at Bis as he pushed back from the table, wondering what Ivy would say if she knew the gargoyle had been using her computer. Silent, Jenks pointed to a bowl hanging from the overhead rack.

Bis's pushed-in face smiled as he flew to the rack, his wings sending the loose papers on the table flying. Jumoke took flight, yelling that Bis was as dumb as a downdraft, but Jenks squinted through it, not moving as the gargoyle dropped to the counter with the larger bowl.

"We've got lots of nitrogen at the basilica," Bis said, grinning at him through the settling papers. "I'll ask my dad about nymphs and dryads, too."

Alarmed, Jenks clattered his wings. "Hey, this is a run, not a job," he called, and Bis hesitated, flipping in midair to cling to the archway to the hall with the bowl dangling from a hind foot. "You can't steal it from the gardener shed."

Bis made his wheezing laugh, looking evil as he hung upside down with the white tuft of his tail twitching. "No problem. They can't give this stuff away. Thirty minutes." Instead of dropping to fly out, he slithered up to the hall ceiling, going nearly invisible as he shifted his skin tone to match the shadows. Only the glint of the copper bowl gave him away. That, and the faint scrabbling of claws. Jenks would be really worried about the scratches on the ceiling if he didn't know where they came from. The ceiling, the walls, the window ledges . . . He had to get Bis to start wearing some clothes. A bandanna or something.

Stifling a shudder, Jenks turned back to Jumoke, seeing him pale and wide-eyed. "It gives me the creeps when he does that skin thing," the small pixy said, and Jenks nodded.

"Me too. But we need to figure out how to mix this stuff up in one batch before he comes back or we'll be here all night. I know Vincet's going to keep his kids up, and Sylvan might burn another one of his newlings. And carefully!" he added when Jumoke tipped the bowl with the lighter fluid to look in it. "The last thing I need is Ivy coming home and finding fire trucks at the curb. She'd have hairy canaries coming out her, ah, ear."

At his shoulder, peering in at the lighter fluid, Jumoke shook his head. "Women."

That one word jerked Jenks's attention up, and his own smile grew to match Jumoke's. Pride filled him. Jax hadn't been like this. He wasn't making a mistake teaching Jumoke his skills. This was going to work, and his son would have a unique talent, one that would help him find a wife, and then all his children could have their happy-ever-after.

Jenks clapped him across the shoulders. "Can't live with them, can't die without them," he said, beaming with pride. This was not a mistake. Not a mistake at all.

5

"**P**igeon poop?" Vincet exclaimed, aghast as he hovered with his three children clustered behind him, clearly frightened of the sight of Ivy reclining on the nearby bench. "You're going to save my family with pigeon poop!"

"Pigeon poop," Jenks affirmed, concentrating on the silvery goop in the bowl Bis was holding steady. The moon was up, making it easy to see Vincet's horror as he dug his hand into the softly glowing mess. Taking another oozing wad back to the statue, he slapped it onto the smooth stone with the rest. "That and pixy dust!" he said cheerfully, trying not to think about it as he wiped his hands off on a fold of stone. He'd never be able to handle a mixture of lighter fluid, soap, and nitrogen like this without the pixy dust to act as a stabilizer. It was the dust that made it go boom so spectacularly, too.

"That's disgusting!" Vincet said softly, and Bis, holding the bowl, rolled his eyes.

"Tell me about it," the gargoyle said. His voice was stoic, but Jenks could tell he was almost laughing. The white tufts of fur in his ears were trembling.

Ivy, too, smirked. The living vampire had driven them out here on her cycle—Bis on the gas tank and grinning into the air like a dog—but now she looked bored, lying back on the bench with her knees bent to gaze up into the branches of the tree. It was obvious that she'd been at someone earlier tonight; her color was high, her motions edging into a vampire-quick speed, and her obvious languorous sultriness, which she tried to hide from Rachel, poured from the slightly Asian-looking woman in a flood of release. Even Vincet had noticed, wisely not saying anything when the leather-clad woman had strode up to Daryl's statue, hip cocked as she pronounced she could take the nymph—if she had the brass to show up.

Right now, though, Ivy looked more inclined to seduce the next being on two legs she encountered, not fight them, her long straight hair falling almost to the cement as she lay on the bench, and a sated smile on her placid face. No wonder Ivy satisfied her blood urges during Rachel's weekly absences. Seeing Ivy like this might blow everything to hell. An emotionally constipated Ivy was a safe Ivy.

"This would go faster if someone would help me," Jenks said, eyeing the goop remaining when he flew down for another handful.

In a smooth motion, Ivy sat up and swung her boots to the cement to stand. "I'm going to do a perimeter," she said, heels silent on the sidewalk as she headed out. "And don't put that bowl in my cycle bag. Got it?" she shouted over her shoulder.

Jumoke landed atop Bis's head and fell into wide-footed stance that would allow him the best balance if the wind should gust. "Mom made me promise not to touch it," the kid said, clearly proud of his new red belt.

"I'm holding the bowl," Bis said quickly, eyes darting.

Vincet took his daughter's hand, pretending he needed to watch her.

"Chicken shits," Jenks muttered, scooping out a handful and throwing it at the statue. It hit with a splat, and Ivy, somewhere in the dark, gasped, swearing at him.

At that, Bis grinned to look like a nightmare. "Pigeon shits," he said cheerfully, and Jenks smeared another glowing handful on Sylvan's statue's nose.

The chiseled face looked as if it could see him and knew

what he was doing. "It's not *that* bad," Jenks muttered, but his nose was wrinkling at the stink. It seemed to be sticking to him even if the modified plastique wasn't. His gaze dropped to Rachel's bowl, glinting in the lamplight, and his wings hummed faster. Ivy wouldn't tell Rachel, would she?

Hovering backward, he looked over his work, almost putting his hands on his hips before stopping at the last moment. If he'd done it right, it'd shatter at the base and out toward the walkway. Sylvan would be free. Jenks's gaze shifted to the small opening under the dogwood that was Vincet's home. It was too close for his liking.

"Jumoke," Jenks said tersely, and the young pixy rose on a glittering column of sparkles. "Set down a layer of flammable dust on the plastique. I have to get this crap off of me."

"You bet, Dad," he said enthusiastically, zipping to the statue. Jenks had put a heavy layer of dust in the mix already, but a top dusting would flash it all into flame faster than any petroleum product made from dead dinosaur.

Bis was stretching his neck to get away from the smell, holding the bowl and being more dramatic than Jrixibell pretending to have a sore wing so she wouldn't have to eat her pollen. He'd used only about half of what he had made. Maybe he should blow both statues up. That would piss off Daryl.

"You got a problem?" Jenks asked, and Bis shook his head, breath held.

"No," Bis said, his thick lips barely moving. "You done with this?"

"For now," he said, and Bis shoved the bowl under the bench, then scuttled to the middle of the sidewalk, gasping dramatically when he stopped in the puddle of lamplight.

Frowning, Jenks wiped his hands off on his red bandanna, then wondered what he was going to do with it. He couldn't put the symbolic flag of good intent back around his waist. Not only did it stink, but taking it back to Matalina to wash wasn't an option. Glancing at Vincet, he dropped it into the bowl. If Vincet had a problem with it, he could just suck Tink's toes.

Just off the sidewalk beside Sylvan's statue, Vincet was on one knee, trying to get his kids to go inside. The triplets were clearly unhappy about being told to go to ground. Vincet was just as reluctant to leave Jenks alone to take them there. Even now, he was eyeing the bow and quiver that Jenks had brought with him to ignite the explosive.

Give me a break, Jenks thought dryly. Like he'd take the man's garden? Frowning, he reached for his bow peeking from the small bag beside the dung-filled copper pot. Vincet stiffened when Jenks put the quiver over his shoulders and strung the bow. Maybe he shouldn't have gotten rid of his red bandanna.

"Go inside," Vincet said tersely to his children, but they only clung to him tighter.

"Papa? I'm scared," Vi said, her eyes riveted to the crap-smeared statue.

Irritation flashed over Vincet, and taking her hands, the young father faked a smile for his eldest and only daughter. "Go wait with your mother so Jenks can fix this," he said. "I can't leave another man alone in my garden with a bow, Vi. Even Jenks. It isn't right."

"But Uncle Jenks won't touch the flowers," she whined. "Papa, please come with us. Don't let the ghost out. Please!"

Smiling, Jenks gestured for Jumoke, who was bored and flying up and down like a yo-yo. They had time before the moon hit its zenith point. Daryl wouldn't appear until Sylvan did, and hopefully the statue would be demolished before then. Jenks had to give Jumoke something to do. That darting up and down was irritating.

"Come here," he said as he brought out from the bag a pot the size of two fists. "I want you to hold on to the coal pot," he said, handing it to the excited pixy.

"Got it," he said, wings clattering, and Jenks reached up, snagging his foot when he started to flit away.

"Keep it lit, Jumoke," he said, yanking him back down so hard Jumoke lost his balance and had to scramble to find it again. "Give it sips of air, nothing more. If it goes out from too much or too little air, I'm going to have to ask Ivy for a light, and that would be embarrassing."

"Uh, guys?" Bis interrupted, claws scraping as he slid to a stop beside them.

"Just a minute, Bis," Jenks said, turning back to Jumoke. "When I ask, take the top off, okay? Not before. The coal won't last long given full air." His voice was severe, but Jumoke was holding the small pot with the right amount of care now, and Jenks was satisfied.

"Go wait with your mother!" Vincet shouted across the way, and his two boys darted away to leave a heavy dust trail. But Vi . . . Vi didn't look so good.

"Jenks?" Bis said, clawed feet shifting, but Jenks's attention was riveted to Vi. Her dust didn't look right, and as he watched, her eyes rolled back and her wings collapsed. And her aura—went silver.

Shit.

"Vi!" Vincet shouted, scooping up the girl as she fell into convulsions. "The dryad's taking her!" he exclaimed, eyes wide in horror as he held his daughter. "She wasn't even asleep! Blow it up! Blow it up now!"

"Sorry," Bis said, ears pinned as he looked sheepish. "I tried to tell you."

Feeling betrayed, Jenks looked at the moon. It wasn't anywhere near its zenith! Reaching behind him, he fumbled for one of his arrows tied with dandelion fluff at the tip. Wings clattering, he turned to Jumoke, finding him . . . gone.

"What the hell?" he stammered, rising up to scan the area, but there wasn't a single twinkle of dust anywhere. He was gone! "Jumoke!"

Vincet flew to him with Vi in his arms, his wings clattering and desperation falling from him like the dust he was shedding. "He's hurting her!" Vincet shouted, Vi's skin red and her dust white-hot. "Blow it up! Free him!"

"I can't! Jumoke has the firepot!" Jenks hovered, poised and scanning. Bis waited on the sidewalk, tail lashing, but Jumoke was gone. Ivy was gone. By the dogwood, Noel was a faint glow gathering the two boys and pulling them underground. They were safe. *Where the hell is Jumoke!*

"Jumoke!" Jenks shouted, exasperated, and Bis took to the air with two heavy wing beats to find him. They didn't have time for this, but as Jenks started off in the other direction, he jerked to a halt in midair. Something smelled like honey and sun-warmed gold.

Tink's dildo, the warrior woman was back.

"You will not!" echoed a vehement voice off the nearby townhouses, and there she was, standing on the sidewalk beside her statue, her bare feet spread wide and her robes shifting. Her expression was frantic, and upon seeing the bow in his hands, she flung her hand out.

"Look out!" Bis shouted, leaping for him.

A blast of honey-smelling air hit them. Tumbling into the air, Jenks felt his heart pound, but he fought with his instinct, folding his wings against him and tightening into a ball as he flew out of control. Holy crap, he was heading right for the trees!

"Gotcha!" came Bis's faint exhalation, and the wind shifted as the gargoyle caught him, pulling him close.

Jenks's eyes opened to see the world dip and swoop. In Bis's other hand were Vincet and Vi. Vincet looked terrified, but Vi's expression held a shocking amount of hatred. It was Sylvan. That's why Daryl had appeared! The stupid dryad. Couldn't he have waited a few more minutes?

With a sharp drop and a wrench that hurt Jenks's neck, Bis dropped to the ground beside the sidewalk next to a large rock. The wind died. Daryl was coughing with her hand to her chest, shaking as she tried to catch her breath in the pollution-stained air.

Jenks unwedged himself from Bis's grip and flitted down to feel small beside him. Taking to the air was too chancy, and he could hit the statue from here.

"Why didn't you shoot it!" Vincet yelled at him, angry as he struggled with Vi, they, too, firmly on the earth.

Where the hell is Jumoke! Jenks thought, still not sure what end was up yet.

"I warned you," Daryl wheezed, pulling herself straight again. She wiped her mouth, then hesitated, shocked at the sheen of blood glinting in the lamplight. Gathering her resolve, she hid it, shouting, "You will *die* before I allow Sylvan to perpetrate his abuse on another!"

"You're a whiny little nymph!" Vi shouted as she struggled to be free. "The gods are dead, and actors play their rules! You're alone! Give up! The world's too ugly for your kind!"

"That's the trouble with you dryads. You talk too much," Daryl said. Eyes narrowed, she raised her sword. The nearby light flickered and went out. The one behind it went black, too, and like dominos, the townhouses across the park went dark. A distant chorus of complaint rose, joined by the beeping of smoke detectors.

Bis shifted his wings, his back to the rock. "I got a bad feeling about this!" he squeaked.

"Hey! Golden girl!" Ivy shouted from behind them, and Jenks rose up, wings flashing red when he saw the silver dusting of Jumoke with her. "Pick on someone your own size!" she added as she strode forward, boots clacking aggressively.

"Dad!" Jumoke exclaimed as he darted to him.

"Where have you been?" Jenks shouted, his relief coming out as anger. "We can't blow up the statue without that pot!"

Jumoke's wings drooped as he landed beside him, pot hugged to his middle. "I'm sorry. I was getting Ivy. I saw Daryl, and I just . . ." The boy's face screwed up. "I'm sorry, Dad. I shouldn't have left."

"Blow it up!" Vincet exclaimed, jerking when Vi got her arm free and smacked his face. He caught her wrist, and Sylvan howled. The white-hot dust spilling from Vi was turning the moss black, burned.

"Let me out!" she said, her childlike voice sounding wrong. "Before that bitch stops you!"

"Ivy's in the way," Jenks said tightly. Giving both Jumoke and Vincet a look to stay grounded, Jenks darted after her, coming to a halt at her shoulder as his partner stopped eight feet back from Daryl. The spicy scent of vampire spun through him, seeming to shift his own dust a darker tint. Ivy was pissed. Hell, even her aura was sparkling.

Seeing them together, Daryl dropped her sword, flushed as she looked at Ivy's tight clothes and anger. "You're aligned with the pixy? Who are you? A goddess?"

"Ooo! Ooo!" Jenks said, looping the bow over his shoulder so he could have both hands free for his own sword. "I've heard this one before. Just say yes, Ivy."

Ivy was eyeing Daryl with the same evaluation. "Worse," she said softly, and Jenks shuddered. "I'm heir to madness. Vessel of perversion. Your nightmare should you cross me."

Daryl's chin lifted, trembling. "Indeed. We might be sisters then, for I'm the same."

Ivy hunched slightly, eyeing the woman almost hungrily. "You hurt my friends." A long hand went out, beckoning. Her lips drew back in a horrible smile, and she let her small but sharp canines show. "Can you hurt me?"

The nymph blinked as the moonlight hit them, then she tightened her sword grip.

The air seemed to hesitate, and when Bis's nails scraped, Ivy jerked, jumping at her.

Jenks shot straight up, yelling, "Get her away from the statue so I can blow it up!"

"You can't!" Daryl cried out, moving impossibly fast as she dodged out of Ivy's attack. Her sword was swinging toward Ivy's back, and Jenks yelled a warning.

Ivy dropped. Daryl's sword point missed, but just. Rolling backward, Ivy tried to knock Daryl down, but the nymph jumped straight up. Ivy was standing when she landed, and the two women hesitated, looking at each other in surprise and what might be respect.

"Blow it up, Jenks!" Ivy called out. "I'll get out of the way!"

Jenks's mouth dropped open. Holy shit. Ivy didn't know if she could take her or not.

Darting back to the rock for protection, he sheathed his sword and pulled an arrow from his quiver. "Everyone get behind the rock!" he shouted. "Jumoke, the firepot!"

Leathery wings shaking, Bis scrambled behind the rock. Vincet fought his child as he dragged her to safety, the freedom-hungry dryad screaming. Vi was only a year old. Her tiny body couldn't take this. She was dusting heavily, glowing like a demon as the energy of the ley line ran through her. Vincet's own tears turned to dust as he fought to keep her from attacking Daryl—but he looked up at Jenks with hope.

"Here, Dad!" Jumoke shouted, taking off the lid. The scraping of the lid was loud, and Jenks buried the tip of the arrow in it. Immediately the wad of dandelion fluff ignited. *Matalina was the real archer*, he thought as he took aim and the arrow arched away. Fortunately, all he had do to was hit the statue. "Fire in the hold!" he shouted. "Everyone down!"

"No!" Daryl screamed, stretching her hand out. A flash of wind came at him, and he went tumbling backward, but a pained cry echoed, and the force immediately died.

When he found air again under his wings, his arrow was lost and the statue untouched. Daryl was writhing on the cement, downed by Ivy in the instant the nymph lost her concentration. Ivy herself looked winded, holding her arm where the nymph's sword had scored on her.

"Rhenoranian, help me!" Daryl said, coughing as she got to her knees, undeterred.

Expression pinched, Ivy strode forward, but Daryl groaned, kneeling as she shoved the air at her with both hands.

"Watch out!" Bis cried as Ivy was flung back to land in the flower bed beside Sylvan's statue as if having been pulled by a string. Frustrated, Jenks lowered his next arrow, not yet lit.

"Let me be your strength, Rhenoranian!" Daryl said, staggering to her feet. "Let me be your vessel!" She turned to Jenks, and his wings went cold. "Let me be your vengeance!"

Worried, Jenks darted up, then down. He couldn't see the ley line she was pulling on, but the force of it made his wings tingle. Daryl pointed at him with a new confidence, and then Ivy's scream echoed against the dark windows across the street. Motions blurring, the battle began again. Twelve feet up, Jenks watched, useless bow in hand and knowing he wouldn't be able to shoot until Ivy downed the nymph. Daryl kept pushing Ivy back to the statue.

Moving faster than seemed possible, Daryl ducked Ivy's crescent kick, only to fall when Ivy continued the spin and knocked her feet out from under her.

The nymph hit the ground, coughing. Ivy jumped into the air, elbow poised and clearly ready to slam it into Daryl's throat as she fell to hit the dirt beside her.

Daryl saw it coming and pulled her sword up to protect her throat. Ivy screamed, knowing she couldn't move enough to avoid being cut. The blade nicked Daryl's face, too, upon impact, but it protected her throat. Ivy was hurt more.

The small success seemed to galvanize the nymph, who staggered to her feet when Ivy rolled away holding her numb elbow. Swinging her blade in a wide arc, she waited—grimacing.

Like a mad thing, Ivy rushed her, plowing her foot right into her solar plexus between the gaps of the blade.

Daryl bent, and Ivy lashed out with a front kick, snapping the nymph's head back.

And still the woman wouldn't go down, falling back as she tried to find her breath.

"Now, Jenks!" Ivy called out, and Jenks dropped down to the rock and the firepot.

One hand to her middle, Daryl groaned, staggering to a stand. "Help me, Rhenoranian!" she screamed, shaking hand outstretched.

The wind came from everywhere. The black roared. It beat at the trees. Jenks tumbled, fighting it.

"Stop!" Ivy shouted, and when Jenks squinted, he saw she had yanked the nymph up and was pinning her to the tree across from her statue. "Stop, or I will fucking kill you!"

"Let me go, or I will pierce your liver," the nymph said, her teeth gritted.

"Oh, shit," Jenks whispered, seeing the glint of metal at Ivy's side.

Screaming down from the hills, the wind circled them like wolves. A small spot of stillness grew, surrounded by a wall of gray and black fury. The lights of Cincinnati vanished as if behind water. Even the ever-present thumps of industry were gone, overpowered by the chugging of the wind.

But here, in Daryl's sacred grove, the moon shone down in perfect stillness.

Jenks glanced to Jumoke peeping up from behind the rock as the torn leaves drifted down, gesturing for him to stay. Vi had stopped struggling. Her breath rasped like oven air, and her wings were starting to smolder by the acrid smell now pinching his nose.

Ivy still pinned Daryl to the tree, her arm against her throat. One in white, one in black, one in silk, the other in leather, both unmoving apart from their lungs heaving.

Slowly Jenks started to drop toward the firepot.

"Why do you stand against me?" Daryl whispered.

"It's honor that gives your limbs the strength to best me." She took a careful breath. "It glows in you, and you hurt from it."

Ivy flinched when Daryl touched her jaw. "I'm not hurt," she said quickly.

"Sylvan went against the gods' law," the nymph was saying, her cracked lip starting to bleed. "Taught himself to exist in cold stone, then used the knowledge not to live, but to kill for enjoyment. Why do you free him? I don't understand."

"She lies!" Vi shouted, elbowing Vincet. "She's touched! Break the statue! Now!"

Sylvan was in jail? Not imprisoned by a jealous lover? Jenks hesitated, his wings going cold as Vincet struggled to hold her wildly struggling body. Had they had almost let him free? A murderer?

"The demons imprisoned him in stone," Daryl said, her fingers opening. The knife dropped to the grass, and Ivy flinched. "His heart remains as cold, even now when the fire of the demon's blood burns through him. I begged for the honor to guard him as it was my sisters he murdered. I fought for the right, learned to kill, to be heartless, only to fail here when it counts. If you free Sylvan, kill me as well, for I'm too cowardly to live when honorable people give such filth freedom."

Around them, the wind died to let the clamor from the townhouses and city beat upon them once more. The lights were on again, and people were talking loudly. "You're not a coward," Ivy said softly, and Daryl's eyes met hers, widening at something only the nymph could see.

Abruptly Ivy let go of her and stepped back, frightened. Holding her arms to herself, she looked for Jenks, now hovering right over the rock, Jumoke below him with the firepot. "We need to reassess this," she said, white-faced.

"No!" Vi exclaimed, exploding into motion and hitting her father right between the legs.

"Ooooh," Jenks said with a wince, then yelped when she scrambled up the rock as if she didn't have wings, snatching his bow and yanking an arrow from his quiver.

"Jumoke!" Bis shouted as the little girl jumped at the boy, screaming wildly. Jenks's son took to the air, frightened, but she crashed right into him. The coal pot hit the grass. The lid popped off and coals scattered, flashing orange with the new breath of air.

Screaming in victory, Vi ran for them, burying the tip of an arrow against one. It flared to life even as she pulled the bow back, arrow notched.

"Get her!" Jenks shouted as he tackled her about the knees.

He hit her hard, and they slid across the grass, his arms scraping. Taking a breath, he looked up to see the flaming arrow was arching true to its target.

"Drop!" he shouted, trying to cover Vi from the coming blast. Panic iced his wings as he saw Jumoke still hovering in midair, shocked into immobility. He'd never reach him in time.

Then Bis raised his hand, cupping it before him.

The night turned white and orange, and an explosion pulsed against his ears and echoed up through the ground into him. Hunching down, Jenks tried to bury himself in the grass, feeling the blast push the blood from his wings for an instant. Jumoke fell to the ground in front of him.

"Why didn't you drop!" Jenks shouted, his own voice sounding muffled from his stunned ears as he got off Vi and went to his son, bewildered on the ground. "Jumoke, are you okay?"

Panicking, he pulled his son up. Frantic, he felt Jumoke's face, then ran his hands down his wings, looking for tears. Jumoke yelped, wiggling to get out from under Jenks's hands.

"Oh, that was everlastingly cool," the boy said, grinning from under his dark hair.

Jenks smacked his shoulder in relief. He was okay. "What's wrong with you!" he shouted, glad his hearing was coming back. "I told you to drop!"

Bis's thick skin on his brow was furrowed in worry, but Jenks didn't think it was from the cut he was looking at on the back of his hand. In the distance, a car alarm was going off. "Um, Jenks?" he said in question.

A quick glance told him Vincet was okay. Vi was in his arms looking stunned but herself. Sylvan no longer possessed her, which meant he was probably free. Great, just freaking great. He only wanted to help, and he freed a murderer. Rachel and Ivy were not going to be happy.

Ivy.

Alarmed, Jenks darted up. Chunks of marble the size of apples and melons littered the sidewalk. A few pieces were embedded in the tree that Ivy had pinned Daryl against, and the scent of cracked rock pervaded. Vincet's home and Daryl's statue looked untouched. But no Ivy. No Daryl, either.

"Ivy!" Jenks shouted, realizing he was about to fall from exhaustion. Damn it, he'd let his sugar drop. Immediately he found a sweetball in his pocket and sucked on it. The sugar hit him fast, and his wings sped up. Across the street, people were starting to come out of their homes, aiming flashlights at the park. They had to get out of here.

"Ivy!" he shouted again. "You okay?"

Bis poked his head up from behind the rock, his ears pricked as he looked at the tree, and Jenks wasn't surprised when Daryl stumbled out from behind it. Ivy levered herself up from the ground, having found a dip to take shelter in. They both picked their way carefully to the sidewalk, taking in the damage with a numb acceptance.

"He's free," Daryl whispered, her smooth features bunching in distress.

A crack of noise made them all jump. It was the snap of breaking stone, and the sharp sound echoed off the town homes across the street. As they watched, a huge slab of broken rock slid from Sylvan's statue, falling to crush the flowers.

"I didn't do it, Papa!" Jumoke exclaimed, eyes wide as he darted close. "It wasn't me!"

"It was me," a new voice said, sly and wispy.

Startled, Jenks turned in the air even as Daryl caught her breath only to start coughing. Ivy held her back from attacking him, but her lips were pressed in anger. A thin figure was standing in the moonlight, his feet on the moss beside the dogwood tree. It looked like Sylvan's statue. Moving as if it might be hurt, the shadowy figure edged out into the moonlight, drawing back as one bare foot touched the concrete. It was Sylvan. It had to be.

"You lied to me," Jenks said, loosening his sword.

"I'm free!" the dryad exclaimed, and he leaped lightly onto the concrete, exuberant as his robes furled.

The glow of Vincet's dust was a sickly yellow as he hovered beside Jenks, his broken sword in hand. The dryad probably didn't know it, but it was a real threat.

"Is Vi okay?" Jenks asked, and Vincet nodded.

"But I fear we have let loose a demon."

"You are trash, Sylvan!" Daryl shouted, sagging in Ivy's arms as she wheezed. "I will not rest until you are *dead*!"

Sylvan stopped his twirling. Looking at Jenks as if seeing him for the first time, the dryad smiled, his gaze alighting briefly on Vincet, Jumoke, and finally Bis, all fronting him. "Daryl is a crazy bitch," he said softly, pulling himself to a dignified stance. "I didn't lie." Glancing at the people coming across the park from the town homes, he added, almost as an afterthought, "Not much, anyway."

"Now!" Ivy shouted, springing into action. Jenks darted forward, sword in hand.

"No, wait!" Bis exclaimed, but Ivy was already pinwheeling to a stop. The spot of air where Sylvan had been, was gone.

"Where did he go!" Ivy asked, turning back to them.

Bis shook himself, resettling his wings as he looked at the people coming closer. "Into the line," he said, clearly unnerved. His ears were pinned and his tail was lashed about his feet. "He shouldn't be able to do that," he added, meeting Jenks's gaze.

Daryl slumped on the bench to look totally undignified and out of character. "It's why he was imprisoned in stone," she said, pushing a chip of his statue off to clatter on the cement. "Now I'll never find him."

Jenks stifled a shiver as he met Ivy's eyes. Tink's contractual hell, he'd made a big mistake. "Let's get out of here," he said. "We can worry about Sylvan later."

"Right behind you." Bis flew to their satchel, ducking behind Daryl's robes and coming out with it and the grimy, dented bowl. A bobbing flashlight across the grass caught his eyes, and they glowed red. Seeing it, someone called out. More lights angled their way.

"Jenks, I'm taking Daryl to the hospital," Ivy said. "Can you get home from here okay?"

Jenks looked at Daryl, struggling to breathe, and he nodded. "See you there."

Daryl was complaining she wasn't going to go to the butchers and leechers when Vincet dropped down to him. "Thank you, Jenks," he said, his expression solemn in the dim light. "You saved my family."

Wincing, Jenks looked to Vincet's front door where his wife and sons were silhouetted in the warm glow of a fire. "You're welcome. I don't think Sylvan will be back."

"Tomorrow," Vincet said, shaking his hand. "I'll come tomorrow. Thank you. I can't ever do enough."

Jenks managed a smile as he thought of Vi. She'd be fine, now. "Just be nice to some pixy buck who needs it," he said. "And build me an office."

Vincet's head was bobbing as he drifted back, but it was clear he wanted to return to his home. "Yes. Anything. Tomorrow."

"Tomorrow," Jenks agreed, then darted up when a flash-light found him, bathing him in a bright white light. "Sorry about the mess!" he shouted.

Vincet went one way, Ivy and Daryl another, and in an instant, even their dust was gone. He waited until he heard the soft sound of Ivy's muffled engine before he turned his back on the demolished grove and rose higher. Like a switch, the sounds of chaos went faint and the air turned chill. An uncomfortable mix of success and failure took him. And as Jenks quickly caught up to Jumoke and the slower-flying gargoyle winging his way back across the Ohio River, he had a bad feeling that this was far from over.

6

Hands on his hips, Jenks hovered a good five inches above the damp moss, newly transplanted from somewhere half across the Hollows. He gazed in satisfaction at the freshly scrubbed, upside-down flowerpot buried halfway into the soft soil. The sun was high, but here, under the shelter of an overgrown lilac, it was cool. It had taken almost a week working the four hours before the sun rose, but Vincet had finally called his office done.

While Jenks's children watched, Vincet had chipped out a door in the upside-down flowerpot, built a hearth, and laid a circle of stone that said "welcome" in pixy culture. Seeds had been planted from Vincet's own stash, and Jenks wasn't sure how he felt about another man putting plants into his own soil. How was he to know what was going to come up?

Watching Vincet had been a good lesson to his own kids, who up to now had only seen their parents work, and when Jenks rubbed his wings together to signal the all-clear, his children swarmed down in a wave of silk and noise. The babble grew high, and he fled, darting to where Matalina was on the wall with Jrixibell, again refusing to eat her pollen, having stuffed herself with nectar. He hadn't a clue where she was getting it. The little girl probably had a stash of flowers somewhere that even her mother didn't know about.

"Go!" the woman relented as the little girl whined, her wings down in a pitiful display. "But you're going to eat twice as much tonight!"

"Thank you, Mama!" she chimed out, and Jenks watched for birds until she reached her brothers and sisters, already buzzing in and out of his new office.

Happy, Jenks settled himself beside Matalina, thinking she was beautiful out here in the dappled sun. She handed him a sweetball, and he took it, pulling her close to make her giggle. "I'd rather have you," he said, stealing a kiss.

"Jenks," she fussed, clearly liking the attention. "I'm pleased it ended well."

A flash of guilt darkened his wings. "Yeah, as long as Sylvan doesn't come back and Rachel doesn't find out," he said, gaze going to his kids as they doused Jumoke in pollen from an early dandelion, temporally turning him blond until he shook himself.

"You're such the worrier," Matalina teased. "Let the future take care of itself. Vincet's family is safe, and Jumoke is considering a career outside the garden. I'm proud of you."

He turned to her, his guilt easing. "You think it will be okay?" he said, and she leaned in, putting her arms around his neck and her forehead against his.

"I'm sure of it. That dryad is long gone. No need to worry."

Jenks sighed, feeling a knot untying, but still . . . "How do you like the office?" he asked, trying to change the subject. "I'll get a little bell and they can ring it. I don't think anyone will come, anyway."

Matalina smiled as a shaft of light found her face. "They'll come, Jenks. Just you wait."

The sound of one of their children wailing drifted to them, and together they sighed.

"Not today, though," Jenks said, giving her a kiss before he took to the air, his hands leaving hers reluctantly. "Today, I belong entirely to you."

And, happy, he rose up, scanning his garden, assessing in an instant what had happened and darting down to make things right.

It was what he did. It was what he always did. And it was what he would always do.

RECKONING
JEANIENE FROST

PROLOGUE

February 16, 2004
New Orleans

Eric swallowed the last of his beer and then set the empty bottle on the sidewalk. *Not my fault there isn't a trash can nearby*, he thought, ignoring the glare the tour guide gave him. The brunette off to his right didn't seem to mind. She smiled at him in a way that made him glad he'd blown off his buddies to take this stupid haunted tour.

". . . in front of us is the LaLaurie house," the guide went on, gesturing to the big gray structure on the corner of Royal Street. "This is reputedly one of the most haunted places in the French Quarter. Here, in the mid–eighteen hundreds, an untold number of slaves were tortured and murdered by Dr. Louis LaLaurie and his wife, Delphine . . ."

Eric sidled closer to the hot brunette, who didn't seem to be paying any more attention to the guide than he was. She was thin, the way he liked 'em, and though her tits weren't big, she had great legs and a nice ass. Her face was pretty, too, now that he noticed.

"Hey. I'm Eric. 'S your name?" he asked, fighting back his slur. *Smile. Look interested.*

"Where are your friends?" she asked. She had an accent that sounded French, and it was a weird question. But she smiled when she said it, her eyes raking over him in a way that woke his cock up.

"They're at Pat O'Brien's," Eric said, with a vague wave.

The guide was glaring at him more pointedly now, going on about the LaLauries' medical experiments on their slaves and other weird, gross shit he didn't want to listen to. "You wanna grab a drink?"

The brunette came closer, until she was right next to him and her nipples practically brushed his chest. "I'm in the mood for more than a drink. Aren't you?"

Oh yeah. He had definite liftoff in his pants. "Baby, like you wouldn't believe."

Eric glanced around to find a few people staring at him. Okay, he'd said that a little loud.

"I've got a room at the Dauphine," he tried again, softer. "We could go there—"

"My place is closer," she interrupted him, taking his hand. Firm grip, too. "Come with me."

She led him down the street, weaving past people and throwing those fuck-me smiles over her shoulder at him every so often. Eric was excited. He'd been here three days and hadn't gotten laid yet. It was about time he got some strange on this trip.

The girl took him down an alley, walking just as quickly as before, even though he had a hard time seeing where they were going. He tripped on something—a bottle, probably— but she just tugged on his arm at the same moment, keeping him upright.

"Hey." He grinned. "Nice reflexes."

She muttered something he didn't understand, and not just because he was drunk.

"Is that French?" Eric asked.

Her dark hair swung as she glanced back at him. "*Oui.* Yes."

"Cool."

She led him up a fire escape at the end of the alley, opened an unlocked door at the landing, and propelled him inside. The lights were off, wherever they were, but this must be her place. She locked it behind him and then her smile grew wider.

"I am going to eat you," she said in a sexy, accented purr that made him even harder.

Eric grabbed her, squeezing that beautiful ass while he kissed her. She opened her mouth, letting his tongue explore inside while he ground himself against her. *Rubber's in my back pocket*, Eric reminded himself. *A chick this easy might have something.*

She put her arms around his neck, holding on to him like she was desperate for it. Eric fumbled with the front of his pants. *Right here, right now* worked for him, too.

He'd gotten his pants unzipped and his hands up her short skirt, when she clamped down on his tongue with her teeth. And yanked her head back.

Eric screamed, staring in horror at the blood around her mouth when she smiled at him again. His tongue throbbed like it was on fire.

"Crazy bitch," he tried to say, but it came out sounding like "'aaazy 'itch." Blood was still pouring from his tongue, and when he felt the tip of it . . . there wasn't one anymore.

"You fucking whore!" Eric spat, not caring if she understood the garbled words or not. His fist came up—and then he was falling end over end, until he reached the bottom with a thud that made his head feel like it had split.

For a stunned second, Eric lay there. *Stairs*, it occurred to him. *Bitch pushed me down a flight of stairs.* He felt the first stirrings of fear mixing with his anger.

A light flicked on in the room and Eric jerked, blinking for a minute at the brightness before the images focused.

There was a tall, thin man standing over a mannequin. He looked like he was assembling it, since its leg was on the ground next to the man and its arm was in two pieces farther away. Then the mannequin's head turned. Its eyes blinked, mouth opened . . .

Eric screamed, trying to scramble to his feet, but a scalding pain in his leg prevented him. The tall man ignored Eric's screams and frantic attempts to back away as he gave an inquiring glance up the stairs.

"*Mon amour*, I was getting worried."

The girl appeared at the top of the stairs. "Why? No one knows we're here."

Eric managed to stand. Agony shot up his leg even though he had most of his weight on the other one.

"Don't either of you fuckin' touch me," he gasped, looking around for something, anything, to use to fight them off.

The girl smiled as she came down the stairs. With his blood still around her mouth, it looked more like a hideous leer.

"Touch you? *Mon cher*, I already told you—I am going to eat you."

I

Bones didn't spare a glance around as he strode rapidly up the streets of the French Quarter. Scents assailed him; countless perfumes, body odor from all manners of hygiene, food cooking—or rotting in the trash. Centuries of decadence had given the Quarter a unique, permanent stench no vampire could completely ignore.

A close second to the cacophony of scents was sound. Music, laughter, shouts, and conversations compounded into a constant white noise.

As he rounded a corner, Bones wondered again why Marie had summoned him. He didn't have to come; he wasn't under her line, so he owed her no loyalty. But when the queen of New Orleans called, Bones answered. For starters, he respected Marie. And he reckoned his head wouldn't enjoy sitting atop his shoulders much longer if he snubbed her.

Though chances were, what Marie wanted would involve Bones killing someone.

He had just rounded another corner when instinct told him he was being watched. He jerked to the side—and felt searing pain slam into his back in the next instant. Bones whirled, knocking people over to dart into the nearest door. With his back safely to a wall and the only entrance in clear view, Bones looked down at his chest.

An arrow protruded, its broad head hooked on three

sides where it had punched through his chest. The shaft was still sticking out of his back. He touched the bloodied tip and swore.

Silver. Two inches lower and it would have gone through his heart, ending his life the permanent way.

"Hey, buddy," someone called out. "You okay?"

"Capital," Bones bit off. He looked around and realized he'd stumbled into a bar. The patrons were goggling at his chest.

He paused long enough to pull the arrow out of his chest before ducking out the door, moving at a speed that would have been only a blur to the onlookers at the bar. He wasn't concerned with them, however. His attention was focused on finding whoever had fired that custom-made arrow. From the angle it skewered him, it had been fired from above.

One vertical jump had him on the bar's roof, crouching again while his gaze scanned the nearby structures. Nothing. Bones ran along the tops of the buildings for two blocks, until he felt certain that he was standing where the shooter had been. There was a faint, residual energy in the air that confirmed what Bones already suspected: whoever fired that arrow wasn't human.

He took another moment to survey the rooftops, but there was no one to be seen. He or she was fast; it had been less than a minute from shot fired to Bones standing where the would-be killer had crouched. No amateur, this. And whoever this was had been alerted quickly to Bones's presence in the Quarter. He'd arrived only last night.

Bones gave a mental shrug as he jumped down to the street, warier now to stay within clusters of people, but not forgoing his appointment. He'd already died once. It tended to take the edge off fearing it afterward.

Bones waited outside the wrought-iron gate of St. Louis Cemetery #1. His back was to a post, and he'd been eyeing the rooftops, ready to spring at the slightest hint of movement.

Ghosts bathed the cemetery and its surrounding streets like spectral cobwebs. Bones ignored them, though they could to be as noisy and bothersome as the tourists. New Orleans Quarter was the last place for anyone to rest in peace, be it the living, or the dead.

It wasn't five minutes before a gigantic man walked toward him. His aura announced him as a ghoul, though he looked nothing like Hollywood's interpretation of one. No, he had smooth brown skin, a bald head, and a barrel-like chest, the very picture of health and vitality. Except his walk, which had a noticeable awkwardness that was at odds with the normal, graceful gait of the undead.

"Bones," the man greeted him.

It had been decades, but Bones remembered his name. "Jelani." He nodded. "I am here to see Majestic, at her request."

Jelani swept out a hand. "Follow me."

Moonlight glowed off Jelani's black gloves, their shape too perfect and too stiff. Prosthetics. Both his legs below the knees were missing, too. Bones didn't know how Jelani had lost his arms and legs, but he knew it had happened before Jelani became a ghoul. The only thing that didn't grow back after being cut off from a vampire or a ghoul was his head.

But what he didn't know was why they were moving away from the cemetery, instead of inside its gates.

"You're not lost, are you, mate?" Bones asked with cool geniality. He'd had meetings with Marie before, and they were only ever held in the cemetery's underbelly, right below where her empty grave was. Marie Laveau had nothing if not a sense of irony.

Jelani half turned, but didn't slow his stilted pace. "If you fear to follow me, then by all means, walk away."

A snort escaped Bones as he stopped. "Trying to shame me into stupidity? Not bloody likely. Half an hour ago, someone made a very credible attempt to kill me, and now you want me to meet Majestic somewhere aside from her normal place. Tell me why, or I *will* walk away, and then you can explain to her why you felt it beneath you to prevent that."

Jelani paused, his face still in profile. "Majestic is not here. She bid me to speak in her stead."

Bones's brows rose. Marie was notorious for handling requests, threats, or punishments herself, but she'd sent her lackey Jelani to meet with him? It made him even more curious to discover what this was about.

"Right, then," Bones said. "After you."

Jelani led him to Lafitte's Blacksmith House, the oldest bar in the Quarter. Bones ordered a whiskey, neat. The ghoul didn't order anything. His gaze kept flickering around, either waiting for something, or from nerves. Bones moved his hand to rest almost casually near his pockets. He had several silver knives lining his trousers and sleeves, in case of vampiric trouble, though nothing but decapitation would kill a ghoul.

"Marie," Bones prodded him.

"Majestic," Jelani corrected at once.

Bones resisted the urge to roll his eyes. *The formalities are over, so do pry the stick out of your arse.*

Instead he said, "What does she want from me?"

Jelani reached in his jacket. His movement was slowed by his stiff, plastic hands, so Bones didn't feel the caution he normally would have at the gesture. Then Jelani pulled out a manila envelope.

Bones took it, slipped the photos out discreetly, taking only a moment to flick his gaze over them and the pages underneath. Then he slid them back in their envelope and gave a hard, flat stare to the man opposite him.

"What makes you think they're even still alive? There's been hardly a whisper about the pair of them for half a century."

Jelani's eyes were dark brown, almost the same color as Bones's, and his stare was equally hard. "They are alive, and they are in the city."

"Because of some blood and bits of body parts found in an apartment?" Bones asked dismissively. "Any human could be responsible for the same."

"It's them." Jelani's tone was emphatic. "They're repeating what they did forty years ago. Majestic was overseas then, too, and they came here just before Mardi Gras. By Ash Wednesday, fifteen people had disappeared. Now once again, the queen is away, and they've returned."

Bones considered him. Either Jelani was a very good liar or he believed what he was saying. That didn't make it true, however.

"I need more proof than missing tourists during Marie's absence. Why didn't I hear that they returned to New Orleans back then, as you claim? It's not like such news wouldn't have made the rounds, mate."

Jelani was also careful not to say their names. "I smelled them both times," he replied, not bothering to correct Bones calling her Marie again. "Majestic wants you to handle this quietly. Once it's done, she will take the credit for their punishment, so it will not seem that she's twice let murderers hunting in her city escape during her absence."

Bones tapped his chin. It wouldn't be an easy job. The LaLauries were infamous in both human and undead history. Louis was rumored to be around four hundred years old, and a powerful ghoul. Delphine was not quite two hundred, but what she lacked in Louis's age, she made up for in viciousness.

"One hundred thousand pounds," Bones said.

It was a steep enough price that Marie wouldn't feel she owed him a favor, but low enough that she'd also know it was a friend's rate. In truth, he might have done the job for nothing. The LaLauries were as nasty a pair as some of the other sods Bones had shriveled for free.

Jelani didn't even blink. "If you finish the job by Ash Wednesday, the money is yours."

That gave him just over a week. Bones finished his whiskey. No time to dawdle, then.

"You'll give me full run of the city," he said, setting his glass down. "And you'll stay out of my way unless directed. Do we have an accord?"

Jelani gave him a thin smile. "We do."

2

The townhouse smelled of death, blood, urine, and random police officers, in that order. Bones grunted as he knelt next to one of the reddish-brown stains on the floor.

"With the stench from all the different coppers in here, I'm amazed you could even decipher the LaLauries' scent."

Jelani stayed at the top of the stairs, not venturing down to the first floor.

"They weren't only down there. They slept in the bed up here"—Jelani pointed to a room down the hall—"and sat on the couch here"—with a stiff finger at what Bones supposed was the family room.

Bones inhaled deeply, making a mental catalog of the scents. Then he leaped up the stairs in one bound, noticing Jelani's inadvertent flinch as he watched.

Right. No need to remind the fellow of what he couldn't do anymore.

"The bed and the sofa, you say?" Bones asked, changing to walk with the slowness he used when around humans. The sofa faced the telly, with a view out the balcony to the left of it. Bones went over to it and inhaled again, noting the differences—and the similarities—from the smells downstairs.

"The owner of the flat. The girl. Has her body been found elsewhere?"

Jelani gave him a slight smile. "What makes you think this wasn't the boy's place?"

Bones shot Jelani an annoyed look. "There's a feminine scent all over this flat. This wasn't where the boy lived, though it's mostly his blood on the first floor."

"There's a picture of the girl in her bedroom." Jelani's voice was neutral, as if they were discussing the weather. "She's beautiful. I imagine she's still alive. For now."

Bones stared at Jelani. All his instincts told him that the ghoul was hiding something. Bones wondered if he'd known the girl. Jelani was acting as if none of this affected him, but his scent was of fear . . . and hatred. If he'd been emotionally attached to the flat's owner, that would make sense.

Or he could just be frightened of what would happen if Bones was unable to kill the LaLauries by the time Marie returned. Since Marie had left him in charge, it would be considered Jelani's failure as well.

"You've never told me how you know Delphine and Louis's scent to recognize it," Bones stated.

Something flashed across Jelani's face before it became smooth as dark glass again.

"I was married in the eighteen sixties," Jelani replied. "She was a slave in the St. Francisville house, which happened to be where the LaLauries fled after they left the Quarter. While I was fighting in the Union Army, Delphine and Louis tortured and ate my wife. I arrived too late to save her, but I'll never forget their scent."

Bones didn't blink. "Your arms and legs?"

"Amputated after the battle of New Market Heights. They told me it was a miracle I survived at all. Majestic changed me afterward, at my request. I wanted to live long enough to one day see the LaLauries die."

Jelani's expression was pure defiance now, as if he expected Bones to berate him for changing into a ghoul solely for revenge.

"I was turned into a vampire against my will," Bones replied evenly. "Brassed me off for a good long while, then I got over it. Can't change how we ended up as we are, so why bother fretting over it? If you're looking for judgment, look elsewhere."

Jelani seemed surprised. "I hadn't heard that about you," he murmured.

Bones let out a short laugh. "Why would you? It's not the sort of tale to be bandying about, is it?"

"Don't you hate your sire for that?"

I did.

For years, Bones had hated Ian for turning him into a vampire. But Ian hadn't done it to be malicious—he'd done it out of a twisted sort of gratitude. If not for Bones sharing his meager food, Ian would have died on that long voyage from London to the New South Wales penal colonies, where they first met as prisoners.

But Bones wasn't about to share that with Jelani. No need to air those particulars to a ghoul he barely knew.

"I don't hate him anymore," was all Bones said.

"You have a house in the city," Jelani noted, changing the subject. "Will you be staying there?"

Bones shrugged. "Not after tonight. You can ring my cell, if you need me. I'll send word when it's finished."

Jelani smiled, and it was cold. "Don't underestimate them. Delphine took the boy during an evening walking tour of the Quarter. He was seen leaving with a dark-haired girl right after the tour had stopped at her former mansion."

Has a sick sense of humor, does she? Bones thought sardonically. Their old home was about the last place he'd expect to find the LaLauries hunting, but it told Bones quite a bit. They were arrogant, which was good. Arrogance and a sense of invincibility were two large points in his favor toward killing them.

"How many ghouls and vampires live in the city?" Bones asked.

Jelani mulled it for a moment. "Year round, a few hundred. At Mardi Gras, that number doubles, easily. Humans aren't the only ones to enjoy the city's festival."

Bugger. Which was why it was an ideal time of year for the LaLauries to hunt, of course. The abundance of people, alive and undead, made them blend that much more into a crowd.

Of course, it would make Bones blend, too. He felt confident he could catch them. What he wasn't certain about, was how many people they might kill before he did.

"I'll ring you when it's finished," Bones repeated to Jelani, and walked out of the blood-soaked townhouse.

3

The afternoon sun glinted off the countless beads people wore around their necks. The streets weren't completely clogged yet. More people would venture out once it got dark. It amused Bones that a vampire could be about at this time of day, yet some humans let their excesses from the night before trap them in bed until dusk.

Bones's only concession to being out in daylight was to wear shades and sunscreen. He wouldn't burst into flames if the sun touched his bare skin, as the movies so comically claimed. Still, an hour in the sun for a vampire was akin to all day at the beach for an albino. He'd heal almost instantly, but there was no sense using his strength over something as trivial as a sunburn.

He'd already walked the length of the Quarter and back, noting the differences since the last time he'd been here— three years ago? No, it was four, because he'd celebrated the new millennium here. Blimey, the years were blinking by. It had been well over a decade since he'd set foot in London. *Once I kill the LaLauries and finish tracking down Hennessey and the other miserable blokes he's involved with, I'm going home*, Bones decided. *It's been too long. I'm even sounding more like a Yank than an Englishman these days.*

Only a couple blocks down was the LaLauries' old house. Even in daylight, there were shadows shifting around it. Residual ghosts. Any sentient spooks who'd died there stayed away from the place, not that Bones blamed them. At night, the house positively crawled with old, despairing energy from its gruesome past. It was no accident that the house had changed hands so many times over the past hundred and seventy years. It was now empty and for sale again as well. Humans might not be able to see the residual manifestations, but they could sense them, on some deep level.

And Delphine LaLaurie, at least, seemed drawn to the house as well. Why else would she pluck one of her victims right in front of it during a tour? Was the irony just amusing to her? Or did she still, after all this time, miss her old home? Was that why the LaLauries kept returning to the Quarter, despite the danger of Marie's wrath?

Bones came closer to the house. The strong smell of chemicals wafted to him from a store to his right. *Salon*, he diagnosed, then glanced at his reflection. His hair had been brown for quite some time. Since someone was obviously hunting him, it wouldn't hurt to alter his appearance.

He entered the parlor, not surprised to find a few people waiting. Every business in the Quarter enjoyed a boost from Mardi Gras, except perhaps church services. He put his name on the list, took a seat, and waited. Forty minutes later, he was brought back by the hairdresser.

"Hi there, what'll it be?" she asked in a friendly way.

"Color, trim, and wash, if you please," Bones replied.

"You English have the loveliest accents." She laughed. "Makes everything you say sound so proper."

After she washed his hair, she led him to her cubicle. Bones read her name on her beautician's certificate and gave a snort of amusement.

"Rebecca DeWinter. Was that an intentional reference?"

She looked at him in surprise. "Yeah. My parents loved that book. You're the first person who's tied my name to it. Not many people are big readers of the older classics."

Bones stifled his next snort, because telling her that he

still considered *Rebecca* to be new fiction would require too much explanation.

"I go by Becca, though," she added, giving his head a last toweling. "So, what are we doing with color today?"

What shade hadn't he done recently? "Make it blond."

She blinked at him in the mirror. "Really?"

"Platinum, the whole lot of it."

Her hand was still in his hair, absently fingering his curls. Bones met her eyes in the mirror. She turned away quickly and threw "Let me just mix the color" over her shoulder.

A smile tugged his mouth. He had no false modesty about his looks. They'd been his trade in the seventeen hundreds when he was human and survived by selling his body to women. Since then, they'd ensured that he didn't spend many nights alone, but by his choice, not for need of coin anymore. And at times, he'd used his looks when he was hunting lethal, feminine prey. They'd been a useful tool, but Bones placed far more importance on maintaining his wits and strength.

Becca came back and applied the color to his hair. Bones chatted with her, learning that she'd worked here for a couple of years, lived just outside the Quarter, and—interestingly enough—had been closing up the night Eric Greenville was murdered.

". . . such a shame," Becca continued. "I can't tell you how many times I've seen those tour groups by our window while the guides talk about that old house. They can't stand on their corner, since that's private property, so they hang out in front here. How awful for someone to be robbed and murdered by a person he met on one of those."

"Is that what the papers say happened?" Bones asked, though he already knew the answer.

She shrugged. "Yeah. Weird stuff always happens during Mardi Gras."

That might be true, but Bones was more interested in how Becca might have caught a glimpse of Delphine LaLaurie that night, whether she realized it or not. He'd intended to track down the tour guide from that evening, for the same reason, but that person would be much more recognizable to Delphine. Becca was anonymous. She could be right useful, and judging from her scent—and the lingering looks she snuck his way—she wouldn't be averse to spending more time with him.

"I'm in town on business," Bones said casually. "Leaving soon after Mardi Gras ends, but I wondered if you'd fancy having dinner with me?"

He'd been watching her in the mirror as he asked. Her eyes widened, then she broke out into a smile.

"Um, sure. That would be nice."

She was quite pretty. Shoulder-length brown hair with blond highlights, a nice full mouth—and arse—and she looked well into her twenties, so not a novice when it came to dating.

Infinitely biteable, Bones decided with a speculative gaze. "Are you free tonight?"

She glanced away. Funny how many otherwise confident women shied under a direct look.

"Yeah. I get off in an hour, but you know, I'd want to go home and change . . ."

"Smashing, I'll pick you up at your house 'round eight," Bones stated, giving her his charming smile. It worked well enough. She didn't argue, as it were.

When he left the salon, his hair was champagne blond, he had Becca's address in hand, and a far different plan for tonight than he'd started out with. *You might turn out to be my homing beacon for Delphine*, Bones thought, giving Becca a peck on the cheek while promising to pick her up later. *Or at the very least, we'll both have dinner tonight.*

4

Becca ordered a salad for her entrée. Bones, used to the baffling tendencies of women on first dates to pretend they didn't eat, said nothing. He just ordered the large prime rib with three sides and cajoled Becca into eating half his food. Aside from being thinner than he preferred, Becca could also use the extra iron from the red meat, since Bones intended to lower her blood count by a pint before the evening was finished.

After dinner, they walked along the streets of the Quarter. Bones gave Becca his coat, since her short dress with spaghetti straps did little to keep out the chill. Around them, the crowds were getting livelier as alcohol mixed with the veil of darkness, and the primal vibe of the city urged people to lose their normal inhibitions.

The hum of energy and excitement coming from the writhing banquet of humanity brought out the undead in force as well. Bones, under the pretext of joining in the festivities, bought masks for himself and Becca. His hid half his face, but hers was a silly little thing with feathers that covered only the area around her eyes.

With his aura of power carefully in check, new hair color, mask, and persona of being just another blood drinker strolling with his future meal, Bones was as disguised as he could be. Somewhere in this seething mass of people, the LaLauries could be hunting, choosing their next victim. Time for Becca to assist him.

Bones drew her a few feet into the next alley they came across. Even above the raucous noise around them, he could hear her heartbeat speed up as he leaned down.

Instead of kissing her, however, Bones brought his face close to hers, letting green spill out of his eyes while he spoke low and resonantly.

"Remember the girl, Becca? The dark-haired one you saw that night walking with the murdered boy, can you see her face in your mind again?"

Bones knew she could. Determining that Becca had seen Delphine with Eric was the first thing he'd done when he arrived at her house earlier. A few flashes of his eyes, some help regressing her to that evening, and Bones was sure Becca had gotten a clear view of the female ghoul. Now to focus Becca on Delphine's image, so she'd recognize her on the spot if she saw her again.

Becca nodded, transfixed by his gaze. Bones caressed her cheek.

"If you see her again, you'll tell me at once. If I'm not with you, you'll ring me straightaway, but you will *not* go anywhere with her, ever."

"Ever," Becca echoed.

"You won't remember this conversation, either; you'll only remember to act as I've told you if you see her. And no matter the circumstances, you won't notice my eyes being anything but brown, or my teeth being anything but normal, right?"

Another nod. "Right."

"Good." Bones smiled. The emerald light left his eyes. Once free of their entrapping glow, Becca blinked, her awareness returning. Her gaze flicked to his mouth, and she licked her lips.

Bones closed the few inches between them, settling his mouth over hers in a firm, leisurely kiss. She tasted of wine and prime rib, and beneath that was her own taste. Sweet, like crushed flowers.

A scraping sound from above made Bones yank to the side with a curse. Someone was up there.

In the next moment, pain seared his back, just a few inches below his heart. As Bones spun around, he spotted a redheaded vampire perched on the roof on the other side of the alley.

"Ralmiel," Bones muttered, recognizing him. He jerked away in the next split second before another arrow was fired off. This time, it landed in the building instead of his flesh.

"'Allo, *mon ami*," the vampire called out genially. "Stand still so I can kill you."

"Oh my *God*," Becca gasped.

"Go into the parade now," Bones ordered her, shoving her in that direction.

Another arrow came at him, striking him in the arm he'd extended to push Becca safely away. Bones yanked the arrow out, spun to avoid another one, and propelled himself straight up in the air. Since he was in the alley, most bystanders wouldn't see him, and the ones who did would be too drunk to remember it clearly, anyhow.

Ralmiel gave an infuriating chuckle as he sprinted away, leaping over the roofs in gravity-defying strides. Bones chased him, drawing several knives from his sleeves. He flung them at the vampire's back, but only one landed, and not in his heart. Bloke was fast.

"You cannot catch me, *mon ami*!" Ralmiel laughed, darting across the next roof onto the steeple of St. Louis Cathedral.

"Too right I can," Bones growled, crossing the same distance in an aerial leap. He reached inside his sleeves, grasped two more knives, and rocketed them at the vampire.

The knives landed in Ralmiel's chest, but he'd jerked

back in a life-saving microsecond that meant the difference between them piercing his heart and burying less harmfully into his sternum.

"*Sacre bleu*," Ralmiel swore, yanking them out and tossing them off the roof. Then he smiled at Bones. "Close, though, *non*?"

Bones reached in his sleeves again—and came up empty. Right, he'd given his coat to Becca, and it held the rest of his knives.

Ralmiel aimed his crossbow, then gave a snort as he saw that he, too, was out of silver.

"Normally it takes no more than four arrows, *mon ami*. I wasn't expecting you to be so quick. We'll have to continue this another time."

Bones jumped onto the church's roof. "We can settle this without weapons. Come on, mate, afraid to only use your hands in a death match?"

Ralmiel had an odd grin. "I think I will let you live tonight and kill you tomorrow. Or the next day. I get paid the same either way."

Bones let out a short laugh. "Decided to take one of the many contracts out on me, did you? After I kill you, mate, I'll be curious to see what *your* corpse is worth."

Ralmiel sketched a bow, squeezing something in his hand. "I think not." Then he vanished in front of Bones's eyes.

Bones stared at the spot where Ralmiel had been. *What kind of trick was this?*

Since they were in New Orleans, the heart of magic and voodoo, perhaps it was a sort of spell. The few other times Bones had run across Ralmiel, he damn sure didn't have the power to dematerialize on his own. Bones didn't figure he'd hide such an ability, either.

Though that begged the question of why Marie would allow Ralmiel, a known hit man, in her city to hunt the hitter she'd hired. If Bones was dead, then he couldn't take care of her problem with the LaLauries, could he? He'd have to inform Jelani of this. Perhaps Marie wasn't aware of Ralmiel's presence.

But now to find Becca, and erase from her mind all the things she'd just witnessed.

5

The next day, Bones went out of the Quarter to a shop titled The Swamp Rat, noting with amusement the layer of ground brick sprinkled across the threshold of the door. It was a voodoo defense barrier, supposedly capable of keeping out anyone who meant the shop owner ill. Pity it didn't work against people who didn't believe in voodoo. Or vampires.

As soon as he stepped inside, Bones flipped the OPEN sign to CLOSED and locked the door behind him. A wizened little man behind the counter glanced up, blinked . . . and then, of all things, tried to run.

Bones was across the room and over the counter in less time than it took the elderly shop owner to clear his seat. He chuckled as the man let out a spate of Creole that cursed Bones, his parentage, and several of his ancestors.

"Remember, Jean-Pierre, I speak Creole, so anything you say can and will be held against you and all that rot."

"Debil," Jean-Pierre said in English with a hiss. "I 'oped I'd seen the last of you years ago."

"Now, mate, you'll hurt my feelings. Don't know why you take such an aversion to me. Your grandfather and I got along splendidly, and I know I'm glad to still find *you* here."

Jean-Pierre's eyes flicked around the shop, but it was empty of anyone but Bones and himself. No surprise there; the wares he had on his shelves were ugly, shoddy T-shirts and other miscellaneous gimmicky items, all in questionable condition and priced higher than most of his competitors.

But Jean-Pierre's real business was voodoo. The shops along the Quarter were for the tourists or the uneducated. Jean-Pierre supplied genuine ingredients for the practiced, discerning buyer, and his family had been in the business since almost the inception of the city. He was someone who knew many of the city's darkest secrets. And because Jean-Pierre had inherited the family trait of being immune to vampire mind control, Bones couldn't just use his gaze to glare information out of him, more's the pity.

"Now then, what did I want to ask you about? Ah, yes, redheaded bloke who goes by the name Ralmiel. Vampire, 'round my height, and has the most amazing new trick of disappearing into thin air. What do you know of him?"

From the expression on Jean-Pierre's face, he did know something about Ralmiel, but he didn't want to share the information.

Bones didn't lose a fraction of his smile. "Need me to bash you about a bit before you answer? No trouble at all. Just let me know which bone you'd like broken first and I'll get to it straightaway."

"Debils," Jean-Pierre hissed. "Nothin' but grave walkers, the both of you, 'cept even the earth don' want you."

Bones waved a hand. "Yes, right, we're all wretched blokes forsaken by God and Mother Nature herself, now get on with it."

Bones really had no desire to start beating on the little man. That would take too long.

"Redheaded debil, he come 'round every so often," Jean-Pierre said, spitting out the words. "He have fetishes made for him, use magic."

"Vampires are forbidden from using magic. It's one of the few laws Cain laid down for his people. I'm surprised Ralmiel uses it so blatantly."

Jean-Pierre's mouth curled. "Cain. God should have killed him for murdering Abel, not made him into a vampire as punishment instead. As for Ralmiel, those who see 'im use magic don't live long enough to tell about it, I think."

That would keep word from spreading, true enough. But a few people had to know aside from Jean-Pierre. "This magic Ralmiel uses, who makes it?"

"Don' know."

Bones gave Jean-Pierre a measured stare. "I won't enjoy it, but I'll either beat the answer out of you, or I'll take you with me and keep feeding off your no doubt dreadful-tasting blood until you tire of being my snack and you tell me then."

"Hope she curdles your blood to dust," Jean-Pierre spat, but gave Bones a name. And her location.

"You ring me if you see Ralmiel again," Bones instructed Jean-Pierre, writing his number on the back of one of the sloganed coasters for sale on the counter. This one had a tagline of "It won't lick itself!" Quite true, that.

"And don't make me end my long, friendly association with your family by doing something foolish," Bones added, letting green flash in his eyes as he handed him the coaster.

Jean-Pierre took it. "I don't cross debils. Too much bad juju afterward."

Bones just nodded as he left. Quite true, that, as well.

It was Bones's fourth day in the city when another murder was discovered. As before, Bones went to the scene to see what, if anything, he could use from it to track the LaLauries.

Jelani spoke with the detective assigned to the case. From their muted conversation, Bones picked up that the detective thought Jelani was an associate of one of the city's biggest donors, and that Bones was a private investigator.

Bones made Jelani empty out the flat before he went inside, ignoring the rubbish the detective sputtered about him contaminating the scene. He'd leave the scene a sight less muddled than those blokes.

Once alone, he walked through the flat, breathing deeply every few moments. *Same male and female scent from the other flat. Spent less time here, though, and made a grand mess of things in their haste. Those blood spatters are from an arterial spray, arced wide enough that the girl would have been running when they tore open her throat. Not the same girl they finished off in the kitchen, though. She's the poor lass who owned the other flat, and she didn't have any legs left to run on.*

The boy was watching. His blood's fresher than theirs, and the stench from his fear is smeared all over both rooms. From the shallowness of his wounds, he was likely still alive when they ate his arms . . .

Bones felt the shift in the air right before Ralmiel appeared behind him. He spun, his knife flashing out, but the other vampire wasn't pointing any weapons at him this time. No, Ralmiel was staring almost sadly around the carnage of the room.

"*Mon Dieu*," he breathed, then gave a censuring glance at the knife in Bones's hand. "Put that away. There's been enough death in this room, *oui*?"

Under normal circumstances, Bones would have disagreed, and then proceeded to stab the hell out of Ralmiel. But the scents, sight, and aura of despairing horror in the flat also made him loath to add to it. Bones lowered his knife, but didn't let it out of his hand. He wasn't so affected that he'd lost his wits.

"Why are you here, if not to attempt to kill me again?"

Ralmiel walked around the room, inhaling just as frequently as Bones had. He held another small, dark satchel in his grip. Ah yes, that would be Ralmiel's voodoo version of a teleporter.

"This was not done by human hands. It is one thing to kill such as you or I"—Ralmiel's dismissive wave encompassed their mutual lack of worth—"but these are innocents. It is not right."

Bones almost rolled his eyes. A hitter with a conscience.

If Ralmiel wasn't out to kill him, he'd buy him a drink and they could talk shop.

"You didn't hear about the other murders? You should pay more attention, mate."

"I heard about the last one, but didn't know our kind was responsible. New Orleans is my city. It has its darkness, but not like this. You know who's doing this?"

Bones met the other man's green gaze. "Yeah, I do."

Ralmiel waited. Bones said nothing else. Finally, Ralmiel gave Bones an assessing glance.

"But you are here to kill them, *non*? You are not too bright if you think Marie will thank you afterward for stealing her vengeance."

Bones shrugged. "I'm doing it regardless. Call it a slow business week."

Ralmiel laughed, but it had a harsh edge. "Tell me who is behind this, so when I kill you, you can go to your rest knowing I will prevent it from happening again. You have my word."

"Thanks ever so, but I'll take my chances," Bones replied, green glittering in his eyes.

Ralmiel didn't know it, but those magic pouches of his were numbered. Bones had paid a visit to Georgette yesterday, the maker of Ralmiel's fancy exits, and had persuaded her to switch the ingredients for Ralmiel's new batch. It barely required any threatening at all. Georgette knew using magic was against vampire law, and as the provider of the product, she was guilty by association. Once Ralmiel ran out of the real fetishes, Bones would have him right where he wanted him. Forced to fight—and die.

Ralmiel bowed. "As you wish." Then he squeezed his pouch and vanished from where he'd been standing.

Bones looked at the empty spot and smiled. *Two more down, mate. I suspect your genie impersonation will soon be coming to an end.*

6

Becca chewed her lower lip. "You're quiet tonight."

Bones glanced up. "Sorry, luv, I'm just a bit preoc-
cupied."

She pushed her plate back. At least, three dates later,
she'd quit pretending that a bowl of lettuce was all she
wanted for a meal.

"Problems with your client?"

Becca thought he was a consultant for a corporation
looking to save finances by downsizing its nonessential
employee positions. It was close to the truth, in a twisted
sort of way.

"Something like that."

The real problem was, Bones still wasn't any closer to
finding the LaLauries. They didn't appear to have their own
residence, but just moved from flat to flat of the people they
murdered.

And despite his walking Becca up and down every street
in the Quarter the past three nights, she'd caught no glimpse
of Delphine LaLaurie. Bones had come across several
ghouls on those jaunts, but they were having a bit of harmless fun. Not looking to savage the first person thick enough
to follow them inside a building.

Becca reached out, touching his hand. "Do you know
where you're going to be next, after this job? And, ah, will
you be leaving right away when it's done?"

He knew what she was really asking him. "I'll be leaving straightaway when I'm finished. My work takes me all over the world, and leaves precious little time for anything else." *I'm not what you're looking for, Becca.*

Hurt flashed on her face for a moment, quickly masked behind a false smile. "Sounds exciting."

Does it? In point of fact, it can be bloody lonely.

"You know," Becca said as the silence stretched, "I'd understand if you just want to drop me home after dinner . . ."

"No," Bones said at once, softening his tone when she blinked at how emphatic he sounded. "I'm sorry, I've been a right glum fellow, but I do want to spend more time with you tonight. If you're willing."

He almost hoped she'd say she wasn't. If the circumstances weren't so dire, Bones would drop Becca at her house and compel her not to set foot in the city until this was over.

But he couldn't stand over the next freshly chewed body and know he might have been able to prevent it. Bones couldn't sniff them out, not with the river of humanity thronging the streets, but he could have Becca give a good look at any female ghoul he found. One of these times, it would be Delphine.

"I'd really like to spend more time with you, while I'm here," Bones said, giving Becca a smile filled with possibilities.

She smiled back, her scent of unease melting away from her.

"I'd like that, too."

Rotten bastard you are, Bones thought. He didn't let any of that show on his face, however. Instead, he signaled for the check.

Power raised the hairs on the back of his neck. Bones turned, muttering a curse when he spied a familiar face headed their way.

"Excuse me," he ground out to Becca, rising.

"'Allo," Ralmiel called out, sliding into the seat opposite Bones's. He gave a charming smile to Becca. "Who might you be, *ma belle chérie?*"

"No one that concerns you," Bones said curtly.

Becca's mouth dropped. Ralmiel looked offended. "As if you would need to protect such a lovely flower from me. My business is with you, *mon ami*. Not with people who happen to be around you."

Ralmiel didn't have a reputation for harming innocent bystanders, but Bones wasn't pleased at Becca being exposed to him. This whole situation was putting her at more risk than he'd intended. He'd have to change his plans for tomorrow night. But first things first.

Bones sat down, keeping his hands close to the silver knives in his coat.

"Is everything okay?" Becca asked, glancing back and forth between them.

"Quite," Bones replied, not letting his eyes stray from Ralmiel's. "My friend just forgot his manners, interrupting our dinner."

"I was going to wait for you outside," Ralmiel said, settling back in his chair expansively, "but when I saw your *chér amie*, I decided to conclude our business tomorrow. After I learn more about *la belle* here."

"I don't like being spoken about as if I'm not even here," Becca said, with a sharp glare at Ralmiel.

The waiter came with the check. Bones dropped several bills onto it without counting them, not tearing his attention from Ralmiel for a fraction longer than needed.

"Join us outside?" Bones asked, with an arched brow.

Ralmiel nodded. "Of course."

Becca got her purse, still giving them wary glances. "Do you two need a minute alone to talk?"

No, Bones thought coolly. *But I'd like a minute alone to kill him.* He picked up his whiskey glass, noting with satisfaction that it was near full, and rose from the table.

"We're fine, luv. Be finished up shortly."

Bones and Ralmiel kept their attention on each other's every move as they walked outside. The tension was thick enough to slice. Almost casually, Bones took a sip of his whiskey. Next to them, a group of smokers waited to get into the restaurant.

"What's your plan, mate?" Bones asked. "Going to skulk after me and wait for your best chance?"

Ralmiel smirked. "*Non, mon ami.* I'm going to follow her home and *then* skulk around after you."

Becca gasped. Bones just smiled. "I think not."

Then he flung his whiskey on Ralmiel, using the lighter from the smoker nearest him to send Ralmiel up in flames.

Ralmiel screamed, swatting at the fire that covered the front of him. Several bystanders yelled as well. Bones didn't wait to admire his handiwork. He yanked Becca with him through the crowd, ignoring her horrified sputtering. Once he found an alley, he propelled himself up in the night, covering both of them with his coat. Less chance of being noticed, since his coat was black against the night's sky.

Ralmiel wouldn't be following anyone, not in his condition.

Becca's scream at being airborne was cut off by Bones clapping a hand over her mouth. He didn't bother with the rooftops this time, but flew over the Quarter and beyond. He glanced back a few times, but there was no flying form chasing him. It would be too much to hope that Ralmiel hadn't managed to douse the fire and was dead, but at least now he wouldn't know where Becca lived.

She kicked and squirmed the entire way, making terrified grunting sounds against his hand. When they reached her neighborhood, Bones glanced around, saw no one loitering about, and set them on the ground by her front door.

"Shh, you're fine, Becca," he said, lasering her with his gaze. "I drove you home after dinner, and nothing out of the ordinary happened."

She smiled at him, the fear melting away on her face.

"Thanks for a lovely evening," she said.

Bones sighed, again regretting the necessity of using her. *When this is over,* he promised her silently, *you're getting a large donation in your bank account. It's the bloody least I can do.*

"No, luv, thank you," he replied, brushing his lips across hers.

He'd intended it to be only a brief kiss, but she opened her mouth and twined her tongue with his, the scent of desire wafting from her.

Bones kissed her with more intensity, letting his hands slide to her waist. She gasped, and then groaned when his hips rubbed against hers.

Money isn't all I can give her, Bones reflected. Becca didn't want him to leave her at her door tonight. Her heartbeat and scent were screaming that to him.

She pulled away long enough to whisper, "Come inside."

Again, it was the least he could do.

7

The float rounded the first street corner to the clamor of cheers. It was a mock-up of an opera stage, with a faux upper balcony and a piano in the forefront. Becca, barely recognizable in curled wig, theater makeup, and a long, Victorian dress, beamed at the crowd. Seated at the piano, Bones ran his hands over the keys while the float's speakers blared out the familiar score from *Phantom of the Opera*.

More cheers came from the street's onlookers, especially when Bones stood up and bowed. He wore a black tuxedo, with that trademark half-face mask obscuring his features, and a dark wig on his head. The other actors on the float mimed a musical rehearsal as Bones stalked toward Becca with the exaggerated seductiveness—and menace—of the Phantom.

It hadn't been hard to switch himself and Becca with the original couple for this float. Just a few flashes from his eyes, and those people were happily drinking rum instead of playing Christine and the Phantom. None of the other actors argued, either. There were days when it was good to be a vampire.

Perched as she was on the fake balcony of the float, Becca had a bird's-eye view of the people up and down the streets. This parade went all through the Quarter, and in their costumes, even Ralmiel would be hard-pressed to recognize either of them. Becca was as anonymous as Bones could make her, having no idea that, subconsciously, she was scanning faces in the crowd looking for Delphine.

After lip-synching a snippet from "Music of the Night" with Becca, Bones jumped down and walked around the outside of the float. This kept Becca's attention where it should be; away from him, and on the faces upturned at her. If that deviated from the scheduled act for the float, so be it. It was only three days until Fat Tuesday. Soon the LaLauries would finish their murderous scavenging and leave the city. There were more important things at stake than following a parade script.

It was after eleven at night, which meant the crowds were at their peak. The parade was halfway down Bourbon Street when Becca suddenly stopped waving and flinging beads. Her eyes took on a glazed look as the directive Bones had instilled in her a week ago kicked in and bore results.

"The woman from that night. There she is."

Becca didn't even seem to be aware that she'd spoken. Bones swung his gaze in the direction Becca was staring, cursing the crush of people around him. There was a sea of faces, half of them female, and every third of those with dark hair. He jumped up to where Becca was, muttering, "Show me."

Becca ignored everything around her, fixated on the directive Bones had compelled in her before: find the woman from that night. With a stiff gesture, she pointed into the crowd. Bones searched the faces ahead of them, looking for that faint, telltale luminance of undead flesh.

A woman about ten meters ahead turned around. Her hair was black and curly, her smile was wide, and her beautiful features were set off by pale, perfect skin.

Delphine.

Delphine noticed him, too. At first her eyes flicked over him disinterestedly, but then she paused. Narrowed her gaze. And turned around and began walking away.

"Stay here," Bones ordered Becca, reaching inside his coat to pull out a large, curved knife. The crowd gasped, thinking it was part of the act. He ignored them as he jumped down, roughly shoving people out of his path.

Her dark head slipped below the crowd as she ducked and vanished from his sight. Bones increased his pace, almost throwing people to the side. Soon the police would notice the disturbance, but he didn't care. His attention was focused on one goal. *Don't let Delphine escape.*

He glimpsed her again, darting quickly through people with her head lowered. Delphine glanced over her shoulder, and their eyes met once more. She smiled, lovely and evil. Then she punched the person closest to her and ran.

Bones gave up pretending to be human. He chased after Delphine with all his supernatural speed. In the next moment, he was upon the young man Delphine had struck. The man was on his knees, blood pouring out between hands clutched to his stomach. She'd punched him hard enough to tear right through the bloke's guts. It was a mortal injury—unless Bones stopped to save him.

He made his decision in an instant and kept going. It was worth the sacrifice of one innocent victim to save countless others. Delphine had underestimated her hunter by thinking this would secure her escape.

Another burst of speed brought him closer. Delphine was fast, but he was quicker. Savage anticipation coursed through him. His hand clenched on his knife. *Almost there . . .*

Just as Bones was nearly upon her, an arrow ripped through his chest, bringing an explosion of pain. He roared as he tore it out, plowing through people well below eye level to make his heart a far harder target. *Ralmiel.* He'd kill the sod for his wretched timing.

Another arrow landed in his back, missing his heart again, but showing Ralmiel hadn't given up. The silver burned, yet Bones didn't slow to pull it out. He couldn't risk losing Delphine, pain be damned.

Every person he jostled by in the crowd felt like he was giving the arrow a good twist, however. Bones gritted his teeth and continued on, cursing the people in his way, the blaring music, the bloody beads, the myriad smells that made Delphine impossible to track by scent, and the Cajun hitter determined to mount him on his trophy wall.

Bones caught another arrow to the neck, skewering him clean through and spinning him around in rage. Blast it all, Ralmiel would get lucky with one of his shots soon, and Bones couldn't kill Delphine if he was dead himself.

He took his knife and hacked the front of the arrow off, then ripped it out of his throat. Fiery pain throbbed for a moment until the wound healed. Bones kept moving, zig-zagging, until he reached the side of a building and then shot straight up. Once on the roof, he tore his mask off; his gaze was sizzling emerald as he sought out his target.

Ralmiel was on the roof across the street, over the MAISON BOURBON sign. The Cajun didn't smile or crack any jokes this time. He fitted another arrow in his crossbow and fired.

Bones whirled to the left, leaving the arrow to sail past him, then whirled again when another rapidly fired. And another.

Sod this, Bones thought. He folded one arm across his chest and then vaulted at Ralmiel, his other hand holding the curving knife. Ralmiel fired off two more arrows, but they landed in Bones's arm, not his heart. Then Ralmiel jumped back, but too slow. One hard slash cleaved the cross-bow in two. Another swipe split open Ralmiel's chest. The blade was steel, not silver, since Bones had intended it for decapitating a ghoul instead of killing a vampire.

Still, the wound was deep. Ralmiel floundered, trying unsuccessfully to wrest away. Bones held on to him and raised the knife again. *This one takes off your head*, Bones thought grimly, swinging the blade. *And that kills everything, doesn't it?*

But the knife swept through thin air instead. Bones snarled in frustration, his knees hitting the roof as the vam-pire under him disappeared. He spun around, just in case the blighter was about to reappear behind him with silver at the ready, but there was nothing.

Cold fury filled Bones. He hacked off the end of the arrow still piercing his back, then yanked that through as well, ignoring the starburst of pain it caused. Either Ralmiel would soon run out of magic pouches or Georgette had decided not to switch the ingredients in them. He'd deal with that later, though. First he had to try to find Delphine again, and God help Ralmiel if he interfered one more time.

Bones darted along the Quarter's roofs for more than an hour, using the higher vantage point to better see the faces of the people below. No sign of Delphine. He cursed himself for not simply flying over the heads of the crowd to get to her before, but hiding the secret of his species was so ingrained in him that his first instinct had been to follow her on foot. It would have been sufficient, too, if not for Ralmiel. Bloody bastard.

But now Bones knew what she looked like. Becca's part in this could finally be over. Bones would try scouring the Quarter again tomorrow, and hope like blazes Delphine hadn't been scared out of the city.

Bones left the Quarter and went to his hotel at the outskirts of city, doubling back several times to make sure he wasn't being followed. With all his backtracking, the sun was almost ready to rise by the time he made it inside his room. He stripped off his clothes and sat on the bed, eyeing his laptop. Better check now for any important messages. Sleep could wait a bit longer.

Bones logged onto his e-mail, quickly reading through his messages. "Bloody hell," Bones swore when he got to the last one. *What was the ghoul up to?*

8

That afternoon, Bones opened the side door to his townhouse to let Jelani in. He went through the foyer, listening to the clicks from Jelani's plastic and metal legs as he followed. Bones stopped in the townhouse's inner courtyard. It was beautiful, with a large fountain in the middle surrounded by flowers planted specifically to bloom even in winter.

"Very nice," Jelani complimented, looking around.

Bones was silent. Jelani waited for a few minutes, but then impatience got the better of him.

"You said you had some news?" the ghoul prompted.

Bones gave him a thin smile. "I do indeed. About you."

Then Bones crossed the distance and grabbed Jelani, holding the bigger man several feet off the ground.

"This is your only chance to tell me the truth. Lie to me and I'll kill you right here. Ever since I arrived, I've had Ralmiel after me, with no fear of Marie's reprisal for it. Strange, that. Then your story didn't check out. Did you think I'd just take your word and not do my own investigation? There's no record of the LaLauries ever being at the St. Francisville house, so they couldn't have murdered your wife there. What kind of game are you playing?"

Jelani didn't bother to struggle. His false arms and legs left him as helpless against Bones as if he'd been human.

"I was the LaLauries' slave," he spat. "Both me and my

wife were purchased from them shortly after they moved to the Quarter. The stories of what they did to their slaves aren't even half the truth. My wife and I tried to run away. They caught us and tortured me. Cut off my arms and legs and ate them in front of me, but that wasn't the worst of it."

Jelani looked away. The scent of pure torment wafted off him, but Bones didn't loosen his grip.

"Go on."

"Delphine changed me into a ghoul," Jelani continued, his voice trembling with remembrance. "Then she kept me chained inside that hellish attic for days, until I was mad from hunger. She finally brought my wife up, chaining her, too, so she couldn't run away. That night, I killed my wife. *I killed my wife and ate her.*"

Bones let him down. Jelani staggered for a moment on his prosthetic legs until he found his balance. When he did, he shoved Bones back.

"I'm sorry, mate," Bones said quietly. "But you know it wasn't your fault. It's their crime, not yours."

Jelani gave a bitter snort. "Oh, I know they're guilty for her death. But every time I go to sleep, I can still hear her screaming in my dreams. Over a hundred years later, I can still hear it." Jelani met Bones's gaze squarely. "I want it to end. I want all of it to end."

Bones let out a slow sigh. "Marie has no idea the LaLauries are even here, does she? That's why Ralmiel is so brazenly after me. He has no fear of repercussions from her."

"When Delphine and Louis were hunting in the city decades ago, Majestic told me not to act until she was back. She didn't want anyone knowing for fear that news of it would weaken her power. But the LaLauries got away before Majestic returned. This time, I couldn't risk letting them get away again. So I lied to you when I brought you here."

Bones ran a hand through his hair in frustration. "Marie will kill you for this. But you must already know that."

The big man's shoulders slumped. "You can't know what it's like, living among our kind crippled this way. Majestic has made it bearable, but once the LaLauries are dead, I want to die, too. My only hope is that Majestic is kind enough to make death my punishment for my betrayal, instead of casting me off without her protection."

Bones's gaze traveled once more over the stumps that made up Jelani's arms and legs. Jelani couldn't wield a knife in defense of his life or in defense of Marie's, which was the expectation of any member in an undead line. He couldn't even walk, if someone were to sweep those prosthetics out from under him—and that would be the first thing any hostile vampire or ghoul would do.

Looking at it coldly, all Jelani had to offer Majestic in return for her protection was his loyalty, and he'd just burned that by going behind her back over the LaLauries. Even if Marie sympathized with why he did it, she'd still have no choice except to kill him for it. Not if she didn't want to be regarded as a weak leader.

And if Bones was being practical, now that he knew none of this had been sanctioned by Marie, he'd leave the city tonight. Then once Jelani's deeds were revealed, Bones could truthfully claim ignorance of the man's betrayal.

But if he didn't, any further actions he took would be held up to judgment by the queen of the city. Bones was a trespasser, hunting on Marie's grounds without her permission. He knew she wouldn't look kindly on that. Furthermore, while he was here, he was providing a damn fine target of himself to Ralmiel, since he couldn't very well hide and hunt at the same time in the same small area.

Though neither could the LaLauries. Not for much longer, as it were.

There was only one choice, wasn't there?

Bones stared at Jelani, not letting any emotion show on his face. "I don't believe I'll see you again, mate, but I'll promise you this—you'll have your vengeance."

Jelani gave him a tight smile. "It won't just be my vengeance. It will be shared by my wife, and everyone else who died at their hands."

Bones walked away, not replying to that. Death he could give, yes. But at the moment, he wished he could give hope, too, even though there was none for Jelani, and perhaps none for himself, either.

9

Bones walked up the street to Becca's salon. He'd tried her cell earlier, but she didn't answer. She was probably annoyed with him for what she'd think was his disappearing last night. Or she was busy with customers and hadn't been able to get to her phone. Either way, he thought a gesture was in order, so he'd picked up a dozen roses on his way.

And just in case Ralmiel was on a roof sighting down a crossbow on him, Bones was wearing a Kevlar vest underneath his shirt and coat. Let Ralmiel try to shoot an arrow through *that*. The next time that scurvy bugger pulled a Houdini and popped up, Bones intended to separate his head from his shoulders. If he could kill Delphine and Louis at the same time, he'd consider it a capital evening.

Bones was a few shops down from the salon when he smelled it. He inhaled just to make sure, then quickened his pace, running the short distance to the salon and flinging open the door.

The girl behind the counter looked up in surprise. Bones ignored her, stalking through the salon and yanking open every closed door, much to the consternation of a customer getting a massage in the back room.

"Becca's not here," the girl called out.

Bones stalked over, letting the roses drop to the floor as he grabbed her.

"When did she leave? Was she alone?"

"Hey, not so rough," she protested.

Bones let her go and asked very precisely, "*Where* is Becca?"

"She called in sick. Or she had her new roommate come in earlier to say that Becca wasn't working today, but when you showed up, to tell you to come over for dinner. So I guess Becca can't be *that* sick."

Even though he already knew, he had to confirm it. "This girl, what did she look like?"

Shrug. "Black curly hair, thin, about my age. Had an accent, I think it was French . . ."

Bones walked to the door. The girl continued to call after him.

"Tell Becca she's in trouble with our manager. It's Mardi Gras, we can't afford for her to just decide to take a day off."

Delphine hadn't just run off last night. No, she'd doubled back and found Becca first.

Once outside, Bones inhaled again, deeply. Even with the scent of countless people trampling through the air, he could still smell Delphine. It was if she'd deliberately rubbed against the side of the shop to make sure he smelled her. Bones walked across the street to stare up at the LaLauries' old mansion. Then he went to the gate and took in another long breath.

She'd been here, too. Again, the trail was so strong, it had to be deliberate. Delphine's scent hadn't been on it before, the many other times Bones had walked past this house. And now he could hear a heartbeat inside the normally empty mansion.

Becca. *Come over for dinner*, Delphine had said, and she was making sure Bones knew where dinner would be held.

A bitter smile twisted his mouth. *No, Delphine. I'm not making it that easy for you. Ghouls are stronger during the day, while vampires are weaker. I'll wait till after nightfall to accept your invitation. It's not as if you have any inten-*

tion of letting Becca go free once I arrive anyway, you murdering bitch.

Bones turned on heel and walked away, wondering if Delphine or Louis was watching him.

It was past nine when Bones came back. His coat was lined with several knives, both steel and silver. No telling whether Delphine and Louis might have vampiric help with them, so best to have all bases covered. He was still wearing the Kevlar vest underneath his shirt, even though it would slightly hinder his movements. Still, its benefit outweighed its liability.

Bones stared at the LaLauries' old house. Even with all the noise around him from partiers enjoying the last few days of Mardi Gras, if he concentrated, Bones could still faintly make out the heartbeat inside the house. True, that heartbeat might not be Becca's, but she might yet be alive.

Now for the last addition to his ensemble.

Bones turned and walked into the reveling crowd, pulling out the first few people his hands laid on, dragging them from the thick of the merrymakers and hitting them with his gaze. The alcohol they'd consumed helped with that, since none of them could claim exceptional mental willpower at the moment. Bones didn't care if anyone looking on bothered to wonder why his eyes were glowing green. Let them think it was a special effect from the *Phantom of the Opera* mask he had on, if they bothered to ponder it at all.

After giving the three bespelled people their instructions, Bones went back into the crowd and pulled out another three, repeating the process. And then another three, then another, until he had more than a dozen obedient bystanders. Finally, Bones walked back down the street to stand on the corner in front of the house.

The shadows around it were darker now, throbbing with the memory of suppressed rage from centuries ago. It was almost as if those shadows knew their former tormenters had returned. Bones took off his mask, then rolled his head around on his shoulders.

"Now," he told the waiting men and women at his back, and vaulted up into the air.

Below him, they began walking to the front of the house and hurling things at it. Beer bottles, their shoes, their masks; whatever they could get into their hands, they flung it. Windows broke on the first and second floors, the sound drowned out by the yells and hollers from the people. They didn't go within a dozen feet of the house, though. No, they stayed just far enough away so that anyone who wanted to stop them would have to come out and get them.

Drawing out Delphine or Louis wasn't the point. The racket they made while they smashed up the house was. Hidden behind the chimney on a nearby roof, Bones waited for his chance. When two windows smashed simultaneously, Bones sprang forward, streamlining his body and diving through the second floor windows.

Bones rolled as soon as he hit the floor, staying low and searching the room, careful not to let any green shine from his eyes. He wasn't going to make it easier for them to find him, if they'd determined the noise they'd just heard was him instead of more objects being hurled through the windows.

The room was empty of all but furniture. Bones inhaled, trying to track Becca by scent, and then swore. The room stank of embalming fluid, a noxious scent that masked damn near everything else. *Clever bastards*, he thought. That was all right; he could still pick up the heartbeat as a beacon, though now that he was inside, it sounded like there were two heartbeats. Both in opposite directions from each other.

He chose the one that sounded stronger. Since Becca was their most recent victim, it made sense that the other, fainter heartbeat belonged to someone the LaLauries had acquired before her. While Bones felt pity for that unknown person, Becca was his primary concern.

He crept forward in a low crouch. The lights were off, not that ghouls needed illumination to see. There was no sound inside except for those heartbeats, his own stealthy movements, and the occasional smash from whatever item was still being flung at the windows.

Yet Bones could feel the energy in the house. Delphine and Louis were here. Waiting. Whatever trap they'd set had been sprung as soon as Bones entered the house. Now all he could do was see it through to the end. *Everyone's got to die one day*, Bones mused with grim determination. *Come on, you sods. Let's see if you've got what it takes to make today* my *day.*

10

Bones edged down the hallway toward the sound of the heartbeat, careful to watch for any hint of an imminent attack. So far, he didn't see anyone, but all his internal alarms were ringing. The trap would be where Becca was, true, but he couldn't just abandon her. After all, it was his fault Delphine took her in the first place.

The heartbeat was coming from the room at the end of the hall. Four menacing, open doorways stood between him and it. Bones pulled two knives from his coat, one steel, one silver. He gripped one in each hand as he kept low and moved forward. *Come out, come out, wherever you are . . .*

Everything in him tensed as he crept up to the first door, his nerve endings anticipating a sudden slice of pain from a knife or other weapon. Bones sprang into the room, braced to counter an assault—but there was nothing. Just more furniture with dust covers over them and that noxious embalming odor that neutered his ability to track anything by scent.

One down, three to go.

Bones repeated the same routine with the next door. This time, he was hit in the face by a spiderweb, but nothing more threatening than that. The third room was empty, as was the fourth room, but the fourth room had blood in it. A lot of blood.

Bones knelt by one of the wide, pooling spots, giving it a deep sniff. Even above the chemical fumes in the room, he knew it was Becca's blood. Which meant the pieces of bones tossed almost casually in the corner were hers as well.

He rose, the swell of killing anger in him making him calmer, not crazed. Bones approached the last room with the heartbeat just as slowly and cautiously as he had the others. If the LaLauries had thought the grisly display of their left-overs would have him dashing in with reckless abandon to save her, they were wrong.

This room was empty of furniture except for one long, dark coffin where the heartbeat came from. Bones waited before entering, his senses tuned for any nuance of noise or movement. Nothing. Then again, a ghoul didn't breathe, and could hold as still as a statue if need be. Delphine and Louis could both be in there, waiting for him.

Bones dove into the room, rolling immediately to counter any frontal assault, the blades gripped in his hands seeking flesh to bury themselves into. Nothing. Not even a whisper, except for that steady heartbeat. The closet in the room had no doors, so no one was hiding in there, and unless Delphine or Louis had acquired Ralmiel's dematerializing trick, they weren't in this room.

He approached the coffin, taking in another deep breath. There was the scent of the embalming fluid, Becca's blood, and something else. Metallic, though too faint to decipher over the stink of the chemicals. Muffled noises consisting of *mmph, mmphh!* interspersed with ragged breathing from inside the coffin. Someone was alive in there. Gagged, from the sounds of it.

Bones ran his hand along the coffin's lid. This was too easy. Was Delphine in there with Becca, waiting to thrust silver in his heart as soon as Bones lifted the lid?

If she was, she'd soon find out the futility of that.

He cracked the lid, heard a faint click—and then flung himself away the instant before the blast. Silver fragments from the specialized bomb were embedded all over the back of him. So were the body parts of whichever unfortunate soul had been in that coffin. Only Bones's Kevlar vest kept the ragged silver pieces from shredding his heart. For a stunned moment, he lay on the ground, mentally calculating his injuries. Then Delphine and Louis burst into the room, swinging away with silver knives.

Bones staggered to his feet, wincing at the pain in his legs where chunks of flesh had been torn off by the bomb. His head was both ringing and throbbing; some silver must have embedded in his skull. He whirled, making the stab Louis aimed for his heart slice into his shoulder instead. But it was a mistake, since the blade pieced deeply into his skin when it would have only bounced off the Kevlar on his chest. Bones shook his head to clear it, mentally lashing himself. *Quit being stupid, or you won't have long to regret it.*

He'd lost the knives in his hands during the explosion. Bones received two more deep swipes before he could secure a blade and attack back. Louis LaLaurie was quick, dodging the blade and kicking Bones in the thigh, where a particularly large piece of silver was still lodged.

It cost him a step as he spun again to avoid Delphine's attack from behind. Her knife cleaved into his upper arm instead of through his neck. It bit deep, though, almost severing the limb. Delphine was strong, and she wasn't fighting like a novice. She slashed at him while Louis attacked from the front. All the silver in his flesh was using up his strength as his body automatically attempted to heal itself—and heal the new injuries that were being inflicted, one after the other.

Delphine and Louis forced him back, causing him to almost trip over a piece of rubble. His left arm, hanging by a few ligaments, took a few seconds to repair itself, but those seconds were costly. Bones couldn't use the arm to fight, and Louis and Delphine were pressing their advantage. More silver hacked at him, until every inch of his body felt like was burning and his blood spattered the ground around them, weakening him further.

Sensing victory was close, Delphine leaped onto his back, savagely tearing at him with both her teeth and her knives. Bones couldn't dislodge her and keep Louis at bay. He couldn't even get more of his knives, since Delphine had managed to rip his coat off in her rabid attack. He couldn't reach the ones strapped to his legs, either, without Louis taking his head off as soon as Bones bent down.

Louis smiled, feral and satisfied, as an upward swipe bit deep into Bones's gut, making him hunch instinctively at the blast of agony. Delphine redoubled her efforts and focused on hacking at his neck, realizing she couldn't penetrate the Kevlar on his back or chest.

A blur in the corner of the room made Bones drop down on one knee. Louis let out a triumphant laugh, but Bones wasn't kneeling in defeat. It was because he'd seen what Louis, with his back turned and his attention fixated on Bones, hadn't noticed.

Delphine saw it, too. She started to scream even as Bones sprang back, slamming both of them against the wall behind him—while a long, curved blade arced its way through Louis LaLaurie's neck.

Louis's head turned to the right and kept going. It rolled off his shoulders even as he slumped forward, a dark, viscous hole facing Bones where his head used to be. Ralmiel held a red-smeared blade behind him.

Delphine screamed again, in a piercing wail of rage and grief. Bones didn't hesitate. He reached into his boots and pulled out the two oblong canisters they contained, ripping the tops off and stabbing them into her chest.

The twin flares erupted, lighting her clothes on fire as they burned her from the inside out. Bones held on to them, pitilessly pushing them deeper. A ghoul's body didn't have enough blood in it to put them out. Delphine's screams became frenzied, her legs and arms scissoring madly as she tried to escape. Bones pinned her to the floor, ignoring the licking flames on him as she continued to burn. He'd fed well before tonight; he wouldn't burn as easily. The fire spread through Delphine's body, splitting and blackening her skin faster than she could heal.

Something savage in Bones made him want to prolong this. To keep shoving flares into Delphine and burning her until there was nothing left but ash, except there wasn't time. Sirens wailed, getting louder. The police would be there soon. That bomb, though relatively small, hadn't gone unnoticed.

Bones pulled a long blade from his boot, letting Delphine see the gleam of the metal as he held it above her. Then Bones cut deeply through Delphine's neck, feeling little satisfaction as her head rolled across the floor to stop at Louis's decapitated corpse. After all the evil the two had committed, it was too quick and merciful an end for them.

But Jelani, at last you have your vengeance.

Ralmiel walked over to him and held out a hand. Bones, after a pause, took it and let the other vampire pull him to his feet.

"Aren't you supposed to be trying to kill me?"

Ralmiel didn't smile. He glanced at the ceiling and shook his head. "I came in by way of the attic and saw her. She doesn't have much time."

Becca.

Bones ran out of the room, following the sound of the other, fainter heartbeat. The explosion actually helped in this regard. The chunk it blew out of the hallway revealed a metal staircase inside the walls, Becca's heartbeat sounding louder in there. Bones pulled back some of the drywall to slip through, then raced up the narrow stairs. He flung back the hatch at the top of the stairs that opened into a small, box-shaped room on top of the house's roof.

Becca was lying on a bench. Bones's face twisted as one glance revealed the extent of her abuse. He knelt beside her, turning her head so she could see him.

She was awake, though in her state, that was a curse instead of a blessing. Bones stared at her, letting the power in his eyes capture her mind. In her condition, it took a few moments. He waited, murmuring, "It's all right, luv. You're safe now," until the horror and terror left her gaze and she quit trying to move or talk.

She couldn't do either, though. Her lips were sewn together with what looked like fishing line, and her arms and legs were gone. The only reason she was still alive was that Louis—or Delphine—had used some of their own blood to seal the gaping wounds left where her limbs used to be. What used to be her arms and legs were now hideously smooth stumps.

Bones closed his eyes. He could save Becca's life . . . by taking it. She wouldn't survive the transition if he tried to turn into a vampire, but he could make her a ghoul. All it required was her drinking some of his blood before she died, and that wouldn't be long. She was very near death as it was.

He thought of Jelani. Of the ghoul's admitted pain over trying to live as someone who would always be helpless compared to even the weakest of their kind. And Becca didn't know there was another world that existed on the fringe of hers. How could Bones condemn her to wake up trapped in that body, changed into something she didn't even know existed?

A slow sigh came out of him, then he forced himself to smile. His gaze brightened while he harnessed all his energy into making Becca believe everything he was about to tell her.

"It's all right," Bones said again, stroking her face. "You're safe, Becca, and there's no pain anymore. You're not injured. You're not even here. You're in a beautiful field, flowers all around you. Can you see them, Becca?"

She nodded, her features slipping into relaxed planes that were completely at odds with the ragged stitches around her mouth.

". . . you're warm, and you're lying on the ground looking up at the sky . . . look at it, Becca. See how blue it is . . ."

Her stare became more fixed. Bones leaned forward, his mouth settling on her throat. Her pulse was so faint, he could barely feel it against his lips.

"Sleep now, Becca," Bones whispered, and bit deeply into her neck.

11

Ralmiel met him at the front of the salon where Becca worked. From there, they had a clear view of the police swarming over the LaLauries' old house and the bomb unit being called in. Blokes didn't want to chance that anything else might explode in the place, not that Bones could blame them.

After a few minutes of silence, Bones turned to Ralmiel. "Why did you come there tonight?"

Ralmiel shrugged. "Jelani offered to pay me double the highest bounty on your corpse, if I let you live instead. So I thought to help you kill the scum fouling my city. It was easy to know where you were, *mon ami*, once the house went *boom*."

Bones couldn't contain his snort. "Mate, I've got some bad news for you. Jelani's skint broke, and Marie hasn't authorized any of what he's done the past several days, so don't expect her to reimburse you, either."

Ralmiel stared at him. "There's no money?"

"'Fraid not."

"He lied to me. I will kill him," Ralmiel said in outrage, pulling a pouch from his pocket and squeezing it.

Nothing happened. Ralmiel looked down in surprise, then squeezed again. And again.

A slow smile spread across Bones's face. "Having some difficulty, are you?"

Understanding bloomed on Ralmiel's face. "You found Georgette," he murmured.

"Never underestimate your opponent," Bones replied. "You know you're not to be trifling with magic, and if anything happens to Georgette for coming to her senses and refusing to participate in your crimes again, I'll be forced to make them public."

Ralmiel said nothing for a long moment. Bones waited, wondering if now that Ralmiel knew he wouldn't be collecting any quid for "letting" Bones live, he'd dare to take him on in a fair fight, without the chance of one of his magic escapes.

Finally, a faint smile creased Ralmiel's mouth. "*Non, mon ami.* That time is past. Money is not everything, *oui*? One day, perhaps, you might assist me."

Bones inclined his head. "I hope you're not lying. I rather like you, but if I ever see you on the other side of a silver weapon again, I'll shrivel you."

Ralmiel shrugged. "Understood." Then he nodded at the mass of people in the street. "Thirsty?"

Another snort escaped Bones. Did he want to plunge into that crowd and glut himself on the throats of nameless, countless people who'd never know they'd been bitten by the time he was done with them? No. He wanted to take Becca to his townhouse, clean her body up, and then bury her in his courtyard so no more indignities could be committed upon her.

But he couldn't do that. Becca's family had the right to bury her, not him. The best thing Bones could do was leave Becca where she was. The police would do their investigation, tie it into the other murders, and perhaps decide they had a copycat killer who'd taken his obsession with the LaLauries' dark history too far. Since Delphine and Louis's bodies, in death, would have regressed back to their true ages, the police might reckon they were old victims unearthed in that hidden room from the bombing. They'd never realize they were looking at the killers themselves.

So, in truth, he had nothing to do *but* throw himself into the crowd that had no idea of the horrors committed just a block away. Besides, Marie might just try to make this his last Mardi Gras. The scale of her retribution had yet to be determined. *Eat and drink, for tomorrow we die*, Bones thought sardonically.

He swept out a hand to Ralmiel. "Lead the way, mate."

12

Underneath the cemetery, the air was damp and cool, with a heavy scent of mildew. Almost an inch of water stood on the ground. These tunnels never got completely dry, no matter how hard the pumps worked. A single candle broke the darkness, illuminating the face of the woman who sat in the only chair in the room.

Jelani knelt in front of her, which hadn't been an easy task, considering his prosthetic legs. But now his huge frame was in a posture of submission and resignation. He'd just confessed his crimes and was waiting for his sentence.

And after him, Bones was next.

Looking down at him, Marie Laveau's expression was blank, hiding whatever thoughts were swirling in her mind. After several tense minutes she stood.

"You betrayed me."

Her voice was as smooth as her skin, making guessing her age difficult.

"Yes, Majestic," Jelani murmured.

Power blasted out from her frame as her temper slipped. Bones didn't react, but he felt like the air had just become littered with invisible razors slicing into his skin.

"You are not sorry."

Despite her anger electrifying the air, when Jelani raised his head, he was smiling.

"No, my queen. I am not."

Christ, Bones thought. *Intending to go out with a bang, are you?*

Something flickered across Marie's face, too quickly for Bones to decipher if it was pity or rage.

"Good. If you are to die for something, then you shouldn't regret what it was."

Her arm flashed out, so fast that Jelani's smile never had a chance to slip. It was still on his face when his head rolled off his shoulders and his body slumped forward.

Marie didn't move out of the way, even though Jelani's slowly oozing neck was now pressed against the hem of her skirt. That long, curved blade was still in her hand as her gaze met Bones's.

"What about you? Are *you* sorry?"

Bones thought about the question, and not just because he knew his life might hinge on his answer.

"I'm sorry I didn't kill the LaLauries sooner," he said at last, holding Marie's stare without flinching. "Sorry an innocent girl met a horrible end because I involved her. Sorry for the bloke at your feet, who felt revenge was worth more than his life. But if what you're asking me is, would I do it all over again to stop Delphine and Louis . . . the answer is yes. And I'm not sorry about that."

Marie tapped the knife against her leg. Bones glanced at it and then back to her dark eyes. *If you want my head, I won't kneel for you to take it,* he thought coolly. *You're not my sire and I didn't betray you, so you'll have to fight for it.*

With a knowing look, Marie wiggled the knife. "Do you think I need this to kill you? Do you think I need any weapon at all?"

She dropped the knife and stepped around Jelani's body. The air around her changed. It thickened with power, becoming icy, despairing, and angry. A faint keening noise seemed to come from nowhere and everywhere at once.

"You know what happens when a voodoo queen becomes undead?" Marie asked. Her voice echoed, like multiple people were somehow speaking through her vocal cords. "My ties to the otherworld were strengthened. Those consigned to the grave filled me with their power. Listen to them roar."

Marie opened her mouth and there *was* a roar, rage-filled and eerie enough to make Bones shiver. Dark swirls appeared around her, as if her shadow had multiplied. Those swirls moved to curl around Bones, stroking him with freezing, malevolent, hungry hands. His strength seemed to melt out of him with their touch while the memory of his death, so long ago, flashed in his mind. He felt the same way he did then; cold, weak, succumbing to that inevitable slide into nothingness.

Then the power around Marie faded. That unearthly keening stopped, the shadows curled back into her, and in a rush, the strength returned to Bones's body.

Marie watched him, a small, brittle smile on her mouth. "I wish you would have lied to me. Then I could have justified killing you."

Bones recovered enough to shrug. "You already knew the truth. Lying would only have insulted us both."

She studied him again, her expression giving nothing away. "You are banned from New Orleans for five years," she finally stated. "If you violate this ban, I will kill you. If you speak of these events to anyone, I will kill you. As far as what everyone else will know, I contracted you to take care of the LaLauries while I was out of town, and Jelani was killed by them in defense of his city. Furthermore, you owe a debt to me equivalent to the value of a life, since I'm letting you keep yours."

Bones didn't argue Marie's assertion that she could kill him. Her display of power moments ago made it plain that there were things about New Orleans's queen that few people knew—or lived to tell. All things considered, Bones was getting a slap on the wrist. Then again, it was also in

Marie's best interest to leave Bones alive to back up her version of events.

As for Jelani, at least Marie was giving him an honorable legacy. There were worse things to die for than securing a long-denied revenge. Sooner or later, everyone died. It just took death longer to catch up to those it had already visited, like vampires and ghouls.

"Done," Bones said.

Marie dropped her gaze to look at the dead man near her feet. "Get out."

Her voice sounded huskier. She knelt by Jelani's withering frame to stroke his shoulder. Even though she'd killed him, her grief was clear. That sort of ruthlessness combined with her level of power made Marie truly frightening. If meting out Jelani's death had meant nothing to her, Bones wouldn't have found her chilling. But even though it had hurt her to kill Jelani, that hadn't stopped her from doing it.

Yes. Best be going quickly.

Bones left without looking back. His flight out of the city was already booked. By tonight, he'd be on his way to Ohio, searching out the undead accountant he'd been tracking before he got involved in this mess.

This was over, but it was time for the next hunt.

DARK MATTERS

VICKI PETTERSSON

For Dennis Stephenson.
A wonderful father, grandfather, and man.

PROLOGUE

It was a normal moment, and barely worth note. Which, of course, was what made it so noteworthy. But after weeks, and a barrage of demands and pleas, JJ would finally be allowed to wave sparklers and an American flag and cheer until his throat burned. And when darkness blanketed the sky, fountains of color so amazing and loud and powerful would rip it open, dulling even the Las Vegas Strip visible in the distance. For a child born, reared, and hidden in an underground lair, it was an absolute dream come true.

So that was why a family of superheroes were having a simple picnic on a grassy hillside, blanket-edge to blanket-edge with the mortals they'd been born to defend.

"Born and sworn to deflect and protect" his father would say, in a booming baritone that made his mother throw back her head and laugh. JJ would steal glances at them—at the giant man with honey-colored eyes identical to his own, and his mother with her quiet strength and noble lineage—and wonder if he had what it took to do that, to make them proud. He didn't know. In a world that honored women, he was not yet a grown man, but he was the strongest five-year-old he knew. And all the kids in the sanctuary said his high jump—already ten feet—was better than most of the girls'.

A born leader, he'd overheard the new soothsayer, Tekla, claim of him, and while he wasn't sure what he was supposed to be leading—a parade like the one they'd seen earlier today? Maybe a band like the one with the drums that'd rumbled down the street?—he'd liked the sound of it.

So while his parents sipped from plastic cups, making small talk with the mortals gathered on the highest green of the SandStone golf course, JJ waved a rope he'd found lying in the asphalt parking lot, and pretended it was his mother's barbed whip. He would inherit the conduit when it was time, and he'd wield it as deftly as she did, unfurling it in the air to strike at fleeing Shadows and their vicious canine wardens.

JJ became so entrenched in these imaginary battles that he had threaded two bunkers and a green by the time the first rocket shot into the sky. Amid the distant laughter and clapping of the hillside audience, he froze under that pulsing sky, the rope slipping from his palms. He felt the same sort of wonder as when his father blocked a thirty-foot dunk in skyball, or when his mother made a concrete wall appear out of nowhere with the mere flick of her wrist. Who knew mortals were capable of something both beautiful and explosive? Each detonated flare thrummed inside his chest like a second, irregular heartbeat.

He jolted when his father's hand dropped to his shoulder. At some point, as light had carved whorls into the sky, they'd found him. "This is what we're preserving for everyone else," his father told him, his characteristic passion making each word sharp. "Every person has a right to the small things, you see? The little happinesses. After all, those are the ones that make life most worth living. It's what we're fighting for."

He touched his wife's hand as he said it.

And JJ saw that it was good. Cotton candy and popcorn and sticky fingers, and a slightly sick stomach when it was all over. JJ only realized he'd fallen asleep when he felt himself being lifted, then settled again in the car they'd borrowed for the occasion. Outside of their troop's sanctuary, his parents were believed to be too hard-strapped to afford their own vehicle. They took the bus when posing as mortals, but most often, they ran with a speed that would make a cheetah envious.

And this was JJ's dream as they drove back to the hotel where they'd spend the night before returning to their subterranean lair at dawn—he was outrunning a big cat, legs wheeling so fast that the beast eventually slowed, and bowed to him as the superior athlete. JJ climbed atop the animal, his right as the competition's victor, and was carried at breakneck speed along the neon-slicked streets, whizzing past the giant hotels his parents had pointed out to him hours before.

He startled awake when the cat reared suddenly, though they would tell him later that the animal's awful cry was really the screeching of brakes. He opened his eyes to see his mother's face, eyes fierce and burning into his. But it was her lighted chest that riveted him. Normally dormant beneath her skin, her glyph was fired, warning of danger, and her right hand curled tightly around her whip.

"Stay," she said, and then she was gone.

"On the floor," his father snapped, and like the sparklers JJ had waved only hours before, he, too, was only a bright trail for the eye to follow in the night.

JJ's heart thrummed inside his small frame, chest tight, as if his Arien glyph wished to burst to life as well. *Danger!* screamed some primal voice inside him. *Flee!*

But his father had said to stay on the floor.

It will be even safer beneath the car.

He didn't know why he'd listen to some unfamiliar voice over his own father's, but if he was outside he could see his parents, and as long as he could see them, he'd be okay.

Of course, even as he clambered over the front seat, even before the first battle cry ripped the hot, velvet sky— probably even before he'd been tossed from the back of the dream cheetah—he knew they were at war. These were

Shadows. Rotted sulphur and smoke pooled in the night sky, stinging his eyes just as in his ward mother's bedtime stories.

Still, he blinked away the burn, searching for his parents along the rocky desert vista, every outcropping a bumpy threat. Inching forward beneath the car's chassis, he settled in time to see his mother's whip unfurl, barbed tips sparking off the light from her chest, which also threw her drawn porcelain features into stark relief. She was feral.

The Shadow she fought was a charred skeleton.

"Mama!" The word squeaked from him. His strong mother, his laughing and vibrant mother, couldn't be injured by that *demon*! Tears welled and he blinked them away— *keep them in sight!*—so he saw when the Shadow's head swiveled his way.

"No!"

His mother screamed, and she ignored the extended arc of her whip as she reversed, flipping her wrist to shove the metal grip into the living skeleton's teeth. Bone shattered beneath the force, and JJ—and his cry—was forgotten.

Another light appeared, zigzagging like an overgrown firefly. Defying bulk to outmaneuver his opponent, his father's limbs whirled, breaking skin and bone with studded gloves, sending more noxious fumes spilling into the air. The two Shadows fell at nearly the same time, and JJ's parents sidestepped, back-to-back, breathing hard, studying their surroundings.

"How?" his mother asked, voice low.

"Later." His father reached behind with one bloodied fist to squeeze her free hand. "Let's get Jay to safety."

JJ nearly opened his mouth to cheer—his brave parents, his strong parents, had done it again!—but his mother jerked her head, her reply a near growl. "We need to know now."

"Why?"

"Because there might be . . ."

Others.

Suddenly there were. So many circling so fast, the smoke became a black tornado, and JJ quickly lost count. Though outnumbered, his parents continued to guard each other, backs and fingertips touching, searching for a way out. Just before the first cry sounded, his mother shot a look back at the car. A smile touched her lips, briefly, before she let it fall.

Then she fought.

And then she died.

And somewhere, more mortals set the sky alight, burning the heavens for pleasure even as his parents' death cries carved whorls into the air.

The Shadows didn't linger. The deaths of two senior agents of Light would soon be noted, the kill spots as obvious as the constellations above for those who knew how to read them. So JJ squeezed from beneath the car as soon as the last Shadow disappeared, and rushed to his parents.

There was barely anything recognizable at all. It was as if the Shadows were so blighted in spirit and form that they wished to render the Light the same.

"Solange! *Ma* Sola! Come back!"

JJ's head jerked up.

"*Un instant*, Mama! I want a souvenir to mark my first . . ."

The girl's words died in her throat when she saw him. Her gaze skittered like beetles to his hands, braced on the broken things he loved. She wasn't much older than he, maybe eight, but with a darkness about her . . . one that'd called her back in search of a memento.

She had watched as her troop ambushed and murdered his family, JJ realized with a sniff. Studying for her future position as a Shadow agent.

A tear coursed over his cheek, and she winced as if it repulsed her. She frowned, then opened her mouth to reveal his existence. He held tight to what was left of his parents while another tear fell.

"Solange!" came the voice again, causing the girl to jolt.

Solange licked her lips. Their eyes remained fastened on each other. Finally. "Nothing here, Mama."

"So *allez*. Our enemies will soon be here. We don't wish to be trapped within their radius. Leave the *cadeau*, and the cleanup, for them."

Laughter accompanied her retreat, and sapped JJ's remaining strength. He collapsed between what used to be his family, and stared blindly up at the molten, scarred, celebratory sky.

"Solange. Sola. *Ma* Sola."

He mumbled her names over and over. He memorized them. He wondered why she hadn't killed him. And, sobbing—even once he was lifted into the arms of his troop leader—he wished she had.

I

The bar was a college hangout, hardly more than a steel ceiling and a concrete floor. The so-called band had just finished their final set and was now taking their payment from the tap. JJ let his head hang forward as Warren called for another round, and the bartender, who'd only dubiously allowed the last one, frowned. Options flitted over his face like words on a teleprompter. He could be fined if they left this bar and suffered injury under the influence of the whiskey he'd served, but on the up side, they wouldn't come back. Even in a run-down, midtown Las Vegas bar, where transience was an accepted part of life, a guy who smelled like a bum and one who looked like a pissed-off linebacker were undesirable. So he hedged his bets, and brought them the bottle. JJ offered up a lopsided smile. It was the Vegas way.

Once served, his troop leader finally came around to the subject he'd spent the last half hour inching up on. "That, my son, was a close one."

No, JJ thought, tapping the glass and throwing back his head. It had been even closer than that. Trapped in that steel plane, thousands of feet above the ground, JJ had been forced to consider something rare, at least in relation to himself: death. In fact, he'd never been so sure of anything in his life as the commuter flight the Shadows had hijacked flew toward the base, flanked by fighter jets, screams tearing through the air. What most surprised him was the voice, the one he trusted and had named his intuition, had sighed its acceptance. *Finally.*

JJ knew Warren expected some bland agreement, but his overriding thought was, *Just buy me another shot, man.*

Then his troop leader surprised him by squaring on him fully. "It's hard living in the past. Hard to even call it your past if you've never put it behind you."

JJ peered into his shot glass. "This thing still empty?"

Warren motioned, took the bottle from the bartender's hands, and started pouring it himself. "You've broken even so far, but that's just treading water, and today proved it."

Because today, for the first time in the three years he'd been a full-fledged agent of Light, JJ had almost lost.

Obviously, he'd experienced death before. One couldn't live long in an underworld of heroes and demons and not be touched by it, and he told Warren that now without words, using only a shrug and a jerk of his head to throw back another shot. God, but the whiskey was good . . . sharp and warm, and lingering in his belly as if his glyph glowed there. It made him feel alive.

"Death's not important," Warren said in reply.

"I know." Holding out his glass, JJ accidentally caught his reflection across the bar; eyes spent, face sunken on his wide frame, his normally tan skin sallow, like campfire dust mingling with sand. He was built like his dad, though even wider and taller and stockier. His sheer size had drawn such unwanted attention that the troop's physician/magician, Micah, had whittled down his frame once already, but the pain of even that minor transformation was like mainlining mercury. In the hours before he healed, it was as if he'd been skinned alive, then stitched back together, tighter. Even now, if he thought about it too much, he could imagine himself bursting at the seams. JJ refused any additional reduction after that, and Warren hadn't pressed.

Looking at his bleached, military-cut hair through the smoked mirror, he wondered idly if he should shave it to the skull. Would that whittle him down even more? Could walking through the world with less friction smooth out the journey?

"Death also isn't meaningful, not even a violent one," Warren continued, impervious to JJ's thoughts of journeys and friction. "It's what you *tell* yourself about death that's critical. Thoughts shape actions, and actions expose your state of mind."

"Shit." JJ jerked the bottle from Warren's hand, because if he had to listen to a lecture about the past and death and the detonated fate he'd narrowly avoided, he wasn't going to do it sober. Unfortunately, it took a lot for a superhero to get truly shit-faced, a fact JJ currently lamented. "So is this the speech where you tell me my parents didn't die because of me, that there was nothing I could do at the time, and that I need to put it behind me? Because I swear I've heard that one somewhere before."

And it was bullshit. Besides . . .

"What more do you want from me?" he continued before Warren could answer. "I do the best I can at all times. You can't tell me I don't."

"I wouldn't. But your level best is different than your potential best."

"I don't know what the hell that means." His voice was too sharp, his body too rigid. *Dial it back*, JJ told himself, even while downing another glass. Boy, the more you drank, the smoother this shit got.

"It means the heroes of your past should fortify the present. You're engaged in old battles, son. So, in answer to your question, *that's* what I want. For the first time in your life, look forward, not back. What happened tonight should show you what a gift the future really is."

JJ licked his lips slowly, knowing exactly what sort of gifts his future held. Things like metaphorically throwing himself in front of oncoming trains to save countless others, most of whom had gotten themselves into bad situations through faulty logic, poor planning, or pure stupidity. In fact, the majority of the mortal population was spoiled and ungrateful, and continued to piss away the life he fought for them to have. He also didn't say he'd give a limb just to be able to work a regular Joe's nine-to-five, and to come home to nothing more complicated than a pair of squabbling kids and a lukewarm meal. *Instead, I have to beware if I go on something as simple as a fucking picnic.*

Warren misread his silence. "Don't you care anymore, Jay? Don't you still believe you can make a difference, son?"

JJ snorted. Sure he cared. He had no problem helping others—he knew no other life than that—but lately it'd occurred to him that making a difference meant having to always put his own needs and desires second. Or, in a city of two million, was it dead last?

Warren dropped a hand on his shoulder. "I think you're burned out, son."

"Maybe," JJ conceded, rolling his glass between his palms. "Though I've never heard of an agent burning out after only three years." *Some superhero.*

"It's been three years since your metamorphosis," Warren said, referring to that critical moment when a troop member turned from mere initiate into a full-fledged agent of Light. "You've been fighting for over twenty."

Their eyes met, but neither man spoke. His parents' deaths were long ago, and remembered from different vantage points, but horror and sadness still plagued both of them.

"Look," Warren said, "I think you should take some time off. Go fishing. Get laid. Fucking shave, for God's sake."

"I'm fine . . . and stubble looks good on the trading cards."

Warren didn't laugh. "You're cold."

"I'm calm," JJ corrected. His voice was low, but his glance was sharp.

Warren wasn't intimidated. "Well, we need you committed if we're going to acquire our priceless little package before the Shadows do. Understand?"

JJ wanted to say he understood his own life was passing him by, unlived, while he toiled in service to some pampered elite, but he was already talking too loud, and his eyes were probably pinwheeling from the adrenaline still trailing through his system. He could sit here and argue with Warren, or he could agree with the man and get on with drinking. So he nodded his head, hoped he looked contrite, and waited for his leader to leave.

When Warren did—after an order, disguised as a warning, to go home and sleep it off—JJ glanced up at the television, where a local station was reporting on the latest antics of some vapid society sisters: a blond who'd just shown her physical talents to half the Western world in some men's magazine he used to read for the articles, and her sister— her dark-eyed, unsmiling opposite—who had no reason that he could see to look so pissed off. He downed the rest of his whiskey and held up a hand for another bottle.

And then, in a roundabout fashion, the "package" Warren had mentioned appeared on the screen. JJ squinted at the image of one Tonya Dane, a psychic who'd appeared on a local morning show the previous week to predict an earthquake on this side of the Sierra Nevadas. That alone wouldn't have been cause for worry, or even note, not among his kind. But the prediction had come true, which was why the footage continued its loop on the tube.

What they kept cutting was Dane's lead-in prediction, the appearance of the Kairos, a powerful woman who would tip the metaphysical scales in favor of whatever side—Light or Shadow—she chose to endorse. Mortals, having no idea what that meant, dismissed it as nonsense, but those words had been long coveted in his world. Previously, the Kairos had been buried in mythology, but Dane's prediction brought that epoch to an end, and now both sides were searching for her in earnest.

Unfortunately, Dane had since disappeared, without even a tarot card to point them her way.

The bartender—mustached, built, and apparently uninterested in parapsychology—flipped the station. He caught JJ's gaze through the mirror, and quirked a brow. "You watching that?"

"Nah, bro. Flip it." JJ shakily brought his shot glass to his lips, muttered into it. "Here's to free will, and all that shit."

"I'll drink to that."

It was a testament to his drunkenness that he didn't sense the woman's approach. He turned, and she was just there—slim-limbed, doe-eyed, with a cascade of raven black hair. She quirked a brow at the bottle in his hand, clearly accustomed to getting what she wanted. JJ didn't mind, though. She smelled good.

"Have a name?"

"JJ, or just Jay." He didn't bother lying. Unlike his glass fingertips, hers appeared printed, like any mortal's, and again, she smelled like a dream. "You?"

"Yes." She licked cherry lips, coming on strong out of the gate. One way or another, JJ seemed destined for a head-on collision tonight. Besides, he thought, letting his eyes travel the length of her body, Warren had said to take some time off. "That your convertible outside?" she asked.

His focus sharpened marginally. "How'd you know?"

"Anyone else in here look like they can manage that ride? Besides, Mustangs are my favorite. Though I usually prefer a dark-haired man driving it."

"Really? So . . ." He leaned forward, into her space, testing, angling in further. She met him halfway. "You willing to overlook that glaring fault and go for a little ride?"

"If I wanted a little ride," she said, pointedly, "I'd be talking to the guy over there."

He laughed, throaty and loud, surprising himself, then threw down some bills. Draping his arm over her slim shoulders, he turned her toward the door. "Come," he said, already sure she would.

2

She did love the car. She purred when he revved the
engine, laughed when the tires bit into the curb, and
stood in her bucket seat, hands gripping the windshield as
speed and desert air—pregnant with a summer storm—
played havoc with her hair. Bolting up Charleston, he left
the false cheer of Las Vegas behind, driving so fast it was
like he was burying them in the night.

He jerked the wheel right before Spring Mountain
Ranch, the turnoff coming more quickly than he remembered, though the view from the asphalt top was as spec-
tacular as always . . . and theirs alone. Wild burros and
rattlers regularly canvassed the dusty range, but as the first
bolts of lightning pinged off the desert floor, all that flashed
back at them were Joshua trees, sagebrush, and the red
sandstone range framing the basin. JJ killed the engine, and
for a moment they were both silent, enjoying the beginnings
of a storm that would turn the dry washes into rivers sure
to flood the valley.

Then the woman rose, straddling the windshield in one
liquid motion, skirt rising to her hips. She challenged him
with a downward glance as her bare foot carelessly crushed
a wiper. "I love a good desert monsoon," she said, and
licked her lips as the sky cracked open.

JJ moved so fast she was pinned to the glass before the
first raindrop fell. His hands were in her wind-whipped hair,

his mouth eating her laughter. He had to remind himself to be careful with her—she was mortal and more fragile than his kind—but her hunger was spiced, and it fueled him. It was probably just the drink, but with his eyes closed, his mouth open, and his body spread atop hers, he felt pieces of him shifting inside, as if loosening from tethered moorings, suddenly unbound.

When JJ finally opened his eyes, he was surprised to find their positions reversed. He was pinned to the hood, her clothing pushed aside, his jeans half down his thighs. She lowered herself over him, a private smile revealed in a sharp crack of splintered light, but when her hips began pistoning above him, he forgot even to be surprised.

He decided later that despite her aggressiveness, she was a closet romantic. Why else wait until the storm had heightened, and they were both about to climax, to pull out the weapon? The need for symbolism, coupled with raw power, obviously motivated her . . . him, too, which was why he happened to open his eyes in that moment, wanting to watch her rain-streaked face as she cried out into the wild night. Instead he saw her wide, dark eyes hard with intent, and the honed edge of a tomahawk barreling toward his chest.

JJ barely pulled his palms from her waist in time to counteract the lethal blow, but once it'd been deflected, adrenaline lent the sobriety needed to disarm her. He flipped, crushing her against the car she so loved, her slim frame denting the pristine hood. The glyph on her chest began to smoke. "Guess I don't have to be so gentle after all," he said, and made a second, deeper dent.

The impact didn't stop her throaty laughter. "Satisfy a girl's curiosity before she dies?"

"Is this a final request?" he growled, forearm across her neck.

"At least you'll finish off something tonight."

"Besides your life, you mean." He dug a nail into the flesh of her fingertip, and felt a false print pop off. He sucked in a deep breath but still couldn't scent anything of her Shadowy nature. She'd covered it with a synthetic, then. It was easy enough to do.

She smiled weakly. "When did you get the tattoo on your right shoulder?"

She'd seen the yin/yang symbol. The word *desire* was etched out in the shaded side. The other held *fear*. "I was nineteen." He saw no harm in answering now.

"And now you're twenty-eight."

She relaxed beneath him as his brow furrowed, all her strength sinking inward. He remained on guard.

"JJ," she teased in a threadbare croak. "I've known you since you were five."

He froze above her, all the shifting inside of him ceasing, reversing. "And you are?" he asked, voice as hard.

"Solange," she said simply.

Lightning cracked over his shoulder as memories moved through his skull. *Solange. Sola.* Ma *Sola.*

"You've lost your accent."

"Second generation French." She shrugged easily, like they didn't have a past, and she still had a future. "Easy when you're raised here."

"Have you waited twenty-three years to kill me?"

Her tongue darted out, wetting her bottom lip. "I've waited to see why I didn't."

They looked at each other, and JJ inexplicably lessened the pressure. Then he caught himself, and picked up her conduit, the tomahawk. The heft was eerily unfamiliar. He lifted it above his head.

She gave him a slight smile for being able to do what she hadn't. "I'm sorry."

Again, it threw him.

"About . . . my parents?"

She nodded again.

He raised a brow. "So sorry you were going to kill me?"

He felt her forearm flex before her fingertips trailed up

his arm, playing just below his tattoo. "I was going to put you out of your misery."

"Don't do me any more favors, Solange."

But as her fingertips continued to play on his skin, he lowered her weapon. Warren's words revisited him as he stared into the cocoa depths of the woman's eyes. *Death's not important . . . not even a violent one.* Thoughts were crucial, he'd said. Actions exposed one's state of mind.

After a few more moments of staring and still living, Solange lifted slightly and ground her pelvis into his. Still half clothed and, surprisingly, half hard, he swallowed, met her gaze . . . and slid easily back into her warmth.

"Ah. So even superheroes," she whispered in rhythm, "crave the illicit."

Her hot breath sent chills down his arm.

"And you crave . . . ?" he asked, somehow knowing he was giving it to her. He pushed deeper.

"Not much." She waited until she was coming again, breathing the answer into his mouth. "Mere relevance."

Why don't I kill her? Why, despite being natural enemies, did JJ instead lie with Solange on the dented hood of his car, until the full of the high desert storm had passed?

Maybe it was because she, too, had been born into this life of battling sides—good versus evil, Light and Shadow—and she recognized, or was at least willing to admit, that perfection and compulsiveness and vigilance would get them only so far. They could both act like model agents, but if either so much as breathed in the wrong direction, the same gruesome death they'd watched his parents endure would readily be theirs.

Normally his mind shied from that memory, but with his enemy's head on his shoulder, he admitted that *that's* what happened when a person gave himself over entirely to the lifestyle. It was why he was burned out, and why he resented the mortals he'd sworn to protect. He found the thought of continuing to exist for the mere good of someone else unbearable. But . . .

If I had something for myself, something that was mine alone.

"What do you recall?" Solange asked him, the heat in her voice threaded soft.

JJ gazed up at the black metal sky. Not the battle, that was sure. That was muddied with the confusion of a five-year-old's mind, a swirl of color and sound melding into a singular cry of pain. When he thought back to the night his parents died, he didn't even remember the red carnage, or not much anyway. Yet he could clearly envision his parents touching hands, holding to each other until the very last. They'd died because of him . . . but they'd lived because of each other.

"It was my fault," he finally said, in lieu of his truest thought, which was: *I'll never have that.* "I wanted to see the fireworks. They were permitted to take me from the sanctuary because no one could stand to listen to me whine any longer. So we were on the golf course, out in the open, because of me . . . and I think we were tracked because of me, too."

He knew now, eyes following the tail of the receding storm, that his emotions had been high, a young boy's excitement even stronger than the fireworks staining the sky.

"Your joy was like tingling, warm taffy," Solange confirmed, turning her head so she was staring directly into his eyes. "It was the sweetest thing I'd ever sensed."

JJ swallowed hard. She broke eye contact first, nestled closer, and looked back to the now-clear sky, stars so bright they looked scoured. He could snap her neck in one swift jerk.

"I follow the constellations," she said suddenly, as if the words and her voice were at odds. "Never someone else's orders. Not even my own whim. So, in a way, the sky is a map of my mind. Nobody else knows that." She tilted her head up to his, exposing her neck like a dare. He bent, kissed its hollow, and found it salty and slightly sharp. When she spoke again, her voice thrummed against his lips. "So if you know what constellation I'm tracing, you can connect the dots and predict my next move."

"What constellation are you on now?"

She gave him a look like he was crazy.

JJ laughed, liking the way she could surprise him. "Fine, then tell me this. Are you on an upswing or down?"

She shook her head, lifting to lean on an elbow. "You're missing the point. The stars aren't what's important. They're just pivot points to send you off in a new direction. It's the space between them that's relevant. Everything that can actually be seen—the stars, you, me—is less than four percent of what's out there. The rest is . . . dark."

"Because it's invisible?"

She shook her head. "Because it's unknown."

She sat up, turning suddenly so both elbows were propped on his chest, her weight entirely atop his, though he felt little of it. "You know, most people think everything they do is so important. They sweat the small stuff—traffic jams and spilled milk—and get pissed off if things don't come off exactly as planned. Most go their entire lives without realizing plans don't matter one bit."

JJ knew. They were at the mercy of something much bigger and, he often thought, more uncaring than that.

"The greatest mysteries—life, love, loss—are destined to remain a dark matter." She jerked her chin at the crystalline sky. "We don't even know what we're looking at right now."

He dropped a kiss atop her damp, perversely refreshing, cynical head. "It's the Universe."

"No." She nestled closer, and pointed at the sky. "That's a violent, evolving panorama of births and deaths. Just like us. The Universe," she said, pointing to the spot he'd just kissed, "is in here."

Which was the same shit Warren had been telling him earlier. Which was the same shit, he thought, sighing, that he already knew. Except for one thing. He tapped his head. "Which means you think that ninety-six percent of what is up here is dark matter."

"Exactly." Linking her slim arms behind her head, Solange smiled. "And chaos reigns."

3

It was hard to argue against people being predisposed to chaos, JJ thought as he hauled a skinny mortal from a seedy downtown strip club. The idiot had been about to challenge a Shadow over a woman who called herself Destiny. Yeah, JJ thought, posing as a bouncer, Destiny was really worth getting your head ripped, literally, from your shoulders.

"Maybe it's why you guys need protection in the first place," he mumbled.

"What?" the man asked, his tone matching his terrified face.

"I said you should take a serious look at the way you spend your free time."

"Look at you, man!" The scrawny redhead jerked down his shirt after JJ threw him against the wall. "Like you have any right to judge!"

Score one point for the village idiot, JJ thought, because as much as the comparison rubbed, for the first time he was indulging his darker side, too. And enjoying it. Still, he had a job to do, and was finding a perverse joy in that again as well. He reentered the club and headed back to the VIP room to give the lone Shadow a real taste of destiny.

"I don't think the Kairos will be found entertaining a late night stag party," JJ said, parting the curtains of the private room, and dropping into the seat nearest the door. "But that's just me."

The Shadow, a small but stocky man who was all but lost between two manufactured breasts, froze. He swallowed hard, dark eyes darting, the glyph on his chest beginning to smoke, but he otherwise didn't move. When he saw that JJ was alone, visually measuring the distance between them as being great enough, he tried to play it cool. "Can't be too thorough, though, can you?" he said, smiling, as he ran a hand down Destiny's thigh.

"No. You can't." And JJ unfurled his whip with a crack. Destiny screamed even though she'd been a whole four inches away from the nearest barb, and began tottering from the room on Lucite heels. JJ caught her in one arm, pulling her close to his chest as he yanked, snapping her john's neck.

By the time Warren arrived, Destiny was "resting" in a dark corner, the Shadow appeared passed out on the velvet sofa, and the room's security tapes were in JJ's pockets.

"Who?" Warren asked, eyes assessing JJ for injury.

JJ smiled, handing the tapes over. "Shadow Pisces."

"Where?"

He jerked his head back at the club. Warren motioned, and a cleanup crew emerged from the night like ninja warriors, slipping inside the back door. The corpse would be gone in five minutes. The kill spot—with the Shadow's death and JJ's claim to it—would remain forever.

Warren clapped him on the back, a wide grin splitting the furrows of his craggy face. "Nice to have you back, son. On the side of Light."

"The side of might," JJ finished for him.

Though pleased with the night's work, he wasn't sure Solange would feel the same. He arrived at their meeting spot, a motel off the I-15, sure she wouldn't come. If she did, it would only be to end their affair. In fact, she might even break their unspoken truce by bringing her troop with her.

Instead, she met him wearing silk and garters and holding a glass of champagne.

"I'd have been worried," she murmured as he closed in on her, "if you'd wrapped that thing around one of the girls instead of the guy."

The morbid humor stoked their lovemaking like rocket fuel. JJ stroked her hair, remembering how it trailed behind her as she'd fled Gregor. He thought of her tomahawk whirring through the air, and it was all he could do not to laugh into her mouth. How could he explain the rush of knowing this dark, lethal beauty was his? Who would believe that he fought hard and well and heroically to return to that wry, promising smile? Coming together with Solange was, very simply, like riding a cyclone.

"That was wonderful," Sola said after their final collapse, sending him a look that would have sucked the air from his chest, were any left. "But the next time you save me from being cornered by the Scorpio of Light, I'll kill you."

She was referring to a small skirmish two days earlier. He'd been sure she hadn't noticed. Tucking a strand of hair behind the delicate shell of her earlobe, he said, "I know, sweetheart."

"I wouldn't stop any of my allies from slaying you."

He hummed his understanding against her lips.

"And you'll kill me as well?" She pulled back, but said it like she was asking for a date.

He shrugged, dropping his eyes. "If you'd like."

"It's not about what I *like*," she said, biting off the last word. She forced him to look at her. "It's about authenticity. We need to be as honest in that as we are in all else. Otherwise, this means nothing."

"In that case," he said, licking at her skin, "I'll wrap my whip around your middle, let the barbs bite into your organs, and rip it free before you even make a sound."

He kissed her lightly and she sighed into his opened mouth. "You're such a romantic."

JJ swallowed her wicked laugh, and met the lift of her hips.

"Find the Kairos yet?" she asked, licking at the hollow of his neck.

He kissed the top of her head. "Stop fishing."

She put on a pout. "Like you don't care what we're up to."

"Honey, if your side had our world's weapon of mass destruction, I wouldn't be lying here now." And a part of him was careful to keep this in mind, even when he was notched deep inside her. "You guys have no idea where the Kairos is."

Knowing she was beaten, she curled up, back to his chest, leaving JJ to wonder if she wasn't merely a gorgeous, exciting, and, yes, dangerous pet project. Proof that even someone raised by people dedicated to chaos and destruction could choose the right thing, if only provided the opportunity. Perhaps, he thought, stroking her hair, if they had someone to believe they were good.

Playing savior was no basis for a relationship, but as his actions weren't being reported in either the Shadow manuals or the Light, he didn't worry too much. Disguised as comic books and consumed by mortal minds, these manuals were as important for what they omitted as for the battles they recorded. Perhaps his deeds weren't being shown because he was getting through to Sola. He chose to believe the Universe knew she needed anonymity if she was to continue working her way toward good. After all, his side would try to stop him if they knew what he was doing, and hers would kill her outright.

Thus, he decided, the Universe itself was upholding their right to choose—to choose each other or to choose to walk away—and to do it without interference from those who wouldn't know of the affair unless they saw it with their own eyes. That was a natural law; and therefore an obvious sign to JJ that Sola was wrong and he was right.

So he held out hope she would soon realize this, even while unable to fathom such a reversal in his own moral code. The great irony? His involvement with her hadn't lessened his desire to save the world, but strengthened it. So how could it be wrong? Besides, his heart's longing was a small, private matter: he wished only to love whom he wanted, to be with whom he chose.

But she was right about one thing. Why should he be the only one not getting what he wanted? Why should every small pleasure be sacrificed to duty? If he was going to die in the same gruesome fashion as his parents—a risk he took every time he stepped from his sanctuary—then he should be allowed to take joy where he could. So when she woke and turned to him in the middle of the night, asking yet again why he bothered fighting her kind, he smiled against her side.

"I need to," he said simply. "I'm a superhero."

"You're a man," she said, her throaty voice soft as smoke, her hand resting on the tattoo that was both shadow and light. "I have what you need."

Yes. For some reason he needed her, too.

And for some other reason, she was willing to be his need.

"Don't get it."

Sola's eyes were on JJ as he leaned from the bed to check his cell. Warren. "I have to."

"You're putting work ahead of me." Her bottom lip, swollen from his kisses, would be sticking out.

"Ahead of the competition, yes." He smiled as he angled back, but she turned away. Snorting, he putting a hand over the receiver in case Warren came on the line. "Don't even try it."

Solange threw the sheets from her body, backside swaying as she made her way to the bathroom. A few seconds later water began running into the tub. "Yes," he said, tone altering at Warren's voice. His leader had begun calling JJ first, whether it was to assist with recon, stakeout, or especially attack. How ironic that he had Sola to thank for it.

"I've found her."

JJ stood. "You haven't." But he began pulling on his jeans one-handed. "Where?"

"Right where she's supposed to be." Warren laughed, and it wasn't his maniacal spiral, though it couldn't be called tame, either. "She wasn't in hiding or kidnapped by the Shadows or even in jail over a traffic violation. She went to fucking Maui, but now she's back."

Maui. JJ rolled his eyes. Tonya Dane predicted his world's savior and then went surfing. "Where are you?"

"The motel on Fremont."

"I'll be right there." JJ flipped the phone shut and slid it into his pocket. Getting to Tonya first was a huge coup. That woman's mind—mortal, but a psychic's—was a big red arrow on a map that, with luck, could lead directly to the Kairos.

Solange was soaking in the tub, slim and shining legs propped against the faucet, dark tendrils pressed against the damp curve of her long neck. JJ smiled reflexively when he saw her, but she didn't even look up.

"Off to play angel of mercy?" She wrinkled her little nose, and sourly truncated his reply. "I don't understand why you bother saving those who won't lift a finger to save themselves."

Given his recent burnout, JJ was surprised to find himself arguing. "We allow freedom of choice from your influence. We don't interfere unless there's an outright victimization. We simply counteract *your* machinations so the mortal population remains autonomous."

"Shadows can't influence those who aren't already predisposed to chaos," she answered, as quickly. "All you do is delay the inevitable."

"We grant a person time and space to make a better choice."

"You waste your life to better the future of those who are undeserving."

"Everyone is deserving of a chance," he answered simply, hand to her cheek.

She mimicked the movement. "I told you you're a romantic."

"You are, too."

She pulled away at that, the lips he loved to lick pursed in a tight bow. "Uh-uh. I live for myself. I put my life above all others. It will always be that way, mark my word."

"And is that written in the stars?"

"You know the answer to that." It was written between them.

"Go." She lifted a leg in the air, soaping one tight calf, her mouth still thinned in a pout.

He wanted to say he was sorry, that she knew how duty called, and all that, but it wouldn't deter Sola from a mood she was determined to be in, and it was also untrue. He wasn't sorry, because the moment she got wind that the soothsayer was back in town, she and her entire troop would swoop down upon her as well.

Right now he ignored Sola's combative words by lifting her from the water and pulling her to him. She squealed, though he could tell she was delighted. How could one of the softest things he'd ever touched also be one of the hardest people he'd ever known?

"You won't be far behind," he reminded her, circling his hands on her bare hips.

She shrugged one slim, wet shoulder, like she didn't care, but beckoned him forward after another moment. Lifting to her toes as he curled about her, she tucked her hands into the back pockets of his jeans, wetting the front of him with her warm body, her tongue darting gently to meet his lips. He opened to her, but she didn't deepen the kiss, just pulled back to stare up into his eyes, the fingertips of her left hand rising to circle the tattoo that lay beneath his T-shirt.

"Be careful out there."

He reached around to cup her ass, lifted her slightly, and deepened the kiss himself. Her response was fired, and seconds flipped into minutes. "Find me again tonight?"

"That soon?" Surprise lightened her voice. They usually waited at least a day between meetings.

He smiled. "I'm hard now."

"I'll be here."

JJ was still smiling as he let himself out into the morning light. Behind him was an enemy mistress, who made him feel bold, oddly heroic, and shockingly alive. In front of him was a mortal Seer, who might or might not know the identity of his world's savior. He tried not to think of himself as being caught between them. He still wanted it all.

4

Warren had Tonya Dane stashed away at a dilapidated motel on Fremont Street, which, while not a safe zone, was a good enough place to hide, as long as emotions didn't run high when Shadows lurked nearby. There were a number of hidey-holes and nondescript locales used this way by both sides of the Zodiac. Safe zones—like Master Comics, where the troop manuals were created and displayed—were desired, but rare.

But today JJ had to quell the laughter that threatened to bubble out of him when he entered the Lazy Dayz Motel to find a superhero masquerading as a bum getting his palm read by a woman who looked like a cross between a country music star and a stripper.

Tonya Dane stared up at JJ when he entered, blinking a good half-dozen times as she took in his short, blond cut, the skin as naturally dark as her enforced tan, and his overall size. When she finished, her frosted smoker's mouth pursed. "Obviously another one of y'all."

JJ glanced at Warren, who sheepishly withdrew his hand. "It's okay, she knows everything. She's agreed to a full memory cleanse as soon as we're finished. We were just passing the time until you arrived."

Tonya reached over, bright pink nails digging into Warren's weather-beaten hands. "Remember what I said.

She still loves you. She's showing it in the only way she knows how."

Warren cleared his throat and rose. "The others should be here shortly."

That distracted JJ from Tonya's words. "Others?"

"I decided to bring in the rest of the troop after we talked. Ms. Dane here says that different people bring out nuance in her readings, even if related to the same subject."

"Time is more fluid than this world believes. Even future relations can be read in the present."

So she'd be able to read connections between them and the Kairos . . . if there were to be any.

"I figured there was no harm in introducing her to the others as she'll give up the memory anyway. It'll give Tekla a rare opportunity to talk shop with someone who shares her talent, but on the mortal side." He smiled at Tonya. "She's our troop's Seer."

"I know," Tonya said, eliciting a truncated snort from JJ. He sobered when her sharp eyes found him again. "We can start with you."

"Start what with me?"

"The readings." And she held out her hand for his palm.

"Wait." JJ turned back to Warren to find humor threading the man's mouth. "I thought we were questioning her. Not the other way around."

He didn't think a mortal Seer could rival their world's psychic in skill, but with a secret life, and his lover's touch so recently on his skin, it was best to stay away from Seers altogether . . . which was why Tekla's impending appearance was so disturbing. He'd been avoiding her as well.

Warren sobered. "Just give it a try. You may have a residual connection with the Kairos."

JJ wanted to ask how it could be residual if it hadn't happened yet, but knew better from his sessions with Tekla. Ask one innocent question and you'd get a weeklong lecture on the intricacies of quantum physics. He had long since learned to keep quiet.

Still, he remained skeptical of Dane.

"I don't know—" JJ began, but Warren was done.

"Jay, please. I know it's not much to go on, but we need every available advantage. Okay?"

He clenched his jaw, but nodded. "Sure."

Tonya reached for his hand as soon as he settled across from her. "It's better if I touch you."

It's better if you don't. "I don't like to be touched."

She reached out anyway, her cool fingers as fragile as a sparrow's foot in his tensile palm. He couldn't help but compare her touch to Sola's. Though undeniably female, his love's form was merely a streamlined version of his own, as if tendons and veins, bone and muscle, were all concrete-filled. Tonya, in contrast, was air.

Her tone, though, gave her weight. "You're a singularly driven man, which isn't rare of your kind, but you've a compulsiveness that drives you harder, farther, and deeper. You fight where others will stop." Which was when she stopped, her body jolting slightly. For a moment he thought she was going to pull away, but then her voice deepened, the cadence altered. "In many ways, and for many years, you will be the perfect superhero."

So much for her preternatural abilities, he thought, starting to draw away. He'd already screwed that up. "Thank you."

Her airy fingers constricted, catching his again. "You harbor a strong sense of duty, but entertain a private restlessness. Your gift, a talent with your hands, steadies you and helps you to live more in the moment, but it doesn't entirely quiet the internal dissension."

JJ sat straighter, warier now, but intrigued. He was the troop's weaponeer, had been even prior to metamorphosis into a full agent, and was responsible for making the conduits that could kill agents, something mortal weapons could not do.

"You have a tragic past, not unusual for one dealing in evil matters, but yours has shaped you in a strange way. You are attracted to things you fear, and desire to understand them. You have friends, you're well liked, but the one who will know you best is drawn in by your fallibility."

Warren stiffened at that, though he remained turned away, pushing aside the curtain to look out the window. Tonya spoke faster, as if rushing through the words could lessen their impact. "Saving 'all of mankind' isn't enough to motivate you. It needs to be personal. You strip away a person's labels and see the individual. It's very admirable."

"It's very dangerous," said Warren, who always saw things in terms of black and white.

"Yes," JJ agreed immediately, knowing too well how his leader felt. Cohesiveness was desired, the good of the whole came first, the troop was more important than the individual.

"Can be," Tonya said, knowing none of this. "But you desire a deeper involvement. You want to feel more. People, their ability to choose—"

"That's enough," JJ jerked away, her pseudo-strength giving way to his will. "None of this is useful in finding the Kairos."

But her voice continued to rasp from between those frosted lips. "This will allow you to see her. She is a mystery to you. A dark—"

Matter.

The greatest mysteries are destined to remain a dark matter.

Dane wasn't talking about the Kairos, he suddenly realized. She was speaking of Solange.

"You will know she is meant for you before she does."

"No more." JJ shot from his chair, heading straight to the door. He needed air.

"You will recognize her immediately—"

"Later," he said, thinking, *Shut up, shut up, shut up.*

"There is no later. Not for you. Not even for me," she said, tone darkening as JJ threw open the door. "There is only now."

JJ froze. Because now half a dozen Shadow agents fanned across the parking lot in a reverse chevron, Solange at the tip. She had her tomahawk in one hand, his cell phone in the other. Her chest was smoking. She looked through him as if she'd never seen him before, as if he'd never lived inside her.

He probably shouldn't have been surprised, but the betrayal cracked his heart. She'd used their private time, their time of truce—and, he'd stupidly begun to believe, their love—to gain data for the Shadow side.

"Hope you're living 'in the moment' right now," Warren commented, suddenly beside him. "Because these next few are going to be doozies."

When JJ saw Sola standing there, his first impulse was to smile.

You see the individual.

Luckily his instinct was stronger, because he dove sideways just as the tomahawk appeared in front of his face, death inscribed on the blade. Whirring head over handle, it sliced air, then there was a sick, wet thud as it found another bodily home. JJ shifted to find Tonya Dane reclined in her chair, frosted lips rounded in surprise, the tomahawk buried in her skull. The crevasse between skin and gray matter literally split her in two.

The glyph on JJ's chest kicked to life, matching Warren's, who'd dived to the other side of the doorway as the phalanx of Shadows moved closer. JJ reached into his pocket and withdrew his whip, unfurling it as he pivoted. Its length licked out and wrapped around Tonya's chair leg, trapping her body to it as he yanked, whipping both to Warren's side. His leader withdrew the tomahawk quickly, with a murmured apology, and JJ jerked his weapon again, this time spinning the chair like a top, the barbed tips in the strip of leather releasing, ready now for a Shadow.

Obligingly, they continued their advance. JJ didn't aim for Solange. Warren, possessing her conduit, would do that.

Turning a person's own weapon against him was like turning his body inside out. It was personal, destructive, and gave the bearer of the death an additional measure of power. Instead, JJ centered his weight, flicked his wrist, and sent the barbed whip on a snapping journey around the doorframe. He felt the tug of flesh as it connected, and jerked back like he was fly-fishing, instead pulling a man ashore. Once the Shadow was blocking the doorway, JJ pulled his whip free, ripping the man's life with it. Warren and JJ then used the dead bulk to push their way into freedom.

Using his tattered trench as a defensive shield—JJ had made the armored coat himself—Warren covered the rear, deflecting projectiles. Solange's tomahawk still fisted tight. JJ's whip danced. Warren planted his boots into solar plexuses and stomachs, both screamed their battle cries . . . and a part of JJ continued to search for Sola.

"Look out!"

The Shadow dropped from above. Warren drew the trench over them, and JJ swept the ground with his whip, one hand braced on asphalt. Even so, he felt death smiling at him—there were too many enemies from too many directions . . . and all because he had trusted Solange.

The full weight of the descending Shadow crushed his shoulders. He braced, but it didn't move, even while other Shadows yelled warnings into the night. Warren whipped the shielding trench from their heads, and JJ circled his whip, readying for the next attack. But the voices raining around them were familiar, and he recognized the mace lodged in the chest of the Shadow at his feet as Gregor's, an ally.

Arriving in response to Warren's call, the troop had surprised the attacking Shadows, and managed to inflict casualties of their own.

Because Solange hadn't known about them, JJ thought, once the remaining Shadow agents had fled. He stood, breathing hard, whip hanging at his side, and surveyed the lot. Warren's phone call, which Solange had somehow taped or bugged or replayed, had mentioned only the two of them locked in a room with the woman who could deliver them the Kairos. But now that woman, and link, was dead, and they were left to clean up the mess.

And Solange had disappeared. Again.

5

*The perfect superhero . . . attracted to things you fear
. . . it needs to be personal . . .*

Tonya Dane's final prediction, always his first waking
thought, jolted JJ awake again.

He cursed as he rubbed a hand over his moist face, down
his neck, and over his bare chest. That prediction, along
with his mind's betraying dreams—the touch of Sola's
flesh on his, the taste of her tongue in his mouth, the scent
of her lingering on his skin, the sound of her soft moans in
his ears—was why he'd become an insomniac in the past
three months. And he supposed *that* was why he'd accidentally dozed off here, in the lush comfort of the Valhalla
Hotel's Turkish-style hammam. It was a warm and misty
wet sauna with walls and floors of swirling mosaic tiles
in relaxing blues, and the perfect place for JJ to study the
city's partiers . . . though that was hard to do, he thought
wryly, if his eyes were shut.

Pushing himself to an upright position, he took a long
drag from the ice water at his side, and looked around. The
hammam boasted a heated gold slab in the great room's
center, occupied on this day by three blonds in minute
bikinis—including one woman who looked marginally familiar. From his corner, which was both bench and booth, JJ
watched as a cluster of suitors, eager to impress, flexed and
bulged around them. Determining that none of the mortals

were either risky or at risk, he breathed in the scents of eucalyptus and soft mint, and squinted up at the recessed lighting. It was so obscured in the wet haze that it almost resembled the night sky.

The blonds soon left, resulting in the exodus of most of the room's occupants, but not before the middle girl, the one who looked familiar, shot him a smile sweeter than he'd expect attached to that body. He realized belatedly that it was the socialite he'd seen burning up the airwaves months ago. He recalled hearing she'd been keeping a low profile since, but imagined that could be true only if she refrained from stepping outside altogether. When the hammam doors swung shut behind her, the swirling wet haze closed ranks.

JJ shut his eyes.

"If you think this is relaxing, you should try the thermal detox."

He'd imagined her voice so many times—screaming, begging, pleading for mercy—that for a moment it felt like a daydream sparked by the misty environs. But when he opened his eyes she was there, reclined sideways on the smooth, thick center slab, steam-slick from head to thigh, white bikini glaring against her tanned, smooth curves. Her dark hair swung down to reveal her slim shoulders. Only her eyes were indistinguishable, dark in their sockets, like they were missing altogether.

"It would be so much easier on me," he said, before he knew it, "if you'd give me something to beat against." He was a warrior and needed a fight. All this passive aggression was somehow exhausting.

"I know," she whispered, letting her hand trail down her thigh.

"Are you going to ambush me again?"

"Rather hard when I don't know where you'll be," she said, voice wry. "You've done a good job of covering your tracks, Jay. I've been waiting at this spa for weeks."

Because he'd changed up every habit he had. He'd

stopped drinking, moved house, and even sold his Mustang. Took a fiscal beating on it because of the dents in the hood, too. "You must be getting wrinkly."

One corner of her mouth twitched. "It's the hot new place in Vegas. I knew you'd have to come here eventually."

So as to protect mortals from each other, and themselves. Keep the balance so all had a fair choice between virtue and vice.

Scent out the Shadow to exact his revenge.

But he hadn't done such a good job of that, had he? He must have some sort of sensory blind spot where she was concerned, just like the emotional one that had allowed her to aim a tomahawk at his skull, while he never saw it coming. And now that she was in front of him, all he was doing was staring.

"You tried to kill me. After we made love, too. After we said whatever we learned while together was off-limits."

"I was merely following the constellations." She shrugged. "Orion."

"And, let me guess, you hit the dark matter?"

She shook her head. "The apex. I was on a downswing."

This time he didn't think her explanation cute. He stood, crossing the room in full strides to loom over her. "So your decision to take my life was random?"

"*Life* is random, JJ!" Solange was suddenly on her feet, too, standing in the middle of the slab like a pissed-off sacrifice. "The stars and skies are the only things that make sense, don't you see? They're impermeable. They're forever. The light gets all the attention, but the dark matter is the glue of our Universe."

"Would you quit with all the 'dark matter' shit? They're just words someone used to describe something unknown. That's all. Fuck."

Her eyes followed the way he rubbed his hands over his head, and he stopped. She huffed. "People like to label things they don't understand."

"Like Light and Shadow?"

"Like love."

His turn to huff. "*You're* going to talk to *me* of love?"

She lifted her chin. "Don't look so outraged. You enjoyed our time together. Remember, I've seen the way you look at me when you're buried deep. You like it."

"I don't like you."

"But you love me."

He didn't say anything.

"And there's your 'tell.' You're actually quite incapable of a lie, JJ."

"Moral pinnings aren't weaknesses."

"Sure they are. They make you predictable."

He thought about that, took a step forward. "You love me, too."

Her turn to fall silent now, but she didn't move back.

"It means you can change . . . if you choose to." And the thought fueled the first flush of excitement he'd felt in months. How sick was that?

"No," she ultimately whispered. Her dark eyes were buried into his as she looked up. "I no more want to be you than you want to be me. You forgot that, even though I warned you."

"So what now? You're warning me again?"

Solange wrapped her arms around his neck. JJ let her.

Why the hell did he let her?

"What do you want?" he finally said, voice muffled against her neck.

"I already told you that."

He thought back, brows furrowing, then shook his head. There was too much emotion marring his thoughts when it came to her. Like static over a phone line, it kept the real message from getting through.

"The first night," she prompted. "In the desert storm. On the hood of your car."

He'd asked her what she wanted then. *Relevance.* "I can't give that to you."

Her fingers trailed along his back, blindly found his tattoo. "Do you know the meaning of the word *quintessence*?"

"It means typical."

She pulled back, offended. He pulled her tight again, and held her there. For a moment it felt like she'd struggle, but then she relaxed, her hipbones playing just beneath his. And then she pulled him down so they were seated across from each other, legs intertwined on the warmed marble. "It means pure. A highly concentrated and most perfect embodiment of a substance. You know what the basic elements are, right?"

He rolled his eyes. "Air, fire, earth, and water." As an Aries, JJ was a fire sign. Solange was Pisces, a water sign. Maybe that was their problem.

And she's a Shadow agent.

"So think about it. Quint-essence. The fifth essence, or element. The Pythagoreans called it ether. They claimed it flew upward at creation to comprise the stars."

JJ furrowed his brows. Another piece in the puzzle that was her obsession with the constellations . . . but it still made no sense to him.

She smiled softly. "You, JJ, are the perfect embodiment of Light. I smelled it all those years ago, a mixture both warm and sweet."

Oh, now he saw. "And you are quintessential Shadow, right? Never swayed, unchanging?"

"You tell me. Scent me again."

Though an agent's every sense was heightened, their noses were perhaps the most keen. Enemies were easiest to scent when emotions were high; an evolutionary gift, but JJ didn't need to sniff to know Solange. His olfactory nerve had memorized her unique blend of heat and spice and that's what he said.

"You sure?" she asked, tilting her head.

He hesitated, then tentatively sniffed at the air. Lifted his chin. Sniffed again. "You smell . . . different."

Her scent had turned, not soured, but altered. Her spice had softened, the biting hooks melting into peppered waves, as if buried in something as heavy and sweet as melted caramel.

She wants relevance.

And in a matriarchal society such as theirs, the best way to achieve that was to mother a child of legacy, one of both Shadow and Light . . . the Kairos. "Oh my God. But the soothsayer said she's already here, in this city."

"She is." Solange placed a hand on her belly. "Inside of me. And has been from that first night under the stars."

A child of Shadow and Light. A baby who would be mothered by a Shadow. But *his* baby.

"Her name will be Lola. She will be the Kairos."

Then the glossy door burst open and cool air rushed in. The man framed in the doorway wore a ratty trench and smelled like soured sweat. He had no place in an upscale spa, but JJ knew he'd moved so fast the reception staff hadn't seen him. Sola's glyph smoked to life, and JJ's glyph burst with light, though whether it was in response to her or Warren, he didn't know.

"Step back, JJ."

He did it automatically, used to obeying his leader.

"Oh," she said, turning her face up to his. Tears brimmed in her eyes, and JJ realized then what it looked like. "Touché."

He reached forward, grip tightening on her arm. "No—"

She didn't fight, and she didn't look away as Warren advanced.

"Your emotion is up, son. Didn't I warn you about that?"

"How long have you been following me?" JJ asked him, as if Solange—his enemy and lover—wasn't right there.

"Since Tonya Dane told me you needed following." He halted in front of them, looking with distaste at Solange, eyes taking her in like she was a snake. "So. You're it."

Like she was a thing, an intangible, trash to be discarded. Next to Warren she looked tiny.

"No," JJ said, before his leader could act. "Wait—"

"I don't think so."

But as Warren stepped forward, arms reaching to snap Sola's slim neck, the strangest thing happened. JJ's fist shot out, slow-mo and of its own accord, and Warren's head snapped back so fast it hadn't righted itself before he hit the ground. JJ didn't even feel his fist lower. It was as if he'd blinked and reality shifted, and he now existed on an entirely different plane.

Shaking, he looked down at his leader, splayed on the heated slab. What had he done? This was Warren, as close to a father figure as he'd ever had, and the leader of the agents of Light. His troop. His family!

"I should have killed you," he told Sola, who hadn't moved. "That first night. I should have slain you with your tomahawk and walked off with the power and prestige that would provide."

"And I, you," Solange said lightly. He glanced up to find her eyeing Warren speculatively. The visual that slid through his mind—a bronzed, bikini-clad warrior carving bodies with a tomahawk—would've been laughable were there anything funny about the situation. Yet all Solange did was swallow hard, and leveled her gaze at JJ. "So what are you going to do now?"

It wasn't worry that had her asking, but confidence . . . and perhaps curiosity. She didn't believe he'd kill her while she was pregnant, and she was right. Shadows were not innocents, and innocents were never Shadows . . . but this was *his* child.

And she will be Light.

So if he really thought he could make a difference in the world, a superhero in deed as well as name, and if he really believed that a Shadow could change—despite her obsession with the Universe's dark spaces—then this was the time to prove it.

No, he thought, not prove it. Make it happen. Because Solange wanted to believe as well. Three times now she'd come to kill him, and hadn't. She could have disappeared, had this baby on her own, and raised it as Shadow without his knowing. But she was here now. She had chosen him. She had chosen goodness. And he needed to do the same.

Solange smirked, as if reading that thought, but the expression dropped as soon as he reached forward, throwing her over his shoulder in one swift motion.

"What are you doing?" She started to struggle. He held tight.

"Finishing what I started that night."

6

A union between them—a contractual one to accompany the physical one growing in Sola's womb—was the best way to show her it could work. Their baby wouldn't just be their world's highest power, the Kairos, she would possess the best of them. She would represent the purest essence of a balance between their two sides. Quintessence . . . and choice.

And Solange was his. That was his foremost thought as he bent his head and placed his mouth to hers, sealing them forever. The female minister, with her shock of purple hair, clapped along with the two showgirls flanking her from the previous hour's "Vegas Package" wedding. Since Solange wasn't exactly sentimental, the feather- and crystal-encrusted women were also their witnesses for the ten-minute ceremony. When they finally pulled away, there wasn't a dry eye in the house.

"Obviously this changes everything," he said afterward, shoving a stacked fork of pancakes into his mouth, though he didn't clarify if he meant the wedding, the baby, or the way they'd both betrayed their troops. They were at a pancake house, both ravenous and wild-eyed with what they'd done . . . and what had yet to be done.

"We can't keep all of it out of the manuals," she said, primly cutting her own food, creating the perfect bite. "Identities are one thing, and even a relationship can be hidden. Anything short of out-and-out treason will remain concealed until we show our hand, but this is different. It's too big."

But what wasn't? JJ thought, as she spoke. Walking down the street was a big thing if there happened to be a drunk driver heading your way. Throwing an innocent smile at a stranger was big if she later became your lover. Everything was big, but then, he thought, watching Sola with her furrowed brow, everything was small, too. And the small things often mattered most.

Still, she was right. Things were omitted from the manuals because for knowledge to be useful it had to be earned, same as for mortals, but not all of this would be left out. And, ultimately, it might be better if it was revealed anyway. Because that would mean they'd gotten away.

"We must either part ways," he said, wiping his mouth, "which is not going to happen, or disappear—"

"Difficult, but not impossible," she interjected. In some cases, rogues blended with humanity for years.

"Harder once the baby comes," he pointed out. As rogue agents, they'd both be disavowed, which meant they'd be driven from the city. Or killed. Not the most ideal circumstances under which to raise their child. "Or we change our appearances entirely."

Even if the manuals showed them doing that, and they probably would, the drawings wouldn't depict their new identities. Universal checks and balances were still in play.

But Sola had stopped chewing mid-bite, a wistful expression blanketing her face as she stared at him.

"What?"

"You. You," she said again, giving it a lover's inflection, as her eyes gained a sheen. "I just wish I could see you."

He frowned. "You mean—"

"I mean before this." She indicated the length of his body with a nod of her head, her sigh spiced with regret. It smelled like her, him, and his child.

"It's not much different. Just bigger." He reached over to squeeze her hand. "Besides, you did. Once."

"As a child," she said dismissively, before squeezing back. "But who did that child become? What would you have looked like if you'd been allowed to remain entirely you?"

"It's still me, Sola. I'm in here. What does it matter what's on the outside?"

"Because I want to make love to you. I want *you* buried inside of me. Not a facsimile, not a mask hiding you from me as if I'm just another person in this world. I'm your wife now, and our child will have your features. I'd like to be able to recognize them in her, that's all."

Her sentiment touched him, and he bent to place his forehead to hers. "I'm sorry. I don't know how to do that."

She bit her lip, fought back her tears, and nodded. Glancing at her plate, she pushed at her food with her fork, before stilling. Then she looked up again, tilted her head, and narrowed her eyes. Her tears fell, squeezed out by the considering look.

"What?"

"Well, I might . . . there may actually be a way. But . . . no. Too risky."

"What is it?"

"No. I can't ask it of you. Not now, after you've done so much. Let's just move forward, okay?"

"Please, Sola, just tell me. If I can't be heroic for my own wife, who can I act for?"

It surprised a laugh from her, but it took a minute more of convincing. When she finally told him, he sat back in his chair, mind spinning. She was right; it was dangerous. It was also taboo.

Each side of the Zodiac possessed a human ally called a changeling, a child young enough to still believe in comic book heroes and epic causes. Their job was to protect an agent from his or her enemies when within a safe zone, and not just the agent, but the agent's identity as well. When the changelings willed it, they could mold their aura around an agent's form to hide the person's current identity by revealing the original.

Despite this ability, the kids were truly mortal. As soon as they reached puberty, the willingness to believe in comics and superheroes waned. They lost their powers, practically overnight, and put the Zodiac world behind them as they would a toy train. Their posts and duties were then passed on to another.

Asking a changeling to perform this function outside a safe zone was taboo because it was also dangerous. An agent could survive injury by a mortal weapon, but if the agent was attacked while wearing a changeling's aura, the child would still suffer mortal damage. There was also the issue of securing the changeling's earthly body. When an agent was using the aura, the child's was immobilized, as fragile as an egg until the aura was returned. That emptied mortal body couldn't survive beyond twelve hours.

All these considerations raced through JJ's mind as he studied Sola. What ultimately settled it was putting himself in her position. If she were clothed in a fleshly disguise, wouldn't he want to see his true love beneath? The way her body moved below his, how her face looked when focused solely on him? Besides, despite the warnings, a changeling had never been harmed before. The warnings were just that: like notices on the back of poison. Only dangerous if it fell into the wrong hands.

"And only once, right?" he asked, though he wasn't really talking to her.

"It would be enough," she said simply, and that was it. She didn't want to hurt anyone, she only wanted him. And this would be her sole opportunity to see whom she was giving up her entire world for.

"Well, as long as we're living dangerously," he said, and a small jolt at the illicit—the same dark desire Sola had known lived in him from the beginning—thrilled through him as they kissed, sealing the decision.

7

It was JJ's responsibility to acquire the changeling, but Sola set the stage. She chose a penthouse downtown, one with an old-school feel but new-city glamour. In the bedroom, she'd created a cocoon of pillows to shelter the fragile shell the changeling would become once JJ borrowed his aura. Their room, he assumed, was up the winding staircase she descended when JJ and the boy arrived.

"I'm going to put on something a little more comfortable," Sola whispered, her body twining with his, already smelling of wet heat. "I suggest you do the same."

She ascended the staircase like a wisp of smoke, and JJ smiled after her, until the kid, Ricky, finally cleared his throat. He was watching Solange with narrowed eyes, but he trusted JJ enough to follow.

"Right. Come with me."

Once inside the bedroom, they wasted little time. The kid reminded him that it was imperative to return his aura within twelve hours, then, making it look easy, shrugged off his aura as simply as he'd remove his clothes. His body elongated into a shimmering outline of JJ's, thinning to a finger's width to achieve the same height, the transformation reflected in the mirror across from them. The boy's glimmering form deepened to opaqueness, so that his features disappeared. Now JJ's could appear through him.

What are you doing?

JJ, watching all this as though from a distance, immediately dismissed the voice. He was being transparent, that's what he was doing. Being truly seen, perhaps for the first time since Solange had looked at him across the distance of his parents' broken bodies. How appropriate that it was she who would see him again now, not as an enemy or superhero, just him and her and the child they'd created between them.

He stepped forward, through the elongated form, and felt the aura mold to him like wet gauze, healing and cool. He avoided looking in the mirror as he made sure the boy's now lifeless body was safely cradled on the bed before heading upstairs. He wanted his wife to be the first to see him. The first in years.

She killed in black silk. Though the staircase surprisingly led to a rooftop terrace that mirrored an outdoor bedroom with the sky spread above, and downtown Vegas winking below, he marveled only at her. It was a toss-up as to what possessed a deeper sheen, her hair or the chemise, or perhaps, JJ thought, it was her eyes, fixed on him as she handed him a glass of champagne, then clinked her glass to his.

"To quintessence," she said softly.

"To relevance," he added, which made her smile. She lifted to her toes, mouth open and inviting on his. JJ moved to deepen the kiss, but she pulled back and held him at arm's length, studying the man who was really her husband.

JJ shifted under her stare. "Well?" he finally asked, sipping nervously at his glass as her eyes trailed him from head to toe. He felt vulnerable, small beneath the night sky they both loved. Though he knew the stars were there, they were unreadable from the city, and he had a sudden flash of being suspended amid all that dark matter, not knowing if he was on an upswing, or a down.

What are you doing? His inner voice again, more urgently, but his eyes had already slid to Sola's smooth legs as she poured more champagne, the black silk rounding out her behind, cutting low on her back to reveal the ridges and muscles and strength he so loved. He caught his reflection in the oval floor mirror and startled at the sight. But he was only sizing himself up in relation to her, and in his eyes—scotch-colored, the same as always—they were a perfect fit. And that's what she commented on.

"She'll have your eyes."

He lifted her, kissing her neck as he dropped her to the center of the bed, also draped in black, so only her limbs shone in the ambient light. Her lips and eyes were dewy, and so was her body as his mouth trailed downward. She was his drug, he decided, as he grew dizzier with her taste and scent and sight. Her moans echoed like a shifting wind as he lingered at her thighs, her desire driving his need. Champagne poured over her torso, and he licked it clean on the way back up to her mouth, where he entered her, dividing her twice. She spread her limbs like a five-tipped star, encouraging him to mirror her with her hands and hips. He did, and she sucked and sucked at him, like she was trying to pull his soul loose and bury it inside her. Already dizzy, he actually became breathless, but her need was relentless. She wouldn't stop.

And he couldn't stop it.

His eyes winged wide—sent another wave of dizziness through his head—and found she was already watching him. He tried to pull away. The strong arms he loved tightened, and her heels hooked around his. She sucked harder.

The wine.

More dizziness as the realization coursed through his body, and into his loins. Too late now, he couldn't help it. He came. She took—his seed, his breath and, he realized as he finally passed out, the changeling's aura from his body—all in a small, inaudible pop.

His last thought before all faded to black? *The small things mattered the most.*

* * *

He searched. God, did he search. And as he did—stumbling across the highway, racing down stinking alleyways, and canvassing all the places he knew Solange had once been— the scales fell from his eyes.

Solange had convinced him to gain the changeling's aura, knowing full well the boy, as who championed the Light, would never trust her. It made sense that she hadn't tried the same with the Shadow changeling. That would compromise *their* side, angering her leader, and it was obvious now—as it should have been all along—that she was still very much a Shadow.

What JJ couldn't understand was what she needed with the aura anyway. By the time the twelve-hour window was almost up, and he still hadn't found Solange and the aura she was hiding beneath, he knew he'd never know the answer to that question. He returned to the penthouse, determined that the boy who'd trusted him so completely wouldn't die alone.

Yet he did die.

JJ entered the bedroom where Ricky lay, instantly shocked at how tiny he looked. Curled into the fetal position, hands tucked prayerfully beneath his chin, his head was bent low as if braced for a blow. He was so small . . .

Every person has a right to the small things.

His father's words burst through his mind like the monsoon that had raged on the night all this had begun. Surely it was only his own guilt rearing, but it seemed the completion of the thought coincided exactly with the boy's final mortal moment. The slight quiver that overtook the small body was as unnatural as if it were made of rousing snakes, and JJ shuddered, swearing he could hear a rattler's shake.

The little happinesses.

The quiver strengthened into a quake, and the cells comprising Ricky's skin began separating, looking pixilated at first, some sinking while others slipped and scattered across the ridges and angles of the young body before dropping to the cotton bedding. JJ's gut twisted, and his hard exhalation scattered those loosened cells into a fine coating of dust.

Those are the ones that make life most worth living.

The boy settled more firmly, burrowing into his final resting place as his sandy insides softened, and he even looked peaceful before his small smile, and his lips, too, fell away. JJ refused to avert his eyes as the freckles dropped, the eyelashes fell. He saw the spiky hair flatten, dissolve, and leave behind a powdery skull. JJ's unblinking stare was obscured only when he began to cry, and he eventually realized between convulsing, open-eyed sobs that his wet sorrow was melding with the boy-shaped dune. He could literally build a castle with his tears. It made him cry harder.

It's what we're fighting for, came his father's last, late reminder.

When, and how, had JJ forgotten to fight?

The shell of Ricky's body was now totally depleted, drained as if dehydrated, lacking life force instead of water. From somewhere in the suite a clock chimed off the last of the twelve-hour mark, and JJ reached out to touch a small hand, to say good-bye. In one moment there was a child. In the next, dust mounded the bedding, a handful finely ground as beach sand in JJ's fist.

An innocent. A child. Dead because of him.

And JJ did bow his head now, unable to form thought or words, but sending up a prayer of emotion into the Universe, hoping someone, something, somewhere understood the regret squeezing his chest, the sorrow burning in his gut, and the hopelessness that made him want to lie down, too, and embrace a dusty death.

Weeping openly, not even trying to hide the scent of his shame and sorrow and misery, JJ didn't turn at the soft sound behind him. Unguarded emotions were easy for his kind to pick up. Kneeling bedside, he bowed his head and welcomed blessed death. But the enemy he'd drawn back to him had something else in mind.

JJ turned his tear-streaked face, and found Warren's unsurprised gaze locked hard on his. Tonya Dane's prediction—the one Warren hadn't wanted to believe and had been trying to prevent—had finally come true. His troop leader put it together quickly, eyes slipping mournfully to the mound of dust on the bed, as he inhaled to take in both the boy and Solange on JJ's skin.

"You should kill me," JJ said flatly, still kneeling.

"Yes." Warren's reply was, if possible, even flatter. "At the very least, exile."

"No." JJ's mind stumbled over the unacceptable thought. "I don't want to live. I don't want—"

"I don't care what *you* want." Warren remained still, so enraged he was all but quivering. "From now on, you want what I want."

"And that is?" JJ said it casually, but inside he was braced against the idea of living. He glanced at the plate-glass window, but a dive from the penthouse balcony wouldn't be enough to kill him. Warren, clearly intuiting his thoughts, moved between him and the window.

"I take responsibility for this," he surprised JJ by saying. "I made a mistake. I allowed you too much autonomy and granted you a position with too much power. I favored you because of your childhood, your parents, their deaths. When you wanted the position of weapons master I allowed that—"

Now something did spark inside JJ. "Because I'm the best."

Warren nearly snapped back, but closed his eyes instead, his head and shoulders drooping. "But I should have had someone apprenticing with you. I just never thought you would . . . I should have thought."

JJ didn't bother saying he was sorry. An apology meant nothing in the wake of an innocent's death. Besides, Warren was admitting he would exile or kill JJ if the troop didn't need him so badly, and one thing that could be counted on by Warren, he always acted in the best interest of the troop.

When Warren lifted his head again, the fatigue was gone and that hard truth was branded in his gaze. "You will give yourself over entirely to me," he said, voice harder than JJ had ever heard it.

Because living with the knowledge of what he'd done would be harder than dying over it.

"You'll tell no one about your *wife*"—he spit the word— "or the changeling. You'll do what I say, no questions asked, no argument, no explanation."

"Okay," JJ finally agreed, head bowed, fingers dusty.

"That wasn't a request." Warren's voice regained its strength and rhythm as he strode forward.

JJ nodded, staring at the floor. "And then I'll find her. I'll make this right . . ."

"You'll do no such thing." Warren said, jerking JJ to his feet. Their faces were so close their noses nearly touched. "She's poison to you, boy. Besides, do you think you deserve *any* sort of happy ending after what you've done?"

No. He didn't. No happily-ever-after . . . including revenge.

"She won't find you, either. We'll change your identity in full this time. Micah will make you over into something new, something better, some*one* who won't make this kind of mistake again."

JJ recalled the fiery pain following his last surgery, and the ghost of his old bulk trying to squeeze from beneath his current flesh, but he only stared at Warren mutely before nodding again.

"You're no longer your mother's son. Not JJ, or Jay . . . or Jaden Jacks." Not his mother's son, not his father's, either. Warren was stripping him of that connection and past, but in a way it was a relief. He had failed them, too.

"Solange won't ever find you. We'll make it so that even

your own troop members won't remember you. It'll be as if you never existed."

JJ did step back now, unable to keep his mouth from falling open. Would Warren really do that? He knew Micah could erase the memories of mortals, rewire their minds so that new pasts defined their futures. It was especially useful if one had happened upon an event or object derived from their hidden world. But could Warren really convince Micah to alter the troop's collective memory? It'd be a huge undertaking . . . not just rewiring the minds of the twelve senior star signs, but the ward mothers who'd helped raise JJ in their underground sanctuary, and the flexible minds of the initiates, too—the children of the next generation who so looked up to him now. Would Warren do that?

He looked at his troop leader's gaze—level again, and cool. Yes, he would. None of them would have a choice in the matter, and most wouldn't even question it. If they ever read about JJ in the back issues of the manual of Light, it would be like reading about someone else entirely. And it made JJ wonder: had Warren ever done this before?

But he'd be alone in his wonder, JJ realized. That would be his punishment. To remember what he'd done, to know the failure forever, and to live among his peers as a fraud. So it was almost as harsh as a death sentence.

JJ nodded yet again.

"You will take the appearance and job I determine for you, you will return to the sanctuary every night without fail, and you will log your activities for me down to the last detail."

"Yes," he replied woodenly. He no longer cared where his needs and desires ranked in his own life. In fact, it would be a relief to follow orders and let someone else do the thinking for a while. He would give his life over in service to mortals, and he'd do it wholeheartedly . . . or at least with what was left of it after Solange's betrayal.

Warren continued, voice thick with everything he wasn't allowing himself to say . . . and do. "You will be the exemplary superhero in every way. If I even suspect you're faltering, I'll kill you myself."

JJ nodded numbly. Then Warren punched him so hard he fell into the sea of pillows. A cloud of dust rose around him, and he coughed, tasting loss and death and a dry guilt that smothered any burning desire to fight. Warren didn't want his numb acquiescence, he realized.

Not when there was so much dust.

"I'm not doing this for you." Warren hissed, pointing a finger at JJ, tears rolling down his cheeks as he said it. "This is for your parents and what they meant to me, and what they sacrificed for us all."

"I won't forget again. Ever."

Though his parents were gone, he would live for them, as they'd once lived for each other. And he'd learn to listen again to his intuition, the inner voice he'd muted while reaching for his own selfish dreams, reaching until Solange had snagged his palm, and pulled him into all this dust.

His answers, his sorrowed scent, seemed to mollify Warren. His leader turned to the bedroom window, trench billowing at his ankles, and looked out at the city he was charged to protect. "You may choose your own name."

JJ stood and joined Warren at the window. "Hunter."

Warren looked at him sharply.

"Hunter," he repeated, sending back the steely gaze. Warren wanted the perfect embodiment of a superhero, so that's who he'd be. The purest predator in the city. The most concentrated essence of good, he thought, looking up at the sky.

The quintessential hunter.

Because somewhere out there was a woman with a thing for dark-haired men, a preference for Mustangs, and a need for relevance. She took action based on the constellations, her deeds steered by the dark matter in between, and she did it with his daughter, his Lola, in her belly.

And a child, Hunter decided, rubbing faintly dusty fingers together, was a damn good reason to continue the fight.

THE DEAD,
THE DAMNED,
AND THE FORGOTTEN

JOCELYNN DRAKE

I

A body was waiting for me at the morgue.

That wasn't the type of message I was expecting to receive when I awoke at sunset, but there was no avoiding it. My voice mail contained a semi-polite message from Archibald Deacon, Savannah's coroner, informing me that a nightwalker had just been delivered to his morgue. The message was followed by one from homicide detective Daniel Crowley, also informing me of the waiting corpse. A final message was from the now frantic coroner, who wanted me to deal with the corpse immediately. Unfortunately, there was nothing I could do until the sun had finally set beneath the horizon, allowing night to reclaim the world.

The private examination room was in the basement of the morgue, away from the main room that held the majority of the dead. It was one of the few buildings in Savannah with a basement, given the city's high water table, and it came at a great cost. Due to moments like these, I had been more than willing to make the contribution to the city.

The cinder-block walls had been covered with a thick coat of white paint that had begun to yellow with age. A handful of narrow windows lined the walls more than six feet above the floor. The glass had been painted black to deter any inquisitive people who happened to wander too close. A window-unit air conditioner sputtered and coughed randomly from its perch at the far end of the room, spewing forth a semi-steady stream of cool air.

I looked up from the coroner's report to watch Knox as he leaned over the body of the dead nightwalker. His lips were curled in disgust, revealing faint flashes of fang. The opposite wall from where I stood was covered with a stainless steel refrigeration unit for corpses. There were only four doors that opened to slide-out drawers. A larger unit was in the main examination room on the first floor.

"Are you sure there were no other wounds on the body besides the main two?" I inquired, turning my attention from the disgruntled nightwalker to the coroner, who hovered close by. Archibald was a short, round man who stood on stubby little legs. His dark brown hair was thinning, leaving the top of his skull nearly exposed. Archie, as I preferred to call him, had been the coroner for Savannah and the surrounding counties for nearly twenty years and we had known each other for almost as long.

"Mira," he snapped. His bushy grayish-brown brows bunched together over his large, bulbous nose. "Half the body was destroyed! How could I possibly answer such a question?"

"Can you at least tell me if the body was burned before or after he was beheaded?"

"After," replied a new voice.

Archibald jumped at the unexpected appearance of Detective Daniel Crowley, but I didn't flinch. I had sensed him walking through the building toward our location in the basement.

"How do you know?" I asked, looking over at Daniel as I closed the file folder that held a copy of the coroner's report. It was the real copy, one that would never be officially filed with the police department. Archibald would create a second version that would carefully omit any questionable details like the elongated canines, the sensitivity to sunlight, and any kind of genetic abnormalities he was already aware of.

"I talked to some of the guys who were first on the scene," Daniel continued, closing the door behind him. "When they found the body, one of the officers opened some curtains to let light in and the body started being reduced to ash like a slow-burning ember."

"They saw him burn?" Knox demanded in a harsh tone. Daniel took a hesitant step backward and looked over at me again. Knox and Daniel had never worked together. In fact, I was the only nightwalker in contact with Daniel and Archie, but it was time for that to change. If Knox was going to aid me with managing my domain, he needed to know the humans I was in contact with.

However, the corpse was unnerving Knox more than I had expected, and the nightwalker was losing some of the cool, unshakable logic that I had come to depend on him for. This unexpected rough edge couldn't be seen by these trusted humans.

Nodding once to Daniel, I dropped the folder on a nearby desk and slipped my hands into the front pockets of my worn jeans. The relaxed stance helped to ease some of the tension from Daniel's shoulders.

"It was weird, they said." Daniel ran his fingers through his sweaty hair, causing large chunks to stand on end. "There was no fire, but they said it was like the body was burning. No one commented that it was the sunlight. They thought the killer might have doused the body with a chemical in an effort to destroy the evidence."

"I've got a couple things I can put in the report that could potentially work as an explanation," Archie interjected.

"Write down the names of the cops," Knox ordered. "We may need to adjust their memories."

Again, Daniel looked at me, frowning. I nodded slightly, approving the request while inwardly I wished I could smack Knox on the back of the head.

Pushing off the wall, I pulled my hands out of my

pockets and stretched my arms over my head, extending my entire body into a long, straight line. "Excellent. Anything else I should know?" I was still trying to fully wake up—I hadn't expected to find myself at the morgue first thing in the evening, especially without even time to shower.

"The call came in at around nine A.M. Anonymous male caller from a prepaid cell phone," Daniel replied.

"The killer?"

Daniel shrugged, acknowledging the possibility.

"That's about three hours after sunrise," Knox muttered in a low voice. He took a few steps away from the corpse, brushing his hands against his pants even though he had never actually touched the body. "Plenty of time to get in and get out after he was unconscious for the day."

"We're still trying to dig up which cell tower was used to see if the person was still in town at the time," Daniel said. His frown deepened as he watched Knox start pacing between the stainless steel table and a wheeled cart loaded with different sharp instruments.

"Anything at the house?" I inquired, dragging the detective's keen attention back to me.

"No, we didn't find anything of interest."

I watched Daniel from under the brim of my baseball cap. The fluorescent lights in the morgue tended to give my pale skin an inhuman pearlescent sheen. It was why both Knox and I were dressed in long-sleeve shirts and baseball caps despite the fact that it was still above eighty degrees outside.

"Knox and I will check it out tonight."

"Do you know who did this?" Daniel asked. Sweat stains stretched from under his arms and lined his collar. His tie had been loosened and he looked oddly out of sorts without a cigarette in one hand. It was still early in his shift but it looked like he had already been through hell. He must have either come in early after hearing about the strange murder or hadn't gone to bed yet from the previous night.

"I've got some guesses. We'll take care of this. Get some rest."

"Mira, I can't just walk away. If there's a murderer within the city, I need to track this bastard down and stop him before he kills someone else. That's my job."

A smile lifted my lips. Daniel didn't see the half-burned remains as some bloodsucker that got what it deserved. He saw him as a person who had his life unjustly ended and believed that the rest of the population (humans, night-walkers, and all the others) needed to be protected from the murderer. I was doubtful many humans would be so open-minded.

"I appreciate that, Daniel," I said, stepping away from the wall to stand between the corpse and Archibald and Daniel. "And normally I would let you get your man, but this time it's a nightwalker that's been killed. You're not equipped to handle this problem. Knox and I will handle it. We won't allow the killer to endanger the citizens of Savannah."

"What about the body? We can't . . . People are going to want tests run and . . ." Archie started, turning my smile into a smug grin.

"I'll sign the paperwork indicating that his sister dropped by and demanded that the body be cremated immediately for religious reasons. You will then declare that the tests are inaccurate due to a contaminated sample. The cause of death is obvious and we'll identify and dispose of the body before we leave. Your jobs are nearly done, gentlemen." The plans flowed forth easily, as if I did this every other night. But the fact was it was rare that I had to deal with the death of a nightwalker. Most of the time, it would turn out to be a lycanthrope or a warlock that was a very heavy magic user. As Keeper of this domain, I was the first and last line of defense for all the supernatural races when it came to protecting our secret.

Both men hesitated, but Daniel finally muttered some-thing under his breath before walking out of the room, his hands shoved into the pockets of his trousers. Archibald said nothing as he waddled over to the desk and pulled out the necessary forms. His white lab coat fluttered behind him, nearly dragging the ground. He marked X's where he needed me to fill out information and sign. Spreading the paperwork out on the desk, he left Knox and me to the corpse.

Now that we were alone, I pulled off the blue-tinted sunglasses I had been wearing and hooked them over the top button of my shirt. "That could have gone better." I wanted to snarl in frustration.

Knox paced away from the corpse, his arms crossed over his chest. "They're unnerved by what we are. It can't be helped."

"Bullshit. They were unnerved by your behavior. I've seen you easily sway anything with nice breasts and a tight ass. What happened here?"

"Maybe it's because those men lacked the aforementioned items," he commented dryly, making me want to throw something at his head.

"Well, you better learn to widen your scope because they're not going anywhere and we need their assistance. You need them and they'll be far more helpful if they're not worried about you grabbing a snack."

"If you want, I can go tweak their memories," he offered.

I waved my hand at him, stopping any movement toward the door. "No, don't go messing with their memories. You need their trust and you don't get that if you're mucking around in their brains."

"They'll never know."

"I'll know."

Knox nodded, removing his dark sunglasses so that I could look into his brown eyes. "I'll do better next time."

"Thank you," I murmured as I stepped up to the body. It was highly unusual for Knox to be so gruff and harsh when dealing with humans. His nature was very ingratiating, and his dark, handsome looks tended to win over the reluctant. His maker had the same manner. Because of his uncharacteristic behavior, I was beginning to worry that Knox had been well-acquainted with the victim.

Looking down at the steel tray, my eyes skimmed over the badly burned face. The skin was blackened and the eyes were now gone as if they had melted in their sockets, sending the fluid down in to the back of the skull. It looked like he might have had short-cut, brown hair. But the condition of the head wasn't the disturbing part. It was the fact that it was no longer attached to the body.

It was likely that that was the killing blow, but the murderer could have removed his heart first and then his head. The nightwalker's chest cavity had been ripped open and the heart cut out using some kind of serrated blade that had torn the edges of the flesh into ugly shreds. At least it was likely that the victim had felt no pain. It appeared that it all happened during the daylight hours, meaning that the vampire had been dead to the world.

"I'm assuming that you recognize who this is," I said, my own mood growing more sour and anxious as I continued to examine the corpse. I vaguely knew all the nightwalkers within my domain. There were more here than in most cities this size, but then I maintained a tight control over my domain. It afforded those that lived here more of a sense of security and peace than what many cities could offer.

However, during the past few years, I had begun to withdraw from my own kind, no longer wanting to be faced with them. I didn't want to hear their thoughts in the night, or feel their cool presence as I moved silently through the city searching for my next meal. Knox had taken over much of the night-to-night management. Of course, that simply required him making regular appearances at all the nightwalker hot spots.

"His name was Bryce." Knox leaned his back against the refrigeration unit, his arms crossed over his chest. His shoulders were stiff and his normally neutral expression was twisted into a frown.

With my hands braced on the table before me, I looked up at my companion. "What's your problem? Did you know him well?"

A faint shrug briefly lifted his narrow shoulders. "I knew him, but not well."

"Then what has got you so on edge?"

"He was executed," he hissed, waving one hand at the severed head. "His head was cut off and his heart removed. He was executed during the day when he was defenseless. How are you not unnerved by this?"

"He was possibly killed during the day," I corrected, trying to keep both of us calm and rational. "We won't know for sure until we check his house." The truth was that I *was* unnerved and more than a little concerned. If Bryce had been killed at night, it was highly likely that the murderer was another nightwalker. And then my only reason for tracking down the murderer would be punishment for allowing the humans to catch wind of it and threatening our secret. However, if Bryce had been killed during the day, we had a bigger problem. But we had to tackle one thing at a time, and a panicked Knox would do me no good.

"How old was he?" I demanded, attempting to refocus Knox's attention.

"Less than two centuries."

"How long has he been in my domain?"

"About a decade. Maybe a little more."

"Was he involved in anything recently that I should be aware of? Changes in allegiance? Was he a part of a family?"

Knox pushed away from the wall and stood, shoving one hand through his sandy blond hair. "I-I'm not sure."

"Concentrate," I murmured, looking over Bryce for any identifying marks. Some families were known for branding their members. We couldn't be tattooed because we always healed, but we could retain some scars if we were low on blood and were unable to heal properly. The process was generally painful and ugly, but then most families were painful, ugly affairs. I didn't find anything on Bryce, but I wasn't surprised. Most of his body was either singed or blackened from its exposure to the sun.

"He's a part of the Ravana family, I believe. He came to Savannah alone and immediately got sucked into Justin's clan," Knox replied. His voice grew steadier the longer he spoke, as if he were finally detaching himself from the gruesome death of the nightwalker that lay before him. Nightwalker flocks were like high school cliques, each with its own set of rules and bizarre tastes.

A low, steady hiss escaped me as I turned this new bit of information over in my brain. I had been hoping that he wasn't a member of one of few families that existed within my domain, but of them all, Justin Ravana's clan was the most undesirable. Cruel and vicious, Justin was one of the oldest within my territory and had been practically raised by the Coven. I hadn't thought much of his petition to live in my domain decades ago, but I had regretted agreeing ever since. Justin specialized in brutality, torture, and control. No one that entered into his family ever escaped it alive.

"When Bryce was away from his family, he tended to associate mostly with fledglings," Knox continued. "During the past few years, I've seen him mainly with this small group of nightwalkers, mostly females, all less than a century old."

"Not exactly the best list of suspects you've got for me." I stood, pulling away from my examination of the corpse. "A group of fledglings? It's possible that it was Justin, but it's not his style to hand off the murder to someone else who could do it during the day. He'd want to be part of it. Justin would have taken the time to handle it personally over a series of weeks if possible."

"What? You've never seen a fledgling kill another nightwalker?" Knox scoffed. The comment finally caused some of the tension to roll off of his shoulders.

"I've seen the remains of plenty of fledgling kills, but I've never known of any fledgling that could accomplish the feat during the day. And I've never known a fledgling to kill a nightwalker in this style."

"Really? Fledglings have a style? A preferred method of murder?" he mocked.

"Don't we all?" I batted my eyes at him.

"We all know your preferred method, Fire Starter," Knox said, shoving his hands into the pockets of his worn jeans. He leaned against the cooler, careful to keep his eyes on me and not on the corpse. "What about fledglings?"

"I guess I have something in common with them. Fire is their preferred method. It's fast, effective, and relatively easy. Of course, I've seen just as many fledglings go up in flames with their intended victim because they weren't careful."

"So you're saying one of the fledglings that knew Bryce didn't kill him," he suggested, earning him a grin.

"I didn't say that. It's possible, but unlikely, particularly if he was killed during the day." I wasn't willing to say out loud who I thought had killed Bryce—we were both on edge enough.

An easy silence settled between us as I contemplated our dead friend and his potential attacker. Knox stood nearby, ready to offer up information. He was careful to look anywhere but at the half-burned, beheaded corpse. "Did you ever do this with my maker?" Knox softly asked, fiddling with his sunglasses.

"What? Look at corpses with Valerio?" I asked, my brow furrowed at the unexpected question. "All the time. It was how we spent most of our nights."

"Ha. Ha," he said, rolling his eyes at my sarcasm. "I can imagine how you spent most of your nights. But you know what I mean. He said you and he investigated strange things for the Coven back when you were in Europe?"

A smile drifted across my lips before I could stop it. I had too many good memories of Valerio, but that didn't mean I was willing to share. Some were too embarrassing or too gruesome. And others were simply too private. My time with Valerio wasn't always filled with happy memories and I was frequently horrified by some of the things we did, but I would never trade the moments I had with Knox's maker.

"Yes, Valerio and I frequently looked into a strange death or a corpse that needed our unique attention to keep the secret protected. During that time, we never found a fledgling that could kill during the day." I smiled at my companion for lightening the mood and shook my head. How had Valerio ever stood to part with this child? I was becoming far too attached to him.

"Is there anything else I should know about our dead friend?" I asked, resting my hands on the edge of the stainless steel table next to Bryce.

"The only other thing I can think of is that about six months ago he petitioned you to allow him to bring over his lover," Knox added.

My head snapped up at this bit of information. "I'm assuming that I said no."

"You denied the request," Knox confirmed. His brow furrowed slightly as he turned over my sudden interest. "You think she had something to do with this?"

"I'm hoping such a thing is impossible since her memory was wiped," I said in a hard, cold voice.

"It was."

"Did our headless friend tell you that or did you check for yourself?"

"I checked. There were no memories of Bryce or nightwalkers in her brain," he replied.

Biting down on my lower lip, I stared down at the blackened remains of Bryce, still wondering if his would-be fledgling had found a way to murder him because he had refused to make her into a nightwalker. Though equally unlikely, there were still a number of ways she might have been involved in Bryce's death.

"Is she a magic user?"

"The woman?" Knox's perpetually even, dry tone jumped several octaves. "I don't think so."

"If she is, she may have been able to hide her memories from you."

Knox's whole body stiffened at my comment while his expression went completely blank. "Do you honestly think Valerio didn't show me how to pick apart the mind of a magic user?" he demanded in a brittle voice.

A ghost of a smile flitted across my face at Valerio's name on his tongue. "Would it have occurred to you that she might be?" I countered, but quickly waved my hand at him. "I don't doubt your ability and I think it's highly unlikely the woman is a magic user. However, I find it strange that six months ago he was denied the right to make a vampire and now he's dead using a very human form of execution."

"Could have been a nightwalker," Knox suggested, putting his sunglasses back on again.

"Maybe," I whispered. Had Justin not approved of Bryce's request to create a fledgling and decided to act against the nightwalker in some fashion? The time issue still needed to be confirmed. "We won't know until we get to Bryce's place."

"We?"

"Of course! You think I would leave you out of the fun of ransacking a murdered vampire's lair for clues as to his killer? Not a chance." My outrageous teasing left a smile tugging at the corner of his mouth. "Besides, there will be plenty of time for you to track down the woman and anyone known to associate with Bryce," I continued, crushing the smile before it could actually form.

"You're too kind, Mira," Knox sneered. He took a step backward as I placed Bryce's head on his stomach. I then picked up the dead nightwalker and carried him over to the oven. Setting the nightwalker inside, I closed the door and summoned up my powers. Within seconds, the body was consumed with flames hotter than any that could be produced by the crematorium. The remains were reduced to ash. Bryce was no more.

As I looked up at Knox, a cold grin stretched across my lips. "You have no idea how *kind* I can be." I was the Fire Starter, scourge of our people. The protector of our secret. Kindness was all relative.

2

A crunch of gravel was my only warning as we walked across the parking lot of the morgue to my car. I hadn't scanned the area for other nightwalkers. This was my domain, and no one would dare to attack me in my own domain. I was wrong. Pain exploded in my ribs just before my body slammed into the side panel of a dark blue station wagon, denting the metal and breaking two of my ribs. With a snarl, my head snapped up to see who attacked me. Knox was squared off against a dark-haired nightwalker in leather pants and a black T-shirt. Other than his porcelain white skin, he looked as if he was a part of the night itself.

"Stand down, Knox," I ordered, pushing back to my feet. My body protested the movement as my ribs attempted to mend.

"Mira?" Knox paused in his circling of the other nightwalker, but his brown eyes still glowed; he was ready to attack if I said the word.

"This is my fight," I stated, taking a step toward the nightwalker. "It's been a long time, Bishop. I don't remember inviting you into my domain."

The nightwalker smiled, but had yet to take his gaze off Knox. Bishop was nearly five centuries old and a very skilled fighter, making him one of the most valued servants of Macaire. The Coven Elder wouldn't dispatch Bishop without a very good reason.

"As an emissary of Macaire, I go where I wish," he announced. He sidestepped to his left so that he could look at both me and Knox at the same time. Unfortunately, Knox still stood between us. Bishop might be here on business with me, but he would have no qualms over ripping through Knox just for the fun of it.

"Knox, go inside and see if there is anything else that Archie needs to complete his paperwork," I commanded, but Knox didn't move. If anything, he seemed to sidle slightly in front of me.

"Not a chance. I'm not leaving you out here alone with this guy," Knox said.

"No wonder I'm here. Your people won't even listen to you," Bishop mocked, straightening from his defensive stance.

"Go, Knox. I know him. We have some business to settle," I said, pushing the words past clenched teeth. Normally, Knox's loyalty and readiness to protect me at all times would be flattering, but not now, not in front of a member of the Coven's court.

Knox hesitated a moment before finally edging around Bishop and heading back into the morgue where he would make sure that no one came out to the parking lot while Bishop and I discussed whatever business had brought him into my domain.

We both waited until we heard the door to the morgue slam shut before we were in motion. My nails raked across his chest, tearing his shirt and leaving four ragged cuts across his skin. He backhanded me, throwing me into the side of another car. Pain spread across my face, leaving me with the feeling that he had broken my cheekbone. With a growl, I pushed away from the car and launched myself at him. Ducking his swinging fists, I landed a punch to his gut that broke a rib or two before he managed to grab my throat with his right hand. He squeezed, effectively closing off my airway. I didn't need to breathe, but from this position he could quickly rip my head off, ending this contest.

I grinned at him, my eyes glowing an eerie shade of purple as in nightshade. Around us, a circle of fire sprang up from the ground, closing in so that there was barely a foot of open space between us and the crackling flames.

Bishop pulled me close to him so that the tip of my nose touched his. There was no escaping his hard, black gaze. There was no light, no glow of power, just a black empty pit as if his power were bottomless. "Do it, Mira!" Bishop whispered. "Incinerate me. I swear you'll awaken tomorrow night back in the hands of the Coven in Venice, and this time Jabari will not be there to save you."

A shiver ran through me at his cold words. The Coven was the ruling body of the nightwalker nation, and it was an ugly place of pain and nightmares. It was a place I had escaped centuries ago and rarely visited, particularly since Jabari, one of the four Elders, had gone missing.

Bishop's grip on my throat loosened slightly so I could talk. "What do you want?" I asked in a ragged whisper.

"Besides the opportunity to rip your head off?" he asked with a dark grin that revealed his perfect white fangs. "I'm here to make sure that you clean up the mess that is currently your domain."

"What mess?" I demanded. I reached up and dug my nails into his large hand, trying to get him to release my throat.

"You're joking, right?" he said, dropping me. "We've heard from people within your domain. There is no order here."

"That's a lie."

"There has been an increase in Daylight Coalition–related deaths within the New World, recently," he continued to list.

"It's not my job to police all of the New World," I quickly countered.

"And now you have a fresh death found by the humans. From what I've heard, it looks like another Coalition kill. Can you not even protect your own?"

"I'm looking into the matter," I growled. I had nothing that I could say about Bryce's death. I didn't know the why behind it all just yet, but I would with time.

"I'm here to make sure that you clean up this mess and deal with the nightwalkers within your domain," Bishop said, taking a step closer to me as I stepped backward. With a thought, the flames were gone and the parking lot was plunged back into darkness.

"Other than the matter with the fresh body, there's no mess here."

"The Coven doesn't believe that to be true."

"You mean Macaire doesn't believe it. Who's been talking to him?"

"Now that would be telling," he said, a fresh grin lifting his thin lips. "Convince me that you have everything under control here, and I will leave along with everyone else that I brought with me. Fail and you'll be coming back to Venice with me."

A fresh stab of fear shot through me, seeming to pierce down to the bone, and it was nearly a minute before I could speak again. "What do you want me to do?" I found myself asking in a shaky voice. I wouldn't go back to the Coven. I couldn't. The place was a nightmare of death and endless screams that echoed through your brain even in your sleep.

"Catch the killer. Settle the chaos within your domain," he said, making it sound so simple. And for him, it was. He was simply waiting around for an excuse to drag me back to Venice. That was his job.

"Fine," I reluctantly agreed. "Just stay out of my way. This is still my domain and I will handle this *mess*."

"As you wish," he said with a slight bow of his head. With a parting grin, mocking me one last time, Bishop strolled out of the parking lot, heading back for the main street.

I sat down on the ground against one of the cars I had crashed into earlier. Resting my elbows on my bent knees, I dropped my head into my hands. *Damn it.* A flunky of the

Coven was dangling a sword just above my neck, simply waiting for an excuse to chop my head off. My hands were trembling and my stomach was twisting into knots as I sat there, mentally listing every nightwalker I knew of within my territory. Who could it be that was talking to the Coven? Someone was betraying me, betraying my trust and my protection.

Knox . . . I called out mentally for my companion. Less than a minute later he was kneeling at my side.

He rested his hand on the back of my head while the other was on my knee. "What happened? Are you all right? Who was that?"

"Someone from the Coven. We're being watched. We need to clean up this mess quickly before it becomes an even bigger problem."

"How did they find out so fast about Bryce? He was killed this morning."

"I don't think Bishop is here because of Bryce. I think the timing just ended up being convenient for whoever has the Coven's ear," I said, lifting my head so that I could look at Knox. "We need to get going. We're officially running short on time."

3

According to Daniel's information, Bryce was found in a house out past Bonaventure Cemetery, not far from Wilmington Island. Knox and I jumped into my little silver BMW Z4 and zipped out of the city like a mercury tear sliding down a clown's cheek. The convertible top was down and we shoved our baseball caps in the center console area between our seats so we could enjoy the feel of the warm summer air rubbing against our faces and tangling our hair. The night was alive, pulsing and squirming, demanding to be noticed.

Yet it wasn't the fact that Bryce had been murdered that had us both unnerved. It was the fact that someone had contacted the police regarding the corpse, potentially looking to expose us. It was the fact that the body had been found in the middle of the living room. No nightwalker was stupid enough to sleep out in the open, even when in the safety of his own lair. It was the way Bryce had been killed—by the old mythological methods, head and heart removed.

The whole thing stank of the Daylight Coalition and yet I felt confident that no branch members resided within my domain. The Daylight Coalition was an all-human organization that believed in the existence of vampires and other supernatural creatures. They saw it as their duty to hunt us all down. Their aim wasn't too good, however, considering they had killed as many humans as they had nightwalkers. The rest of the human world thought they were a bunch of crackpots who had watched *Van Helsing* one too many times. I tended to agree.

I downshifted the car into second as I turned onto Bryce's street. The houses were spaced relatively far apart, with large yards filled with massive honeysuckle bushes and white jasmine. The air was thick with the rich scent of flowers and damp earth. Across the street from the two-story, redbrick house, I parked the car and turned off the engine. Using my powers, I briefly scanned the region. There were only a few nightwalkers in the area, and one of them was Bishop. I suspected he was going to be my shadow until this little investigation was finally concluded.

Another was standing just at the end of the block. Her name was Heather, and she was also a member of the Ravana family. Word traveled fast among telepaths. Without my needing to say a word, most of the city nightwalkers knew that a vampire had been murdered. In general, they were willing to give me a wide berth so I could investigate the matter, but I had been expecting someone from the Ravana family. Bryce's death was their business.

I hesitated, my right hand still clutching the key in the ignition. Something felt off. We sat in the car, waiting for the brunette to finally reach us. She stood in the street a few feet away from where I sat in the car. She looked lost and afraid, with her right hand gripping her left elbow.

"Do you know if he had anyone else staying with him in the house?" I asked.

"No one on a permanent basis," she said shaking her head, sending her long brown hair down around her face. "I think he had nightwalkers that stayed for brief periods of time here and there, but nothing permanent."

I was willing to guess that Bryce was one of the few within the Ravana family that was permitted to keep a residence outside the main family home. Justin believed in spreading out his clan throughout the city so that his influence could be felt everywhere. Older, trusted members were allowed their own homes as long as they checked in on a regular basis. This wasn't an original idea within the nightwalker world, just rare.

I listened into the thoughts of all the humans with a one-block radius, but they were all consumed with their own problems—bills, sickness, doubt. No one was thinking of the body that was taken out of the lonely redbrick house. Even all the lycanthropes had left this section of the city. I had a feeling I had Barrett Rainer, Alpha of the Savannah Pack, to thank for the extra space.

Sitting in the car for another minute, we all stared across the street at the dark house. The feeling of foreboding was irrational. I was unnerved by the way Bryce was killed and I was afraid of what I would find inside. We were all completely helpless during the daylight hours; unable to awaken, unable to defend ourselves. That was our greatest fear—to go to sleep one morning and not awaken the next night.

"Let's get this done," I announced gruffly, jerking the key from the ignition with a soft jingle. We both alighted from the tiny car and crossed the street in silence. There was only the sound of the wind rustling the leaves in the trees and a distant wind chime singing a forlorn melody. The air was still hot and heavy even after nightfall.

"Why would someone kill Bryce?" Heather softly asked, walking a couple steps behind me.

"*Who* and *why* are the questions we're trying to answer," I said a bit irritably. Stopping short, I spun around on my right heel to face the young fledgling. "Why did Justin send you here?"

"He . . . I . . . he said I was to help you in any way I could. Bryce was part of the family. Justin cares about us," she replied in an almost mechanical manner.

I snorted and turned back toward the house. She had been sent to spy on me and report back to Justin.

"You go in through the back and search the second

floor," I said, looking over at Knox as we walked up the sidewalk and past a pair of stone urns overflowing with what appeared to be a fuchsia plant. "I'll go in through the front door and search the first floor."

"Anything in particular I'm looking for?"

I paused with my foot on the bottom step leading up to the front porch. The wooden board was warped from age and covered in peeling white paint that crunched under my running shoe. "We're looking for any sign of a struggle. Also, look for Bryce's daylight chamber. Was he taken out of there or did he actually fall asleep out in the open in the living room?"

Knox stared at me for a second, his blond brows bunched together over his nose. "You think the killer knew exactly where to find him?"

"Maybe. We won't know until we get in there and look around."

"What should I do?" Heather asked.

"Go with Knox. Help him, but stay out of his way."

Heather quickly nodded, her arms wrapped around her middle as she moved to follow after the other nightwalker. I mounted the warped stairs to the front porch, watching Knox out of the corner of my eye as he circled around the porch and headed toward the back door. A mechanical whir caught my attention, drawing my gaze toward the ceiling above the door. The tiny red light on the remote video camera blinked once.

The world around me exploded. I flew backward through the air and bounced once before finally landing on my back in the yard. Bricks, chunks of flaming wood, and other bits of debris followed me, crashing to the ground and on top of me. My head throbbed and there was an annoying ringing in my ears. A hundred different pains radiated through my body. Groaning, I rolled over onto my side to find most of the house in the yard with me, while what remained on the foundation was engulfed in flames. So much for our investigation.

Reaching out with my powers, I searched for Knox. He was still alive, but his thoughts were consumed with terror. He was on fire. Pushing to my feet, I ran as fast as my protesting body would allow. My vision blurred as I ran around the side of the house, blood flowing into my left eye from a gash on my forehead.

I found Knox rolling on the ground, struggling to put out the fire on his right arm and on his pant legs. Panic overwhelmed him. With a wave of my hand, the fire immediately went out, but he continued to roll. Kneeling next to him, I grabbed his shoulders and forced him to sit up.

"Fire! I'm burning! Please! Stop it! Help!" Knox babbled desperately, still trying to pat his legs.

"The fire's out!" I shouted at him, giving him a hard shake.

The nightwalker blinked a couple times before his gaze focused on me. His whole body was trembling, and tears had begun to streak down his cut, bloody face. Some distant part of me could understand his fears. Most nightwalkers burned so easily, like dry kindling, and the moment Knox had caught fire he was sure that he was dead. And maybe he would have been if I hadn't been here to control the fire.

"You're going to be okay," I murmured, relaxing my hold on his shoulders. My stomach twisted at the feeling of him shaking violently in my hands. Knox nodded his head slowly and looked down at the palms of his hands. They were blistered and burned from where he had tried to beat the fire out. "It could be worse," I announced, drawing his gaze up to my face. "The fire could have started at your crotch."

"You're sick," he snapped. He scowled at me, which was better than the terror that had gripped him earlier. "What happened?"

"A bomb."

"No kidding. I mean, what set it off?"

That was the real question. I wagged my eyebrows at him once before pushing to my feet.

"Where's Heather?" I asked as I helped Knox rise as well. We found her lying dead a few feet away from where Knox had landed. A brick from the house had crushed the back of her skull, splattering her brains. There was no recovering from such a wound in our world. She was gone so quickly, and only because she was in the wrong place at the wrong time.

This was not going to go over well with Justin. First, a member of his family is murdered by some unknown killer. Then a second member is killed while kindly helping me in the investigation. If I had any sense, I would have sent her away, but as a member of the Ravana family, she had a right to be there as well.

The cry of a fire engine off in the distance seeped into my thoughts. It was getting closer. We needed to get out of here before too large of a crowd gathered—we'd have to alter the memories of a handful of humans as it was. Picking up Heather, I tossed her into the fire that was growing in the remains of the house. She would be incinerated along with the rest of the evidence of Bryce's existence and any evidence related to his killer.

With Knox hobbling along beside me, I increased the fire eating away at the remains of the house once we were in the street. If I wasn't going to be able to get into the house then no one would. By the time the fire department got this fire out, there would be nothing left but hot ash.

We were speeding back to the city when Knox started speaking again. However, his brain wasn't totally functioning yet. "I don't understand," he muttered. "Why destroy the evidence after the police had gone through the place during the day?"

"That wasn't the purpose of the explosion."

"What do you mean?"

"You think it was a coincidence that the place blew up when we just happened to be there?" I laughed.

"You think someone was trying to kill us?" Knox

twisted in his seat, sending his blond hair flying in wild disarray in the wind.

I was beginning to think that someone was trying to kill me. First the Coven flunky's arrival, and now the explosion just as I was entering the house. The timing was too perfect.

"There was a camera on the front porch," I explained, keeping my theory to myself for now. No reason to upset Knox just yet. "The same person that killed Bryce knew someone would be by to investigate. I think this person was waiting for someone that didn't look like a cop." And for the murderer, I fit the bill. I didn't look like a police officer in my blue jeans and black button-up shirt. But then, there was enough otherness in my lavender eyes and ultra pale skin to make some people wonder if I was even human.

"But I didn't sense anyone . . . I mean, I scanned the area and no one wanted us dead."

"It could have been done by remote, allowing the person to be miles away."

"And now he knows you're associated with Bryce. If he knew Bryce was a nightwalker, he's going to assume you're . . ."

"Yeah, I've got a brand-new problem," I grumbled. It had now become even more imperative that I find Bryce's murderer. This person had seen my face. If the murderer knew Bryce was a nightwalker, I now fell under that same classification. As a result, anyone I associated with would now come under scrutiny. I slowed the car to a stop at a red light. We were just outside of town, driving along the Savannah River headed toward the riverfront district. "I think a member of the Daylight Coalition killed Bryce and tried to kill us tonight."

"Because of how he was killed?"

"As well as the timing and the call to the police. Regardless of the reasons for killing Bryce, no nightwalker would risk a human discovering the corpse. Someone knew he was a nightwalker and wanted proof to get out to the rest of the world. This murder was done during the daylight hours when Bryce wouldn't have been able to fight back."

"Then why not a shapeshifter? They can walk around during the day," Knox argued, drumming his fingers on the armrest. I doubted he actually believed it, but he was doing his job and playing devil's advocate.

"A lycan would have the opportunity, but the risk of exposure is too great. No matter how pissed you are, we all know not to reveal our secret to another human. If the lycan was discovered, not only would his life be forfeit but there's a good chance that the whole pack would be destroyed." I shifted the car into first and pushed on the accelerator as the light changed to green. "You're right that it is a possibility, just not a very strong one," I conceded. "I'll check in with Barrett and see if he knows anything about Bryce or if the nightwalker was known to associate with any shifter. At the same time, I want you to check among the nightwalkers. I want to know who he associated with."

"You think someone tipped off the Coalition?"

"Maybe."

"Anything else?"

"Yeah, what's the name of the girl Bryce wanted to change?"

"Katie Hixson. She's about thirty-two years old. Medium height, slim, with short blond hair and blue eyes," Knox listed succinctly.

"Do you know her address?"

"No, I'm afraid I don't."

I downshifted the car as I pulled over to the side of the road just outside the Dark Room, a nightclub in that catered only to nightwalkers and lycanthropes. A long line had already begun to stretch outside the bar as a mix of shifters and nightwalkers hoped to get in tonight. It was one of the few places you were likely to run into the nightwalker you were looking for.

"That's okay. Daniel can locate her for me. You start digging around in Bryce's past. Call me if you find anything interesting."

Knox nodded once and slowly got out of the car. By the expression that flashed across his face, each motion was painful. After closing the door, he leaned forward on it, wincing as it cut into his wounded hands. "I'm sorry about the morgue and how I . . . performed at the house. I—"

"Let it go, Knox. This job takes some getting used to. I'm not Valerio." I was quick to cut him off. I didn't want his apologies, particularly out in the open where any night-walker might be able to hear him. We needed a strong front or there would be the chaos Bishop was so confident was everywhere within my domain. "Just get to work. I'll be in contact."

"Mira, you realize that if the Daylight Coalition is behind this, there is a very good chance a member now has your photograph," Knox grimly pointed out.

"Well, I guess we're going to have to get this bastard, because I'm not moving," I said with a smirk. "Get to work."

The thought chilled me to the shreds of my soul. I had lived more than six hundred years and had never come close to exposing what I was to the world at large. But now it was a very real threat that my identity was in jeopardy. At the very least, I would become the main target for all of the Daylight Coalition.

As I drove off, heading to a quieter part of the city, I pushed the speaker button on my steering wheel and said Daniel's name into the open air. The Bluetooth connection to my cell phone quickly dialed the number.

"I'm a little busy right now," Daniel's voice growled from the speakers of my car.

"I have no doubt you are, but I need your help," I said, pulling into a dark parking lot. "I have a lead in the case we discussed, but I need you to track her down for me. Name's Katie Hixson. Slim build with blond hair—"

"And blue eyes," Daniel finished in a suddenly weary voice.

"You know her?" I was stunned. What were the odds that Daniel knew this nightwalker wannabe?

"Yeah."

"Do you know where I can find her?"

"Yeah, I'm with her now. She's dead, Mira."

4

A dozen profanities tumbled past my lips, filling the air. It was a good thing that the residents of Savannah didn't know seventeenth century Italian curses or I might have blushed.

"Are you sure she's dead?" It was a stupid question, but I couldn't afford for Katie to be dead. Sure, I had planned to kill her if she had anything to do with Bryce's murder, but that was only *after* I had managed to extract some information from her still-living brain.

"I know dead, Mira," Daniel snarled. "Her neck has been broken and she's been drained of blood. She looks like a gray raisin. She's dead."

I pounded the steering wheel once with my fist and swallowed a fresh round of curses. This was not how my night was supposed to go. I had hoped to have this whole mess settled before sunrise, but I was beginning to have serious doubts. Bishop was going to serve my head up on a silver platter to the Coven if I continued at this rate. That was assuming the Daylight Coalition didn't get ahold of me first.

"Where did you find her?" I bit out, trying to rein in my temper. My hands had begun to tremble and it felt as if my throat was starting to close up in fear. I wouldn't let the Coven take me.

"At home. Her neighbor called. She got concerned when she saw the front door left open." The scrape of Daniel's shoes on concrete could be heard in the background. It sounded like he was pacing outside, the one place he could get a little privacy at a murder investigation.

"A wild guess, but the neighbor didn't see anything?"

"Not a thing. Not even sure when Ms. Hixson got home."

"Has Archie arrived yet?"

"He's on his way."

"Tell him to stall if necessary. I want to look at the body before you move it. What's the address?"

Daniel gave me quick directions as I shifted back into first and drove out of the dark parking lot. Once I found the right street, the house would be easy to identify. It would be the one surrounded by flashing cop cars and decorated in yellow tape like a giant Christmas tree.

I flew through the gears, zipping across town as fast as I could. Katie's house was just on the outskirts of the city on the opposite end from where Bryce's nighttime lair was located. While Bryce's death had annoyed me, Katie's obvious murder had caused a knot of worry to start growing in my stomach. Had someone else known about her involvement with Bryce and killed her in fear that she knew something or saw something? Or maybe someone thought she was responsible for Bryce's untimely demise and had murdered her in revenge?

Yet all these concerns and speculation were pushed to back of my mind as I parked my car at the end of the block from Katie's house. I had briefly hoped it would be in a questionable part of town so her death could be pawned off as a flash of random violence in a violent neighborhood. Unfortunately, Katie had owned a house in a quiet, family-oriented part of town with its neighborhood watches, window boxes, and decorative flags celebrating the upcoming start of summer. Not the type of place a body was supposed to be found drained and broken.

Popping the trunk, I walked around to the back of the car and pulled out a black blazer. I quickly tucked my shirt into my jeans and pulled on the jacket. I briefly tried to straighten my hair and wipe away some of the blood that covered the side of my face. Without seeing a mirror, I knew I looked like I had been dragged through hell. Yet part of convincing a human that we were something other than what we really were was giving them a good reason to believe us. And right now, I needed to be able to convince the cops milling around this crime scene that I was just another detective.

With my shoulders back and my head up, I walked down the street and past the threshold of the house, pausing long enough to wipe my feet on the brown and black welcome mat. As I passed each police officer, detective, and forensic investigator, I mentally pushed the image of my being another detective into their brains. It took a little extra push because my jeans were torn and dirty. There was also dried blood on my temple and along the side of my face from where my scalp had been cut by flying debris at Bryce's house.

The process was tiring and the strain was already causing my head to throb along with all the other aches in my body. There were close to a dozen people in the area, not counting the neighbors that were standing in their front yards with looks of horror stretched across their faces. Normally, I wouldn't dare to come into a crime scene littered with so many people, but three people were dead in less than twenty-four hours and I was beginning to fear that the body count was going to continue to rise if I didn't find the killer soon. My people didn't need to be drawn into the spotlight by some psychopathic loose cannon.

In the living room, I found Daniel standing on the fringe of the group huddled around the body sprawled on the floor. His lips were drawn into a frown, causing deep lines to crease his face. An unlit cigarette dangled from his fingertips, waiting for him to finally step outside again so he could light it.

The room was a cheery affair in pale orange with a darker orange acting as an accent. The sofa and chair were covered in white linen and surrounded a honey-wood coffee table. Pictures of flowers in black metal frames lined the walls.

Katie lay on the floor with her arms folded over her chest. It was strange. There was no look of strain on her face, no fear. From what I could see, there were no bruises, scratches, or signs that she had fought for her life. It looked as if someone had lovingly laid her on the ground after he or she was done with the distasteful task of killing the young woman.

But Daniel was right. Her head lay at a slightly odd angle, and broken bone poked and stretched the skin. Her neck had been completely snapped. Not the easiest of feats, and it was very likely that it had been done by a nightwalker. Her skin was also a stomach-turning shade of gray that sagged and hung loose on her body. Someone had drained her of all her blood. But I didn't know of any nightwalker that could do such a thing in a single feeding, and this whole thing felt too neat for several nightwalkers to be involved.

"Forced entry?" I murmured as I came to stand next to Daniel. We both watched as one of the investigators snapped a series of pictures of the body and the rest of the room.

"No," Daniel said, pulling the cigarette box from his pants pocket. He returned the loose cigarette back to the box and put the box in his pocket again. "It looks like Ms. Hixson let the murderer in. There's no sign of struggle. She probably had no idea she was in danger."

Katie probably knew her attacker. She let the person in when he or she arrived. And when she turned her back on her attacker, the murderer snapped her neck with no pain and little fuss. I frowned. I just couldn't figure out who the killer was or why Katie was killed shortly after Bryce. Maybe they weren't necessarily related.

Daniel finally looked over at me and nearly stumbled a step backward. I hadn't bothered to adjust his perception of me. There was no need, and I had enough on my plate already. "You look like shit," he whispered, trying to avoid drawing the attention of the others.

"So kind of you to say so," I muttered.

"Trouble at the house?"

"It's not there anymore."

Daniel sighed as he rubbed his eyes and the bridge of his nose. "Did you cause that?"

"I wouldn't look like this if I did," I grumbled.

"Same killer?" he whispered.

I shook my head slowly, frowning. "No." I knew without a doubt that a nightwalker had killed Katie, while a human had been responsible for Bryce's death.

"Linked?"

"I . . . I don't know," I admitted, wishing I didn't have to.

Shaking my head, I left Daniel's side and approached the corpse. I knelt down, ignoring the strange looks I was receiving, and bent over to sniff the body. Before I could get my face close to her, I picked up the overwhelming scent of perfume. It was everywhere; on Katie's clothes, her hair, her skin. Whoever had touched her was smart enough to douse himself or herself in perfume so I couldn't pick up the individual scent. Only a lycanthrope might have a strong enough sense of smell to pick it out, but there was a good chance that he wouldn't recognize the scent of the nightwalker. Otherwise, Katie's body did not yet reek of death and decay. She had been dead for less than two hours. Her neighbor had just missed walking in on the murder.

The one thing I was sure of was the fact that Katie had been killed by a nightwalker and the murder had occurred shortly after sunset, by someone the woman had possibly known. Katie's death was too neat and tidy, and there was a lingering feeling of mercy and compassion. This was done by someone who knew her.

Pushing back to my feet, I walked back over to Daniel, keeping my back to the rest of the room. "Tell Archie to call me if anything interesting turns up."

"You think something will?" he mocked me. We were looking at a woman that had been killed by the breaking of her neck and then drained of her blood, but there wasn't a drop on the pale tan carpet.

"Like no puncture marks on an exsanguinated corpse?" I offered. When I was kneeling next to Katie, I noticed no puncture marks on her neck or in the interior of her arms. It was possible they were somewhere else on her body, but it was unlikely. It was more likely the nightwalker had healed the wound out of habit. "Yeah, he'll find something interesting. You might want to also check the bathtub. Some of the blood might have been sent down the drain. I'll be in contact."

I quickly left the house and headed back to my car. This wasn't good. I had a third dead body, and this one was caused by a nightwalker. The peace in my domain was crumbling around me, and the worse it got, the better the chance of humans discovering our secret.

Popping the trunk of my car with my remote, I tossed the blazer inside and pulled my shirt back out of my jeans. The night was not going well and it was about to get worse.

"I don't think doing a striptease in the middle of the street is going to convince me to allow you to slide on this mess you've got in your domain. That's the third dead body tonight, isn't it?" Bishop asked from where he leaned up against a tree just a few paces from my car. I hadn't noticed him there when I walked up because my mind was stuck on the problem at hand.

"You realize that I'm being set up," I snarled at him, my temper getting worse as fear flooded my veins.

"You're saying that all these people are being killed just to make you look bad so that you'll be sent back to the Coven," Bishop sarcastically said, scratching his chin. "It's a possibility."

"Damn it, Bishop!" I stomped over to where he stood leaning against the tree, his arms folded over his large chest.

"You know me. You know what we're capable of. I'm being set up."

"And it's working."

Snarling, I took a swing at him, but he was expecting it. Pushing off the tree, he grabbed both of my wrists and pinned them over my head against the tree. He pressed in close so that his face filled my field of vision. I positively itched to put my knee in his groin, but I waited to hear what he had to say.

"It's working, Mira. Someone probably does have it in for you and they're successfully setting you up. How many enemies could you possibly have here?"

"A few," I admitted. Justin Ravana instantly came to mind. While he had never made any play to seize power of the domain from me, he had always been a steady voice of unrest. But in the end, he kept to himself so I let him be.

"Would any of these enemies have a reason to kill this poor human?"

"One would," I growled. Killing Katie would be Justin's way of wiping out the last of Bryce's ties while potentially making me look bad in front of the Coven. Justin was my next target, and I was happy to take the fight to him.

Frowning, I stared at Bishop for a moment, trying to suppress my few memories of the nightwalker. Too many nights washed in blood and violence. "You know I can clean this up and get the territory back under control. This is about Macaire wanting me under his thumb in Venice," I said, shifting slightly so that the tree bark wasn't biting into my back. Macaire had hated me since Jabari had taken me under his wing five centuries ago. With Jabari now missing, the ancient nightwalker now thought it was safe to make his move against me, and if I didn't think of something fast, it was going to work.

"Why does it have to be about only Macaire?" Bishop shifted his hands so that my wrists were held loosely in one of his large hands. His left hand came down and moved some hair away from my face. "Admit it, Mira. We had fun in Venice together. You used to enjoy our games with the fledglings. Hell, they feared you more than the entire Coven. You thrived on their fear. Why don't you just come home? Macaire will leave you alone if you listen to him."

"I can't go back to that life. I've outgrown it. This is my home now," I said. Leaning forward, I brushed my lips across his cheek. "Why can't you stay here?" I whispered. "You've been with the Coven most of your life. You've got to be growing weary of it. Stay here with me. Make this your new home."

"And go from being a messenger for the Coven to being a flunky for the Fire Starter? Not likely," he said snidely.

"No. Just live here. Be your own person."

Bishop stared silently at me for a minute, the skepticism clear on his face, but I could also see the hope in his eyes. The offer was appealing. Bishop had a lot of freedom due to his position within the court, but not true freedom—not like what I was offering.

"It's tempting, but not everyone's master is as forgiving. My leash is not quite as long as yours," he said, releasing my hands as he stepped away from me. And it was true. I didn't belong to Jabari in the same way Bishop belonged to Macaire. Yet if Jabari demanded I return to Venice, I would out of loyalty and a good dose of fear.

"Then all I ask is that you be fair about this," I pleaded, cupping his face with my hands. "Give me a chance to fix this."

"You're flailing."

"Temporarily. I can fix this."

"One more dead body not of your own making and you're going back with me," Bishop warned, gently lowering my hands from his face.

I nodded, pulling from his grip. "The offer still stands. You're welcome here."

"Maybe someday, but not now, not like this."

5

I was done chasing my tail. I was ready to take the fight to the one person who had the most to gain from my removal. Justin Ravana's three-story brick house was located on a hill on the outskirts of the city. Its location not only allowed him to easily sense the approach of any nightwalker, but he could watch them crawl up his hill like a supplicant coming to request a boon.

Driving up the hill, I realized that I had made a mistake in the handling of him. I had thought that he would be content to rule over his family, and for a time he had been, but now he wanted to take all of Savannah from me. For him, the easiest way to claim it would be through the Coven. I had little doubt that he had been the little bird chirping in the ear of Macaire, telling his lies so that I would be drawn back to Venice and all her horrors.

My temper was barely caged when one of Justin's fledglings showed me to the main parlor where Justin sat waiting for me. The air in the house was thick with the scent of blood and fear. Muffled screams and heavy footsteps could be heard on wooden floors about me.

"Mira, this is a surprise," Justin opened, pushing slowly out of his cushioned high-backed chair as if he was reluctant to rise to his feet in my presence.

"It shouldn't be. Bryce belonged to you, didn't he?"

"And so did poor Heather. Savannah has certainly

become a dangerous place to live," he said with a shake of his head.

"I'm sure your fledglings would argue that it always has been."

A smile toyed with his lips as his eyes traveled over the length of me. "Yes, well, one has to do what one must to keep the young ones in line."

"And what did Bryce do to deserve the death he received?"

"You think I had something to do with Bryce's death?" he gasped, looking honestly surprised. "Mira, you know my methods." Again, the same dark grin spread across his lean, angular face, reminding me so much of an animated skull. "If Bryce had crossed me, I would have taken care of the matter here, in the privacy of my own home. I would have kept the matter in the family."

"So the fact that Bryce had come to me looking to make his own fledgling didn't bother you?" I asked.

Justin sat back down in the chair he had been seated in, his sharp gaze drifting away from me to a spot on the floor. His left hand curled into a fist on the arm of the chair, but his voice was calm, even when he spoke again. "I was . . . unaware of his request, but Bryce knew that I would not object to expanding the family. I would have welcomed his fledgling."

"Maybe that's just it. He didn't want this fledgling to be a part of the Ravana family. He possibly wanted something outside of your reach," I said, purposefully twisting the knife in his chest as I struggled to keep the smile off of my face.

"Then I would have killed him, but again I would have done it my way. Here and slowly. I'm afraid if you came here looking for Bryce's killer, you have come to the wrong place."

Unfortunately, I believed him. "No, that's not the only reason why I'm here," I said with a smile. I was about to comment on his recent trip to see the Coven when a bloodcurdling scream rent the air, effectively silencing me and wiping the smile from my face. We both looked up at the ceiling. I got flashes of a naked female chained to the brick wall in the attic being tortured by a lycanthrope and three other nightwalkers. She was streaked with blood, and her face was swollen to the point that she could barely see out of her puffy eyes. One of her tormentors was projecting the fight for Justin's benefit since the master of the family was stuck dealing with me.

"Who—?"

"A new fledgling that has elected to join the Ravana family. She's being broken in. Would you like to help?"

"No."

"But it's been so long since you took the time to appropriately break in a fledgling. These young ones have no concept any longer of what it means to exist in our world. They don't respect you as they should."

"I want no part of your games," I growled.

"But you must. My fledglings ask that you show them what you truly are capable of, great Fire Starter." There was no missing the sarcasm that was etched into every word he had spoken. A knot twisted in my stomach, and for the first time, I fully scanned the house. There were close to thirty nightwalkers in this house. I had walked into a trap he had been waiting years to spring. Justin hadn't been building a family; he had been building an army of fledglings for the sole purpose of killing me.

Two sets of doors opened on the parlor as Justin rose and walked over to stand near the wall next to a fire extinguisher. A smug smile lifted his features at the same time more than a dozen nightwalkers rushed into the room. There was no time for clear thought, no room for delicacy. Each one of Justin's fledglings wanted to kill me.

I dodged fists and clawing nails as I quickly delivered as many blows as possible. There was no time to punch into a chest and rip out a heart. I could only try to knock out as many as possible. I grabbed one snarling body and threw it into the crowd, hoping to create a hole so that I could make a mad dash for the front door. I needed to get out of this room and into a more open area. But the crowd bounced back as quickly as it crumbled, keeping me trapped in the confines of the congested parlor.

There were too many of them. Pain rippled through my body as fists connected with my vital organs and rained on my head and face. I held my own until someone grabbed a chair and hit me in the back, knocking me to my knees. Another kicked me under the chin, throwing me to my back. A cry escaped me as pain flashed through my body. While I was down, a large, hulking nightwalker straddled me and raised his hand with the intent of plunging it into my chest.

Time slowed down for that second and the world drifted away so that there was only that blond nightwalker with a look of triumph on his face. Fear brought a scream to my lips as he erupted into flames. As I expected, he was immediately hit with the white spray of the fire extinguisher, but that didn't stop me. I focused my powers, burning him on the inside and out. He howled, rolling off me. The nightwalker clawed at his chest until fire finally peeked through his blackened skin. The other nightwalkers drew back, but that didn't save them.

Sitting up, I directed my powers to all those around me, burning them on the inside and out, cooking them so thoroughly that Justin and his little fire extinguisher couldn't save one of them. Chaos reigned in the house, but it was my brand of chaos. While I burned any nightwalker that I saw, I also projected the images throughout all of Savannah. Any nightwalker within range would see the bloodbath that was raging through the house.

I am the Fire Starter! I am the Keeper of this domain! This was my answer to the chaos and the threats around me.

I thought I heard Bishop's laughter in my head as I doused the last of the flames and rose to my feet. The room was filled with charred, blackened bodies. Justin was in the far corner, still holding the now empty fire extinguisher. I smiled at him as I approached.

"You were right," I said, grabbing a handful of his brown hair and slamming his head into the wall. "It has been way too long since I properly broke in a fledgling. It's a shame about your family, though. I think I destroyed most of them."

"Mira—"

"The Ravana family is no more. You will return to the Coven and tell them that I have restored order here."

"Y-y-yes," he agreed, attempting to nod, but he couldn't move his head within my grip.

"And when I see you again, I will kill you."

Releasing him, I stepped over the bodies of the dead and walked out to my car. I didn't expect Justin to go to the Coven. It worked to his benefit if they thought that the city was still a mess. But that didn't matter now. Bishop had witnessed the cleansing.

Nice job, came Bishop's taunting voice in my head.

Will that do? I asked, ready to have him out of my hair and back to the Coven reporting the good news.

Not quite. You have no proof that you actually killed the murderer.

Soon.

6

Leaning against my car, I pulled my cell phone from my back pocket. My hands were shaking and my legs were weak beneath me, threatening to buckle. I hurt in a dozen different places, and they all seemed to be healing too slowly for my liking. Hunger gnawed at me, begging me to stop long enough to feed. I had lost too much blood between the explosion at Bryce's house and this fight. I needed to rest and heal, but there simply wasn't time with Bishop lurking around in my domain. I had to press on despite my growing weakness.

I dialed Barrett Rainer's number, grateful that I finally had something work in my favor. With the presence of the lycanthrope at the Ravana house, I now had the leverage I needed to call in a favor from the Alpha for the Savannah Pack. Lycans were not supposed to take part in the torture of fledglings. Justin was correct in that it was part of our breaking-in process, and lycans were not supposed to be around to muddy up the waters when allegiance was on the line.

While I wouldn't necessarily refer to Barrett as a friend, we were on comfortable, civil terms. In general, our contact was limited to the occasional check-in around the full moon and if there was some kind of problem.

"Having a good night?" Barrett's deep baritone filled my ear when he answered the call. The grapevine in the supernatural realm was fast and far-reaching. I wasn't at all surprised that he knew about Bryce's murder and probably the explosion as well. Katie's death would take longer to spread since she was human.

"I've had better," I growled, pacing away from the rear of the car. "I have a favor to call in."

"I've got problems of my own at the moment. Why do I owe you a favor?"

"I caught a lycan at Ravana's taking part in the torture of a fledgling. You know that it's not permitted. I left him alive for you to deal with, but . . ."

"But I now owe you a favor," he bit out.

"I need you to get your boys out looking for someone for me. A member of the Daylight Coalition. There's at least one in town. I'm willing to bet that he's behind Bryce's murder and the attempt on my life."

"Actually, I've got someone here that might interest you," Barrett announced. I could easily imagine the smug smile that spread across his hard, angular face.

My feet skid to a halt in the gravel-riddled street. I stood with my back to Ravana's house and faced the growing darkness. "What do you mean?"

"Someone from the Daylight Coalition just walked into my restaurant and ordered dinner." Barrett owned and operated an Italian restaurant downtown called Bella Luna, which was somewhat ironic since his family's ancestry was mostly German. Apparently, at some point, a member of his family married an Italian woman, and she started the restaurant that has been handed down over the generations.

"What? Did he flash his official Daylight Coalition membership card hoping to get a discount?" I didn't mean to be so snide, but fear and frustration were eating away at me. I was running out of time before Bishop arrived to claim my hide.

"Hardly. I can read his thoughts." He sounded much calmer than me. It was quiet where he was, making me think that he had called from his office rather than standing over a potentially half-dead man. If it was known that someone was from the Coalition, many of our kind would take it upon themselves to immediately cut short his life span. Neither side did anything to put a halt to these activities as long as no evidence was left behind. It wasn't a pretty arrangement, but it was get them before they got us.

"Besides," the lycanthrope said, his voice dropping a little closer to a growl for the first time since he had called. "We get them on occasion. They pop into the bars, restaurants, and shops with any form of the word *moon* in the name. I guess they're hoping to catch us acting like animals so they can do the world a great service and put us down."

I paced back toward the car, shoving one hand through my hair, getting my fingers temporarily stuck. My dirty, blood-matted hair was a knotted mess. "Are you going to put him down or are you going to let me talk to him first?" I needed to know if our unexpected guest to the city of Savannah had anything to do with Bryce's murder.

"Will he survive the interview?"

"It depends on his answers. It's doubtful."

"Then you can have him."

I clenched my teeth and swallowed my next snide comment. I was determined to have this man regardless of what Barrett's wishes were. Two nightwalkers were dead, a house had been blown up, and a human was dead in connection to one of the dead nightwalkers. And now I had some unknown Daylight Coalition schmuck wandering around in my territory. He had to be connected to this mess in some way. I just had to figure out how he fit in this puzzle.

"How much longer do you think he'll be at the restaurant?" I demanded as I reached into the front pocket of my jeans and pulled out the keys.

"Probably another thirty minutes at the most. He's already ordered his dinner and it should be arriving within a couple minutes."

"That's fine. I can be there by then. I'll park behind the restaurant and follow him after he leaves."

I paused as I was about to jump in the car and looked up at Ravana's house. The fledgling was still in the attic, chained to the wall. For a moment, I wondered if I should go up and free her, but I quickly shook off the thought and got into the car. If she couldn't find a way to free herself, then she would never survive in my world.

Back in the car, I was flying across the city. The restaurant was downtown, not far from the Dark Room. I planned on swinging by to get Knox before arriving at the restaurant. I didn't particularly need the backup, but this was Knox's investigation, and I had a feeling we would be able to get a lot out of this human if we could keep him alive long enough to pick his brain.

"I have to get back," Knox announced as he fell into the passenger seat beside me. "Gregor knew Bryce and Katie." I had filled him in about Katie's death when I called to tell him I would pick him up. He already knew about what happened at Justin's; all the city's nightwalkers knew about that.

"Hopefully, he'll stay alive long enough to be questioned," I said under my breath.

"Another body?"

"Not yet, but our luck hasn't been that good tonight." I looked over my shoulder at the front entrance where a nightwalker bouncer by the name of Adam stood glaring at the crowd. His brown hair was cropped short on his head and his black T-shirt was stretched over bulging muscles, making him an impressive figure even if he hadn't been a nightwalker.

Adam, tell Gregor that I want him to remain here when he arrives. Knox and I want to speak with him. This message was conveyed with a brief touch of my mind to his. Yet, no matter how brief, I could still feel the flood of fear that shivered through him at my touch. I tried to ignore it, but there were times when it ate at me nonetheless. I was trying to protect him and all of my kind, but he feared me like most nightwalkers feared the Coven. And after what had happened at Ravana's, it was worse than usual. I could feel a wave of fear crashing off all the nightwalkers that saw me outside the club.

Turning my attention back to the road, I let off the clutch and jumped out into the traffic. We rushed down to the river, cutting down and around one street after another as we drew closer to Bella Luna. It took only a few minutes to reach the restaurant, leaving me to settle the car in a shadowy area in the back where the deliveries were made.

"Do I scare you?" I asked without warning after sitting in silence for several minutes.

"I beg your pardon." Knox turned in his seat and looked at me, his lips twisting slightly as he was fighting to hold back a smile.

"Do I scare you?" It was harder to say the second time, but I forced the words out.

"Scare me?" Knox stared at me for a moment before a sigh finally escaped him. He leaned his right elbow on the door and shoved his fingers through his dirty, bloody blond hair. He had taken the time to clean up slightly while at the club, but he still looked ragged. "Mira, I feel like there's no right answer here."

Slumping in my seat, I relaxed my grip on the steering wheel, letting my hand fall into my lap. "You know me, Knox. I want the truth."

"Yes, you scare me. You know you do. After the show of power at Justin's, how could we all not fear you?" Knox said in a sudden rush as if the words were stampeding from his chest. "You're the Fire Starter. You can kill us all with a thought. And even if you weren't the Fire Starter, you're still powerful enough to wipe the floor with any one of us. So, yes, you scare me."

"But . . ." I inserted, prompting him to continue when he seemed to hesitate.

"But I know Valerio. I spent more than two centuries with my maker. You've known him for even longer. I think you're more like him than you sometimes realize. You're more emotional, but you can be just as methodical. Whether

Five
Nov

anyone else realizes it, there's a method to your madness, like Valerio. You're about protecting the secret and being honorable. As long as a nightwalker doesn't cross those two lines, he's going to wake up the next sunset. The others don't realize it, do they?"

"I can feel it when I enter a room or when I touch their minds. I can feel the shiver of fear, the recoil when I get too close. I feel trapped. I don't want them to fear me, yet the only way I can get their complete obedience is for them to fear me." Each word was forced out between my clenched teeth. I was tired of being the outsider after more than six centuries of life. I was tired of being the outsider within my own domain.

"Do you know what would make it easier for them to accept you?"

I shifted in my seat slightly and looked over at my companion, surprised that he was willing to offer me a suggestion. "What?"

"Date another nightwalker."

I chuckled softly to myself and shook my head. "You're kidding, right?"

"No, I'm not. I've been here awhile and I've never heard of you with another nightwalker."

I looked over at Knox again, stunned to find that he was absolutely serious about this ridiculous suggestion. "Not a chance."

"Mira, dating another nightwalker within your domain might convince them that you're not a heartless killing machine. That there is something feeling about you."

"Mmm . . . your comments warm my cold, dead heart," I mocked. This conversation was taking a turn that I wasn't expecting. I turned the key in the ignition enough to get the clock radio to flash on. We had been sitting there for only a couple of minutes. *Damn it!* I had started this nightmare conversation.

"I'm serious."

"So, what? Are you offering to be my boyfriend?"

Knox stared at me for a long time, his eyes moving over

my face. I knew I looked like a mess. All the wounds I had
sustained while at Bryce's and Justin's had healed, but I was
still covered in my own blood along with dirt and a little
of Knox's blood. There was nothing attractive about me at
this moment in time. But it was more than that. Knox knew
better than most who I was. He knew of me before we had
ever met. His maker, Valerio, and I had run together for a
few centuries back in Europe. I had no doubt that Valerio
had told his fledgling more than a few entertaining tales of
the old days. Beyond that, Knox had been brave enough to
try to get to know me when he arrived in Savannah. Unlike
anyone else within my domain, I felt like a rejection from
Knox would actually be a rejection of who I was, not necessarily of the image I presented to those in my domain.

And in truth, it had been a couple of centuries since I had
last been involved in a serious romantic relationship. The
last one had ended badly, and I wasn't entirely sure I wanted
to put myself in that vulnerable position again. Certainly not
when the peace of my domain was being threatened.

"Do you honestly want me to offer to be your boyfriend?" he finally asked.

I was saved from having to reply to his strange question when the heavy metal door leading into Bella Luna's
kitchen exploded open, banging against the brick wall of
the building. A large mass came flying out of the doorway
and landed halfway across the back parking lot. It rolled a
few feet before stopping and groaning. Whoever it was, was
still alive . . . for now.

A series of low growls filled the darkness, drawing my
gaze back toward the restaurant. Three men stepped out of
the restaurant, their eyes glowing a frightening copperish-
red. They were all dressed in black slacks and pristine white
shirts. The trio was followed by Barrett, who stood outlined
by the light coming from the doorway. His broad shoulders
tapered to a narrow waist. He was one hundred percent hard
muscle, and by the way he clenched his fists at his side, seriously pissed.

"Did the guy try to leave without paying his check?" Knox whispered below the blood-chilling growls.

"No," I murmured, my concentration elsewhere. I had already reached out to the creature to discover the mass was human; he had pulled a knife on a female server in the restaurant—a female shapeshifter. Sifting briefly through the thoughts in his mind, I discovered that his name was Franklin Thomas and he was from the Daylight Coalition. "Shit," I hissed. This lump of blood and stupidity was the one I had come to fetch.

Putting one sneaker on the soft leather seat, I launched myself over the door of the convertible. I had to get between the schmuck and the lycans before they tore him up. My stomach knotted and I struggled to keep my voice firm and even. "You can't do this, Barrett."

"I'm sorry, but our agreement is off," Barrett replied in a low voice, not at all sounding sorry. "He attacked Erica, threatened her."

Damn it all to hell. I didn't know most of the lycanthropes by name, but I had made a point of learning the names of Barrett's immediate family. Erica was Barrett's younger sister. Of all the people the human could have picked, he chose a blood member of the ruling family. I was no longer sure I could delay his execution now.

"Barrett, we both know that business comes before personal in our world," I countered in a gentle yet firm voice. With four lycans spread out before me, I wasn't sure I could keep them all at bay. "The secret comes before personal vendettas."

"I'll not let you tie my hands like this!" Barrett took a step closer to me, and the other werewolves closed in as well. The air seemed to shimmer with power. They wouldn't bother to shift, but they would call on whatever energy they had at their disposal to take me down and get to the human.

Slowly walk over to the man and get him to his feet, I directed Knox telepathically.

"I need your patience. This man owes me answers. He

may have killed Bryce and I think he attempted to kill Knox and me earlier tonight."

"No!" The sound was more of a snarl than actual English, but I got the point and so did his compatriots. They all thought I was going to kill the human because he potentially attacked me first. It would be my right, and Barrett was pissed because his sister's slight would never be properly avenged. But, no, I didn't plan on killing the human. I had a much better idea in mind.

As the werewolves lurched forward, I threw out my hands to my sides, creating a semicircle of fire between me and the lycans. It wouldn't stop them for long, but I needed only a few seconds.

Get him out of here, I ordered Knox. *I'll catch up.*

I heard the man groan once and then there was only the soft whisper of fabric. Knox had lifted up the human and run to a safer location. I didn't need to tell him to be careful. My main concern was the man doing something stupid to anger Knox, who could kill him before I'd had my chance to question the Coalition flunky.

The moment I felt that Knox was a few blocks away, I lowered and extinguished the flames. The lycanthropes didn't hesitate. I narrowly dodged one fist flying toward my face and answered by slamming the heel of my palm into his solar plexus. The air exploded from his lungs, dropping him to his knees as he gasped for air. Balanced on the balls of my feet, I spun to my left and ducked down as another charged. I landed two blows and dodged one before I finally sent him flying across the parking lot.

The third stood back, his body hunched over as he struggled to find a way to take me down when his two companions so quickly failed. Barrett also remained in the background, his large hands clenched into fists. He was still smart enough to know that if he attacked me it could cause an all-out war between the shifters and the vampires in my domain. For now, this was just a little scuffle and I was simply defending myself.

I was shaky on my feet and there was a fine trembling in my fingers, but the rest in the car had given me the strength I needed to face off against Barrett if it came down to it. "I won't kill him, Barrett," I called out, my eyes locked on the one lycanthrope besides the Alpha that was still standing. "I need answers, and that man dead won't help me get those answers."

"Mira—"

"You can have him back when I'm done, I promise."

"Are you serious?" The hardened edge had left his voice—he seemed surprised by my offer. The change in tone was enough to get his people to give me a little more space.

"Dead serious."

"Leave us." Without another word, the three werewolves filed out of the parking lot and back into the restaurant, closing the door behind them. The power that had flooded the small parking lot instantly left with the light breeze that blew through, shifting the leaves in the nearby trees. "He tried to kill you?" Barrett said once we were alone.

"He's not the only one."

"We didn't —"

I knew what he was about to say and I cut him off. "He's not the only one who's tried to kill me tonight and he won't be the last. There's always someone trying to kill me. It's the world we live in."

"Your world, not mine," Barrett corrected.

I smiled at him as I walked over to my car. "I'll contact you when I'm done with the human," I said, then drove off before he could say anything further. Whether Barrett wanted to admit it or not, we lived in the same world, with rules that threatened to choke those that could not accept it. I loved this world and its tight boundaries. Finding ways to manipulate the system we all lived in was one of the few things that still got the blood pumping in my veins, so to speak.

7

I located Knox at a warehouse a few blocks away from Bella Luna. It seemed as if he was reluctant to stray too far considering I had been outnumbered by a group of angry lycanthropes. But then, Knox still had a touching tendency to underestimate me.

After my car was properly stowed, I joined him in the nearly empty warehouse with the Daylight Coalition member. The dark-haired man paced the open area, his eyes never straying long from Knox as he looked for possible exit routes.

"There are two doors on the ground floor and a third on the second floor that leads to the roof," I announced as I soundlessly walked across the main floor. I knew the warehouse because I owned it. It was kept empty for meetings just like this one.

The overhead lights remained out, but patches of light spilled through dirty windows into the gritty expanse filled with large crates and warped wooden pallets. I stepped into a square of light and stayed there so Franklin could see me clearly. "But you won't make it to any of those exits unless I want you to."

"Why'd you kidnap me?" he demanded in a harsh, ugly voice. His accent didn't contain any of the soft Southern drawl that I had become accustomed to when dealing with humans. He was from somewhere up north originally.

"Kidnap you? I think you mean saved your sorry ass." Knox laughed deeply, shoving his hands into the back pockets of his torn jeans as he leaned against the wall. "You threaten the sister of the owner of Bella Luna, and you expect to walk out with your balls still attached? Very unlikely, my friend."

"I'm not your friend!" he raged, taking one step closer to Knox before backing off again.

"I know what you are!" Franklin shouted. He paced toward me as if his courage had returned for a second before it left him and he paced away. "You're a vampire."

It was on the tip of my tongue to deny it, but I let the comment pass. If he was the one that blew up Bryce's house, then he mostly likely saw me at the house seconds before it exploded, and now I stood unharmed before him. Was there a better explanation than the fact that I was a nightwalker? Well, none that would make any sense.

"And you're a member of the Daylight Coalition," I said with a light shrug of my shoulders. He honestly seemed shocked by my sudden pronouncement. He stumbled backward a couple steps and shook his head, causing me to laugh. "You know about us, but do you honestly think we wouldn't know about you?"

I stopped laughing suddenly, letting the silence overwhelm him before I started speaking again. "You kill nightwalkers. This morning, you killed one by the name of Bryce at the edge of town. He was tall, slender, with brown hair and freckles. He looked like he was nineteen. You killed him and made sure the body was left in a spot where the sunlight could reach it." As I spoke, I watched the memories playing back in his mind like a silent movie. In a slightly broken jumble, I saw Franklin drag Bryce's unconscious body up from the basement. With an enormous knife, he sawed opened the nightwalker's chest and cut out the heart. He then removed the head. The whole time, Franklin was grinning as he was washed in Bryce's blood.

Bryce had been asleep and completely helpless when the

human struck just after sunrise. Nothing in heaven or earth could have wakened him. Some would argue that at least he felt no pain. But he also had no chance to fight back. No chance to fight for his right to exist.

I suppressed a shiver that bit at my muscles and ignored the ache in my fangs. I couldn't kill this coldhearted monster. I needed the answers he held. He knew the *why* and the final *who*.

"How did you find out about Bryce?" I asked, doing the best I could to swallow back my anger. "I can't imagine you found him on your own considering that you're not from around here." I squatted like a toad among his memories, waiting for the image of the person who had betrayed Bryce. Yet I was momentarily distracted by the smile that blossomed on his face. The scowl that twisted his features melted away, and his eyes widened as a grin split his mouth.

"I didn't know about him until one of your kind told me about him," he proudly announced, hoping to get a rise out of me, but I didn't react. I had already suspected that a nightwalker was somehow involved in this mess. But hearing those ugly words fall from his lips didn't stop the flash of anger that ripped through me.

"Who?" I whispered.

"Why would I tell you?"

"In hopes of getting a quick, merciful death." I took two quick steps out of the light, approaching my companion. He lurched backward, nearly stumbling in his awkward haste. I smiled as his own smile faded. "You can tell me or I can pick it out of your mind. Besides, why would you want to protect this nightwalker?"

"What do I care about some stupid fucking vamp? She came to me bitching about being turned against her will and that she wanted me to kill the bastard that did it. She was some blond bitch. Said her name was Katie."

As he spoke, I watched him mentally replay the moment when she had approached him at night in a lonely parking lot. But something was off. Katie was not now nor was she ever a nightwalker. And yet the image of the nightwalker was blurred so that I could only pick out the figure's slight form and blond hair. The person was definitely female, but the face was unclear. The nightwalker that spoke to him had tampered with his memory, but had not done a very good job of it.

Did you see? I silently asked Knox, who was still watching from the other side of the room. I never heard him move, but I could feel that he was now closer to me than he had been only seconds earlier.

Yes. That's not Katie. She wasn't a nightwalker, unless . . .

I saw the body. She's not rising tomorrow night. She's gone. Even if Katie hadn't been drained of all her blood, it was unlikely she would have been able to heal her broken neck in the process of being reborn. In general, the human had to be in working order if he or she was going to be brought over. We could heal nearly any wound once we were nightwalkers, but we all had to start off in good shape.

"You've been lied to, my friend," I commented, turning my attention back to the human. It wasn't Katie. Furthermore, the nightwalker had lied about the reason for having Bryce killed. It was impossible to be made into a nightwalker against your will. If you didn't want it, you died. And sometimes, even if you did want it, you died. You had to fight death for your soul during the process and he wasn't the most congenial loser.

"What the hell do I care? A vampire is dead. One less to prey on humans."

"Yes," I hissed. "One less." Turning on my right heel, I headed back toward the entrance of the warehouse with Knox at my side. I was done with the human. Between his uninformative answers and his damaged memories, I had gotten from him all the information I was going to be able to get. I was content to hand him over to Barrett. I had a bigger target in mind at this point. While combing through Franklin's mind, I had caught the address for a Coalition safe house in Atlanta and a second one in Memphis, Tennessee. I'd see to it that that information was put to good use.

The shot was like an explosion in the silence of the warehouse. Pain punctured my back to the right of my spine, ripping through flesh and organs, before exiting through my chest. My whole body bowed and jerked forward. I slid a couple inches on the tips of my toes before my knees gave out on me and I collapsed to the floor. The bastard had missed my heart, but the bullet cut through one of my lungs. Lucky for me, I didn't need my lungs any longer, and it wouldn't take long for the damage to repair itself.

Knox knelt beside me, one hand on my arm while I pressed a hand to my chest to stem the bleeding. "Are you okay?" he demanded in a snarl. He was simply waiting for me to say that I was okay before he launched himself at Franklin.

"You forgot to search him?" I bit out.

"I'm sorry. I . . . I forgot. I'll take care of him now."

"He's mine," I replied in a low growl. Gripping Knox's arm, I jumped to my feet and rushed across the warehouse to where the human stood, attempting to unload the contents of his handgun into my body. However, all the bullets went wide. There was no hitting me. I was moving too fast. A grim blur of color in the dimly lit warehouse. He didn't know I was there until my hands closed around his throat and I threw him against one of the support beams. By then, his gun was clicking sadly, out of bullets.

"You have my undivided attention now," I said, leaning in close enough that my breath brushed against his ear. "Is there something you wanted?" My chest pressed against his shirt, soaking up some of my blood. I pulled back just far enough that he could now see my fangs, sending a shiver of fear through him.

My hands clenching his shirt trembled as I fought the urge to sink my teeth into his throat. But it was more than just the need to drink in his blood. The monster that lay deep within my chest roared to life, demanding that I rip flesh and break bone. I wanted to hear him scream in pain until the sound echoed through the empty warehouse. I needed him drowning in pain, instead of emitting the terrified little whimpers that escaped him now.

Slowly I regained control of myself. In my world, I had the right to tear and rend and shred. He attacked me first. He tried to kill me at Bryce's and again here. Unfortunately, I had other plans for this shivering sack of flesh that would serve me better than a moment's joy in killing this bastard.

"I thought so," I said, shoving him a little as I released his shirt.

Again, I turned and walked away. Knox accompanied me out of the warehouse. His mouth opened the moment the steel door closed with a solid clang behind us. "We forgot to ask about the video camera," Knox said, sliding to a stop in the gravel.

"He'll only lie about it, wasting our time," I said, halting him before he could go back into the warehouse.

"But if they have your picture —"

"I'm screwed, I know." Screwed was an understatement. If it got out that I was a nightwalker, even as a joke, the Coven would have my head and heart on a platter before sunrise. "Do we have anyone who might be able to hack into the Coalition database?"

"Hackers? Nightwalkers, no. But Barrett has at least a pair."

"Perfect." I pulled my cell phone out of my pocket and dialed Barrett's number. "He's at the warehouse, but won't remain here for long. He's all yours now," I announced as soon as he picked up the line.

"Thank you," Barrett murmured in a low voice. He was grateful, but he wasn't particularly happy. He owed me now and it sat heavy in his stomach.

"You can track him by the scent of my blood," I added, twisting the knife.

Barrett knew the only way my blood would get on Franklin would be if he managed to wound me. He now owed me a very big favor considering I had walked away from a very personal slight so that he could have his revenge. And if there was one thing that all the other races had in common, it was the fact that not one of us liked to be beholden to the other.

"What do you need?" he said as if he were grinding the words up in his clenched teeth.

"A favor. He may have gotten me on film earlier. I need all evidence of it erased. Files, e-mails, and possibly data removed from the Coalition database. Do you have people who can handle it?"

"You know I do," he replied. His voice sounded a lot less gruff than earlier. As favors went, this one was fairly easy. His people were potentially getting access to our enemy's files while he was evening a score with me.

"My fate is in your hands."

"Don't worry, Mira. I'll keep you off YouTube."

Smiling, I shoved the phone into my pocket and pulled my keys out of my other pocket as we walked around the side of the building to where my car was parked. Opening the trunk, I dug around in my little bag for a fresh shirt. "So did we learn anything of value tonight?"

"That a nightwalker was the one to contact Franklin," Knox replied.

He was right. A werewolf would never have been able to blur a person's memory like we saw and it was extremely unlikely that a warlock or witch would be able to find where Bryce kept his daylight sanctuary. However, nightwalkers frequently shared that information when they allowed other nightwalkers to bed down with them during the day in rare moments of trust or when seeking to start a family.

"Whoever it was didn't know how to properly mask her appearance. She vaguely looked like Katie, but it was very shaky as if the person was struggling to either hold the illusion or was unable to properly mend Franklin's memories."

"A fledgling?" Knox asked. He sounded skeptical and I couldn't blame him.

"Possibly." I quickly unbuttoned my shirt and looked down to find that the wound had completely healed, but now there was a trail of drying blood running down into the waist of my jeans. Wiping off as much blood as possible, I threw the shirt into my trunk to destroy later and pulled on a dark gray T-shirt.

"It could just be an older nightwalker that never had any proper training," Knox suggested.

"A fledgling seems unlikely," I agreed, shutting the trunk of my car. "Bryce didn't have any fledglings of his own and he should have been old enough to easily defend himself from any of the fledglings within the area."

"Which is maybe why a fledgling got the Coalition to do the dirty work?"

"Could a fledgling be so stupid? She had to know that we would look into this and track her down." I turned and leaned against the car for a minute, my arms folded over my chest.

"And maybe that was a part of her plan," interjected a new voice. I looked up in time to see Bishop step from the shadows beside the wall of the warehouse. "Maybe this fledgling's goal is to kill you as well as this Bryce person."

"She's getting closer if that's the case," Knox added, making me scowl at him.

"Don't make faces at the boy, Mira. He's right," Bishop teased. "You've been nearly killed three times already tonight and you've yet to catch this schemer."

"I can understand killing Bryce for some reason related to our world and even the attempts on me. It's all involved with our world. But why kill Katie Hixson? All she wanted to do was to enter our world."

"Don't know," Knox said with a shrug of his shoulders. He stood before me, his hands shoved into his front pockets. "Jealousy? Maybe the fledgling didn't want Bryce bringing over Katie or maybe she was jealous that he would rather spend time with Katie than with another nightwalker."

It wasn't a new story. A fledgling was hurt because a

nightwalker fell for a human and wanted to turn him or
her. I'd seen it all play out like a Shakespearean tragedy—
everyone dead. "We need the answer to those questions."

"Only one place left to get them."

"Gregor." The name escaped me in a low growl. If there
was one nightwalker I wouldn't mind seeing with his head
and heart removed, it was Gregor. He was a few centuries
old and controlled a clique of nightwalkers that I found
more than a little annoying.

For now, I would have to put aside my distaste for him.
If Bryce was known to travel with Gregor on occasion, then
the nightwalker would be able to give me more information
as to who might have had Bryce killed and Katie Hixson
drained.

8

Gregor wasn't at the Dark Room. Adam quickly informed me upon arriving that when Gregor discovered I was looking for him, he left the Dark Room and asked that I meet him at the Docks. I could only guess that the nightwalker didn't want to be seen being questioned by me. I could understand his hesitance, but that didn't make me happy about it.

The Docks was a nightclub near the riverfront that catered to the local Goth scene with its dark, smoky decor and nonstop industrial music blaring in the background. It was one of my favorite places to spend an evening. The clientele were content to just let me enjoy the music and the dancing. It was a good place to hide when you were trying to avoid the world around you.

Slipping ahead of the crowd that waited to get into the club, I slapped a fifty on the counter per my usual no-questions policy with the management of the club. They didn't ask to see my identification and didn't attempt to put one of those paper strips on my wrist indicating that I was over the age of twenty-one. I didn't come to this place to drink alcohol.

Gregor sat alone at a table in a dark corner of the night-club. He wore a dark red, knee-length jacket over a black shirt and black double-breasted vest with large silver buttons. A gold chain for his pocket watch hung from his vest pocket. His whole attire screamed of Victorian aristocracy, making him appear to be horribly out of place in this bar filled with black leather, silver chains, and tattered lace. Regardless of the fact that Gregor had actually survived the Victorian era, he was now part of the Steampunk generation, which was a somewhat distant cousin to the Goth movement that refused to completely fade away. While I doubted he believed in their mentality, the Steampunk generation did fit his taste in clothing.

"Mira, it's so good to see you again. It's been ages," Gregor said, easily rising to his feet as we approached his table.

"Hmm . . . yes, not since you suggested that a number of nightwalkers go running with the shifters on a full moon. How many fledglings did we lose that night? Six?" I said with a frown as I took a seat opposite him.

A grin spread across his face as he returned to his seat. "Eight."

"And four lycans were badly injured," Knox added from where he stood just behind my right shoulder. There were only two chairs at the tiny table, and I was surprised that he had chosen to stand behind me rather than pull over another chair. But then Knox was from the Old World and had been raised by an Old World nightwalker. Standing indicated that he was my assistant rather than my supposed equal sitting beside me.

"But it was fun. I'm sorry you missed out," Gregor continued, nearly chuckling.

"It seems I missed out on some other fun, too," I said, preferring to finally switch the subject. There was nothing I could do about Gregor's twisted sense of humor. He had convinced a group of young nightwalkers to go running with some werewolves on the night of a full moon. There was the inevitable scuffle, and eight nightwalkers got shredded in the process, as Gregor knew would happen. My concern was the four lycans that got hurt. Barrett had not been happy about it, but then we both knew there was nothing we could do about it. We had to give our people some room to make stupid mistakes so long as humans weren't involved.

"If you're referring to what happened to Bryce, I had nothing to do with his demise as I'm sure you know. I heard that he was killed during the daylight hours," Gregor said, sitting back in his chair. The music shifted at the back of the nightclub where the dance floor was located, moving to a heavy thumping beat that vibrated in my chest. I would rather be dancing, surrounded by smiling, sweating humans caught up in the music, than dealing with Gregor and this entire mess.

"For once, I believe you," I said with a frown. "I need to know who Bryce hung out with. Particularly females. Someone killed him and Katie Hixson."

For the first time since we walked into the Docks, the smile that filled Gregor's face slipped away and he honestly looked confused. "I don't understand. Katie was murdered?"

"Shortly after sunset. It was a nightwalker," Knox interjected.

"You knew Katie?" I demanded, drawing Gregor's stunned gaze from Knox to me again.

"Yes, Bryce and the rest of his group brought her in to the Dark Room a few times. She was a lovely young lady. Very polite and sweet. Not the usual Goth, living-dead nonsense that you see hanging on our kind as if we were their long-lost messiah."

"Was there anyone jealous of Bryce and Katie? Anyone who might have wanted them both dead?" Knox inquired.

"Bryce, yes. I can think of one person who would want Bryce dead, but not Katie. Lauren was the one that introduced Katie to Bryce and the rest of his small group. Lauren had known Katie while she was a human and had brought her into the fold as a human. It could have been anyone within the group he hung with. There were three females: Lauren, Bridgette, and Kari. And then Charles traveled with that flock on occasion, but not so much within the past few years."

I was familiar with Bridgette. She was about fifty years old and had moved into the area with my permission more than twenty years ago. However, the other two I wasn't overly familiar with. "How old are Lauren and Kari?"

"Kari is nearly thirty, I believe. She moved here with Charles. Lauren is really fresh—five or six years, I think. I'm not sure who her maker is. She's never mentioned him and I've never seen her with anyone but Bryce and the rest of his group."

"Are any of them a member of Ravana's family?"

"Kari and Bridgette are, I believe."

"Where can I find them?" I demanded, drumming my fingernails on the sticky surface of the small circular table that separated us.

"All three ladies are back at the Dark Room. Charles is—"

"Thanks, Gregor." I pushed to my feet. I had heard enough. I knew who had killed Katie and set the Daylight Coalition on Bryce.

"Mira, you don't think it was one of those girls?" Gregor demanded, lurching awkwardly to his feet in his surprise. "They're just fledglings. They couldn't have . . ."

"Stay here, Gregor. You don't want anyone to know you ratted them out," Knox said, earning a low snarl from the nightwalker. I bit back a smile as I walked out of the nightclub and into the fresh air. It wasn't much cooler than the uncomfortably warm nightclub.

Knox was as irritated with Gregor as I was. The nightwalker seemed to parade himself around my domain as if he ran it. He made sure that he was acquainted with everyone within the Savannah area and made himself up to be more powerful than he really was. However, those within my domain that were more powerful and stronger (including myself) tended to ignore him since he was just an annoyance. He also proved to be a valuable source of information on the rare occasion, so we all let him be. Regardless of all his pomp, he knew where the line was and he was very careful not to cross it. Dance on it, spit on it, and kick dirt on it—sure. But he didn't cross it.

"So, you know who the killer is?" Knox said, walking beside me as we headed back to the Dark Room.

"Yes, and you're going to end her bloody reign for me."

I looked over at Knox to find him smiling at me, a faint glow touching his eyes. "As you wish."

9

I paused just off the entrance of the Dark Room, beyond the two empty coat check rooms, and looked over the club. The main floor was lit almost entirely by candles in wall sconces and in hurricane lamps on the tables. The walls were lined with booths that were cloaked in deep shadows that could be easily penetrated by our superior night vision. Thick burgundy curtains made of heavy velvet lined the entrance to each booth, ensuring just a little more privacy for its occupants. The music was a low, hypnotic beat, burrowing its way into the brains of the dancers as they swayed and moved with it.

The Dark Room was an alluring den of seduction and peace in a world that seemed to be passing with greater speed. In here, everything stopped for those few night hours and we were able to stop pretending to be something we were not. Of course, it meant that we had to find a way to live in harmony with each other while within the confines of the bar, but even that was a temporary arrangement as Bryce's death had proved.

It was nearly midnight and the place was busy. The dance floor in the center of the main room was packed with writhing bodies and the booths were filled with others. It seemed as if they majority of the lycanthrope and nightwalker population had showed up. I hadn't planned to make this a performance for both races, but then an audience had never deterred me when something important had to be accomplished. And in this case, it might prove to be useful.

Tilting my head back toward my right where Knox was standing behind my shoulder, I asked, "Do you know the group that he spoke of?"

"They're in the booth at the far corner toward the right," he replied in a low voice so that no one could hear us over the music that was pumped through the cool air. "Do you seriously know who we're looking for?"

"Without a doubt. I'm just not completely sure of the *why* at this point, but I imagine we'll know before the night is out."

I descended the stairs down to the main floor and strolled back to the booth that Knox had indicated. Lycans and vampires both skirted me as I passed through the crowded region. Everyone knew of Bryce's death by now. Everyone would suspect that I was looking for the killer, and no one wanted to fall under my searching gaze.

The booth consisted of two long benches that ran parallel to each other with a low table in the middle. It was easy to figure out which one of the three women that sat in the booth was Lauren. Her short blond hair and petite figure made her a relatively close physical match to not only Katie, but also the image that I picked out of Franklin's mind. She lifted her blue eyes when I blocked the entrance to the booth, and she didn't at all look surprised to find me standing there with my fists on my hips.

"So, I guess it's safe to say that Franklin failed in his task," she announced, drawing some confused looks from her companions.

"No, he managed to kill Bryce," I corrected.

Her bright pink lips twisted into a moue before she coolly corrected my wrong assumption. "He was supposed to kill you, too."

Her companions gasped and started to move as far from her within the booth as possible before encountering me.

I had wondered if she had worked alone or if any of her companions had helped, but their utter shock and horror was easily picked out of their respective minds. This plot was Lauren's alone.

I shrugged my slim shoulders, frowning at her. "He nearly did, but then, I've survived worse. Why do it? Your life is forfeit for involving the Daylight Coalition, for attempting to kill Knox and me. Why kill Bryce and Katie? Because I wouldn't allow her to be reborn?"

"You stupid bitch!" she exploded, all her rage suddenly rising to the surface to mar her beautiful face. "You think that's all. If it had been simply not allowing her to be reborn, then I would still have Katie. But that wasn't enough for you. You had to have her memory wiped as well. Bryce took her from me!" Lauren's fingers curled into shaking fists and she raised tear-glazed eyes to me.

I was beginning to realize exactly how wrong I had been about this entire situation. Katie had not been Bryce's lover, but Lauren's. Unfortunately, Lauren was too young to bring a human into our world so she convinced Bryce to secretly handle it outside Justin's knowledge.

It was common practice to wipe the memory of any human that had been denied access to our world. It was too risky to leave them walking around with knowledge of our world. In a moment of anger at being rejected, they could strike out and talk to many of the wrong people, spreading knowledge of the nightwalker and even lycanthrope world. I had never considered what would happen to someone who hadn't that intention but truly had a connection with a nightwalker.

"I'd been with Katie since high school. He took all her memories of me. There was no getting her back. She didn't know me! Didn't remember us!" she moaned.

It was all gut-wrenchingly clear now. Lauren had killed Katie rather than face what she saw as a horrible eternity without her. Katie might not have recognized Lauren, but her appearance was deceivingly sweet and innocent. Katie wouldn't have hesitated to open the door. Lauren had gone to the woman's house, broke her neck from behind so that she would feel no pain, then drained her completely dry so that no one else could ever have her blood. Afterward, Lauren lovingly arranged her companion on the floor as if she was simply resting. Sleeping Beauty waiting for her lover's kiss to awaken her.

"I'm sorry. I didn't know the situation, but—" I started, but rage had finally overtaken Lauren's grief.

"You're sorry? You ruined our lives!" Putting one high-heeled foot on the table, Lauren pushed off the wall and launched herself at me, her fingers raised toward my face like claws. I tried to sidestep her, but hunger and fatigue had made me slow. Her nails scored four long cuts along my arm and another across my cheek before we crashed through the outer ring of tables. Still struggling, we smashed into the crowd of people on the dance floor. There was a cacophony of cries, curses, and hisses that went up at the collision, but we ignored them all as Lauren worked to regain her feet. Her eyes were locked on me.

Still lying on my back, I swung my leg around into her, knocking her back to the floor. I rose faster than her and slammed my fist into her face, breaking her jaw, before taking a step backward. Lauren howled in pain but still took another blind swipe at me with her long fingernails in hopes of drawing blood again.

Knox stepped in front of me, ready to take over the fight. To my surprise another combatant had jumped into the ring, and I hadn't even noticed her in the nightclub. But then, that was Amanda's special gift. She had a special way of fading into the background so that you didn't immediately notice her there. It made her all the more dangerous.

Amanda had one fist wrapped in Lauren's hair, pulling her head back so that the long expanse of her neck was exposed. Her right hand held Lauren's right arm, twisting it behind her body. Hovering inches from Lauren's throat, Amanda's fangs were poised to tear it out if I so much as blinked my approval.

"Hold," I said, brushing off my hands. "This is Knox's fight."

Amanda frowned, sheathing her fangs for the moment. I knew the look of disappointment. There was a truly heartless, vicious quality about Amanda. She reveled in their pain and the violence that our kind was capable of. Yet it was more than that. While Knox saw to the night-to-night workings of my domain in many ways, Amanda was an enforcer for me among the fledglings. She saw it as her duty to keep the young ones in line, and somehow Lauren had slipped by her. Amanda felt responsible, and now she needed to be a part of Lauren's demise.

"Mira, please." Amanda's plea came out in a wavering whisper.

Slipping my hands into the front pockets of my jeans, I nodded. "Help him clean up." I watched as Amanda and Knox ushered Lauren to a hallway toward the back of the nightclub where they would destroy her in the basement. As the trio disappeared behind a door, Adam appeared at my elbow. With another nod from me, he ushered Kari and Bridgette from the club. There was such a thing as guilt by association in my world. While they may have been innocent, I simply didn't want to look at them.

I settled into the back corner of the empty booth and set my crossed feet on the low table as I waited for Knox. Something twisted in my stomach as I listened to Lauren's screams just under the throbbing beat of the music that had once again started. The dancing seemed a little more frenzied as the occupants of the nightclub either enjoyed the rush from her painful end or fought to block out her death with music and dancing.

Our world was a delicate balancing act. We held these amazing powers in the palms of our hands, but in a moment of carelessness, we could lose everything to the humans that surrounded and outnumbered us. Over the long centuries, we created a series of rules and laws that we all had to abide by, from fledglings to the Elders in the Coven. But I've seen these rules crush those they were attempting to protect just as frequently as I've seen them save us.

Lauren broke our most sacred rule of never informing a hunter of our existence. Even if she hadn't attempted to have me killed, she would have been dead tonight.

Bishop sat down at the table and handed me a linen tablecloth. With a grateful nod, I pressed it to the line of claw marks Lauren had scored on my right arm. He gazed at the assembled crowd, a frown teasing at the corners of his mouth.

"Didn't quite accomplish what you set out to, did you?" I announced, drawing his gaze back to me.

"I can still take you back to Venice with me," he threatened, his dark eyes narrowing on me.

"No, you can't. I'd never willingly go, but it might have been easier if I had been mentally or emotionally broken by the events here." Drawing a deep breath, I lowered the napkin that was stained with my blood. I was sore and tired from the various fights that had filled my night, but this one was going to be my most dangerous. "Were you the one to introduce Lauren to the Daylight Coalition member or did you handle that all by yourself?"

"I don't know what you're talking about," he blandly said.

"Of course you do. You've been in town for months now, watching and listening. I know what's happening in my own domain. Only the urging of someone older and stronger would have gotten a fledgling to actually plot out my death. Involving Justin Ravana's family was a nice touch, though. He never actually contacted the Coven, did he?"

"No," Bishop finally admitted, flashing me a smile full of fangs and menace, as he realized that I had figured out his part in this plot to end my existence. "Fledglings are meant to be used."

"And Ravana?"

"I didn't want to deal with him when I take over your domain."

"Which you get if I go back to the Coven."

"Or simply die."

Bishop lunged across the short distance between us, as he drew a small wooden stake out of his pocket. I grabbed his wrists, but he was bigger and stronger than me, and I was already weak from the night's encounters—something I'm sure he was counting on.

The chunk of wood bit through my flesh as he put his entire body weight behind the stake. Pain lanced through my body as it dug into my chest, grinding closer to my heart as I pushed against him.

A part of me didn't want to kill him. I thought I had known Bishop, but I had been wrong.

"Don't do this," I cried in a pained voice.

"It's too late to plead for your life," he said past gritted teeth.

"I'm not. I'm pleading for yours." Bishop increased the pressure on the stake so that the tip punctured my heart, winning a scream from me. Closing my eyes, I conjured up flames so that they instantly consumed his body. I continued to hold his wrists, trapping him in the booth with me. His screams rose above the music, add their own unique chorus to match Lauren's screams coming from the next room. When he was reduced to ash, I removed the flames and opened my eyes. With a grunt, I pulled the stake from my chest and grabbed the napkin to once again stanch the bleeding.

I looked up in time to see Knox crossing the dance floor toward my booth. Fresh blood was splattered across his clothes and skin. Knox's eyes glowed with an almost frightening light as he stepped back onto the main floor. Dropping the napkin on the table, I slowly pushed from my seat and walked toward him, meeting him in the center of dance floor. Energy vibrated from his slender form, born from the rush of killing another creature in what I was sure was a brutal death. Valerio would have taught him well.

Cupping his head with my right hand, I stepped close and ran my tongue along his neck and up his jaw, drinking in some of Lauren's blood from where it had sprayed across him. A shiver ran the length of his body, and his right arm locked around my waist. "Dear God in heaven, Mira," he uttered in a husky voice. "You can't do that."

I simply chuckled as we began to sway to the beat of the music, his body hardening against mine. Knox tightly wrapped both arms around me, pulling me tight against him as he buried his face in the crook of my neck. His fangs scraped the bare, tender skin there, lifting a sigh from my parted lips.

The murder was solved and the plot to dispose of me had been unraveled. We could relax for a few minutes before the next disaster hit, threatening to tear apart our fragile world. We could afford this moment to forget about it all as we stood safe in our own sanctuary listening to music that pulsed through and around us.

Did she tell Franklin anything else about us? I silently asked after a couple minutes.

Nothing. His right hand squeezed my waist in what was meant to be a reassuring gesture. *Just the address of where to find Bryce and to kill anyone that came to the house that night.*

Barrett and the lycanthropes would see to Franklin. We would need to watch for anyone else during the next few months looking for Franklin or any signs that he had sent information to his companions at the Daylight Coalition. We still weren't out of the woods, but we could see moonlight at the end of this dark journey.

"Bishop?"

"Disposed of."

After the song ended, I pressed a kiss to Knox's cheek and started to pull out of his arms, but he stopped me.

"I got a call while you were away looking into Katie Hixson's murder," he began, erasing our light moment of relief. "It was from a contact I have up in Cincinnati. She said that a hunter rolled into a town a few days ago looking for you."

"By name?" I asked. It was extremely rare for anyone to know me by name outside my own domain. Most simply referred to me as Fire Starter. Any hunter that knew of me would know me by that moniker.

"Yes."

I understood why the call was being made. Knox's contact was looking for permission to send the hunter my way and get the person out of that domain. A dark grin spread across my face. "Tell your friend to send him my way. I'll be ready for the hunter."

TWO LINES

MELISSA MARR

To J, Vicki, and Mark,
for far more than I can ever say. You're the best.

I

Eavan pushed through the crush of dancers at Club Red: sweat-slicked, alcohol-saturated prey swayed and gyrated in time with the music pulsing out of a wall of speakers. It was—as it had been every other night—tempting, but lately, Eavan had been letting herself be carried away by the crowd, enjoying the too-brief touches of strangers, near-drunk on the energy on the dance floor. But tonight wasn't for indulgence. Daniel was in the club. She'd felt it the moment he crossed the threshold, felt *him* in an unacceptable thrum under her skin. For reasons she didn't know, she could find him in a crowd without looking.

He was moving through the room, a beacon among the waves of swaying bodies. In another life, she would've run away from—or perhaps to—him. Instead, she waited, proving to herself that she still held some measure of self-control. Each time she caught him mid-crime, she whispered a silent prayer that he'd stop poisoning girls, that he'd become innocuous, but hoping and praying were no substitute for action—not that action was proving particularly effective, either. Trying to single-handedly rescue the worst of Daniel's zombies was futile. For every one she saved, there were a dozen more she couldn't reach.

He was only a few bodies away from her now. Tiny electric zings bounced over her skin as she came closer to him. He was tempting enough that it hurt. *And he knows.*

Foam poured onto the dance floor as Daniel took a far-too-high girl into his arms, and the time for waiting passed away. Swirling violet and crimson lights gave an ethereal cast to the humans who squealed and writhed around them as the dance floor became a slippery mess. *A predator's banquet.* The question of which of them was the better predator wasn't one Eavan wanted to answer: either answer meant she lost.

Daniel glanced back at her and then moved toward a side door with the girl. He cut through the crowd with an ease that made him seem Other. He wasn't though.

He's just another mortal. She had repeated that asser-tion every night these past six months. There was nothing particularly exceptional about him. *Except for the way he provokes me.* Putting a final end to him made good sense, but she couldn't be the one to do it. There were two steps needed to wake up her maternal heritage—sex and death. So far, she'd avoided both, but if she did both in the same month, she'd become a full-blooded glaistig.

In another few moments, he'd be out of the club, out of reach, and the girl would be lost.

Not this time.

Some nights, she'd lost their quarry. Many nights, she was at the wrong club. Once in a while, she found his prey before Daniel could. Tonight, she'd decided to step up the confrontation.

She intercepted Daniel and grabbed the hand of the barely conscious girl.

"Chastity!" Eavan squealed her name with false excite-ment, an act for the crowd around them. She had no clue what the girl's *real* name was. It didn't matter. All that mat-tered was that Eavan was taking the girl from Daniel. The two men on either side of him stepped closer. If they wanted to, there was a good chance that they could take the girl out of reach. Eavan was banking on Daniel's dislike of scenes.

She smiled at him, a flash of teeth that animals still understood as aggression. She didn't bother glancing at his employees. Daniel waved them away as usual when she was near. He either didn't see her as a true threat or was amused by her efforts. She hadn't figured out which it was, but she knew that he preferred to be alone with her when he had a chance.

Once the men vanished into the sea of bodies, Daniel stepped closer to Eavan. He didn't let go of the girl, but he didn't do anything obvious to keep her out of reach, either. "She's with me, Eve."

"Is that what you really want?" Eavan let her conservative habits slip farther away and turned her full attention to Daniel. It wasn't a hardship to look at him: he was a pretty specimen, wrapped up in Armani and attitude.

For a few heartbeats, he said nothing, but he wasn't immune. Real humans never were.

"*She's* not meant for my bed."

"I know," Eavan admitted, enjoying his momentary meekness. "I know your taste, Daniel. Unconscious isn't it."

"So tell me, little Eve, what *is* my taste?" He came closer, still holding the barely standing Chastity. "Say it aloud for a change. Give me that much."

It was painful to let those tendencies come closer to the surface; hungers best left unfed were already omnipresent when he was near. Eavan sized him up openly, caught and held his gaze just long enough to be too-bold. "You look good tonight."

He smiled then. "Admitting you're tempted?"

Ignoring that challenge was hard, but Eavan had been too close to the edge with him for weeks. If she didn't know he was a monster, she'd want him. *I do anyhow.* If she had been thinking clearly, she wouldn't be talking to him at all. *I'd miss it.* If she didn't want to stay human, she'd take him to her bed and kill him tonight. *I am* not *a monster.*

She reached out and lifted the girl's eyelid to peer into her extremely dilated pupil. "I'm taking her with me."

"Fine." He relinquished his hold on the girl. "There are dozens more just like her."

Chastity was swaying, barely sober, and soon to attract attention. She was so far gone that Eavan wasn't convinced she could be saved. Anger threatened to surface—at herself, at him, at the inability to make a real difference.

Daniel stepped closer, invading the bubble of personal space she usually kept between herself and regular humans. "You need to start saying hello when you arrive at the clubs, or say good-bye and come home with me . . ."

Despite her growing anger—or maybe because of it—Eavan enjoyed his aggression. Something about him made her want to push the rules a bit further, made her want to see how close to forbidden she could get without crossing over. *Nice girls don't hunt; human girls don't like murder.* She knew the boundaries; she knew she wanted to stay on the right side of them. *He'd be such fun to kill though.*

Daniel's smile made clear that he sensed her interest, even though he undoubtedly read it as merely sexual. He was close enough that she could taste scotch on his breath. "Can I give you a lift tonight? Anywhere you want to go. Or we'll call someone for her so we—"

"No." She moved so the girl was farther out of his reach, so *she* was farther out of reach too. Glaistigs drank down a mortal's last breath. He'd sweetened his with a peaty scotch.

I'm not hunting him.

"We could go to the Chaos Factory." He reached out and ran a finger over her bare midriff. "Tell me what you want, Eve. What's it going to take to get you home with me?"

"It would be a bad idea," she said—not a lie, but not an answer. She stepped backward, retreated from him. Not everything was about dominance. She'd rescued Chastity; she'd taken the prey from his hands. Now she needed to get away.

"So we'll do this another night." He leaned in and brushed a kiss over Eavan's lips, unknowingly teasing her with his sweetened mortal breath. "Unless you're planning on running already?"

"I'll be back." She couldn't do otherwise, and they both knew it. "I'll be at your clubs."

"And I'll find you." And then he vanished into the crowd of feverishly dancing mortals. It was easy to see why people came willingly to his feet. He was everything a man should be—dangerous, sexy, and just ever-so-slightly aware of it. In many cases, he'd be the alpha predator.

Which is why I want to kill him.

Logic insisted that her macabre fixation on him was basic animal law, but it was outside logic to stalk Daniel. He dealt in magicks that made the Other community—at the prompting of Eavan's own matriarch—set a *geis,* a ban forbidding fraternizing with him. That ban on contact with Daniel was as law for Others.

But Eavan wasn't purely Other. Glaistigs were female only, each one born of a human father and glaistig mother. Unless she crossed the two lines into adulthood, she was technically mortal—with a few extra traits. *Geasa don't apply to mortals.* That was her excuse, at least. *Not that I'm going to "fraternize" with Daniel. No sex. No death. I can do this.*

2

Muriel opened the door before Eavan could knock. She didn't quite scowl at the sight of the mostly unconscious girl in Eavan's arms. Her usually welcoming expression vanished, but she kept her tone light. "For me? You spoil me."

"I'm sorry." Eavan carried the unconscious girl inside the apartment. "She's . . . I know better. I know we talked about it . . . I just . . . Daniel had her and—"

"Later." Muriel's blue robe was the only color in the black and white room. It made it impossible not to stare at her as she closed the door. The generous bit of bare skin didn't help matters.

"I had to," Eavan whispered.

"I know. That's the problem, isn't it?" Muriel took the girl and carried her into the den.

As with every other time, Eavan went to the kitchen and fixed herself a drink. She couldn't drink on the hunt, but afterward she was shaky enough that she needed a few fingers of whiskey. Tonight was worse than usual. It had been growing worse every time she saw Daniel.

Chastity whimpered.

Muriel's voice was too muffled to make out the words, but the tone made clear that the words were some comforting lie. Muriel could do that, lie at will. Eavan didn't have that luxury: partially fey things could lie sometimes, but it wasn't a predictable sometimes.

After glancing toward the closed door of the den, Eavan emptied her glass.

If Chastity survived, she'd be slipping into withdrawal soon; if she didn't survive, she'd still be better off than with Daniel. Girls like Chastity went to bidders with sadistic habits that Eavan couldn't bear pondering . . . not when so many Chastitys had been sold already. They had no control over their sexuality. Drugged to the point of being zombies, they were reduced to nothing more than sex toys to be used until they were destroyed. The beauty of sexuality was something she cherished—and couldn't have; to have it sold for base coin was beyond intolerable.

Or Muriel's right and I just have a fucking savior complex. Several more ounces of whiskey splashed into the glass. *Or a death wish.*

Eavan hated that there wasn't a better answer to the problem, but if not for Muriel, she wouldn't have much of a solution at all. Muriel drank enough of the girls' blood to pull the poisons out. If they survived, Muriel had ways to get them wherever they needed to go next. Alive and out of reach: those were the goals. Beyond that, there were no constants.

It depended on who Chastity really was. If she had a home and resources, Muriel would have one of her coven use those funds to set the girl up in a new city. If not, Muriel would see her to a shelter or halfway house under some pretext. *Or she'll put her into the ground.* There were far too many that ended up dead despite Eavan's efforts. That was how Muriel got involved in the first place: the vampire had a system for dealing with corpses. Eavan had needed that system one night, and the only other resource she'd had for disposal of bodies was her grandmother, and asking Nyx for such a favor had too high a price.

Muriel's willingness to remove the toxins was an added bonus—one that gave Eavan the ability to try to rescue

girls who were much further gone on Daniel's drugs. If not
for Muriel, Eavan would've been at a crisis months earlier.
Even with Muriel's help, the situation was akin to attempting to hold back a wave with a single hand: it was impossible. Eavan couldn't stop Daniel from destroying people;
she couldn't stop herself from hunting him; and she couldn't
see any way to avert the disaster that would follow if something didn't change.

Eavan poured a drink for Muriel as the petite vampire
came into the kitchen. "Well?"

"She's alive." Muriel took the glass and emptied it. She
swished the whiskey around her mouth and spit it into the
sink before adding, "You're going to have to ante up something clean if you're going to keep asking me to drink all
these toxins, or"—she gave a coquettish grin—"you could
give me a taste."

Eavan blushed and looked away. "No."

"You can't really kill me, and maybe it doesn't count as
sex if it's—"

Eavan shook her head. "Sex with women is real sex,
and we're not crossing that line. Casual sex wouldn't be my
thing even if—"

"You're a glaistig, darling; of course it would." Muriel
lowered one hand, sliding it over the blue silk covering her
hip.

Transfixed, Eavan watched—and then scowled. "No, it
wouldn't. I don't want casual, and you don't do commit-
ments. Discussion closed."

"Really?" Muriel stepped closer, much as Daniel had
earlier, and whispered, "Your heart is racing awfully fast for
someone who doesn't do casual."

"Interest doesn't mean consent." Eavan forced herself to
look at Muriel's face. "I can say no. I've been saying no for
years. No sex. No death."

"If I tried you tonight, truly pushed you, could you still
say no?" Muriel was gentle, but she knew that the answer
was liable to be different than it had been before the Daniel

obsession. The more Eavan hunted Daniel, the harder it was control either appetite.

Being mortal means keeping control. Over centuries a few glaistigs had tried to stay human, to not kill, to not fuck. Eavan knew about them from journals and letters Nyx had hidden away. They'd all failed or were simply killed by their matriarchs. *"Culling the weak, Eavan."* Nyx had stalked her *as she lectured and punched her when Eavan admitted to seeing the forbidden texts. "Is that what I need to do with you?"* Eavan forced away the memory of Nyx's fists and said, "I want to be mortal, Muriel."

"That doesn't mean refusing both sex and blood, Ev," Muriel said. "Just have one to take the edge off. Too many rules and hang-ups will be your downfall . . . sooner than later if you keep stalking him."

"If I can't live by my own rules . . ."

"Friendship is *like* a commitment." Muriel tilted her head and gave Eavan her best disarming look.

Eavan laughed at her best friend's faux innocence. "It is, but it's not enough for me."

They'd been having the same discussion for several years. Muriel had a host of partners. To her, it was like shoe shopping: there were many choices for many moods. It wasn't an emotional thing or a cruelty thing. It did mean, though, that their occasional boundary pushing stopped short of sex.

Teasing set aside then, Muriel took the bottle of Middleton from the counter. "The junk Brennan's peddling ruins even virgin blood."

"Virgin?"

"As pure as you." Muriel took two clean glasses, added a couple cubes, and poured the whiskey.

Eavan shuddered. The idea of an innocent—especially one who had her will stolen by Daniel's zombie mix—being sold to a sadist was more revolting than normal. "He's a sick bastard."

"So kill him," Muriel said. A drink in each hand, she

hopped up on the counter. Neither drink spilled. She kicked her feet in the air like a child on a swing and held out a glass. It was hard to remember that Muriel was a monster; she looked like a hand-crafted doll, one of those delicate pieces of art that belonged safely on a shelf.

Eavan took the whiskey. "No. I'm not going to sacrifice myself over him."

Muriel snorted. Now that the flirting was out of the way, she could relax into her less charming habits. "Some sacrifice . . . It's not like you'd be throwing yourself on a sword, Evvie."

"No, I'd just be throwing away my humanity."

"Humanity's overrated." Muriel warmed to the old argument. She'd been Other for more than a century now and saw nothing wrong with it. "Humanity means *dying.*"

Humanity meant a lot of things. It meant ethics, joy in the brevity of life, compassion . . . and yes, dying. Dying didn't seem as oppressive as the alternative. *At least for me.* Muriel wouldn't understand though: vampires didn't grow cloven hooves when they stopped being human. They didn't have tendrils of hair that writhed like serpents or need to sate not one but two depraved appetites.

"No. Humanity is wonderful," Eavan insisted. "It's what I am. Daniel isn't going to steal mine."

"So maybe you should stop trying to save the girls he gives the zombie powder to?" Muriel's voice grew cold. "Something's going to break, Ev. You keep pushing and he'll push back, or your family will find out what you're doing . . . You're walking a foolish path taunting Brennan."

"I'm handling it."

"You think Nyx would agree?" Muriel put a hand on Eavan's wrist. "Your grandmother finds out you're taking risks without any safety nets, and she'll be livid. You need to kill him or back off."

"Just a little bit longer, Muriel? I need to find a way to get him to stop. I can't just let him sell those girls . . . I *can't* . . ." Eavan leaned her head back on the cabinet behind her, putting a bit of artificial distance between her and Muriel.

"If Nyx comes calling, you know I can't cover for you." Muriel's expression was gentle, but the words were anything but reassuring. "I won't."

"I know." Eavan closed her eyes. Thinking about her matriarch's reaction was the last thing she wanted to do, but it was sobering. "But until then?"

Muriel took her hand away. The only sound in the kitchen was the soft slide of feet on the stone floor as Muriel walked away. Eavan didn't follow, didn't open her eyes. She waited.

Ice clicked together in Eavan's now empty glass. The splash of whiskey followed. "For now, yes," Muriel whispered, "but not forever."

Eavan opened her eyes and accepted her glass.

Then Muriel added, "*But* the next time you go to the club, I'm coming, too."

Before Eavan could object, Muriel raised the hand not holding the bottle. Perfectly tinted nails and understated rings flashed through the air. "No invitation, no help. Either you hunt or you don't, Evvie. Either you persist at this I-want-to-be-mortal nonsense or you accept your heritage. This half-assed thing is going to stop."

"But—"

"Tell me you aren't right there at the edge with Brennan?" Muriel's sweet exterior was gone. *This* was the vampire that had gone toe-to-toe with Nyx and survived. Her doll-pretty exterior was a façade; her coquettish charm was a ruse. Muriel was every breath the monster Nyx was. "Tell me, Evvie, and we'll discuss it further."

Eavan wanted to argue, but there wasn't anything that she could say without lying. "No more club trips without you."

"I'll stand by you if you want to be mortal. I'll help you if you want to be glaistig." Muriel's more familiar, kinder expression returned. She widened her blue eyes in a pleading way. "I just don't want to see you regret whichever it is because you were being foolish."

If I stop, what happens to the next Chastity? Eavan didn't bother saying that though; Muriel wouldn't be swayed by that concern any more than Nyx would. *Family first.* That was how the Others thought, and mortals weren't family.

3

Cillian walked toward Dorothea Dix Hospital on his nightly mind-clearing stroll. He'd spent the past several hours going over his file, but still had no clue how to get closer to Brennan or how he got the unknown powder he cut his coke with. Whatever the silvery talcumlike material was, it wasn't matching anything on the periodic table or the existing databases at the Crypto Drug Administration.

The drug was appearing in other areas around the country, and Brennan was the closest thing to a source that the C.D.A. had found. The I-85 and I-40 intersection tended, like many such interstate crossings, to be a drug-heavy region. Durham had a definite heroin business. Volumes of marijuana and cocaine slid through, but those weren't issues for the C.D.A. Crypto Drugs dealt exclusively in the chemicals that utilized or targeted the Others that hid in mortal society. Brennan's powder was an anomaly even in an organization established around coping with the unusual. The C.D.A. didn't like anomalies.

Or lack of results.

No one in Brennan's immediate circle seemed approachable. None of the victims was around long enough to be of use. The only one who seemed like a potential *in* was one woman Brennan kept circling, but she seemed to be stalking the drug dealer when he wasn't stalking her.

So I stalk the stalkers.

Cillian thought about the dark-haired girl. *Eve.* He'd stared at her picture frequently enough that he'd begun to feel like a perv. He wanted her not to be a victim *or* a criminal, but he couldn't find any evidence to suggest which she was or any logical way she wasn't one of the two. Nice girls don't flirt with drug dealers. Nice girls don't spend inordinate amounts of time at strip clubs. He was pretty sure of that—except everything else he could find on Eavan made her seem like a nice girl. She worked at her jobs for short periods, but her employment records were all flattering. She was average: modest clothes, nondescript reading habits, no odd purchases, not a single unexplained trip; in sum, there wasn't anything at all that would flag her as criminal.

Still thinking about Eve, he let himself into the apartment he'd rented.

Just inside the door, he stopped. A cream-colored envelope sat propped up against a book on his kitchen table. No one knew he lived here other than his supervisors, and they weren't the sort of people to leave notes with calligraphic lettering on his table.

A quick search of the tiny apartment revealed that he was alone. After donning a pair of gloves, he carefully opened the letter. *Mr. Owens, If you'd like to resolve the D.B. problem you're having, contact me. Nyx.* Under it was an address in the historic district and a meeting time that was just late enough to be private.

Several hours later, Cillian parked up the block from the address on the note; he glanced again at the sheet of lilac paper sealed in the bag on his passenger seat as he cut off the engine. The paper, the calligraphic writing, the lavender scent on the paper—it wasn't covert. It didn't seem apropos of intrigue.

At least not any sort I'm used to. Prior to this assignment, he'd worked in the research and clean-up divisions of the C.D.A.

He closed the car door quietly and made his way up the flagstone path. A woman sat on the front porch. She looked to be in her thirties at most. She was stern, eyes too flat, smile too calculating; everything about her was predatory in the true sense of the word. Whispers of caution rose from that instinctual part of the mind: walk carefully, mind the escape routes.

"Mr. Owens, so nice of you to visit."

"Nyx?" His voice was steadier than his emotions. He'd walked into altercations that resulted in hospital visits, but this beautiful, polite Southern woman in a semi-public location was setting off the same sort of alarms usually reserved for the truly unsavory.

What is she?

"Come." Nyx patted the swing beside her. Then she reached over to a crystal decanter sitting on a side table. "Whiskey?"

"No thanks."

"It's not poisoned, dear." She smiled a courtesan's smile. "Poison isn't a method I prefer. Too distant."

Cillian paused midstep and looked around the porch and azaleas that lined the front of it. There were no other people he could see, nothing that looked dangerous. *Except Nyx.* He'd learned before his first year with the C.D.A. that criminals didn't all look dangerous. Usually, though, they weren't this odd combination of ballsy, blunt, and beautiful. "Is there another method I should be watching for?"

She laughed and poured herself a drink. "Sit down, Mr. Owens. The neighbors needn't see you looking at me so cautiously. They're used to my business, but discretion is always wise . . . especially in *your* business."

He sat next to her, but not so close that he couldn't reach his gun. "I'm not sure what you think you know, Ms.—"

"Nyx." She sipped her drink and smiled. "It's just Nyx."

If not for the fear he felt as he sat beside her, he'd find

her attractive. She was all curves and muscles, and none of it hidden. Thick dark hair fell around her like a cloak. She was near-naked from the waist up, clad in a sheer top over bare skin; dark aureoles and pert nipples more than visible. Not an inch of flesh was bared below the waist. A long skirt and boots hid her legs.

Why hide the rest of—

"I see the temptation in your expression," Nyx said softly. "Trust me, Mr. Owens; you're much better off not following those thoughts to completion."

He was here on business. Ogling someone he might have to kill was bad form. He forced himself to hold her gaze.

And Nyx smiled then. Her posture hadn't changed. Her spine was arrow-straight, making her very not-sagging breasts—

I'm not like this. He felt positively amoral. His libido was healthy enough, but he didn't mix business and recreation. *I'm not going to start, either.* He caught and held her gaze. *Like being held in the gaze of the snakes in the reptile house . . . without the safety of the glass.*

"What do you want?" he asked.

She handed him a picture. "This is Eavan."

Eve.

Cillian kept his face blank. "And?"

"The girl, my cousin Eavan, is getting mixed up with a man I'd rather she didn't. You're stalking him, so I thought we might help each other." Nyx folded her legs up on the swing, angling her body so she was facing him. "I'd rather Daniel Brennan die. I find him . . . unpleasant, but Evvie would be cross with me if I killed him."

"Do you often murder people you find unpleasant?" The words were out before he could think better of them. Despite looking like an ingénue, Nyx spoke with a callousness that made Cillian certain that the woman beside him was, indeed, capable of murder.

Nyx laughed. "I think we'll both be happier if you don't ask too many questions like that, Cillian. I know who you are. I know about the C.D.A., and I know that Mr. Brennan is a person of interest to your organization." She lifted a folder from the floor and extended it to him. "Here's a list of others you might want to investigate."

She held it there while he reeled from how casually she listed top security clearance C.D.A. information.

Cillian reached out and took the folder. "Do you have any idea what sort of trouble you'd be in? We're talking about treason."

She waved away his remark with a flick of her wrist. "Your government isn't a concern of mine. I know what I know, and you'll not let anyone find out about me. Do you think that there aren't people who would erase the entirety of your organization if they realized that your superiors know about . . . *people* that treasure privacy? History is filled with stories of strange groups of people, secret societies if you will, vanishing. Your sort exist only because we've yet to decide how much of a threat you might be. I believe you can be harnessed and made useful. I need my cousin looked after, and you are getting nowhere with Mr. Brennan. It's a simple business exchange." She ran a finger absently through the beads of sweat sliding down her glass and licked a droplet from her fingertip before adding, "I'm trusting you, Mr. Owens."

In seven years for the C.D.A., he'd never experienced anything quite as surreal as this meeting. Admitting that he understood that she was Other was a breach of several papers he'd signed under strictest security. *She's not human. She's just admitted as much.* That didn't mean he could admit it though. He tucked away the questions he wanted answered and focused on the issues he could address: "A single phone call and you'll be in jail or worse for the rest of your life. You can't summon a government agent to your house and just . . ." He shook his head.

"I trust you because if you expose me or reveal the other *unusual* things you learn by accepting my offer, I'll kill you, your sister in Miami, your nephew in Chicago . . . and your dear sweet father in"—she paused and tilted her head—"where was it? Phoenix, I believe?"

Cillian had his hand on his 9mm before she was halfway through the threat.

"Lower your hand, boy."

He did, not by choice, but he lowered his hand as obediently as the women addicted to Brennan's drugs. He couldn't disobey. "Wha—?*Who* are you?"

Nyx sighed. "The answers to that don't matter to you today. What you need to know right now is that neither you—nor your loved ones—would stand a chance if I asked you to obey me . . . and no, you may not ask why just now. Put your hands out here where I can see them."

When he did so, she nodded placidly as if he'd hadn't been seconds away from trying to shoot her—and he couldn't force the questions of *how* and *why* from his lips.

"I can be a great ally. You want to stop Brennan's drugs. I have reasons to want you to succeed at that," Nyx said.

Cillian opened the folder and glanced at the sheets inside. Charts, account numbers, passwords, maps, key codes, names, aliases . . . it was far more information than he'd seen on Brennan after months of workups and considerably more detailed than anything he'd gathered in the six weeks he'd been in Raleigh.

Nyx pinched it closed. "You mustn't tell Evvie that you know me. I'm hiring you as her bodyguard as far as she knows . . . well, *will* know." Nyx's mouth curved in a wry expression. "Evvie will object. She'll attempt to evade you. She'll . . . be difficult."

"I'll need to talk to my supervisors—"

"Talk to them, so they can verify the value of that data . . . but I am an anonymous source." She stood up and stretched her arms over her head, making her sheer top lift up and expose her bare stomach. This time, though, Cillian wasn't even slightly tempted.

"Or what?" he asked.

She laughed, a husky bedroom sound that made him swallow hard despite his utter distaste. "Or I'll slaughter everyone who sees this data."

He stood and faced her, still holding the folder. It was foolish, but he had to say it: "You're not human."

She put her hand on the folder, pressing it against his chest, leaned in, and kissed his cheek. "If you're interested in my help, take the folder and be here tomorrow at seven sharp to be introduced to my cousin as her new bodyguard. If not, leave the folder and walk away. I'll give you an out this once." She kept her hand on the folder, holding it between them as she invaded his space. "If you accept my offer, please do understand that I'm quite serious about the terms of our contract."

Then she turned and left.

Cillian sat silently in the dark for several minutes, debating the consequences of both actions. If he took the folder, he'd have resources the C.D.A. needed, resources that would enable him to do his job better. If he left it behind, he assured his family's safety; of course, they were only endangered if he couldn't keep silent. That wasn't an issue. The things Cillian had learned in his job weren't things he shared with his family. This was no different. If Nyx was honest, he and his loved ones were endangered only by violating her privacy. If she wasn't honest, they were already in danger. Either way, taking the folder didn't change anything critical. All it really meant was that he was becoming personally involved in the world of the Others.

Which has been inevitable since I took the damn job.

He'd expected his overt knowledge of the not-humans to come through official routes, but he'd still expected it from the beginning.

What difference does it make?

He took the folder and walked away. Now he just needed to figure out what to tell his supervisors—and protect a woman who was some sort of Other, and, if he was lucky, stop Daniel Brennan. All told, he was more excited about his job than he'd been in months.

4

Eavan hated family meetings with a passion she reserved for . . . actually, a passion she reserved for family meetings. She stood in the street, staring at her home and trying not to fall under the sway of the neighborhood. Oakwood was a little bit of heaven—houses that weren't prefab monstrosities, people who sunk their roots into their city, a community whose collective energy made this part of the city something pure. Her family always lived in such areas. Unlike the subdivisions that cropped up everywhere, Oakwood and its neighboring Mordecai had personalities, histories, and dark whispers. More than a few of those whispers were tied to the women in Eavan's family. Sometimes an unfaithful husband vanished. Once in a while, a wayward family member returned home meek and eager to be forgiven. Drug traffic never took hold in the several blocks surrounding their home. No one in their immediate area was ever robbed. Of course, no one would speak directly about the belief that Nyx's influence was what kept them safe in home and family. Secrets were all the more poignant for the fact that they were openly known, but never spoken. It was enough to keep the neighbors from looking too closely at the family.

If they truly knew, would they still look away?

The neighbors might murmur about them being "fancy women" and the scandal of women owning strip clubs, but they didn't pursue their talk beyond the occasional, and quickly silenced, remark. They didn't speculate aloud at the family's methods of keeping peace; there were no titillating rumors voiced about the beautiful murderesses who lived inside the modest house.

Eavan's family was a clan of true glaistigs: they devoured people. They were many men's—and a fair number of women's—darkest fantasy, but sometimes with a steep price. They didn't kill many, but they did kill. Glaistigs swallowed the last breath of mortals or strangled them, preferably during sex.

Monsters.

She walked around to the back of the house. It was part of the routine she'd clung to in order to keep herself from believing the façade. Routines were her anchor, innumerable little tricks to keep from believing in illusions, to create her own illusion of normalcy. Going through the front door, the door for guests, was walking into the illusion. The truth was what kept her from surrendering to the role her family wanted for her.

This is not what I am.

Steeling herself for the sensory shock, she pushed open the door.

She wasn't but a step inside the room, when Mother Chloe appeared in front of her. Uncharacteristically, her legs were hidden away. *There must be guests.* Even now, no one in her family seemed able to keep her chest, stomach, or arms covered. Given a choice, they'd roam in lingerie.

Eavan straightened the sleeves of her suit jacket. *I am not like them.* She'd worked hard to cultivate a modest streak and had gone a bit overboard lately with being so close to the edge. No one else at the office dressed as conservatively as she did; even the senior marketing consultants looked at her oddly.

She stood silently for her birthmother's inspection. They were always like this, greeting her at the threshold and assessing her like a stray dog returned to the pack. Chloe glanced at Eavan's stocking-covered calves approvingly. She smiled—until she looked up and saw Eavan's tightly wound bun. "Well, that certainly sets a mood, doesn't it?"

"You asked me to let it grow again," Eavan reminded. She sat her briefcase at the front door and slipped off her pumps.

"I don't understand you." Chloe walked away, her boots striking the tile floor in a regular rhythm, sounding out the familiar cadence, bringing to mind memories of a lifetime of late night music sessions. Chloe insisted on wearing boots that would resonate on the floor as her own cloven feet would. She liked music, even that made of her own movement.

Despite her irritation, Eavan smiled at the sound. For years when she'd lived in the house, she'd been happy. Things had made sense, but back then, she'd known little of what she'd one day become. It wasn't until she was a teenager that she understood the parties, the musicians, and the strange cries. Her mother-family, glaistigs all, fed on acts of sex and death. It was essential that they feed; it kept them alive. Eavan understood it—but understanding didn't equate to wanting to be like them.

Far better to live a mortal lifespan and die naturally than to transform into a monster.

Chloe paused and stamped her foot. "Evvie! Come now. Your grandmother isn't feeling patient tonight."

"Is she ever?"

Chloe scowled. "She's far more patient with you than I would be."

"Yes, Mother Chloe. I do realize that." Eavan followed her mother into the sitting room where the rest of the family would be waiting. Of course, calling it a sitting room was a bit of a kindness. It was something between a bawdy house and the results of a Victorian decorator on acid. Aunt NeNe had her foot propped on an honest-to-goddess stuffed elephant foot that was fashioned into an ottoman. Gold tassels dangled from the cushion atop the atrocity. All around the room, floral patterns clashed with one another; gilt-framed art cluttered walls and shelves. Dressing tables that had no place in a front room were scattered about, like the desks in an untidy classroom. On each table, Eavan could see a jumble of silver hand mirrors, ivory combs, feathered hair barrettes, and crystal bottles of perfume with elaborate atomizers.

And her family sat—in dishabille—on overly plush divans. In the center, like a queen holding court, was Nyx, Eavan's grandmother and matriarch, her judge and torturer. Nyx held herself regally, watching with serpent-cold eyes. "Eavan."

It wasn't a warm welcome, but no one there thought Eavan deserved Nyx's warmth.

Even me.

Ever since Eavan had told Nyx she wasn't moving home after college, things had been more strained. Glaistigs didn't live away from the clan. It simply wasn't done. Of course, no other glaistig clan would be foolish enough to challenge Nyx's decision to violate tradition by allowing Eavan a touch of freedom. The same cruelty that had left scars on Eavan's back allowed Nyx to defy tradition now: crossing Nyx was painful more often than not.

Beautiful monsters. My family.

The three of them looked like sisters, like *her* sisters. They appeared to be only a couple of years older than Eavan—wrinkle-free, lustrous hair, bodies as sculpted as professional dancers. In high school, her "guardians" had incited equal parts envy and curiosity when they attended school events. In college, people assumed they were her sorority sisters or asked if she was part of a modeling agency. Luckily, they hadn't visited her en masse at the office yet. Their unchanging nature would eventually elicit too many questions. *As will my own.* Eavan wasn't sure when it'd started bothering her, but it irritated her more and more—their immutable nature, her own now-unchanging body.

For now. Choosing mortality meant Eavan would eventually age and die. She'd age more slowly than mortals, but it would still happen. Glaistigs didn't. They brought death, but didn't suffer from it.

"What *are* you wearing? It's so"—NeNe fluttered her hands around as she took in Eavan's skirt, which reached just below the knee—"opaque."

"It's wool." Eavan leaned down and kissed her aunt's cheek. They might be monsters, but they were still her family. "Just like I've worn to every other meeting."

"I must've repressed it." NeNe sniffed. Like the rest of the women, with her gauzy camisole and thick tumble of hair, NeNe looked as if she were awaiting clientele, not expecting a visit from the girl they'd collectively raised as their daughter.

"You know, what this place needs is a stripper pole." The words were out before Eavan could stop herself, but no one flinched. Eavan could say whatever came to mind here. Home wasn't where Eavan wanted to be, but she couldn't deny how right it still felt to be there. Glaistigs were clan creatures, and although Eavan was clinging fiercely to her humanity, she was still part of the clan. "A pole would fit right in," she added. "Just like at your clubs."

Grandmother Nyx nodded. "I was just saying that, wasn't I?"

Chloe handed Eavan a brush before answering, "She's joking, Mama."

Nyx shrugged, lifting one delicate shoulder in a graceful move that belied her centuries. "It matters little. She's right for a change."

Eavan smothered a laugh; Nyx knew that Eavan had been only partially joking. It would fit in, and they'd enjoy having it here. Sometimes when all the rest was set aside, Eavan suspected that Nyx was the only one who truly understood her. The older glaistig didn't approve of Eavan's urge to live as a mortal, but she understood the impulse to forge new rules. Following a path simply because it had always been done that way wouldn't make sense to Nyx. Of course, neither would chastity.

Eavan sat on the back of the sofa, perched behind her grandmother, and began unplaiting the woman's thick rope of hair. The tendrils were like living things in Eavan's hands, as if night had taken solid form. "You look lovely, Grandmama."

"Of course." Nyx stretched; muscles that shouldn't exist rippled under her wrinkleless skin. The strength in those muscles would make it a simple thing to crush Eavan's throat—and no one would stop her. Eavan learned that lesson years ago when she stood up to Nyx the first time.

And a dozen times since.

Nyx wasn't callous, no more so than anyone else in the house, but she was in charge. Forgetting that was unwise.

"Bring him in," Nyx said.

The tension in Eavan's body rose. She paused a heartbeat longer. "Him? Grandmama, what have you—"

"You've stopped brushing, Eavan. I don't like that."

Dutifully, Eavan resumed the measured strokes, gripping the olivewood handle, pulling the tufts of boar bristles through the thick tresses, keeping her eyes on her task—and not looking at the man who'd entered the room.

Like a lamb to slaughter.

"I've checked all the windows," he said by way of greeting.

"Lovely." Nyx rolled her shoulders. "Keeping brushing, Eavan."

"Yes, Nyx." Eavan stayed in her increasingly uncomfortable position on the back of the sofa where Nyx was seated. She didn't look up at him. If Nyx had brought him here, had insisted Eavan meet him, he was dangerous. His voice alone, a deep growling bass, was proof of that.

Temptation. Eavan knew her family wasn't above underhanded tricks; treachery was their first instinct. *Perhaps it's not that.* She knew better though. Nyx didn't rule one of the strongest clans of glaistigs by accepting defeat. *Ever.*

"The windows aren't secure at all," the man added. "A screwdriver and—"

"Right, so we'll replace those. NeNe?" Nyx made an imperious motion.

"Here." NeNe held out a blank check. "Fix whatever needs fixing."

"Our home's security is very important, Mr. Owens," Chloe said.

"It's Cillian, ma'am," he corrected.

Eavan paused at the change in timber of his voice; he also sounded almost as assertive as Nyx. When Eavan looked up, her fears were confirmed: he was perfect, a visual feast, lean, confident, and seemingly unintimidated by the nest of vipers he was in. His instincts should be telling him to flee or to bow before Nyx. He did neither. He stood there as if oblivious to her charm, to all of their allure.

Eavan couldn't help but stare, just as Nyx undoubtedly expected. He was fit without being bulky, muscular and toned. If not for his almost pouty lips, his face would be too stern. As it was, he looked just this side of fierce—not easily daunted or foolishly aggressive. It made her want to see what it took to provoke him.

I am above this. I am stronger than instinct.

The older glaistig looked back and caught Eavan's gaze. A guilty blush burned on Eavan's face.

Nyx's posture hadn't changed, but she had her confirmation: Eavan was intrigued.

Too much so.

The man made a note as he said, "I'll have one of my associates drop by to go over the literature on the different options for replacing the windows."

"Whatever. Really, my cousin's safety is really the difficult thing, Mr. Owens. As I said, that's why I needed you here today." Nyx caught Eavan's hand and tugged so that their clasped hands were resting just over her collarbone. "Eavan doesn't seem to understand how dangerous refusing to stay with the rest of the family is. A young girl in the difficult world all alone . . ."

"Is she in some sort of danger, ma'am?"

"Inevitably. She's foolish, you know." Nyx squeezed Eavan's hand until tears threatened. "I worry so over her. Beautiful. Wealthy . . . and with the things I see in the news . . . Did you know there were shootings just up the street from her flat?"

Eavan blinked the tears away. Her voice was clear, though, as she said, "I'm not moving home. No matter what . . . happens."

"I'll accept that," Nyx said mildly. "In fact, I've hired Mr. Owens's firm for that very reason. I've taken a lease on the vacant flat across from yours."

"I don't think—"

"Or you can move home." Nyx looked back at Eavan. "You have choices. Prove to me that you can do as you're told or return to the fold where I can look after you. I'll not have you die to prove a point."

"Nyx," Eavan pleaded, "please?"

Nyx turned away.

"I want to apologize for making you stay in Eavan's dismal building, Mr. Owens. How anyone could want a tiny little nest in some ugly modern thing . . . It's appalling." Nyx's reply couldn't have held more vitriol. She sighed melodramatically before adding, "NeNe and Chloe will go over the other details with you. Eavan and I have things to discuss in private before you two leave."

And with that, Nyx dismissed him, and NeNe and Chloe were at his sides almost instantly to assure that he was removed from the room. Nyx spoke, and the world obeyed.

Except me.

"Tell me about your associates, Mr. Owens," Chloe murmured as she trailed fingertips over his stomach.

"Chloe." Nyx curled her mouth into snarl. "Not acceptable."

"Yes, Nyx." Chastened, Chloe ducked her head and hurried the man out of the room.

Eavan repressed a shiver as everyone left her behind.

Not that witnesses would matter.

Eavan stood. Wordless, she walked over to place the brush on one of the vanities.

Nyx pulled the dark spill of hair over her shoulder, where it coiled into a rope that would've made Rapunzel jealous. She turned her gaze to Eavan. "Do you think it's easy for me to think of you vulnerable to the dangers of the world?"

"I don't have a choice, do I?"

"I'd rather you didn't die."

"I'd rather no one died," Eavan said.

"Sometimes death is necessary." Nyx made a fluttering gesture with her hand as if to shoo away an insect. "Yours is not one I'd like."

Eavan bowed her head. She'd lost. She'd lost months ago, but simply hadn't known it yet. Nyx had concocted some story, hired a bodyguard, and effectively entrapped Eavan. She'd been sentenced to spending her time around a tempting mortal.

How am I to do anything about Daniel now? Eavan wasn't about to admit that she'd been hunting the drug dealer. Nyx was always surly over dealers. She liked her strip clubs well enough, but refused to allow any drugs in her clubs. *Unlike Daniel.*

"He's pretty."

Eavan turned to stare at her grandmother. "What?"

"The man. He's pretty. The type you try not to look at." Nyx stretched her legs out on the divan. "I notice, child. I've been noticing for years."

Eavan didn't dare turn her back on Nyx, so she settled for a shrug.

Nyx laughed, sounding joyous as she often did after long days of partying.

"I'm not like you, Grandmama. I won't be." Eavan's mouth was dry. It'd been months since Nyx struck her, but the possibility was always there. "Putting him in my path doesn't change that. You're wasting money hiring him to 'protect' me."

"I haven't forgotten how difficult that first time is, sweetie." Nyx held out a hand.

Eavan went to her. She took her grandmother's hand as she sat at the woman's feet. Centuries of experience hid under Nyx's flawless skin.

"I'm not going to do it," Eavan whispered.

"You will." With her free hand, Nyx pulled the pin from Eavan's bun. It'd been only a week since it'd been cut, but it was already past her shoulders. Nyx ran her fingers through it, loosening the strands so they drifted freely. "You'll hunt. You'll fuck. You'll kill."

"I'm not like you."

Nyx squeezed her hand—gently this time. "You're a glaistig, love. You're *exactly* like me."

"I'm *not* a murderer."

"It's the natural order of the world." Nyx smiled indulgently. "The higher beasts eat the lower. Do they get upset over eating other animals? The predators thin the herd, taking away the diseased or aberrant or weak. It's natural."

"It's not."

"Humans do it. Kill animals. Raise them like pets and butcher them . . . our way is far more humane. At least we don't wear their hides for garments. We're far more civilized."

Eavan looked at Nyx's hand-sewn leather boots. They were butter soft, custom made of the eel leather Nyx preferred these days. "And if they were able to be crafted into clothing you liked?"

"No." Nyx ran her fingertips over a boot. "Mortal skin isn't as silky . . . Plus, it's just gauche."

"Gauche?" Eavan asked. "And a stripper pole in the parlor?"

"Practical," Nyx said. "If you are so sure you can be a mortal, here's your test. Prove to me that you don't have the same lusts we all do. If not, he seems a good sort to keep around for at least one of your appetites. We picked him especially for you."

Eavan sighed. "Sometimes I really hate you."

"I know, dear." Nyx stood and pulled Eavan into a hug. "It's one of the reasons I respect you. Let's go find your new temptation."

As if I need another one. Resisting hunting Daniel was using up all her self-control. Resisting another entanglement was the last thing she needed.

Maybe he's a bore . . . a girl can dream, right?

5

Cillian waited outside in the overgrown yard behind the house. If he didn't know better, he'd think it was left to grow wild, but like everything, the truth was in the details. There were plants in this yard that he hadn't seen anywhere else in the Triangle area, ones that wouldn't flourish, even in the Raleigh humidity, without attention. The illusion was one of disorder, but the truth was that this was cultivated fecundity. His current job depended on his noticing minutiae, on seeing past the lies people wove, and on creating his own illusions. Those were the skills that would help him pretend to know nothing about Eavan, despite the hours they'd be forced together.

"Mr. Owens?" Nyx stood on the back porch.

"Ma'am?" He turned to face her.

Nyx paused as Eavan kissed her cheeks; then she turned her attention on Cillian. "You'll keep her safe."

"I'll do my best to not let anyone harm her," he said. It was the best he could offer, especially as he had no idea who or what Eavan was. *Was Brennan human?* That information was the sort of thing that the C.D.A. was never privy to, but it did make a difference. The first time Cillian had had his ribs broken, he learned exactly how much it could matter.

Eavan took a step backward. "I'm not that fragile."

"You're more fragile than you should be, Evvie." For a strange moment, Nyx was the one who looked truly vulnerable. Her thus far implacable calm vanished. She licked her lips anxiously. "You'll let him teach you what you need. You'll be careful. He's good at what he does . . . and the things you . . . I picked him for reasons you—"

"Nyx." Eavan backed down the porch stairs and looked up at Nyx. "I'm not actually in any danger. You and I both know that. Hiring him"—Eavan glanced at Cillian—"is a control tactic. It won't change anything, but you don't have to pretend it's a legitimate bodyguard situation."

Nyx lashed out with a closed fist.

Eavan gripped the banister in front of her to keep from stumbling. Blood slid down her chin from a cut lip.

Cillian started forward.

"Stay out of it." Nyx didn't even look his way. Her attention and her next words were for Eavan. "You'll let Mr. Owens guard you as carefully as if there were hellhounds pursuing you, Eavan, or you'll move into this house. I make the decisions in this family, and this one is not negotiable."

Eavan stood motionless, staring at her cousin as the blood dripped from her mouth. They both had all of the affect of statues.

"Don't challenge me, Eavan. The consequences would be very unpleasant." Nyx's hair seemed to move of its own accord; the dark tendrils twitched like restless serpents around her shoulders.

Cillian stood there awkwardly. He wasn't sure *either* of them should be trusted, but instinct told him that there was a threat to Eavan whether she was inside the house or on her own. It shouldn't matter as much as it did, but he had a longtime habit of cheering the underdog.

"Am I understood, Eavan?" Nyx asked.

Finally, Eavan bowed her head. "You are, but I'll prove that I don't . . . *need* him."

"I almost wish you were right, Evvie," Nyx murmured. Then, before anyone could say another word, she spun on her heel and stepped back inside the house. She didn't close the door. Instead, she left it open so they could watch her walk away swinging her hips like an invitation. Her footsteps echoed as she went into the room, a heartbeat rhythm beat out by her sharp heels.

And Cillian couldn't look away. Seeing Nyx go made him feel like he was losing something—even though she made his skin crawl.

"Are you all right?" Eavan's voice drew his attention from the open door.

"Are *you*?"

"I'll be better once I'm out of here." She dropped her shoes to the ground and slipped her feet into them. Then she pulled out a tissue and wiped the blood from her face.

He started down the walk, but stopped when he realized that she hadn't moved.

"Why did you take the job, Mr. Owens?" She watched him as she twisted her hair back into a tight coil. Everything in her posture screamed "challenge." It made him want to refuse any answer. *Which works out well.* He couldn't tell her anything.

"It's what I do right now." He didn't lie, not really. Watching her *was* his job. His supervisors were very clear that he should accept the terms of his anonymous source's offer—including guarding Eavan.

"Guard people against nonexistent enemies?" She almost smiled, and the change was remarkable. She was every bit as tempting as the beautiful monster that had hired—*blackmailed? manipulated?*—him, and based on her family and her association with Brennan, she was also likely to be just as deadly.

He tamped down the softness he was feeling when he'd watched her face off with Nyx.

"Nyx seems certain you're in danger," he said.

"Nyx is sure I'm in danger every time I'm not in her direct line of sight." Eavan shook her head. "If you wanted to simply *say* you guard me, but not—"

"She hired me to watch you. I'll watch you." He tried a falsely friendly smile. They'd do better if they were at least civil to each other. "You could make that easier on both of us if you answered questions."

"Sure. I'll answer what you need to know to do the job Nyx hired you for." She smiled again, not full of promises like the women inside, but with barely curved lips. It was a dismissal, and in case he missed the message, she turned and walked down the flagstone path.

Yeah. This is going to be a cakewalk. He snorted and followed her. Before she had taken a half-dozen steps down the end of the walk, he was in front of her. "Guarding you means you don't go wandering off."

"I'm not an errant child, Mr. Owens. I drove here on my own; I go to and from work every day on my own. I go—"

"No. You *used* to. I'll be escorting you to and from everything for the time being." He'd hoped that Nyx had explained the extent of his role in Eavan's life, but if she did, Eavan wasn't cooperating. To be sure there was no confusion, he added, "Nyx was adamant about that part of my services. I'll be accompanying you everywhere you go, every time you leave your apartment for any reason. It's why she rented the apartment. That way, I'll be within reach the moment you step outside your door."

Eavan made a frustrated sound. "What if you have other things to do? We can come up with a schedule that—"

"Eavan?" He waited until she looked at him, and then said, "This is my job. If I'm not able to keep up with your schedule, I'll call one of my associates, but I suspect I can keep up."

"This is going to be a pain in the ass, isn't it?" She yanked open the passenger door of her Z3 and dropped her briefcase on the seat.

"You won't need that." He didn't wince as he said it, but he did draw a deep breath, bracing himself for the next snarl that was sure to follow his clarification. "We'll leave it here to be picked up later."

She looked over her shoulder. "Exactly what is it that I won't need, Mr. Owens?"

"The car. We'll take mine." He gestured at his car, a nondescript black sedan that looked like the same sort innumerable car services and middle-class businessmen drove. It blended. Eavan's topaz blue BMW didn't. "You won't need yours for a while."

"I won't need my *car*?" Her hands were on her hips. Her lips were pressed together in a tight line.

"Look. I'm not your enemy. I was hired to keep you safe . . . or out of trouble . . . or maybe just drive you crazy so you move back home. You can go back in there and talk to her, or you can cooperate." He wondered briefly if Eavan had the same ability to hypnotize him as Nyx apparently had. If he tried to restrain her, could she control him as Nyx had done when he'd pulled his gun? He needed more answers than he had. "You need to accept that I'm like your shadow now. You aren't going anywhere without me. If that's going to be an issue, go talk to Nyx while we're still standing here."

Eavan's answer was a string of expletives and a glare at the close-curtained windows of her family's house. "Talking to Nyx won't change a thing. It rarely does."

He nodded once. "Okay then. So, do you want to eat while we go over your schedule? Or go to your apartment?"

Cillian felt a touch sorry for her. It wasn't an easy position she was in—not that his was much better. Now that Cillian had sent the data in to his supervisor and been told to work with—*for?*—his "anonymous" source, he had more than a few questions for Nyx. He just needed to get Eavan tucked into her apartment so he could go ask a few of those questions.

"It's your choice," he added. "We could go downtown and grab a bite or—"

"Food first," she interrupted. "Fat Daddy's."

She slid into his car, slammed the door, and stared out the window.

"Right, then," he muttered as he walked around and opened his door. "This should be great fun."

6

Late that night, Eavan slipped out of her apartment window. She wasn't sure if she could get out the front door without Cillian noticing. Odds were that he wasn't staring at her door, but she wasn't sure about video feeds. He'd mentioned surveillance in the hallway, the breezeway, the parking deck, and the back lot. *Safer to slip out the window.* The drop wasn't that far. She might be predominantly mortal—and intending to stay that way—but her genetic heritage still came with a few extra benefits.

After a surreptitious glance to assure that no neighbors were out on their balconies, she hopped up on the balcony rail so she had her back to her apartment and dropped down. The impact of the landing was muffled by the grass-covered ground.

No one the wiser.

With a satisfied smile, she crossed the lot and opened her car door.

It was good that her Z was home instead of still at Nyx's, but when Eavan thought about strangers driving her car, it felt more like injury than insult. She hated the fact that he'd had some stranger drive her car home. She slid her hand over the wheel affectionately.

She left her car door slightly open, put it in neutral, and coasted to the bottom of the hill. Once she hit the intersection, she slammed the door and popped the clutch. The squeal of tires and almost-but-not-quite-out-of-control swerve as she slammed through the gears was exhilarating.

Driving was one of the passions she could indulge. No sex. No murder. No stalking. *Okay, a little stalking, but no killing anyone.* A woman needed releases for pent-up energy, and there was only so much workouts and toys could do to let off stress. Sometimes speed was essential to sanity.

On this, at least, Nyx had always been tolerant. She had reduced rates on a number of vices for the local police in exchange for looking the other way on Eavan's driving habits. It had started as a sixteenth birthday present and evolved into status quo over the last eight years.

Eavan could navigate the streets of Raleigh and Durham and a number of cities within a four-hour radius. Having the I-95 corridor, I-40, and I-85 all but at her doorstep meant that her penchant for speed was easily indulged. Finding a mechanic who disabled Nyx's GPS tracking toys regularly added a layer of privacy the past two years that had made Eavan feel almost like a normal woman.

Not now. Not with Cillian holding a leash. Eavan made her way to the beltline and just drove for a while before she headed downtown. It helped, but the anxiety was still riding her. She took a few side streets, turning at the last possible moment each time, focusing on the importance of control and precision. *It's not going to change a thing. I am not going to change how I live.* This could be a short-term problem, a test to be passed. *Or failed.*

That was the real problem: Eavan felt herself getting closer and closer to crossing lines that she swore she'd never approach. This business with Daniel had become an obsession. It needed to end so that she could regain control of her life. It made control of both appetites feel precarious. If she could scare him away from the drug trade or find some information to get him arrested, maybe she could stop hunting him—because she *was* hunting him. She knew it, even if she wouldn't admit it to anyone else, and she needed to get it in check before Nyx found out.

Eavan parked the car down by Moore Square and headed toward one of Daniel's warehouses. It wasn't any trouble to let herself inside the warehouse: she'd lifted a key one night flirting with Daniel. Soft-soled shoes muffled her steps as she crossed the concrete floor. This was what she did, who she was. Every instinct she'd had told her that she was where she should be—except the ones that told her that naked with Cillian was a better plan.

Equally unhealthy urges.

She could control them though. She'd been doing so for twelve years. A glaistig's dual needs for sex and death—preferably together—coincided with the onset of menses. It had taken her six years to learn to smother those urges until they were just a whisper. She'd slipped and hunted a few times, but she'd never killed or fucked anyone. She'd walked away from every hunt before it became an obsession.

Until now.

Now, both of Eavan's urges were screaming to life.

The smart move was to stay away from Daniel, to stay out of his clubs. Something there made all of her family uncomfortable—and made Eavan feel like electricity was battering all her synapses simultaneously. That sensation had never been quite as all-consuming as it was right now.

Because he's near me.

She stood in the shadowed recesses of a room, half hidden by towering shelves, peering between the wooden crates that were stacked at the end of the aisle of shelves. In front of her in a bare bit of concrete in the center of a darkened warehouse stood Daniel—her prey. He wasn't Other, but he was tangling with things that made him resonate like he was more than mortal. She could feel it. *What are you doing?* There was more to her reaction to him than the actions he'd undertaken. The taint of the magicks he used wasn't enough to explain her compulsion where he was concerned, but she had no other explanation.

She did, however, know she couldn't ignore what he was doing. Drugging women and selling them like chattel was inexcusable.

He needs to be stopped.

The .38 was heavy in her palm before she realized she'd reached into her bag. The stainless steel vein down the back of the grip didn't burn her hands or weaken her as it would if she were truly a full glaistig. With her mortal blood still dominant, iron and steel barely gave her a twinge. Instead, the gun felt right in her hands; the desire to sight down on the tainted mortal was a compulsion inside that grew from a whisper to a roar.

As she watched, Daniel ground the child's bones into powder. It was an odd sight: he stood in a business suit at a table alongside an average-looking barbecue grill. On the grill were bones, a child-size skull, and several small lizards. On the table were assorted plants, an empty mixing bowl, a glass jar of what looked to be blood, and a modern electric meat grinder. Daniel was barefoot in a pile of earth that seemed more out of place than all the rest.

Muttering something and gesticulating, he lifted the skull from the grill. Then he raised a large hammer, closed his eyes, said something in what she suspected was to be a reverent way, and smashed the hammer onto the tiny skull until it cracked. Shards of bone lay scattered in the earth.

"What do you want?" He didn't look at her when he said it, so for a moment she thought he was talking to someone else.

She wondered if he could find her in that unerring way she had with him. They were bound together in a way that made no sense to her. *Is it the magick? Is it because I'm hunting him?* Something existed between them, and she wasn't sure what it was—or if she really wanted to know.

"Eve?" He tossed the hammer aside and began picking up the bone shards. Once they were all gathered, he turned to stare directly at her. "What are you doing here?"

"I . . ." She didn't have words for what she wanted, not

words she wanted to share. She wanted to kill him, wanted to reorder the world, press down the chaos that buzzed in her skin before she crossed a line that would change everything. She wanted to end her hunt of Daniel with something bloody and satisfying. She settled for a socially acceptable statement: "What you're doing is wrong."

He was utterly nonplussed. "Praying?"

"That's not praying."

"Sure it is. It's just an older religion."

An older religion? All faiths had a place, but humans like Daniel were the reason mainstream humanity thought Old Faiths were evil. He was using the veneer of religion to sate his greed.

"What will you do with it?" she heard herself asking, as if his admission to her would change anything. She knew exactly what he did with his poison: drugged people, addicted them, and sold them.

He dropped the bone fragments into the grinder. The whirring noise seemed loud in the empty room. "How about I make you a deal . . ."

She felt like her skin was crawling with stinging things as she stepped toward him. She wanted to go to him, despite everything. "What are you offering?"

He was a bastard. He preyed on the innocent. He used earth and bone to enslave people, not as punishment, but randomly for avarice and malice.

He lifted the corner of his mouth is a sardonic half smile. "For starters, drop that piece in your hand. Then tell me what you want from me."

She glanced at the .38; she hadn't realized she had raised it. She lowered it with effort. Her arm hung at her side, but her finger still rested on the trigger. *Did I take off the safety, too?* She wasn't sure, but she suspected she had. The habitual movement would've preceded raising her weapon.

"I want you to stop mixing that," she told him.

The look he gave her was curious. "And if I don't? Are you going to stop visiting me? Stop stealing my toys?"

She had an intense craving to show him exactly what would happen if he didn't stop. Why this one was different she didn't know, but in that instant she wanted to let her Other heritage reign. *Sex and death.* The room was already filled with death; her body was screaming for sex. If she had both on the same night, she'd become just like the rest of her family—like Nyx wanted, like her mother wanted. She'd have eternity. Steal the lives of mortals, enjoy those dual pleasures, and she'd be stronger, faster, live for centuries . . .

She swallowed against the dryness in her mouth and said, "Please?"

"Please what?" Daniel gave her that same tempting smile he'd offered in the clubs so often. "I don't like them mindless, Eve. No medicine for you. Aren't you tired of provoking me? It's been fun to have someone try to thwart me. Ballsy. I like it. Let me give you what you want."

Her hand tightened until the ridges on the grip pressed into her skin. Her tongue was slow in her mouth as she told him, "You *can't.*"

"Are you sure?" Daniel stood there with a jar of blood in one hand and the stuff of death all around him. "You see what I am, but you're not disgusted, are you? Come closer."

And in that instant, she wanted to swallow his final breath more than anything she'd ever wanted. She reached out her other hand to touch him, but stopped short of actual contact. "You don't *want* to give me what I want, Daniel. Trust me. Please. If you have *anything* good in you, change your path. Stop making these drugs. For everyone."

And then she ran, away from temptation, away from the room of death and blood and bone. She was a mortal. She could walk away. She'd chosen humanity. She just needed to *keep* choosing it.

Eavan went to her car and began one of her tried and true reordering plans. Absently, she drove out to Chapel Hill.

There was the first stop. *Step one. Routine.* It was a strange loop she'd adopted when she was a student—like walking her perimeters, demarcating territories. *Like an animal.*

No, she reminded herself, *proving that I am not an animal.*

It made her feel more focused.

I am not a monster.

At UNC, she measured her steps, pacing them out just so as she crossed campus to reach the courtyard outside Davis Library. That bricked vista felt reassuring—line after line of red bricks. There was order, structure. She clung briefly to that. *Order. Follow the lines.*

They'd just opened for the day.

How long was I driving?

She went inside and wandered through the wide open layout. People, regular mortals, were already going back and forth between shelves and tables. Some were curled into cocoons of their own projects—papers and books and furrowed brows. It was normalcy. It was her world—the one she chose.

The one I'm staying in.

She'd find another way to deal with Daniel—talk to Muriel or one of the lupine-clan or even Nyx if necessary. She had found a limitation she wasn't going to test.

I can't keep stalking him.

She crossed back over the campus, smiling at the green spaces. Even those were in order. The paths were angled. The layout was defined and orderly. Sure, there were people who weren't walking down those paths, but they were following other guidelines. They wore their school colors or their Greek letters on their clothes. They defied grouping by assigning themselves another group. It gave form to the world. It was not-chaos.

She drove past Durham, not wanting to stop by Duke's library when she was feeling so tentative. *Step two. Choosing.* The Perkins Library building was gorgeous, and the order she craved was more obvious inside, but walking through the stacks made her feel predatory. *But I will not hunt.* Good mortals, smart humans, didn't stalk and attack. Knowing what she could be wasn't always reason enough to resist. She wanted it to be, but it wasn't.

For that, she needed her routines, her tried-and-true tactics. She hadn't needed to work this hard in years. She left the library and drove to Raleigh.

NCSU was twisted among the city; the campus twisted between houses and restaurants and stores. University buildings nestled around tattoo parlors and coffee shops and convenience stores. Students and professors ate next to construction workers and strangers. *Everyone is welcome here.* Sure, there were those that wore letters and insignias, but those who didn't could still blend. It was a feeling more than a quantifiable element, and the feeling was one that soothed her unease. Here, she could restructure herself. Here, she could create the order that kept her anchored to the world that she had chosen.

As she walked across the brickyard, she felt herself settling. Maybe it was the routine; maybe it was the familiarity. It didn't matter, not really.

She went inside D. H. Hill Library and went up to the second floor. She walked through the east wing and then the west wing. She went to the study carrels. She stroked shelves and paused at water fountains. It was all about the anchors. It was all about order.

"What in the hell are you doing?" Cillian was behind her; her new temptation was right there in reach.

"Nothing."

"Really? So why were you at Brennan's warehouse the other morning? Why are you here tonight? Brennan's a factor somewhere here, Eavan. I just don't know how."

Eavan bowed her head. If Cillian knew about Daniel, Nyx would know, too. *Unless she already does.* "How did you know where I went?"

"GPS."

"Did you install it?" she asked, although she was pretty sure she knew the answer.

"No," Cillian admitted. "They were preinstalled."

Eavan paused. "They?"

She'd really thought that the car was tracker-free. Her mechanic hadn't removed anything the last time. He'd pronounced her car "clean." He'd lied.

"Your car, phone, the red jacket . . ."

Eavan schooled her face as she turned and said, "Shh."

"What are you *doing*?" Cillian repeated, softer this time in deference to their location.

For a heartbeat, she considered telling him, giving him the answers she'd never spoken to anyone. Instead, she said, "Walking."

"Walking. Driving. Going in and out of libraries. Aimlessly pacing sidewalks . . ." He stepped closer, moving into her personal space as if such a thing was acceptable "At least you don't have a pattern. I can't imagine how your potential stalker could—"

"That *is* my pattern, Mr. Owens." She spoke evenly, forcing emotion to stay in check. She'd need to be more careful; she'd need to figure out how to cope with the cage that was tightening around her—but not now, not when she was still feeling unsettled. She stared at Cillian and said, "I drive. I walk. It's how I make the world make sense."

"Well, next time, you'll take me with you." Cillian looked frazzled. "You drive like you're invulnerable. I thought you were going to get killed coming off the interchange."

She didn't have the heart to ask which interchange. She didn't recall parts of the drive. It was the anchors—red brick, cold metal shelf—that mattered. That was the world.

"I'm going home," she told him.

"Please, Eavan, I need you to try to cooperate." Cillian's expression was about as frayed as her emotions had been. "Even if you don't think you're in danger, Nyx does. Slipping away from me puts us *both* in danger."

"I'm going home," she repeated. "I needed air. Now, I need sleep."

For a moment, she thought Cillian was going to say more, but instead he nodded. "I'm driving. The car will stay here."

And Eavan was too shaky to fight him. She didn't hand over the keys, but she did walk quietly to his car with him.

7

E avan stayed in her apartment for the next three days. She'd called and quit her job without notice; being around mortals right now was untenable. Of course, being around Others wasn't a good idea, either. Nyx had been tracking her; the older glaistig knew something was going on. Eavan couldn't risk going out, couldn't face talking to Nyx, and couldn't be sure she had the resolve to resist killing Daniel. She was trapped by her own biology. Her inability to deal with hunting Daniel was wearing on her. Cillian's kindness only made matters worse. Being trapped with him, a temptation always in reach, was slowly wearing away whatever control she still had left.

"I called the grocery to deliver food. Your kitchen was barren." He stood in her doorway, not crossing the threshold, but clearly expecting her to let him in. "Eavan?"

She blinked at him, aware that she'd been staring. He had the loveliest green flecks in his eyes. *And kissable lips* . . .

She turned sharply and walked away. "I was fine with takeout."

She ordered; he accepted the delivery in the hall, and once the delivery people left, he knocked on her door. *Not that he needed to knock.* She was watching through the peephole every time.

"Groceries are being delivered here. Just go in the bedroom when they arrive and—"

"I'm not in danger from delivery guys," she snapped. Being housebound was not getting easier. Knowing it was self-imposed wasn't helping, either. "I'm not in danger from any . . ." She started coughing. The words weren't ones she could force out: they were a lie.

He stepped closer. "Why are you—"

"Fuck it," she muttered.

And then she pinned him to the wall.

It wasn't her first kiss; it wasn't even the first time she'd lost control this badly. She had a leg hitched around him, pressing herself against his responding body, trying not to grind against him—and failing. He'd wrapped an arm around her, supporting her weight. *A gentleman even now . . .*

With decided effort, she pulled back. "I'm sorry. I'm so sorry."

"Eavan?" Cillian looked stunned.

"I'm sorry." She backed up, bumping into a small bookshelf in the process, sending paperbacks crashing to the floor.

He reached out to touch her face. "It's okay. You're under pressure and . . . it's okay."

Eavan ran to her bedroom while Cillian let the delivery guy into the apartment. She could hear his muffled voice, like a siren's song in her safe harbor. She stood with one hand palm-flat on the bedroom door and the other on the knob. Hunting Daniel had made both hungers all-consuming. For the first time in years, Eavan wasn't sure she could stop herself from losing control of at least one appetite. *Sex is safer.* She hadn't killed anyone; she could bring Cillian to her bed. It was safe.

It's not.

She could wrap her body around his.

And have just a taste of his breath during. *I could stop. Just a taste . . .*

She'd started to turn the knob when the phone rang. She walked over to the bed and lifted her phone from the night table.

"Eve?" Daniel asked. "How are you?"

She sat on the edge of the mattress. Her hands were shaking. "Daniel? How did you get my number?"

"Come see me, Eve." He paused just long enough that she could hear hesitance. "I miss you."

"No." She closed her eyes, wrapped one hand around the bedpost, and tried to focus. It wasn't working. Her whole body shook.

"Do you want to talk to Chastity?"

Eavan's heart thundered loud enough that it roared in her ears, but her voice was whisper-quiet. "What?"

"One of the girls . . . not the *same* Chastity. Just another mindless doll . . . right here in my arms . . . waiting for a rescue." He murmured to someone who moaned into the phone. "She's a co-ed. Well, she *was* . . ."

"What are you doing?" Eavan squeezed the bedpost until the wood cracked and cut her palm, stinging as blood slid between her fingers and trickled down the dark wood. "You can't *do* this . . . Let her go."

"Come see me, Eve. I'll be at Chaos tonight." Then he disconnected before she could reply.

Eavan slowly unwrapped her fingers from the splintered wood of her bedpost. A sliver of wood was embedded in her skin. She stared at it as she sat quietly, trying to force her mind to process Daniel's challenge.

She dialed the only person she could be almost honest with. "Muriel?"

"What's wrong?"

Eavan explained, and then she waited. There was no judgment, no leash that followed. The vampire said only: "I'll be there in thirty minutes. Get dressed."

Even though Muriel was too kind to say it, Eavan knew she was making a mistake, but staying here was a mistake, too. Her body was screaming for something. It didn't matter

which urge she fed. *Staying near Cillian isn't an option.*
She was too tempted before Daniel's call; now her body was
thrumming like something feral.

The delivery guy was still out there. That made it safer to
slip out of the room, to walk past him. It was the best opening she could hope for.

Steeling herself, Eavan opened her door and went to take
a cold shower. She didn't look at him, didn't step nearer
him, although she could feel his gaze on her.

After a painfully cold shower, she went back to her room
and got dressed.

Cillian was at the bedroom door. He had been for several
minutes. "Eavan? Can we talk? Maybe you're feeling too
housebound. We can—"

She opened her window. An alarm went off.

Ten minutes left.

Cillian tried the knob. "Damn it. What are you doing?"

Don't answer. Just go out the window.

She stood looking at the window and then at the door. He
was jimmying the lock.

"How in the hell am I to keep you safe if—" He opened
the door. "What are you doing?"

"Stay back. Please?" She looked at him, too close and
too kind. "I don't want you to get hurt."

He crossed the room and started to close the window.
"If you don't cooperate, I can't keep you safe. We've talked
about this. If it's the kiss . . ." Frustration weighed in his
voice, his movements, his everything. "It's okay, Eavan.
We can pretend it didn't happen. People react differently to
stress, and . . . it's not a big deal."

Not prey.

He was too close though.

"I'm sorry," she whispered.

"It's okay. I *told* you that." Cillian turned to face her. He
was not even three steps away.

She stared at his mouth. *Just another taste.* The tip of her
tongue darted out.

He froze, but he didn't run. "It's okay."

She wasn't sure if he was giving her permission or still forgiving her. It didn't really matter. She closed the space between them. It was all she could do to speak, but she warned him: "You should run now."

He didn't move.

So she kissed him. She had both legs around him, and he walked forward until she felt the wall behind her.

She pushed herself tighter to him. "More." She pressed her lips back to his, lifted herself up enough that she could reach between them and unbutton his jeans. Her skirt was around her hips, leaving only her underwear between them. She ripped it away; the sound of tearing cloth brought an encouraging sound from Cillian.

They were on the floor. She was straddling him, moments from crossing the line she swore she would not cross.

Better sex than murder.

She pulled away and looked down at him.

I could swallow his final breath as he . . .

She lowered herself onto him and shuddered. Sex and death, all at once, she could have it all. She licked her lips and leaned forward.

"Eavan!" Suddenly, Muriel was there, pulling her backward. The small vampire was more than a match for Eavan.

Muriel pulled Eavan off Cillian.

Eavan hissed. Muriel slapped her.

Cillian looked dazed. He scrambled to his feet, naked and somehow already aiming a gun at Muriel.

"Get in the car," Muriel said, or perhaps repeated, if the way she bit off each word was any indication. She stayed like a guard between Cillian and Eavan. "And tell him who I am, Evvie, before he tries to shoot me."

"Friend," Eavan forced out. Forming words just then was a trial, but she did it. "Muriel's a friend. I called her."

Cillian lowered his gun.

Eavan's gaze followed the lowering weapon and fell on Cillian's very beautiful naked, just-out-of-reach body. She tried to step around Muriel. "I'm fine here."

Muriel sighed. "I'm sorry about this, Mr. Owens, but until she's thinking clearly, it's for the best."

Then she punched him.

8

Eavan had a violent case of the shakes by the time she was a mile away from her apartment. It was a little mortifying to think that Muriel had seen her so out of control with a human, but at least she had been there to stop Eavan.

"I owe you," she said, not looking at Muriel yet.

"Sweetie," Muriel drawled, "you *always* owe me for something or other. You just count yourself lucky that I don't call in all those chits."

"Why did you stop me?" Eavan had heard Muriel's lectures on "giving in" often enough that she was a little surprised.

Muriel glanced over at her, taking her eyes off the road long enough that it gave Eavan a pleasant shiver of danger. When Muriel looked back at the road, she answered, "When you choose to cross those lines, I'm good with it, but it's not my place to help you cross them . . . unless you decide in advance . . . preferably with me along for the ride." She flashed a fanged grin at Eavan.

"I'm not sure I'll ever be woman enough for you," Eavan admitted.

Muriel laughed, not cruelly, but in that way that made clear that she knew secrets that the rest of the world could only guess at. "I'll be gentle the first time . . . although I'm not so sure that's what you're looking for. You came near to breaking your mortal."

"I'm mortal, too." Eavan wasn't sure of it just then; she felt pretty far from mortal after the way she'd thrown herself at Cillian. The words, the reminder—to herself and to Muriel—were important though. "I'm *still* mortal."

"You are, sweetie." Muriel reached over and squeezed her head. "You haven't killed anyone, and I don't know if that was sex enough to count."

Eavan and Muriel had discussed what constituted "sex" often enough, but there weren't any clear answers. Things Other were notoriously prone to loopholes, semantics, and arguments of intention. If she considered it true sex, would it be? Or was it the definition of the matriarch? Or was it the interpretation of some long dead ancestor? Eavan had no answers, but she did know that she needed to tread extra carefully the next month. *Just in case.* One month without murder—usually that wouldn't sound so impossible.

"Help me stop Daniel?" Eavan stared out the window into the dimly lit parking lot of the Chaos Factory. Somewhere out there, her prey waited.

"It's a trap." Muriel pulled in and zipped around the line of cars to go to the valet stand. "You know that, right?"

"I do." Eavan accepted a hand as she slid out of Muriel's Vanquish.

Muriel walked around the car and wrapped an arm around Eavan. Then she caught and held the valet's gaze.

"Don't joyride," she warned. Her fangs appeared just long enough to scare the valet. "If any of you so much as stroke the car, you're dinner."

The valet shuddered. He wouldn't remember the words, or seeing the fangs, but he would take good care of Muriel's car.

"This is a bad idea, Eavan." Muriel motioned at the club. "Going in there when you're like this is a *really bad idea.*"

"I need to get the girl out," Eavan insisted. "I can handle it."

Silently, Muriel walked past Eavan.

She didn't need vampire powers to charm the doorman. She skipped the line and went to stand in front of him. Eavan followed. Muriel wrapped an arm around her again. This time, though, she stroked her fingers over Eavan's hip.

Eavan gasped. "Muriel . . ."

As Eavan leaned in to Muriel's caress, she felt the doorman and innumerable mortals in the waiting line respond to the tease of a show.

Not as much as I am.

"Shhh, sweetie," Muriel whispered in her ear. "We'll be able to dance in a sec." To the doorman, she added in a low whisper, "My girl's in a bit of a mood. Can we skip the line? She's not much of an exhibitionist unless the music's on."

The doorman grinned and motioned them inside.

They stopped just inside the door. Muriel's hand slid up and across the small of Eavan's back. "This is where we are, Ev. You're not in any shape to be here."

"Staying here." Eavan swallowed. She fisted her hands, driving small half moons into her palms. "I've been almost as bad before."

"Not in years."

"I can do this." Eavan forced the craving back as hard as she could. "Please, Muriel?"

Muriel shook her head, but she asked, "Tell me the ground rules."

"Don't let Daniel take me anywhere. Get the girl out." Eavan leaned against a wall, feeling the onslaught of music, the thrum of sexual energy, the lure of prey in the club. "No sex with *anyone*. Knock my ass out if you need to."

"Anything up to that point or nothing at all?" Muriel forced Eavan to look at her.

"Nothing with anyone but you. If I need . . . if . . ." Eavan hated to ask Muriel to be her crutch. "I don't want to hurt . . . you're strong."

Muriel laughed. "Woe is me."

"We're friends." Eavan would hate herself if Muriel actually attached emotion to sex. They'd pushed a few barriers over the years though, so it wasn't unheard of. Muriel was the closest to sex Eavan had been.

Until tonight.

"I'm here." Muriel's teasing vanished. "Just like old times, right? I get all the fun, and you refuse to enjoy yourself."

Eavan laughed. "I plead the Fifth . . . actually . . ." She took Muriel's hand and led the way to one of the bars. "Redbreast. Triple shot. Neat."

The bartender looked at Muriel.

"Crown, rocks, with a splash." She paused and looked behind her as if the man standing there was with them. "And a vodka tonic, neat."

"That was mean," Eavan whispered. "I hate vodka."

Muriel sighed. "Vodka's mine, sweets. You can have my whiskey."

With a grateful smile, Eavan took the two glasses of whiskey when the bartender returned. She upended the triple and left the glass behind. It was a start. The whiskey was a comforting narcotic, numbing her senses enough to help block the cravings a little.

For the next two hours, they pushed through the crowd, pausing at each of the bars rather than running a tab, so as not to alarm any of the bartenders with how much she was consuming. *Not enough for a glaistig, but far more than a real mortal could drink safely.* Even still, Eavan was one pulsing nerve after pressing too close to mortals, all but stoned on the pheromones in the club.

Another hour passed. Daniel was nowhere to be found. She could feel him nearby several times, close enough to set her body on edge, but when she turned he was not near enough to find.

What game is he playing?

"Daniel's not here." Muriel yelled the words. They'd just made another circuit of the main dance floor.

He was, but the only way for Eavan to know that was through some creepy affinity that Eavan wasn't about to admit to Muriel. It was stronger now, a compulsion to seek him. *Is this how the zombie girls feel?* She was sure she hadn't ingested any of his drugs, but she felt called to him. It didn't make sense.

She slammed the rest of her latest glass of whiskey, and then took Muriel's out of her hand and downed it, too.

Muriel led the way to the stairs. "Top bar," she mouthed.

Eavan nodded and followed. At the top, Muriel pushed open the heavy door. They went into the lavish room, and the door fell closed with a thud, sealing out most of the noise. It wasn't silent, but the top floor bar was designed to make conversation possible.

"Oh shit," Eavan whispered. Cillian was standing at the bar, looking far from happy.

Muriel put her back to him. "Give me rules, Evvie. Are you okay?"

"I am." Eavan was able to look away from him. "I've had a half a fifth already. Everything is sleeping now."

Muriel smiled at Cillian as he came up beside her. "How's the head?"

"I'm fine." Cillian scowled, but to his credit he didn't do anything else.

Muriel gave him a quick once-over. "I know."

His scowl deepened, so Eavan stepped closer and told Muriel.

"Should I stay?" Muriel asked.

Eavan shook her head. "I'm good . . . because of you. Again."

With a wicked grin, Muriel brushed a quick kiss over Eavan's lips. "Be safe, Ev."

Once she was gone, Eavan turned to face Cillian. "Are you okay? Really?"

He closed his eyes like he was trying to control the temper that was playing in the edges of his expression. "About the blueballs? Yes. About your girlfriend knocking

me out? I guess. About you running out so I can't do my
fucking job? No, not so much."

"I'm sorry," she told him yet again.

"For which part?"

"Everything but the running out," she admitted with a
small smile. In the space between words, she paused. Her
skin was crawling: Daniel was near. Perhaps he'd stayed
away only because Muriel was in the bar.

Cillian took Eavan's elbow and led her to a table
toward the back of the room. "Are you on something,
Eavan?"

"Like drugs? Me?" She felt her mouth curving into a
smile at the thought.

If he knew the truth, what would he think?

The cocktail waitress, thankfully, chose that moment
to stop at the table. Cillian waited while Eavan ordered
another drink. Through a tinted window they could see the
main dance floor. In the middle of the floor, surrounded by
guards, Daniel stood. He stared up as if he could see her
through the darkened glass.

Eavan stood and stepped closer to the window.

In the crowd below, Daniel waited. Cuddled into his
arms was a very malleable young woman. Daniel kept
her upright. He kissed her forehead and then looked up
at Eavan and mouthed, "I'll let her go if"—he stopped
a group of women, gave the girl over to their care, and
then looked back up at Eavan—"you come see me soon,
Eve."

Cillian came to stand beside her; he peered into the
crowd below. "Are you looking for someone? A dealer?
Brennan again? If your family is trying to protect you because you're mixed up in something . . ."

She walked away from the window. Daniel was gone.
It wasn't a trap, but a negotiation. *What do I do now?* She
couldn't chase after him; the idea of seeing him in this state
was sheer foolishness. She couldn't take Cillian, either . . .
or leave him behind. Rage started to build inside her. She

was a glaistig, not some child to be toyed with and broken. Daniel had no clue who he was taunting.

Eavan watched the mortals of the dance floor. It looked so normal. That's the sort of life she'd used to dream of having; it was the life she thought she could have one day. Nyx had seemed to be giving her a little more freedom. Everything seemed to be going well—until Nyx hired Cillian. *Until Daniel.*

She's been watching me the whole time.

There was no normal, only degrees of beautiful lies.

Eavan knew the answer, but she asked all the same: "Did my cousin hire you because of Daniel?"

Cillian didn't reply or flinch, but his silence was answer enough for her.

Eavan held down "1" on her mobile and said, "Grandmother."

Nyx didn't bother with greetings at this hour. "Are you injured?"

"No." Eavan watched Cillian as she spoke. "How long have you known?"

"Long enough to see that you were too far gone," Nyx said. "I don't like Brennan. Not for you or for anyone. Especially not as your first."

"You know what he's doing?" Eavan asked, still watching Cillian.

"Of course I do." Nyx sighed. "That's not your business though, Evvie. Brennan is trouble. The powder he uses . . . it's *really* not good for our kind. It works on some of us, too."

Eavan looked away then. She'd been a fool to think she could hide anything from her matriarch, and in that instant, she had to wonder if she truly could do anything beyond Nyx's control. "This doesn't change the other thing. I'm done with Daniel because I'm not able to—"

"Ask your Cillian what his real job is," Nyx interrupted.

Eavan looked up and caught Cillian's gaze. "What do you do for real?"

"I'm your bodyguard."

On the other end of the phone, Nyx made a rude sound. "Tell him to tell you the rest."

"Nyx wants me to know," she told him. "She said . . ."

Cillian held out his hand for the phone. Silently, she released it.

He held it up to his ear, listened for a moment, and then scowled and hung up. Quietly, he said, "Let's take a walk."

9

Cillian wasn't sure what he hated more, the fact that he had to tell Eavan that he was with the C.D.A. or the fact that he seemed to have picked up a second supervisor. He wanted to tell Nyx to piss off, but his superiors would be anything but pleased if he lost his "anonymous" source so soon—plus that whole threat business of Nyx's echoed in his mind.

Eavan was silent by his side as they walked down the street toward a tiny park that was reasonably well-lit. He stopped at a small cluster of unoccupied benches. It was late enough that they had a bit of privacy.

"I'm here investigating him," Cillian told her. "Your *cousin* offered me a wealth of information on his activities, among other things, in exchange for protecting you."

Eavan laughed, a bitter sound that made him want to comfort her. She sat down beside him. "Threats, sex, or money?"

He didn't pretend to be shocked. "Not sex."

"With her at least."

"With *any* of them," Cillian corrected.

Eavan was silent for a moment. "She hired you in the hopes that I'd sleep with you. It's an obsession of hers."

"Excuse me?" He angled his body so he was facing her. Of all the things he'd been prepared to hear, that wasn't anywhere on the list. "She hired me because she

knew you were spending time with Brennan, and he's
bad news."

"He is." Eavan took a breath. "But Nyx could've simply
broken a few of my bones if all she wanted was to keep me
away from Daniel."

"She could've"—Cillian lowered his voice as a small
group of people walked by—"*broken your bones*. You say
that like it's an everyday event."

"Not these days, but . . ." Eavan shrugged. "Nyx is in
charge. I'm guessing you already know on some level how
terrible she is, else we wouldn't be having this conversation.
She picked you for reasons that aren't about guarding me
from Daniel. She picked you for me to have sex with."

"Does she pick a lot of people for you to sleep with?" He
tried to keep his voice even, but the idea that his family had
been threatened, his life endangered, his career toyed with,
and his peace of mind completely upended over *sex* was infuriating. *It isn't Eavan's fault*, he reminded himself. She'd
been adamant that she did not want him around.

Eavan blushed. "No, you're supposed to be the first."

"Well that's something, at—" He stopped mid-sarcasm.
"The *first* first . . . like . . ."

"Yes." She looked about as comfortable as he felt. "The
very first. My virginity is a matter of family irritation."

"Your family is concerned over your being a virgin." He
said the words slowly. "So you were dating a drug dealer
and your cousin hired me to have sex with you? Is that what
earlier was . . . Never mind."

"No, earlier was about my wanting you. It was a mistake. A pleasurable one but a mistake nonetheless . . . and I
wasn't dating Daniel." Eavan smiled regretfully. "I know it
all seems a bit odd."

"You think?"

They sat there for a moment while Cillian tried to figure
out what to say. On the phone, Nyx had been very clear in
her orders to be "completely honest" with Eavan and then
report to the house to speak with her. *Screw it*. He was

already so far out of his comfort zone that he wasn't sure he'd be seeing level ground again. "Can I ask you what you are?"

"What I am?" she repeated.

"I've met your family . . . and now this. You're not quite like most *humans*, right?"

"I can see where you'd get that. I'm human, mostly," she hedged. "I'd like to stay that way, too."

"Explain?"

"There are a couple things I can't do if I am to stay human." She squirmed, and a blush burned up her cheeks. "My *grandmother* Nyx would like me to do those things. She's not particularly pleased with my intention to live and die as a human."

"And if you do these things, you become something else? Something *Other*?"

She nodded.

"So Nyx hired me to . . ." He whistled and shook his head. "And Brennan? He's what?"

"Daniel is a human. One that my family doesn't like."

"So . . ." He paused and shook his head, trying to make sense of the things she was sharing. He thought he was taking it remarkably well, all things considered. "I'm trying to understand. Help me out here?"

Eavan stood and crossed her arms over her chest. "Nyx wanted my first to be someone I'd remember fondly. She'd prefer I sleep with you than with Daniel, and she, undoubtedly, thinks I'd be in danger if I continued . . . stalking him. He's making some zombie powder that he's using to enslave and sell girls. I was just going to try to scare him, rescue some of the girls, but I got caught up. And Nyx thinks that whatever he's doing with the zombie powder is dangerous to our kind."

Cillian sat speechless, watching the people cross through the park. A preacher or madman perhaps was harassing passersby, calling them "harlots" and misquoting the Christian Bible.

If only he knew what dangers really lived in his city . . .

He wasn't sure which side of the good-evil fence she belonged on—or which side her family was on—but there were nights when he wasn't sure where he belonged, either.

"I'll tell Nyx that you left. Get out of here, Mr. Owens, before you get trapped." She turned and walked away. "Get out, and don't look back."

Eavan was midway across the park before Cillian could formulate a reply. He wasn't sure what to think about the things she'd told him, but he was sure that Nyx—and possibly Eavan—had answers to help him stop Brennan. That's what he'd been sent here to do. He'd expected to do so by ordinary means: the C.D.A. might track and eradicate Crypto Drugs, but he had no direct and open dealings with the world of the Others. The human world still functioned in ignorance. He was to continue to act as if he, too, was ignorant. Other C.D.A. members had a higher security clearance and were thus able to do otherwise.

Did they end up involved this way, too? Was it just a random case gone off the rails?

On a personal level, he wasn't sure if he was flattered or horrified. He didn't want to think long on that detail. He'd watched her at the clubs with Brennan; he'd watched her stand up to Nyx. *And held her in my arms like something molten and too dangerous to touch.* There was something different about her, but getting involved personally with a case was a bad idea.

He caught up to Eavan and said, "You need a lift?"

She gave him a strained smile. "It's a bad idea, Cillian."

He shrugged. "I'm not running—from *either* of my jobs."

"It's a mistake," she said.

"It's my mistake then."

The way she held herself aloof made him want to comfort her, but in light of what she'd just revealed, that was the very last thing he could do. Instead, they walked silently to his car and drove to Nyx's house.

10

Nyx was dressed in the closest thing to proper attire that she ever wore. Eavan knew when she walked in that they weren't staying. She shivered. "Will you let Mr. Owens leave?"

"*Mr.* Owens?" Nyx repeated with a knowing smile. "Your *Cillian* is perfectly free to leave if he'd like to go."

Eavan's distancing tactic was, like most things, utterly transparent to Nyx. How many times had they stood in the kitchen in a standoff? Nothing had changed, not the ridiculously artificial country-shabby decor of the room, not the fear that she felt, and certainly not the fact that Nyx had the upper hand.

Nyx gestured toward the door they'd just entered. "He can go. No strings as long as he doesn't tell anyone what he's learned of our world. I'm not a monster, Evvie."

Before Eavan could dispute that claim, Nyx held up hand and said, "Not now."

"So . . ." Cillian's tone was relaxed, but he stood nearer Eavan with his body slightly at an angle, positioning himself between the two women. He hadn't left. Instead, he'd chosen sides. For whatever reason, he was still acting as if he was there to protect her.

Nyx stepped toward him, each pace measured and timed to give him a chance to back away, to acknowledge her as the alpha predator she was.

Cillian stepped forward, moving away from the kitchen counter to give himself room to maneuver. He grinned. "If you're going to get hostile over her figuring out that you hired me because of Brennan, now's the time, Grandma."

Nyx paused.

Eavan winced.

"You're either brave or foolish, Mr. Owens." Nyx reached out beside him and took a pair of bone carved hair sticks from the counter. "My granddaughter is precious to me. I want you to keep her safe. In exchange, I will help you in your job. That hasn't changed."

Eavan was speechless.

"Done. I'll do my best, but"—Cillian scowled—"I'm not a stud for hire. Eavan told me about . . . the other thing."

"Of course she did. It's a bit sooner than I expected, but this was all inevitable, my dears." Nyx twisted her hair up into a coil atop her head. Tendrils snaked down on either side. Stylists would have to work for the look she achieved in a moment—of course, glaistig hair was a living extension of the body, so that did help.

Nyx stepped between them and put one arm around Eavan and the other around Cillian. "If she needs a bedmate she might not kill—which she seems fixated on—you'll be handy. It's the most progress I've had with her, so I'm content. Now, let's go see Daniel, so that matter can be put to rest, shall we?"

Eavan hesitated. "Grandmama? Do you think that's it's a good idea for *all* of us to go?"

Nyx's laughter was unrestrained. She patted Eavan on the cheek and walked out the door.

They stood in Brennan's living room, after having Nyx charm the doorman, a maid, and two security guards. Cillian wasn't sure at all of the protocol. B&E wasn't outside the parameters of his job, but murder usually required either a series of paperwork or immediate threat.

"Much easier to tread quietly when he covers the floor

with this." Nyx looked gleeful as she walked across the plush carpet. "Poor bastard won't know what hit him."

"He's unnaturally tempting." Eavan spoke softly. "There's something off."

"He plays with voodoo, dabbles in zombification, so he's abuzz with energy, and you're"—Nyx paused and looked askance at Cillian—"you're hungry. The privilege of age, Eavan: I'm not starving or unsure."

Eavan stood, examining an obsidian sculpture to avoid looking at Nyx or Cillian as she admitted, "I don't like this."

"Noted." Nyx didn't bother to hide her amusement. She looked around Brennan's house like an antiques appraiser. "He has good taste."

"I'm not sure this is a good idea," Cillian repeated for the sixth time. Unfortunately, after the second time, Nyx ignored him as if he hadn't spoken aloud. Cillian wasn't exactly sure why she even allowed them to come along. He did, however, know what he was doing there. Months of work would be wasted if Brennan was murdered. Admittedly, it would be satisfying. Having criminals simply arrested sometimes felt anticlimactic, but having them murdered before they revealed the information he needed to proceed on his case was a trouble of a different sort.

He tried again: "Unless he has records here, this will stall the whole investigation . . . Nyx!" He turned to Eavan. "Can she hear me?"

This time, though, Nyx paused. "He's selling mortals. It upsets Evvie, and she's behaving foolishly. He's moving drugs that are causing you complications. If I kill him, she'll be happier; your employer will have resolved a drug flow. I can always use a snack. Where's the downside?"

Then she sashayed across the room and into Brennan's bedroom, humming softly. She left the door wide open, so they could see her when she stopped beside a massive glass-block pedestal bed. With a wicked grin, she watched Cillian as she lifted one side of her skirt. He couldn't look away—or stop the sound of shock. Her legs were not those of a human: they were muscular and furred like an animal's legs.

"Told you that you didn't want all of those questions answered, Cillian," she said as she pulled out her hairpins. Her hair was writhing around her shoulders like angry serpents.

He took a step backward.

Eavan reached out and squeezed his hand. "We should look for his files."

Brennan stirred as Nyx straddled him. The sheet was only partially covering him; his upper body was bare. His hands were under the pillow beneath his head.

"Wake up, Mr. Brennan." Nyx sounded cheerful. "We have to chat."

"Who—"

"Shhh." Nyx put a finger over his mouth. "My dears, perhaps you could close the door before you go looking for whatever documents you needed? Daniel and I need some privacy, don't we, dear?"

Cillian didn't speak as Eavan pulled the door shut, closing in the two predators. He wasn't sure which of them was worse. Good and evil weren't always clearly delineated. Nyx intended to kill Daniel Brennan; Brennan drugged and sold people. *Is it monstrous to kill a monster? Is Nyx evil?* He wished, briefly, that his childhood catechism held up under such questions. It didn't. Moral relativity made clear that black-and-white questions weren't realistic in the world Cillian saw.

The world these people . . . creatures . . . all see, too.

"Come on, Cillian," Eavan said gently. "It's easier if you don't think about it."

"For whom?"

"For all of us." She gave him a rueful smile. "That's my family. My blood. And she's about to kill him."

"Is that *all*?" He hated that he wanted to know, but he did. He'd involved himself in the business affairs of Nyx and her family—not just because of the C.D.A., but also because he felt the stirring of interest in Eavan. That interest didn't die when she'd told him that she wasn't altogether human. He'd been pretty certain of that long before she'd kissed him. "What will she—"

"Don't ask me that right now." Eavan opened a door and peered inside. Fitness equipment filled the room. She walked to another door and opened it. "Here we are."

"And her legs?" He had to ask now while he still could. "I mean, your legs aren't . . . I've felt . . ." He looked at her bare ankles and toned calves. "You're not like that."

She didn't flinch. "I'm still mostly human. I told you that there were things I had to do in order to be like the rest of my family."

"Sex and . . ."

"Murder." Eavan looked at the closed door. "Preferably at the same time."

"And last night when we . . . were you going to kill me?" His heartbeat felt too fast, but he wasn't sure it was entirely from fear.

"I don't know." Her tongue darted out to trace her lips. She looked straight at him and said, "I thought about it for a moment."

"And Brennan?"

She stared at him still, a challenge plain in her expression. "Yes, I wanted to kill him."

Cillian felt a strange—*unhealthy*—stab of jealousy. "And . . ."

"Maybe." She shook her head. "I've never done either one. I can't do both, so I do neither. I want to stay human."

Cillian wasn't sure what to say, other than, "Let's start searching . . . If you see anything that could be business, set it aside."

She nodded, and they searched in silence.

11

Nyx screamed, but not in pleasure.

Eavan was out of the office before Cillian realized she'd moved. He followed her, not as fast as she moved but only a few steps behind her.

When he crossed the threshold of Brennan's room and saw Nyx, he was horrified. Brennan had her bound with thick chains. White powder was all over her face, giving her lips a chalky appearance. She was unconscious. There were gashes in both of her arms and one high up on her thigh. Blood poured from those cuts into paint basins under each arm.

"Eve!" Brennan was blood-covered, naked, and far too happy. "I had no idea you would bring me such a present. Glaistig blood is ridiculously expensive in the open market, and for whatever reason, they're averse to my presence so I can't lure them in for love nor money."

"Get Nyx," was all Eavan said, and then she was on Brennan like a crazed person.

Brennan pushed her back like she weighed nothing and wrapped his arms around her. She leaned forward and bit him, grabbing his earlobe in her mouth.

He laughed joyously. "I *knew* you'd be perfect."

Cillian unwound the chains from Nyx and looked up at Eavan. "She's breathing."

"Go," Eavan said. She was held in an unwilling embrace

by Brennan. "Bind her wounds in the car. Get her out of here before she's too weakened."

Cillian couldn't stand the idea of leaving Eavan behind. "But—"

"Please?" she asked Cillian before turning her attention to Brennan and adding, "Let them leave, and I'll stop fighting."

Brennan kissed her. "Better yet, how about I let them go, and you keep fighting? I don't like my zombie girls; I just like the money I make selling them."

"Done." She looked over at Cillian again. "Get her home. Now. Tell Chloe to call Muriel."

Cillian lifted Nyx into his arms, but he hesitated. *How do I leave her here?* Eavan caught his gaze and asked, "Please? She's . . . she needs help. If she dies . . . please?"

Brennan picked up a knife and held it against Eavan's throat.

She didn't move.

"Listen to Eve, or I'll bleed her out." Brennan drew a heart on Eavan's throat with the tip of the knife. "If you go, Eve gets a fair chance at fighting."

Eavan stood meekly as blood trickled slowly down her skin and vanished into her shirt. "Please, Cillian? I need Nyx safe."

Eavan watched Cillian carry her grandmother out. Daniel held her still. She could feel how happy he was to be entangled with her. He nuzzled her bleeding throat and murmured, "Did you really think I didn't know what you were, Eve?"

"How?"

"I drink glaistig blood. I mix it in my drugs. I knew who and what you were the moment you crossed my path. A virgin glaistig. Do you know what you're worth on the market, lovely Eve?" He licked her throat. "I don't want to share you though. Not now, and definitely not once your hooves are here."

She didn't speak. The words she had screaming in her head weren't words to share with mortals.

"Tell me yes." He traced the contours of her body. "Better yet, tell me no."

"Why?"

He kissed her, and she couldn't deny how easily her body responded. It wasn't the mind-blowing reaction she had to Cillian, but it was a reaction. *But he hurt Nyx.* If he hadn't done that, if he'd have been honest with her, she wasn't sure she'd be able to resist.

"We could skip this whole messy business. Save me having to kill your lovely family . . ." He loosened his grip. "We could keep playing our games, but you'll be stronger." He got more excited as he spoke, rubbing against her. "It'll be fun."

He unbuttoned her blouse. "You can't run." He traced down her sternum with bloody fingers. "That's what I said to your grandmother. A little glaistig blood, powder, and magic, and she was helpless. Just like you . . . I have your kind's blood in me. Just like glaistigs, when I speak, you have to obey . . ."

He kissed her and laid her back on his bed. "Lose the skirt . . . and the gun, Eve."

Over the years, Eavan had felt herself forced under Nyx's will; she'd watched Nyx and the rest of the clan bend mortals to their wishes. No one but Nyx was strong enough to force her to obey. Daniel shouldn't be, either.

He was though.

"Thought you didn't like them mindless?" Eavan ran her thumb along her bellyband holster. *Would death by bullet, not by my actual hand, still mean changing?* She wasn't sure.

"I don't. Once you lose the gun, I'll gladly give you control." His eyes darkened at the thought. "You want me; don't you, Eve? You wanted me the night we met. Tell me the truth."

"I did," she admitted.

"The skirt." He sat up, so she could remove it. "But keep the panties."

"Why?" She lifted her hips and slipped the skirt off. Then she loosened the holster, pulling it apart at the fastenings as slowly as she could. Years of resisting Nyx had helped her to learn the tricks of disobeying glaistig control. It was about finding the loophole that allowed disobedience.

"I want *you* to make the choice." He shivered as he said it.

She slid the gun out of the holster. "I am. I'm still mortal, Daniel . . . with immunity to all but a matriarch's control. I couldn't have survived my family if I wasn't immune. No unturned glaistig could."

But she still let him take the gun from her hand.

"Lucky me"—Daniel licked Nyx's blood from his fore-arm—"I have matriarchal blood right here."

"You know what glaistigs do? I'm going to kill you. Is that what you want?"

"You'd have shot me before if you were going to kill me." Daniel rolled her on top of him. "You can't kill me, Eve. That's the last order I'll give you. You have your will but for this: as long as I'm breathing, you can't ever kill me."

And with that, she had possession of her will. He'd given her complete control, save for murdering him. He knew enough about what she was to say the words that could make her safe. He forbade her, and she had to obey. *Could Nyx have done that?* If Nyx had ordered Eavan not to murder anyone, she would be free to stay human, free to have sex and live like a normal person. She wanted to weep at how basic it could be.

"As long as you're breathing," she repeated. As she turned the words over in her mind, she saw the flaw. She sealed her lips to his and breathed in. Her hands tightened around his throat.

He clawed at her hands, but an instinct centuries in the making held her. He was her first, but her body knew how things were to be. She drew his life into her mouth, sucking his dreams and fears into her lungs, holding him to her with hair that was extending from her in the same serpentine tendrils she'd once thought were beautiful on Nyx.

She did what Nyx could not, what her matriarch had failed to do, what she'd never wanted to do. Then she dropped Daniel to the floor.

"I've worked for *years* to not kill anyone. I've lived like a virgin. I've done everything I could to avoid this moment."

As she stepped over him, she could still see her feet, her normal human toes, her pedicure. She didn't have hooves. *Yet.*

12

Eavan was blood-covered when she walked into her house. Cillian didn't bother asking if Brennan was alive. He couldn't help glancing at her legs, though. *Are they going to change?* He wasn't sure if such a change was immediate or not.

"Nyx?" she asked.

"Sleeping now. Muriel is with her. She says everything will be fine." He didn't know if he should reach out or what to do. If Eavan had been human, he'd have offered a shoulder to lean on; if she was a friend, he'd have offered an embrace. She was something else, so he settled for words: "Are you going to be all right?"

Eavan nodded. She dropped a stack of files on the table. "I didn't know what you needed, so I brought these."

He came to stand beside her. "Do you need anything?"

"A shower." She looked lost, but resolute. "I'm a mess."

He forgot his misgivings, his professionalism, and his common sense. He wrapped his arms around her and held on to her. She didn't resist, but she didn't crumble into sobs, either. For a moment, she stayed stiff, and then she relaxed into his embrace. Drying blood, some of it hers, streaked her skin. Traces of tears on her face made it apparent that she had cried, just not where there were witnesses.

"You should run, Cillian," she whispered. "Being around us is unsafe."

"I'm not going anywhere yet." He wasn't sure where he'd be or when he was going, but until his supervisors assessed the files she'd brought, he was untethered. "My assignment was to come to Raleigh. Until I get new orders, I'm here."

"That doesn't mean you need to be around monsters." She didn't move away from him as she spoke. "Nyx won't force you to stay, and Daniel isn't around to investigate."

"He's gone?" Cillian hadn't wanted to bring it up, but they did need to deal with it. "If he's dead, I'll call it in, and the C.D.A. will clean it up."

She nodded. "He's dead."

"It's not your fault," he said. "You—"

"Hunted him. Brought Nyx there. Left her in a room with him." She made a bitter sound and stepped away. "No, it's not my fault at all."

She walked past him, ignoring the rest of her family and heading into the room where Muriel and Nyx were. She stopped in the doorway and bowed her head. "Forgive me, Grandmama."

Cillian watched for a minute, and then he took the files with him into the sitting room to call the office. "I'll be staying in Raleigh for a while," he said when his supervisor answered. "I need a cleanup and containment though." He filled them in, and then sat down in the gaudy room and started to read. There was plenty to do in Raleigh.

Eavan stood in the doorway and looked down at her matriarch. She'd always been imperious, seemingly invincible, and terrifying. Seeing her weakened was heartbreaking to Eavan. *Why was she weakened by him? Why couldn't Nyx kill him?* Eavan realized that she had done what her matriarch could not. It wasn't a comforting feeling to be the better monster when Nyx was the competition.

"I'm sorry," she whispered. Later there would be time for questions; later there would be room to think about the unpleasant truth that she was going to need to make peace with being a part of her clan. Right now, all that mattered was that her family was unbroken. "I'm so sorry."

"Don't be a fool, Eavan. *You* didn't injure me." Nyx opened her eyes. "Is he dead?"

"Yes."

"By your hand?" Nyx wasn't any less fierce for being injured.

"Yes," Eavan admitted.

"It was worth it then. Now, if you want to make me happy, go celebrate with Cillian. Call it a cure for your guilt." Nyx closed her eyes and drifted off to sleep.

Eavan stood there for several moments. *Some things never change.* Her grandmother was still the family matriarch, still focused on her personal agenda, still determined to save Eavan from dying from the "disease" of mortality.

Quietly, with only Muriel for a witness, Eavan walked over and kissed her grandmother's forehead and whispered the same words she used to whisper as a girl: "You're such a bitch, Grandmama Nyx."

Nyx smiled but didn't open her eyes. "Love you, too, Evvie."

After her shower, Eavan sat in Nyx's room and flipped through a manila folder she'd found in Daniel's office, one she hadn't given Cillian. He had looked up when she walked past the sitting room, but he hadn't followed her into Nyx's room.

Eavan flipped through the pages and stared at the names:

Christophe, James
Imlee, D–?
McKinsey, Rachel
Wall, ???

There were more than a dozen pages on different people

and other thicker packets of information that made no sense to her.

She wasn't meant for a normal life, but that didn't mean she had to give up hope of everything she'd believed. Maybe Nyx was right: maybe she couldn't deny what she was. She was a murderess, a daughter of glaistigs, but she was also daughter to a long-gone human father. She'd commit a few murders to keep her appetites in control. She wasn't going to become fully glaistig. There were choices left to her—not as many as before Daniel, but still enough that she could keep hold her of her humanity.